A SISTER FOR
Venus

PETER ROSSER

A SISTER FOR Venus

CONTENTS

FAMILY TREE

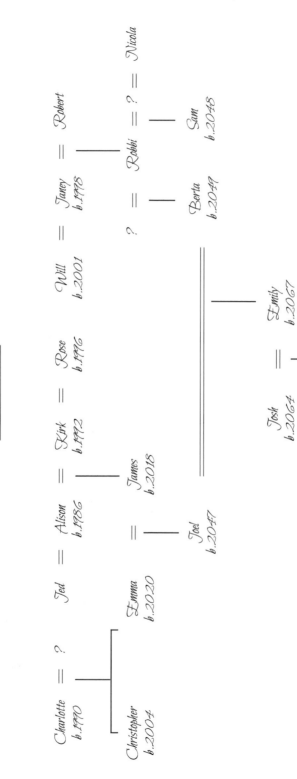

Charlotte b.1970 = ? — Ted = Alison b.1986 = Kirk b.1972 = Rose b.1996 — Will b.2001 = Janey b.1998 = Robert

? = Robbi = ? = Nicola

Christopher b.2004 — Emma b.2020 = Joel b.2047 — James b.2018 Berta b.2049 — Sam b.2048

Josh b.2064 = Emily b.2067

Grace b.2098 — Daniel b.2092

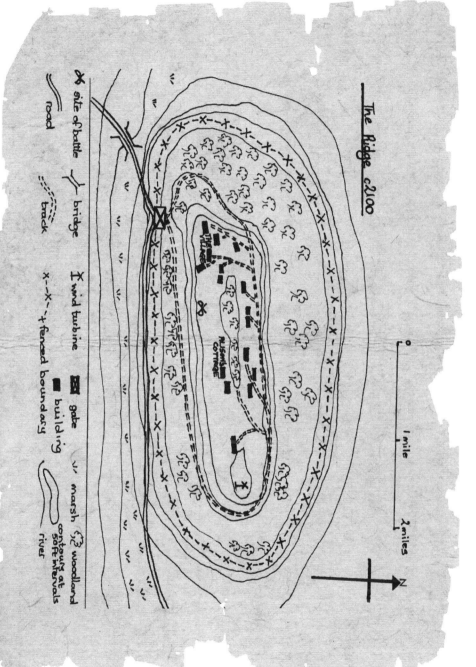

The Ridge c.2100

Legend

- 🏹 site of battle
- ⟩⟨ bridge
- ∿ road
- - - - track

- I wind turbine
- ▩ gate
- ▪ building
- x—x—x fenced boundary

- ∨ marsh
- ⌘ woodland
- ⌒ contours at 50ft intervals
- ⌒ river

TREE VILLAGE

RUSHMEAD COTTAGE

Scale: 0 — 1 mile — 2 miles

N

PART 1

CHAPTER 1

A CRIME IN HALLAMTON

Kirk was alone at home – and worrying. His pay from the College where he worked was now a fortnight overdue. He was already dipping into his savings and although he still had a good reserve in relation to his needs, he knew all too well that the lack of income would soon start to make itself felt.

He was also worrying about the effect on the people around him. The intermittent crises affecting the whole country were making themselves felt in a profound pessimism, which had already severely affected the financial system. He was living on money he had drawn out of the bank nearly two weeks ago. People everywhere were going onto a 'three-day week' or being laid off work. Hallamton was not a wealthy place and Kirk knew that it would not be long before desperation would begin to show itself. The English government seemed to be locked in continuous emergency session whilst a similar situation prevailed in the other countries of the British Isles.

He went to the window and sat on a chair, musing on the lack of activity outside. The window was very grimy – too dirty for him to be able to see anything in detail. Instead, his own reflection – that of a man in his late twenties, dark hair and eyebrows, wide, intelligent eyes – stared back at him.

For the time being, the lack of noise outside told him what he needed to know, for even in the streets there was silence – a strange uncanny silence – when, on an evening such as this, he would have expected bustle, the sights and sounds of people going to the pub or into the city for an evening's entertainment. From his insignificant seat, the earth – and for that matter heaven – seemed to have fallen silent.

He was becoming bored. Looking at his watch, he realised with a small shock that he must have been sitting at the window for about half an hour – and now, suddenly there was noise in the street outside. He tried to peer through the window and dimly made out shapes moving about, rapidly, violently. There was a voice –a man's voice, shouting.

He looked around for something to clean the window but could see nothing. Hurriedly, he scrubbed at the pane with the tips of his fingers until a small arc of cleaner glass appeared and he could peer out into the darkness.

The terraced houses opposite were a mirror image of the row from which Kirk now peered. The street lights imparted an orange glow to the pools of darkness that dwelt between them. It took a moment before he could make sense of the light and shadow. Then he saw what looked like a large bundle of black clothing in the road.

He was not a hero of any kind, but from the noises he had first heard Kirk had suspected that there was a fight going on and curiosity was getting the better of him. Whatever had happened, there now appeared to be someone lying in the road. As far as he could tell, there was no-one else in the street. He padded across the room and down the narrow staircase. He found his shoes by the door and then it took him a few moments more to slide back the bolts and undo the various locks; although this was generally a quiet area, the neighbouring streets were not such safe places to live. However, as soon as he had the door open, he stepped out onto the pavement and, glancing up and down, immediately confirmed that there was no-one else around.

He decided that he was going to investigate. He walked slowly across to where the body lay and as he approached it he could see that it was someone taller and more muscular than himself. He crouched at his side, wondering for a moment what to do, although, by this time, he was also becoming aware that there was a need for some urgency.

Despite this, he approached with a certain amount of caution. Somewhere at the back of his mind were thoughts that the stranger might suddenly leap up and sprint off down the street, or worse, spring up and start kicking and thumping him, but as he drew closer, these ideas began to seem rather bizarre; the apparent lack of vital signs convinced him that he was in no immediate danger. He leaned closer.

Under the street lights, the face seemed to be that of a man who was, perhaps, several years older than him, but whatever his age, his head was bleeding. Somewhere amongst the rather unusual and unfashionable brown curls, was a deep gash from which pumped a steady welling of dark blood. The face also had numerous cuts and a mass of heavy bruising.

He thought he had better check for breathing. Tentatively, he placed his fingers near the man's face and nose. He had no idea if this was what he was supposed to do, but it told him what he wanted to know. He could feel on his skin the faint sensations of breathing – albeit rapid and irregular breathing. He vaguely remembered something about the 'recovery position' from some training day long ago, but the man lay on his side already, huddled in a foetal position, presumably trying to protect himself from the kicks and blows that had been aimed in upon him. Kirk would not look any closer now. It had been a very thorough beating. He pulled out his mobile phone and pressed '999'. He was not sure of getting a response and when it came, it almost took him by surprise. The voice at the other end came from a busy room but was clear and efficient: "Which service do you require…?"

Closing his phone a few moments later, he reflected briefly that there were still a few parts of society that were working as they should.

***

The houses of the street seemed to revolve with the baleful colours of the lights on the emergency vehicles. The street had remained quiet until the police car and then the ambulance had arrived within moments of each other. Up and down the street, new rectangles of light appeared in windows and doorways; a small huddle of people began to coalesce at the kerbside. For a few minutes, reality had burst out of the television and onto the street.

The police had questioned him. They were quite rigorous. It was obvious that the victim had, as they put it, "been given a good kicking". Come the morning he might no longer be in this world. Kirk hoped intensely for a moment that he would survive the night and then felt rather selfish about his motives; the questioning from the police had further unsettled him. He had already been asked to provide a statement and he did not want to go through the intensified version of this procedure, which he assumed would follow, if the police investigation became a murder inquiry.

When he was eventually free to go and to crawl into his bed, it was getting into the early hours of the morning. Obsessively, despite his tiredness, he refused to just throw his clothes down on a chair. They had to be put away tidily in the wardrobe – but he was momentarily aware of irritation with his own behaviour.

The freshness of the sheets and the austerity of the room were reassuring after the crowded events that had followed his call to the emergency services. Despite his fatigue and his desire for sleep – or perhaps because of it – he lay awake, turning over the night's events in his head. The longer he thought about the street incident, however, the more it seemed to him that it was probably just another of the kind that was so often in the local news – a tale of sound and some apparent fury – but which would probably turn out to be meaningless or just inconclusive, to anyone outside the circle of the thugs who had carried out the attack. He wondered vaguely if the victim had known his attackers, but it was his last conscious thought before drifting into sleep.

CHAPTER 2

A TOUCH OF AMNESIA

Over the next few days, Kirk found himself wondering about what had happened to the victim of the beating in the street. Eventually, he was contacted by the local police; it seemed that the injured man was now out of hospital but could not remember much about what had happened. The police also told Kirk that he was still a suspect and that, at some point, they might want to question him again.

Although most of his days were now very similar, he reminded himself that it was Saturday; he drifted about the house doing his usual weekend chores – tidying away books and papers prior to cleaning the house – but continuing to brood about the possible problems arising from the incident in the street.

He was trying not to get too agitated about the police; presumably they were simply following their usual procedures. Up to that moment, his only previous contact with them had been when he was stopped for speeding. However, he could not prevent himself from wondering about the identity of the man he had found in the street and just why he had been beaten up. It was not simply a matter of curiosity. Jostling about amongst the uncertainty was also a vague feeling of anxiety. If he had, in effect, prevented a murder, would the thugs who carried out the attack come after him?

To keep himself away from such feelings, he tried to keep himself at home with such work as he had to do, although his motivation was daily ebbing away.

His mind briefly skimmed over his past year at the local college. He had managed to get a post there, teaching adult literacy, and it had proved to be something of a lifeline.

In the two years before that, he had first separated from his wife and then they had divorced. Within him, there still persisted a large element of surprise, even shock about it all; he and Joanne had always assumed that they would stay together and that, of all the couples they knew, they were the most likely to remain married to one another.

Kirk blamed himself. He had been a slow starter and had not worried much about relationships with the opposite sex until he was in his early twenties. Somehow, at that point, he had overcome a tendency towards shyness and had found that he could talk easily to women. After a while, this seemed to develop into a natural flirtatiousness, although at first, he had always chosen to talk to women who would not, perhaps, be very confident in talking to men.

Celia had been one of the first. She was quite small but had not developed the compensating aggressiveness that he sometimes encountered amongst some of her peers. When he first met her, he had seen her as a rather nervous and mousy woman, but he soon began to appreciate her mischievous sense of humour and ready, unaffected laughter.

He found himself returning to thoughts of her, despite his feelings of loss from the divorce. He briefly remembered the first time that they had slept together, the pleasure of discovering her naked shapeliness and the smooth texture of her skin… He deliberately stopped his train of thought, wondering if his current celibacy was leading to frustration. A loud rap on the door knocker further interrupted his thoughts. He opened the door, thinking that it was probably the postman with a large letter or a parcel.

Then, for a moment, he paused, unsure… His visitor's face seemed very familiar and yet not one that he could really claim to know. Suddenly he remembered; when he had last seen this face, it had been horizontal to the road and then to a stretcher. The eyes had been firmly shut, the skin a mass of wounds and bruising. It was the man he had last seen being lifted into an ambulance. The eyes Kirk was looking at were now wide open, the skin blotchy and discoloured, but no longer looking like something off the meat counter.

"Sorry," said the stranger by way of introduction. "You probably don't recognise me. I'm Mark Ridgeway, the person you found lying in the street about a fortnight ago."

Kirk was not quite sure how to react. Although he had gone to the stranger's aid and now knew his name, he otherwise knew next to nothing about him. As he hesitated, the stranger put out a hand, seemingly to steady himself against the door post.

Slightly alarmed, Kirk found himself saying, "Perhaps you'd better come in. I'm Kirk Hallam by the way – in case you don't already know." He led his visitor into the small hallway and then into the lounge, gesturing him towards a large and rather battered armchair.

"Thanks," said Mark with obvious relief. "I've only been out of hospital a couple of days and walking still makes me feel light headed." He was about to collapse into the chair but then reached out and grasped Kirk's hand, wringing it warmly.

"One of your neighbours saw you helping me. You did me a great service the other week – and I'm very grateful."

"No problem," said Kirk and gestured again towards the chair. "Please – sit down. Would you like some coffee?"

"Coffee would be good," said Mark.

Kirk disappeared into the kitchen and busied himself with the means to make what he called 'proper coffee'. Mark studied the room for a few moments and then stood up again and went to the window, trying to pinpoint the place where he had been set on by his attackers.

Kirk returned with the coffee and found his visitor with his nose almost pressed to the window and the glass misting with his breath.

"I doubt if you'll see much from there," said Kirk. "It's months since I had the windows cleaned. Anyway, I would have thought that you'd want to forget about that particular evening. How do you like your coffee?"

"Just black please – well you would think so, but I've called round to express my appreciation of what you did – and also, because I need to remember what happened. You may be able to help me with some of the details. Unfortunately, I forgot most of them when I was hit over the head." Mark returned to the chair in which he had been previously sitting.

Kirk felt another momentary pang of uncertainty. He wanted to be helpful but there were times when he found it difficult even to remember what day of the week it was.

"I'll do what I can" was his tentative response.

"Good, good," crooned Mark, sipping at his coffee. "I know that you've given your statement to police and so on, but I thought that talking with you might just trigger some memories from shortly before the attack… and that could help both me and the police."

Kirk thought for a moment. "Are you sure that you should be talking to me at all?" he asked. "According to the police, I'm not only a witness, I'm also a possible suspect."

Mark shrugged. "They haven't said anything to me," he said, "but now that we've met, properly that is, I'd be confident in telling them that you were not one of my attackers."

Kirk cocked an eyebrow at him. "Oh, why's that?"

"Because one of the few things that I have been able to work out is that the guy who made the dent in the top of my skull must have been at least as tall as me. His mate was probably of a similar height – so, if you don't mind my saying so, on that count alone you don't really fit the bill."

Kirk smiled at Mark's candid reference to his lack of height. He began to study his visitor more carefully than when he had first admitted him to the house. Big though it was, the armchair did not seem adequate to the task of accommodating Mark's very large anatomy. Like those who had attacked him, he was tall – and, in Kirk's vocabulary, 'solidly built'. He had looked like a young man when first seen in the orange glare of the street lights, but looking at him now, Kirk estimated that he was in his mid-thirties.

Mark had continued talking…

"Did you see any of the people who attacked me?" he asked.

"No, as I told the police they'd gone by the time I got to you."

"I thought there were two of them, but I can't be sure. I caught a glimpse of one of them in front of me. Not that it told me much – he was wearing a balaclava. Then someone hit me from behind. The next thing I knew I was in hospital feeling as if my head was about to explode."

Kirk, who for no particular reason had supposed that it was just another instance of neighbourhood street violence, was surprised. He thought it unlikely that Mark had been the subject of a random attack by two assailants wearing balaclavas, but he kept his thoughts to himself.

"It doesn't sound like the usual sort of street crime that we get around here – but they obviously meant business. Why do you suppose they attacked you?" He had tried to keep suspicion out of his voice, but Mark still detected its presence.

"I haven't the faintest idea…but it certainly seems like they knew what they were doing." He ran his right hand gingerly round the back of his head.

There was brief silence then Mark said, "This might seem a bit of a strange request, but I think it might help if I could get a clear view of the street – perhaps from your bedroom window?"

Kirk thought about it for a moment. He could think of no strong reason to object. He had only the chores and the marking of student assignments to look forward to that morning so the diversion, however brief, would be welcome.

They both stood up together, awkwardly filling the confined space of Kirk's lounge.

"I particularly want to see the view from one of your top windows because I think that I'll be able to see the whole of the street." The comment seemed to be offered by way of explanation.

Kirk, who had occasionally had reason to put his head out of the top window, agreed.

"Yes, it'll give you a good view."

He began to lead the way to the stairs, but Mark had already reached the doorway and was halfway up the stairs before Kirk called after him, rather unnecessarily…

"It's the first door on the landing, almost straight ahead of you."

Kirk followed his bulky predecessor, wondering what had happened to his visitor's initial dizziness and hesitancy. Hauling himself up through the darkness of the stairs and into the light from the bedroom window, he saw that Mark had placed himself at an angle to the window and was gazing down into the street.

"I see what you mean about these windows," he said, scrubbing at the glass with his fingers. "I reckon they must have been waiting at the end of that alley over there. They'd have been well hidden by the hedge. I probably walked straight past them."

"I don't suppose you were expecting to be attacked…?" suggested Kirk.

If Mark noticed the question he also ignored it, choosing instead to set off on a tack of his own. He wrinkled his nose and sniffed the air.

"Smells a bit of damp plaster in here," he commented. "Have you had some building work done recently?"

Kirk was sure that the remark was purely a diversion, but he replied, "No, not me. The previous owners had the walls re-plastered in here just before they sold it to me. I don't like to heat the room too much. I sometimes find it hard to sleep if the house is too warm."

"Right," replied Mark. He stood looking thoughtfully at Kirk for a moment and then said, "You've been very patient, but I've taken up enough of your time. I'd better get going."

Kirk shrugged but Mark was already on his way back down the stairs. He was letting himself out when Kirk caught up with him. He was still unsure about exactly how Mark's visit could have helped him in any way, but he said, "Well, I hope that was of some use to you although I don't think I've told you anything that I haven't already told the police."

"I'm sure you told them all that you could. They're probably still filling in the forms. You might get to hear from them again, but I doubt it. They won't be putting a lot of 'man hours' into an incident such as this one just now."

Kirk thought that he was probably right but did not want to say so.

"You sound quite philosophical about it all."

"Curious perhaps rather than philosophical," observed Mark, ruefully feeling the back of his head again. "I'm staying a few streets away, in Rutland Place. I sometimes drink at the 'Dog and Duck'. Perhaps I'll see you in there? Thanks again for talking to me. You've been most helpful."

He did not wait for a reply from Kirk but instead strode off purposefully towards a car that Kirk could dimly see parked under the colourful, late autumn trees at the end of the street.

Watching him, Kirk noted again that Mark seemed to have forgotten about the dizziness that had accompanied his arrival. He turned the visit over in his mind. It had set up a whole new set of questions – and he felt even less motivated about marking student assignments than before.

CHAPTER 3

ROSE

After Mark's unanticipated intrusion into the morning, Kirk continued to feel at something of a loose end. He went back into the house to make himself another cup of coffee. The pile of students' work that awaited him was still on his mind, but it was now close to lunchtime, and, prior to Mark's arrival, he had kept his own company for the last two days. He decided that work could wait and that he would go to his local pub – not the 'Dog and Duck' but 'The Stanwick Arms' – a place he went to infrequently but which at that moment held out the attractive proposition of lunch. His meagre savings would just have to stand the expense. He shut the front door of the house and set off along the street.

Despite the two years that had passed since he and Joanne had been divorced, he still thought about her every day. In many ways, he was still grieving for her – although he had to admit to himself that it was his own behaviour that had led to the divorce. His self-awareness seemed for the moment to stretch just as far as admitting this, but not to understanding how he had allowed himself to become entangled in an affair.

Then again, if he was really candid with himself, perhaps he could understand. Most men would have thought that Sarah, the woman he had pursued, was beautiful… In fact, Sarah's attractiveness to other men had later become all too apparent.

He pushed his thoughts away. He had spent the last two years trying to make sense of that part of his life and, so far, his efforts had not met with success; he was beginning to tire of a way of thinking that led nowhere. Meanwhile, the facts of his daily existence had changed so much. He allowed himself to wonder what Joanne was doing that day and how she was feeling…

By this time, he had reached the corner close to where Mark had earlier parked his car. It was now but a few yards to 'The Stanwick'. Before going in, however, he went into a nearby newsagent to buy a newspaper, which he felt would provide him with a pretext for sitting in the bar alone when most of the people there were in the company of others.

The barmaid who had a friendly, pleasant face but whose neckline was generous in what it revealed, smiled and said, "Yes, love, what'll it be?"

"A pint of Grenadier, please."

A few moments later, he was sitting contentedly with his pint of beer and a sandwich, generally feeling at peace, admiring the contours of the barmaid – and then self-consciously wondering why he was doing so. He forced himself to concentrate on the newspaper and, after some effort, became properly immersed in it.

***

He had been reading and drinking for some minutes when he became aware of three women sitting at one of the tables opposite the bar. They looked a little like some of the students he taught at the college except that they were some years older – in their late thirties, or possibly early forties. Then again, perhaps they were too well dressed to be students; he noticed that one of them was wearing a dress – which would have been unusual at the College, where jeans and a top seemed to be the order of the day. The conversation was animated and there was already a good collection of glasses, bottles and discarded slices of lemon on the table.

Just then one of the women interrupted their conversation to call loudly across the bar:

"Yoo hoo, Ken! We're over here!"

In response, 'Ken' wove his way across the room and towards the women, stopping first, however, at the bar to buy himself a drink.

"Can I get one for anyone else?" he asked the group.

For the moment, they were on their best behaviour and declined his offer, but soon he was seated amongst them and happily joining in with the conversation, which continued to be lively.

Meanwhile, Kirk became aware that every so often Ken was squinting along the bar. Kirk speculated that perhaps this was because he was feeling outnumbered, but as Ken went to buy his second pint of beer, he edged his way along the bar so that he was closer to where Kirk was sitting.

"It's Kirk, isn't it? We have met – on the induction day at the College."

Kirk nodded. "Yes, I remember. You're in the English Department, aren't you?"

Ken nodded. "That's right. Look it would be a bit anti-social for you to be sitting here on your own. Why don't you come and join us?"

Kirk was not too sure but found himself on his feet and being ushered towards the group. Now it was his turn to stop at the bar first. He ordered himself another pint of beer and then, feeling a sense of obligation, was foolish enough to ask:

"Would anyone else like something whilst I'm here?"

This time, the response was less reserved.

"Ooh, I think I will," said the woman in the middle of the group.

"Yes, I wouldn't mind, since you're buying," chorused a rather smaller, dark-haired woman.

"Me too," came the third voice from the slightly plump woman who peered at him over her glasses, from the right of the group.

Wondering why this had not happened when Ken arrived, Kirk bought the round of drinks and settled himself amongst the group. He noted disappointedly that no-one seemed to be eating, only drinking. Ken took it upon himself to do the introductions.

"Kirk, this is Rachel" –the small, dark haired woman to the right of the group nodded, "Rose," continued Ken – the larger but attractive woman in the centre sipped her drink and smiled at him with her eyes "…and this is Barbara." The plump bespectacled lady on the group's left held out the middle fingers of her right hand, which Kirk duly shook in something of a mock hand shake.

"Well, now we've done that bit – Kirk's at the college as well."

The women seemed vaguely interested.

"We've just signed up to Ken's evening class," said Barbara.

"Oh, which course is that?"

"A-level English. I've always wanted to do it." Rachel smiled at Ken as though she was still being interviewed for a place on the course.

"What do you do, Kirk?" It was Rose who was asking the question.

"I teach Basic Skills."

Rose smiled. "How 'basic' is 'Basic'?" she asked.

***

After a while Kirk began to think that it was fortunate that he had walked to the pub rather than driven. He was feeling quite mellow and a little hazy. He noticed when he went to the bar for another round of drinks that he was not as steady as he had been. He nearly fell over a stool, and he caught a glimpse of Rose looking amusedly at him and then at the other members of the group.

Ken by now had developed a rather strange, fixed smile. Kirk noticed that he slopped some of the drinks as he helped carry them back to the table. There was a lull in the conversation as the various members of the group reached that stage of drunkenness in which they returned for some minutes to 'ground state'.

Then, unwittingly, Ken broke the spell by spilling some of his drink on the table and on Barbara's hand.

"Oh, bugger, I'm sorry, Barb…" he apologised – perhaps a little too profusely.

"S'alright," she said, smiling at him as he clumsily tried to mop her hand with a soggy tissue.

The conversation and mellow state of affairs continued until Rachel slurred, "Well, I don't know about you lot, but I needed to be home hours ago." There were weary nods of agreement round the table.

They finished their drinks and Ken stood to go. It was clear, however, that he was going to need assistance. Barbara had begun trying to put her arm round his shoulders so that she could help him out of the pub, and Rachel was similarly holding on to his arm and guiding him towards the door. Rose and Kirk sat watching them for a few moments and then Rose muttered, "Gawd", and spread her fingers across her face; the trio had reached door and were struggling. Ken seemed to be putting far too much of his weight on the two women, particularly Barbara.

Kirk got up to help them, but the landlady had come round from behind the bar and arrived first.

"Someone needs to go and lie down," she said.

"Too bloody right," agreed Ken.

"Would that be a quote? Shakespeare – 1596 maybe?" enquired Barbara. "Nah – 'Ken, 2026'," said Ken. "Anyway, what d'you know about 1596?" "She probably thinks it was when you were born," contributed Rachel. "Cheeky!" hiccupped Ken.

The three of them staggered their way down the street towards Barbara's house, just a short distance from the pub.

Kirk watched as Barbara fumbled around in her handbag, trying to find house keys. "It's quite touching really…the beginning of a new student/ teacher relationship."

"Yes," agreed Rose. "She'll teach him a great deal, you can be sure."

Kirk laughed and looked sideways at her. There could be more to Rose than he had thought.

✳ ✳ ✳

They sauntered along in close proximity until Rose said, "You wouldn't happen to be following me by any chance, would you?"

"Not at all," responded Kirk. "I live around here."

Rose looked at him. "You surprise me…but then, I think I have seen you around a few times."

"Yes, now I come to think of it I think I've seen you as well."

They had reached the entrance to the unmade road that provided rear access to the terrace in which Rose lived. She turned into it and was about to say 'goodbye' when Kirk also turned into the entrance.

"Well," she laughed. "Where exactly do you live?"

"Second house from the end – number 11." Kirk gestured vaguely in the direction of his back gate.

"This is mine – number 3." Rose had stopped and had her hand on the gate. "I'm not in a rush," she said. "How would like a cup of tea? After all, we seem to be neighbours."

The pile of students' assignments beckoned briefly again – but then, only very briefly.

"Yes, I could do with a cup of tea." Kirk smiled and followed her through the gate, glancing up at the row of bedroom windows and wondering if anyone was watching them, but then the windows were small and in his own house, looking out of them involved a certain amount of contortion. The windows stared anonymously back.

"Go on through," she said, pointing the way from the back door and through a low doorway into the dim interior of a small lounge. He walked through, ducking slightly to get through the doorway.

The room felt cool and looked out from behind thick curtains onto a very small garden and a brick wall which obscured the view of the street. There was a piano in one corner of the room and a dresser accommodating small ornaments and a few photographs. A large bunch of flowers on the window sill further obscured the view of the street so that the room felt cosy and, despite its position, hidden from view.

The furniture – a leather settee and a single leather armchair – took up quite a large proportion of the room.

Kirk called through to Rose, who was still in the kitchen waiting for the kettle to boil.

"Mind if I put on a light?"

"Of course not," she replied. "The switch is on the wall by the books."

He switched on a small table lamp next to the only books he could see in the room, and it provided a soft yellow glow from its corner.

Rose came through from the kitchen bearing two large mugs of tea and set them down on a small side table in front of the fireplace. Kirk had seated himself in the armchair and Rose sat opposite him, on one end of the settee, kicking off her open-toed shoes and tucking her legs under her.

"Sorry," she said, "I didn't ask you how you like your tea."

"It's fine," he said, despite sipping at it rather tentatively.

Kirk glanced at Rose as she sat drinking and holding the mug in both hands.

"So do you live here by yourself?" he asked.

Rose glanced at him. "Sometimes," she said. He must have looked puzzled because she added, "I live with Richard. He's a computer salesman. He travels about a lot. I thought he would be here today, but he rang to say that he won't be back until tomorrow."

Kirk glanced towards the photographs on the dresser. "How long have you been together?"

"Oh, we've been partners for about six years."

There was a brief silence and then Rose asked, "How about you?"

"I teach at the College, as you will have gathered. I've been here about two years."

"Do you have a partner? Are you married?"

"No, no – I live by myself. I was married but I got divorced about two years ago."

Rose reverted to sipping her tea for a moment and then said, "Oh – was it amicable?"

He seemed nonplussed by the question, so she partly repeated her question: "The divorce – was it amicable or acrimonious?"

"Neither" he replied. "Or at least, not on my part?"

Rose hesitated, wondering if her questions had already become too intrusive but then she continued. "Do you still have anything to do with your previous wife?"

"No – nothing at all – we haven't even spoken for the past two years."

It seemed as though he wanted to say more but then when he sat gazing into his cup she asked, "Can I top you up?"

She wondered again if he had understood the question, but he said, "That's kind of you – but I'll have to say no. I must get back and do some work."

He stood to leave, and she showed him to the door.

Minutes later he arrived back in his own house. As he stepped into its quiet solitude with only the prospect of a pile of assignments to mark, he wondered why he had not accepted Rose's offer of a second cup of tea.

CHAPTER 4

A WALK ALONG THE EDGE

"**D**amn it!" exclaimed Kirk. He had peered out of his kitchen window, wondering whether to go for a walk when he noticed that his back gate was swinging loosely on one hinge. He walked down the garden path and found as he arrived that the damaged hinge had remained attached to the gate post but that the wood on the gate had splintered. The winds that week had been particularly strong, so he was not surprised but then he noticed the print of a large boot on the gate and a lump of mud clinging to the wood. "Damn!" he said again, annoyed at the thought of the repair that he would have to make.

He had lived in Hallamton long enough to expect problems with vandalism and casual damage. Feeling irritated, he decided to be more vigilant and keep an eye on who was using the access road at the back of the terrace. Fetching his tools from the shed, he mended the gate sufficiently well to prevent the wind from causing any further damage to it and then glanced at his watch. It was already two o'clock.

Having procrastinated the previous day, he had spent the morning marking more of the assignments that he had given up on the previous evening. He ate a solitary lunch and found himself thinking about Rose, wondering if her partner Richard had returned from his business trip.

Marking the assignments had given him a headache and feeling in need of fresh air, he decided to go for a walk. The walk would help to clear his head but for good measure he decided to take some headache tablets and went to rummage for them in the bathroom cabinet. He gulped down two of them with some water, and although it was not particularly cold, he donned his anorak and then his walking boots and set off from the front of the house.

A strong breeze was blowing, and small cumulus clouds were scudding across an otherwise blue sky. The autumn that year seemed slow to take hold. Belatedly, the leaves on trees and bushes were turning from green to yellows and browns, but despite a pervading sense of the year's tempo ebbing away, he was still surprised at how slowly the season was progressing.

From his house, the road took him in a roughly north-westerly direction before dividing in two – one branch bearing more concertedly north towards an offshoot of Hallamton, and the other bearing left and in a westerly direction towards the countryside. Kirk followed the road left.

Kirk had rarely walked for the sake of it, but ever since his divorce he had often gone off into the countryside trying to organise his thoughts and to make sense of the last few years. He hoped that walking would promote a sense of harmony, but before he reached the track that would take him across the fields, his route was strewn on both sides with rubbish – remnants of 'take-away' meals, plastic bottles, newspapers, sweet wrappers – a huge assortment of refuse blown from houses or lorries, or thrown down by passers-by.

This initial part of his walk only served to heighten the desolation that he still felt when he allowed his mind to dwell on the past. He still wondered why he had 'cheated' on his wife. Sometimes he could understand it; at other times, the huge betrayal of trust weighed heavily upon him, and he wondered how he could have done it.

He reflected that the events about which he was thinking had happened some three years before, but it was taking a long time for their pain to diminish. Some of his memories of them, he had to admit, were already becoming confused – although others still remained strong and clear.

Prior to the affair, he remembered a long running sense of dissatisfaction – and yet he could not say that the dissatisfaction had stemmed from his relationship with Joanne. He had always loved her. How then, he asked himself, had he found himself committing adultery with Sarah that first time? Was it her beauty? She was certainly very beautiful – and when they were first getting to know each other, he had been flattered that she had not simply ignored him or told him to go away.

He had been completely captivated by her – and yet, when he entered her for the first time – well, it had been pleasurable, deeply pleasurable of course – but he had also felt as though a pit was opening before his feet, a point from which there was no return.

After that first occasion, he could never undo what he had done. Instead, he had accumulated a huge morass of deception, which he came to deplore even more than his persistent adulteries with Sarah.

He knew that it must all catch up with him – and had been amazed when it seemed to take quite a long time to do so. In the end, he had betrayed himself. Some saw it as weakness – but the incessant deception had run directly counter to the whole of the rest of his life. He had told Joanne.

He remembered that he had told her late in the evening. The night, the day and the night that followed were probably the most desolate of any that he had known – and around them lay in shattered ruins a relationship that had, until then, seemed to both of them a source of happiness and a buttress against the insecurities of daily life.

Sarah had thrived on the secrecy, the furtiveness of it all and saw Kirk as weak – a feeble little traitor. She had quickly and determinedly brought the affair to an end. Wherever he had looked in his private life at that time, it seemed that he had brought about destruction.

His mood then, as he walked, was consistent with the degradation and disorder of his surroundings. He was seeking the countryside but first he had to get through an area about which no-one seemed to care at all, an area into which people could simply toss all their rubbish without any thought for the ugliness or the sordidness that they were creating.

At this point, he came to a gap in the hedge bordering the road. A track, deeply rutted with tyre tracks, ran through the gap and crossed a small area of rough ground to a tarmac path which it met at a muddy junction a short distance away. The reason for the creation of an alternative entrance was not hard to see: two enormous sections of concrete drainpipe had been dragged across the entrance to the tarmac path in an attempt to prevent the access of vehicles.

Kirk had now explored this path a number of times. He picked his way along the rutted track, pausing here and there to hop over puddles. When he reached the path, he turned onto it and began walking along it to where it apparently disappeared into the woodland that lay about a quarter of a mile away.

To his left was a boggy area, populated with reedmace and sallow; to his right, a margin of firm ground bordered the path but gradually extended into a further area where water could be glimpsed, and water-loving grasses grew in profusion.

This first part of the walk took him through a strange hinterland in which the sordid remnants of relatively recent times had inserted themselves amongst the more picturesque fragments of an older, rural past. Growing on the margin of the path were several old apple trees. Kirk could only speculate as to how they had come to be growing there, but that morning their boughs were heavy with ripe fruit.

Just beyond them was a solid, brick building which at first sight looked as though it might be a small house or office but which, as he approached, had only a single heavy door, barred and locked, and a very grimy window glazed with opaque glass further protected by a set of steel bars. He thought that perhaps it housed a pump or electrical equipment of some kind. Its walls were covered in graffiti, which to him was an inarticulate scrawl but which he supposed was a territorial marker for local youths with time on their hands and little sense of meaning or purpose.

The path continued before him. Access to the areas on either side was delineated by rusting fences topped with barbed wire. Unmade roads and tracks criss-crossed the area to his left, and pieces of industrial debris lay strewn about in the scrubby wasteland that the fences enclosed.

The open aspect of the path now closed in as it pushed its way between dense growth of trees and bushes. Suddenly, his walking reverie was broken by the sound of uncouth shouting. It was coming from behind him. He turned and saw four teenage boys riding on bikes towards him. He looked for a moment at their bikes, which were generally far too small for them; they seemed to spend most of their time standing on the pedals.

The lad at the front of the group, whose face was tinged with red and had a small silver earring projecting from the lobe of one ear, yelled at him.

"Get oot the fookin' way!"

Kirk had already moved to the edge of the path.

Another of the four, similar in looks to the first, also began to shout at him.

"Clear off, granddad! We don't like paedos!"

"Yeah!" joined in a third rider. "We'll kick your fookin' 'ed in!"

For a moment Kirk thought that they were going to stop but their shouting obviously had something to do with their sense of being a group. Coarse laughter ran round the group; they might enjoy beating him up, but it could wait until another day.

"Hey, our Brian, are we fookin' racin' today or what?"

The lad at the front was yelling again but at the one who had diverted from the group's objective – that of reaching the rough tracks and mounds in the waste land to one side of the path.

Their pace, which had slowed to a meandering crawl, began to pick up again.

The youth who had verbally abused Kirk turned partly towards him and spat pointedly onto the path – and then they were off, racing, competing with each other, shouting raucously as though nothing and nobody existed but them. Kirk's heart, which was pounding hard, began to slow just a little.

His course now led him across a broad confluence of tarmac road and various tracks and over to a point where the path squeezed between a long row of poplar trees and another high fence, which, despite the gaping holes and sections of wire that had been detached from their posts, was intended to deny access to a huge spoil heap that towered above the area to his right – a 'Silbury Hill' of waste, reaching baldly out of the landscape.

Kirk hurried along, feeling happier in the knowledge that the ground was soft and the path narrow, so that it was less likely to attract the teenage bike riders. It was usually at this point in his walk that he began to feel that the domain of human beings was slowly tapering away into the fingers of Nature.

As he continued to wander along the path, he occasionally looked back at the wire, the waste tip and the sprawl of an industrial area; seen from this point in his journey, there was limit to the extent of its ugliness. The old adage, supposedly from the north of England, came to mind: 'Where there's muck, there's brass'. The people of the area had their livings to earn. The 'Can-Do-It' Pipeworks Company whose site lay spread out before him in the valley below was a benefactor of the college where he worked. For all he knew, perhaps a part of his salary was paid from money donated to the college by 'Can-Do-It'. Of course, he thought, the people of the area had to earn their 'brass' but he wondered if it necessarily had to involve the 'muck' as well.

Not all the human activities in the area behind him had led to ugliness. By this stage, he was climbing up a long slope towards the top of a hill. Looking back, he could see a series of ponds that had been created when local people had first begun to extract clay from the valley below. It was now a wonderful mixed area of trees, reedmace and a rich variety of other plant and animal life.

He reflected that having come out to try to sort out his thinking about Joanne, his mind had only travelled over the usual, familiar territory, but the exercise and the countryside were proving to be more therapeutic than any amount of thinking that he might have done shut away in his house.

The climb was making him breathless, and he paused, taking the opportunity to gaze back once more – this time, to a small, wooded knoll which lay between him and the ponds. He was now near the top of the hill, so he was able both to look back and down on the small area of woodland which stretched out below him. As he looked, he was slightly startled by six or seven loud popping sounds from the tree-covered area away to his left.

Now that times were hard, people sometimes tried to supplement their diet by hunting for rabbits in and around the wood. He supposed that the sounds he had heard were those of small calibre guns, but then, he was uncertain; he was some distance away and what he knew about weapons could be written on the back of a postage stamp.

It was nearly another ten minutes before Kirk arrived at the point that was locally referred to as 'The Edge'. The afternoon had become early evening and the light was beginning to fade. He looked out over the landscape, sweeping his gaze across the huge conurbation to the north, the thick and meandering limbs of urbanisation as they ran out to the west and then further round again, where, like a vast breath of reassurance, hills could be seen rolling untamed into the fading colours of the sky.

As he returned his gaze, he found himself straining to focus on something that was moving, down by the wooded knoll that he had seen some minutes before. Squinting against the sun and the distance, he thought that he could just make out two shapes, two dark figures moving away from the wood and towards a path which would take them in the opposite direction from the track that Kirk had climbed to the top of the hill.

Caution prompted him to stay back against the trees and to stand very still.

He remained there for several minutes, trying to see where the two people below had gone – but then decided that there was little point in waiting any longer. He checked the small rucksack in which he generally kept a torch. He would need it when the time came to walk down the hill on the other side and along the road back to his house. However, the village of Stanwick lay just beyond the hilltop and the 'Cricketers Arms' always seemed to be open. The welcoming atmosphere and a drink would help to postpone the walk back to the house.

A short while later he was ordering his first pint. The landlord, Rob, recognised him and began pulling the pint that Kirk had ordered; he usually chatted about the weather – or sport. Today, it was the weather, but as Kirk strained to hear him above the noise from a huge plasma screen television in the adjoining bar, it seemed that the landlord was distracted by news of something that had happened in the past few hours – something about a major storm on the south coast – a 'hurricane', he said. Kirk paid for his pint just as blaring music from the other bar announced the arrival of a news programme. Rob hurriedly put the change into his hand and went through to watch it. Kirk's curiosity was aroused and although he generally tried to stay away from the television, he decided to find out what the fuss was about. He arrived just in time to hear a solemn-faced newsreader relating the news that some 300 people were feared dead.

At first, he could not make visual sense of the scenes being presented on the screen. He wondered if they were from somewhere like Texas or Florida or out in the Caribbean perhaps. However, it seemed that the wreckage being portrayed was in Southampton – or what remained of it.

Looking at the scenes before him, Kirk felt at once bemused and disturbed. For some years past, people in the UK had had to accustom themselves to extreme weather – or at least, weather that would previously have been thought extreme – but this seemed to be of a different magnitude.

He knew very few of the people in the bar but the scenes of disaster on the screen brought him briefly together with them. Involuntarily the words, "What the hell…?" escaped from his lips as his mouth sagged open at the devastation unfolding on the huge screen in front of him.

The rest of the small crowd that had gathered watched in stunned silence as the boat from which the pictures were being sent curved its way through the smashed and flooded streets of the city. Cars bobbed about in the flood, together with boats that had been torn from their moorings. The camera zoomed in as a car was borne past with the driver still inside, beating on the windows in a desperate attempt to catch the attention of onlookers. When someone else further along the bar said "Did you see that…? Poor bugger…" he was immediately "shushed" by others in the small crowd.

It seemed that it was the south-east that had been hit hardest by the storm, an area roughly marked off by a line drawn between Bournemouth and The Wash.

The camera shot had returned to the studio and affected areas were being listed on the screen together with emergency contact numbers. Someone muttered, "Oh my God," and rushed out of the bar, mobile phone in hand.

Others in the crowd who had remained silent up to that point began an agitated discussion. Kirk eavesdropped briefly on the comments being made by a small group of drinkers.

The gossip focused on the warnings that had been given, but also that everyone had assumed the storm would produce heavy rain and strong winds but no more.

One man who looked to be in his late sixties asked, "Doesn't anyone remember 1987 – or look on the internet?"

It seemed that no-one in the bar had done either of these things because the comment was met only with remarks such as:

"How sad are you?" and "We're not that old, granddad".

When a middle-aged man related between mouthfuls of beer that over half a million trees had been lost but that storms such as this one occurred about once in every 200 years, the news was also met with derision.

"They can't count that quickly."

"Bugger the trees. What about the people? Who cares about a load of bloody trees?"

25

"Every 200 years? My ass – seems like every five minutes these days."
Kirk thought that he had heard enough and decided to find out more at home. It would probably be the top news item on the BBC news channel – not, he reflected, because it was an environmental story but because its worst effects had been felt along a line running roughly north-east from the Bournemouth and Southampton area to Cambridge and Norwich – a line, he noted, that also took in London.

CHAPTER 5

A NEIGHBOURLY ACT?

Leaving the pub, Kirk reflected that in recent years, he had found himself living in 'interesting times' – 'times' that seemed to be moving ever closer to his own personal point in the cosmos.

The pictures from Southampton had shaken him. He had no friends or relatives there, and as predicted by climatologists, extreme weather had become more commonplace in all parts of the globe – but he still found it shocking when such an event took place in his own country.

Meanwhile, he was shambling his way down the hill from the pub, climbing the bank at the side of the road every so often to avoid the 'boy racers' (a term which had stuck). He swore at one who came particularly close as he roared by and wondered, not for the first time, at the sheer perversity of a society which now generally used hybrids and electric cars as its main means of personal transport, but which had then readily built into them, a device which imitated the roaring of a petrol engine. Then again, he thought, there was a positive side to it; he had no wish to become another piece of 'road kill'.

Although he was still enjoying the air, largely unpolluted as it was by petrol or diesel fumes, he was just beginning to feel the autumn chill and was looking forward to an evening spent by the fire. He rounded the corner of the road that led to his house and decided to take the unmade road that led along the back of the terrace. His eyes were still adjusting to the deeper darkness there when he became aware of a hunched figure at Rose's back gate. The hunched person was also exhibiting a fair degree of agitation, seeming almost to hop about on one leg whilst attempting to delve into a large shoulder bag.

As he approached, he could see that the agitated person was Rose.

"Hello, Rose, are you having trouble?"

"Of course I'm having trouble! What a bloody silly question!"

Kirk gathered from the vehemence of the reply that Rose's agitation probably stemmed from more than just an immediate frustration. As was typical of him, however, he was reluctant to intrude on another person's feelings when they were clearly upset.

"Sorry, Rose," he said and began to head for his own back gate.

He had barely started, however, when he felt her hand on his arm.

"No! No! No!" she said and then followed this with, "Oh bugger, Kirk – I'm sorry."

In the residue of light, she looked into his face.

He was surprised – and almost taken aback – to see that there was an imploring look in her eyes.

"What is it, Rose?" he asked. "What's bothering you?"

"Oh….! I've locked myself out of the house," she said.

Thinking again that the effect seemed out of proportion to the cause, Kirk found himself asking what proved to be an even more inflammatory question.

"Will Richard be home soon?"

"Home? Richard? Home?" She seemed to splutter and gasp at the same time.

Sensing that that the use of words was problematic for her at that moment, Kirk gently put an arm round her shoulders.

"Perhaps, I'd better see if I can help…" he muttered through a face full of Rose's hair as she held him tightly to her and sobbed into his coat.

It was probably only seconds, but it seemed more like minutes before the tremors of Rose's sobs had subsided to the point where he felt he could make a move, however reluctantly, towards the garden path and the back door.

"Is there any chance that the keys are still buried somewhere in your bag?"

He had already glimpsed the chaos of paraphernalia that Rose kept in her shoulder bag and thought that it would be possible to turn over such a jumble of objects many times without actually finding something which had been specifically put there a few hours earlier.

Rose did not reply and, looking at her, he could see that she was not in a mood for a game of 'twenty questions' about how to get into the house. He set off up the garden path with Rose following. Despite feeling that it was rather pointless, he nevertheless turned the handle of the door and pushed. The door did not move but he decided to try holding the handle down and shoving at the door with his shoulder. This time, he thought that he detected a slight movement. He tried this twice then three more times, managing to move the door by increasing amounts on each occasion.

Rose watched with a mixture of surprise and concern. The last shove at the door had hurt Kirk's shoulder and he briefly rubbed it before giving vent to his annoyance by shoving yet harder. The door rattled alarmingly and burst open; Kirk found himself sprawling on the injured shoulder and banging his head on Rose's refrigerator. He managed to smile – just – when Rose appeared at his side, looking down at him but this time with amusement and relief belatedly written across her face. He held out an arm, which she took and used to help him to his feet. Together they inspected the door; there were no signs of damage to the lock and the conclusion that it had not been locked anyway, seemed inevitable.

"Well…" said Rose with a watery smile, but then she turned away from him and he could see that her shoulders were shaking again with a fresh bout of sobbing.

"It's been a bloody hell of a day!" she exclaimed through her sobs, although by now Kirk felt that the explanation was hardly necessary.

$***$

For a while, Kirk bustled about in Rose's kitchen, making cups of tea for them both. Rose had kicked off her shoes and curled up in an armchair with her legs pulled up to her chest, seemingly far away in her thoughts. Kirk sat on the large settee and, together, they sipped at their tea in silence.

After a while he asked, "Is there anything I can do?"

"You've been really helpful already," she replied.

When they had both finished, Kirk stood, picked up his cup and was in the process of picking up Rose's cup when she put her hand on his.

"Do you think that you could stay for while?"

He thought for a moment. He would much rather spend the evening with Rose than sit at home, alone by his own fireside, but there were other considerations.

"I could stay – but what about Richard?"

She looked up at him.

"He usually phones me to say what he's doing. He'll probably phone me quite shortly. Why don't you stay until then?"

Kirk could see no particular harm in staying and Rose still seemed to need company.

"Okay," he said. "Until you hear from Richard. Perhaps there's not much sense in the two of us sitting separately in our own houses when we can keep each other company."

Rose smiled and steered him back towards the settee.

"Right then," she said. "You sit there, and I'll do some food for us both. It won't take long and it's probably a while since you've eaten."

Kirk nodded although he was not used to having someone wait on him.

"Can I help?" he called out to her.

"No, it's alright. I've got some pasta with vegetables, if that's alright for you?"

Kirk thought that it was.

"Whilst I'm doing this, why don't you watch TV for a few minutes?"

He decided that he would do as she suggested. He rarely watched television even though he lived alone, but it would give him a chance to find out more about the storm that had hit the south coast.

'Stand-by' buttons on television sets had been banned some years ago so he walked across and pressed the power switch. The screen, miniscule by comparison with the one at the pub, sprang into life and he found himself watching a quiz show. Despite his very sporadic watching habits, he recognised the programme – and the woman asking the questions. She looked a little older than he remembered, but she was just as rude as ever to the participants and they seemed just as willing as ever to endure the ritual humiliation that she handed out to them. He checked the programme listings. There would be a news programme in just a few minutes so he decided not to 'channel hop'.

Rose bustled in bearing not food but newspaper, a basket of logs and a box of matches. She set to work at the wood burner, laying the fire and then carefully setting light to the paper. After a few minutes it was blazing away brightly and began to dispel the chill of the room. She arrived again shortly with first one tray and then another. Kirk still felt slightly uncomfortable about being looked after in this way but found himself with a tray on his lap – and no excuse for moving from his seat.

"I'm going to have a glass of wine. Would you like some?"

"Yes please," said Kirk.

"I'm not sure if it should be white or red," she said apologetically. "Anyway, it'll be from the Loire Valley."

He could see that she was reading from the labels.

"That must be almost as far south as the French can grow vines these days," said Kirk, remembering the scorching of the landscape and the numerous deaths that had occurred in the south of France during several previous summers.

"I know," said Rose. "It's all changed so quickly. When Richard and I first met we used to go camping down there, but I can't imagine doing that now."

Kirk had turned down the sound of the television but by now the quiz show had finished, a litany of other programmes had been 'trailed' and the news was about to begin.

"I don't watch television much these days," said Rose. "Do you?"

"No, I prefer to get the news from the Internet," replied Kirk. "I did see an earlier TV news programme when I was in the pub. There was something about a disaster in Southampton."

"Yes!" exclaimed Rose. "Here it is now!" She plucked the handset from the arm of the settee and turned up the sound. The newsreader's voice could be heard as the camera panned across scenes of wrecked buildings, floodwater, cars and all manner of debris borne along in deep, surging water.

The cameras zoomed in on scenes of helicopters rescuing people from the roofs of those buildings that still remained. The report then moved to shots of the countryside where vast swathes of uprooted trees could be seen, including some which had fallen onto buildings, cars or power lines.

Watching the scenes of devastation, Kirk felt a resurgence of the astonishment he had felt at the pub.

Rose watched in silence but then after a while, looked at Kirk and said, "What's happening to our weather? It's terrifying! I see all this in the news and I'm terrified!"

Kirk's reply was sharper than he intended. "We all know why it's happening. We've known for years."

Before Rose could respond, her mobile phone burst intrusively into a jangle of sound. She put down her tray and went to rummage in the chaotic shoulder bag, first gasping to find her keys and then, with remarkable speed, also managing to find her phone. She walked through to the kitchen. Kirk heard her say "Hello Richard" but then her words became indistinct. He made no special effort to hear what she was saying since he felt that he could guess the general nature of what was taking place.

Time was passing. Kirk waited but when he could no longer hear Rose in the kitchen, he decided to investigate. She was sitting with her phone in front of her on the kitchen table, tears streaming down her face. She looked up at him.

"The bastard says he won't be home until the middle of next week."

"Why's that?" asked Kirk.

"He says that he's got to finish a big piece of work before coming back down here."

"Do you believe him?"

"Of course not!" she scoffed. Seeing his surprise at her certainty, she said rather bitterly, "I know exactly the 'piece of work' he has to finish. I've known about her for the past two years."

"How do you know about her?" he asked, wondering if it was wise to do so but also feeling that she needed to talk about the situation.

"One of his company's offices is in York. Unknown to him I'm still in touch with an old school friend of mine who moved there when she married. She knows Richard but has never contacted him when he's been on a trip there."

Kirk nodded but still wondered how she could be so sure. She looked at him and continued with the story.

"Two years ago, my friend decided to tell me that she had seen Richard out in the city with a woman. That meant nothing in itself of course, but they were rather indiscreet. She saw them in the street with their arms around one another and kissing before they got into what appeared to be her car. Apparently, she was the one who went to the driver's side, so we assumed that it was her car.

"My friend didn't tell me immediately, but the incident nagged away at her and about a week later she decided to tell me about it. At first, I preferred to ignore it, thinking that she had probably exaggerated a point here or a point there, but a few weeks later, she saw them again at a Chinese restaurant behaving in a very similar way."

"So did you decide to ask him about it?"

For a moment she looked uncharacteristically defensive.

"You have to remember that I loved him," she said, giving Kirk a moment to absorb the fact that she had used the past tense.

"I suppose that I preferred to put my head in the sand, but then, shortly after that, I tried to contact Richard and could get no reply from him. We should have been spending the weekend together, but on the Friday night, he didn't appear and early the next morning in desperation, I rang my friend and asked if she would mind having a visitor for a day or two.

"Three hours later, I'd driven to York, parked a little way from Richard's office and arrived to see him coming out and heading down the street towards a line of parked cars. At first, I was tempted just to run after him, but then I thought that I would wait for a few moments to see what, if anything, would happen. Sure enough, a woman of my friend's description got out of a black hybrid parked at the kerbside and took Richard's arm. I could hardly bear to watch. They were all over each other – like a rash. Despite having the worst kind of feeling in my stomach, I decided to return quickly to my car and to follow them – at a distance, of course.

"Anyway, I had to follow them for some time but eventually we arrived at some bloody awful development, supposedly a 'housing village' on the edge of York. Her car drew up outside a fairly large, detached house and they both disappeared inside. I tried to keep out of sight but walked towards the house. As I got closer, one of them hastily pulled the curtains. I thought about banging on the door until someone was forced to answer – but then thought better of it. If I was going to finish with Richard, I wanted to have worked out what I was going to do afterwards. So I drove round to my friend's house instead and cried all over her."

Kirk had listened in silence to the details of her story. She was a very attractive woman but despite that, he sensed a certain vulnerability which had not been apparent when they had first met in the pub.

"He seems to have caused you a lot of grief," he said. "Why haven't you thrown him out?"

"That's a question I've asked myself many times," Rose replied. "Perhaps because until recently I used to think a lot about how good it was when we first got together – and also because on a practical note, I'd find it hard to pay the mortgage if I was here on my own." She gave a wry smile.

"Even so, you must be living in a state of permanent anxiety, wondering whether he's going to leave – or come back to you."

"Of course I'm anxious!" she retorted. "But we're all bloody anxious, aren't we?"

For a moment the vulnerability had been replaced with a rather fierce facial expression which he assumed to be a sign of her feelings about the general situation in the UK – or indeed, everywhere, at that time.

She stood up and announced that she was going to pour herself another drink.

"Would you like one?" she asked.

"I should go," Kirk responded without managing to sound convincing.

"I was rather hoping that you would stay for a while longer..."

Kirk did not reply but allowed her to take his glass. The truth was that he badly wanted to stay but although it was now two years since his divorce, he found himself wondering if, yet again, he would be making more foolish mistakes.

When Rose returned with two more glasses of wine, she seemed to have made a decision of her own during her visit to the kitchen. She sat down next to him on the settee. So far Kirk had responded carefully to her, but he was out of practice at the game Rose was playing, and it began to get the better of him. He turned towards her and began kissing her gently – around the neck at first but then, as she began to respond, quite firmly upon the mouth.

Somehow, Kirk pulled himself back from the brink on which they were teetering. "Rose, love," he said. "Rose, I know where this is going, and we can't go there."

She continued kissing him for several moments but then sat back on the settee. "I'm sorry," she said. "I... I don't know what I'm doing. You've been so kind and helpful..." She seemed to be finding it difficult again to find the words that she wanted.

Kirk picked up his glass and drank a little more of his wine.

"I'm a neighbour, Rose. Of course I helped and you've been really kind. I enjoyed the meal and I've enjoyed being here with you, but let's just see what happens next. I don't think you've decided what to do about Richard yet."

She looked at him with a smile. "No, you're right," she said. "I need some more time to think – and not just about this but about everything else that's happening."

Kirk looked at his half-full glass of wine and decided that it would not be sensible to finish it. He got up from the settee and began making his way towards the kitchen door. Rose followed him. At the door, she put her arms around him again and he lightly kissed her on the cheek. She let him go and he turned to open the door.

He stepped out into the pool of light just outside the back door and turned back to where Rose was standing on the back doorstep, her arms folded and about to wait for him as he made his way to the gate. "Even if Richard does come back, I don't see why we should stop seeing each other."

"No," said Kirk with a faint smile. "Neither do I."

As he made his way out into the back lane, Rose turned off the light and closed the door before going in search of what remained of the wine.

CHAPTER 6

WORMWOOD RISING

Kirk had lingered over breakfast that morning wondering what to do with the day ahead. He wanted to see Rose again but thought that it would be better for both of them to have some time to themselves.

He decided instead to spend the day finishing off the assignments he had already spent so long marking. As he plodded through them, he wondered if life would eventually return to normal – or what had passed for normal just a short time before, when he had still been making the daily journey to work.

Late in the day, he glanced down from his window to the street below. As he looked out, two huge lorries resembling milk tankers rumbled past in the direction of the fork in the road between Hallamton and the countryside.

They absorbed his curiosity for a moment or two. He was used to milk tankers passing the house but these seemed much larger. As the second of the vehicles disappeared into the twilight, he thought he could read the words 'Dairy Crown Milk' on the rear of its tank.

Deciding that there was nothing other than the size of the vehicles to excite his curiosity, he went to phone one of his friends from work in the hope that he might welcome some company for the evening.

A short while later he had walked up the hill from his house and into the village of Stanwick. Fortunately, his friend, David Holmes, was also at a loose end that evening. As Kirk arrived at the door of his cottage, David greeted him with a bonhomie that suggested he had already been sampling the 'home brew' he had offered to share when Kirk had called him on the phone. Kirk took off his coat and handed it to David, who hung it in the hallway before leading him through to the lounge.

Kirk rarely saw David on his feet so it was always something of a surprise to realise that his friend was a little shorter than him in height. Together with a very large number of other college tutors, they both spent a large amount of time each day working in a large open plan office seated at their computers, planning their sessions and catching up with incessant e-mail.

The view that Kirk usually had of David was of a man in his late thirties, whose oval face was topped with spiky prematurely-greying hair. His regular, usually smiling features belied a rather pockmarked complexion and large teeth that became increasingly evident whenever he grinned with pleasure or excitement. Despite the fact that he spent hours of each working day hunched over a computer, David strode with surprising athleticism into the kitchen to pour two pints of his home brew.

The lounge was softly lit by two large table lamps and was warmed by a large log fire. Seating himself in front of the fire, Kirk was soon sipping his way through a pint of a potent if somewhat pale yellow liquid which his friend assured him was the best home brewed beer that he had ever made. Dreading to think what David's previous efforts had been like, he consoled himself with the thought that at his friend's present rate of consumption he would soon be incapable of realising how much, or how little, Kirk was actually drinking.

For some while, they talked animatedly about the supposedly temporary closure of the college and the lack of news complaining, for the first time that either of them could remember, that they could not access their college e-mails and that for the past fortnight there had been no daily deliveries of post. Having exhausted these rather limited topics, they went on to speculate about events in the news, particularly the storm that had swept across the south-east.

Their conversation continued until, eventually, David remained slumped in his chair, inviting Kirk to 'help himself' whenever he noticed that Kirk's glass was nearly empty. Soon Kirk found himself topping up not only his own glass but also his friend's until finally David wished in a very loud voice that "things would simply return to normal" before falling sonorously asleep.

Hearing the first of his snores, Kirk moved quickly across to prevent David's beer from spilling over his knees and then checked that the fire would be safe when he left. There seemed little point in disturbing his companion, so he went in search of his coat.

He stepped out into the darkness of the street and made his way to the road, feeling thankful that the route home lay downhill. He took a torch from his pocket and set off.

Twice he was made to scramble up the bank when oncoming cars came too close, but it was later than he had thought and there was less traffic than usual. Feeling a little footsore, it seemed an appreciable time before he arrived once more at the entrance to the unmade road that led along the back of the terrace in which he lived. He glanced at Rose's back windows. There was a light in the kitchen, but he quickly decided against knocking on her door.

When he reached the back of his own house, he decided that he wanted to clear his head a little more before going indoors. Rather than go through into his garden, he swung open the large gates that led onto his garage forecourt.

As he did so, the screech of an owl drew his attention, and he went to look over the fence behind the garage.

He stood for some moments, peering into the darkness. The owl had perched on a branch of a nearby tree and was briefly silhouetted against the night sky before swooping down to prey on some small, unseen creature in the long grass at the tree's foot.

He was about to turn back towards the house when a movement away to his right distracted him. As he watched there was a brief wink of light followed by another. Prompted as much by the large quantity of beer he had drunk as by his curiosity, he decided to investigate.

He scrambled up the fence and jumped down onto the rough ground on the other side. Despite an awkward, somewhat drunken landing, he was undeterred and slid down the slope of the perimeter ditch that ran around the area in front of him.

Scrambling up the other side, he came to the high chain link fence that ran left and right for some distance along the industrial area behind the terrace in which he lived. There was another brief wink of light. This time, he was sure that it had come from his right, from the area beyond the far end of the fence.

He followed the fence along until it took a right angled turn to his left. The perimeter ditch followed the line of the fence, necessitating another scramble. He came out into a large open space of rough grassland that sloped gradually upwards towards an area of woodland silhouetted against the night sky. He walked forward up the slope, stumbling every so often over tufts of grass. He began to realise that the woodland, the outline of which he could see ahead of him, was the copse that he had seen during his walk along the Edge the day before. As the events of the previous day came back to him, he was simultaneously aware of small flickers of movement on the edge of the copse. He dropped to his knees and began to crawl forward through the grass.

Gradually, as he drew closer to the trees, he could make out a number of shadowy shapes moving about in the darkness. Given the number of shapes he estimated that he could see – which was perhaps between 15 and 20, the group of people gathered in the darkness seemed to be making remarkably little noise. Now that he was closer to the activity ahead of him, however, he could hear a constant low level noise, a hum, from the industrial area that lay a little to the east of the woodland. He speculated that power was being used for something hidden amongst the trees.

His first instinct was to crawl away in the opposite direction and should any of the proceedings that he was witnessing come to anything, to feign total ignorance. His next thought, however, was that by crawling away, he might attract attention – and that could be far more dangerous than edging forward and then simply lying completely still amongst the trees and undergrowth.

For short periods of time, the people out in the open area which lay just beyond the edge of the wood seemed to be immobile. Then someone would move across to a very large object that lay at the centre of the clearing. The wood was not very large, but Kirk had never ventured into this part of it before. He surmised that, perhaps, the long low shape in the clearing was a building of some sort.

He was soon disabused of this idea. Another hum, closer at hand than that coming from the industrial area, began to pervade the air in the space before him. Kirk smiled grimly to himself as he reflected on his scant acquaintance with the ideas of Freud; ahead of him a very large phallic shaped object seemed to be erecting itself in the darkness. Kirk felt sure, however, that this particular 'phallus' was going to be all about death and destruction.

He felt a sense of delayed amazement at what he was witnessing. The group of people in front of him had a missile – or certainly a rocket of some kind – and from the activity he could hear around him, he guessed that they were preparing to fire it. The missile, now clearly silhouetted against the stars and the night sky, seemed to have reached its intended elevation because the hum from the clearing came to a halt.

Next there was swoosh of sound that built with unbelievable rapidity to a roar and an explosion that brought Kirk close to losing control of his bowels. Clods of earth rained down on him despite the cover of the trees.

Almost immediately, the event was repeated; there was another swoosh and roar, another explosion which seemed even closer than the first. Again earth rained down on him as he lay, trembling in every part, knowing that this was outside anything that he had ever experienced before.

In blind panic, he stood and began to run chaotically through the wood and away from the clearing. Fortunately, the wood largely consisted of birch trees and was fairly open in nature. Running seemed to help; his immediate panic subsided a little. Now he had the presence of mind to wonder what could be happening back at the clearing and what the people there were doing.

As he ran, rapid thoughts flitted through his brain. The clearing seemed to be under attack, presumably in an attempt to prevent the firing of the missile. He had reached the edge of the wood and had to scramble over a wooden fence. Adrenalin leant him an athleticism that he had partly forgotten. He stumbled from the fence and into a field of low-growing crops on the other side.

Running now became more difficult because the field was deeply rutted from ploughing. He was also running uphill, and he felt frustrated by labour of his movements. He consoled himself with the thought that there was an absence of moonlight and that unless anybody attacking the woodland began to widen their focus, he would probably remain concealed for a short time yet…but time, he knew, was of the essence.

This thought had hardly formed itself in his brain when he stumbled over a furrow. He lay pressed against the earth by the sights and sounds that assaulted him, but then he raised his head, preparing to get to his feet again. A crescendo of noise made him turn his head awkwardly towards the woods. As he watched, the nose of the missile rose above the trees and then its tail, as it rapidly lifted from the ground and began to accelerate into full flight towards the night sky. The countryside around resonated to its roar and the atmosphere crackled with the combustion of its fuel. The missile's dark shape became a furious but speedily diminishing fire which was now arcing, ever more rapidly against the fixed pattern of the stars and, as Kirk estimated, towards the south.

Even as Kirk lay in awe, watching the missile disappear across the night sky, a battle seemed to be developing in and around the woodland; opposition to those who had fired the missile seemed, belatedly, to be becoming more organised; beams of light criss-crossed the area, accompanied by solid, earth-shaking thuds. The sound of heavy machine guns began to blast away unrelentingly at the darkness. Crashing sounds of destruction in the wood could be heard. Vehicle lights began converging along the radiating tracks, towards the centre of the woodland.

Kirk stood and began stumbling forward again. Almost ahead of him, a light in the sky was moving rapidly towards him and he could hear the tell-tale thwack-thwack rapidity of a helicopter's rotor blades. Instinctively, Kirk knew that he must now head towards the industrial area that now lay below him and to his right; the helicopter was possibly carrying heat detection equipment and he would find it easier to conceal himself there than out in the fields bordering the woodland.

Fortuitously, much of the area was used as storage space by the pipeline company and large drainage pipes lay stacked in orderly rows across the site. As he moved forward he fell again, this time into the ditch that ran along outside the perimeter of the security fence, gashing his thigh on a large piece of jagged metal that had been discarded there. There was no time to examine the damage. He crawled forward as rapidly as he could and picked his way through one of the many holes made in the fence by local children and into the first large pipe that he could find.

The crew of the helicopter seemed briefly to be aware of his presence. A powerful searchlight swept across the rows of pipes and steadied its attention in the vicinity of where he lay. He guessed that, despite the pipe, the heat of his body was being picked up on the helicopter's equipment. He lay as still as he could.

The once separable sounds of the helicopter's blades now began to merge into a deafening roar as the helicopter began descending towards the pipes, amongst which Kirk lay with his heart pounding as though it sought to burst out of his chest. The helicopter and his own preoccupation prevented him from noticing that by contrast, activity in the woodland and the surrounding area seemed to have fallen into an ominous lull.

Dread and preparedness fought within him; he struggled to suppress a sense of resignation. Then, inexplicably, the mounting blizzard of sound above him was jerked away and the helicopter climbed back into the darkness and began drifting across towards the wood, its searchlight panning back and forth across the trees.

From further out in the area surrounding the woodland, a fresh chatter of automatic gunfire had broken out. The helicopter's searchlight was switched off and the helicopter began veering away. From various points on the surrounding hillsides, rocket fire shot into the trees and the clearing, followed by further deafening explosions and tremors. Fires began breaking out in the wood and soon most of the trees at the focal point of the area were ablaze.

Despite his terror, Kirk had crawled to the end of the pipe and watched the new scenes that were unfolding before him. Suddenly, a single arc of light shot from the earth and towards the helicopter; in the blink of an eye, it became a tragic insect caught in explosion and flame, a ball of tumbling fire which fell to earth in a rain of debris and crater-making impact.

Not pausing to reason about what had happened, Kirk quickly climbed down from the pipe in which he had been concealed and began heading for the opposite side of the site, which lay adjacent to the row of cottages in which he lived. The forced inactivity in the pipe had given him 'second wind', but he had also become aware of the numerous cuts and bruises that his escapades had inflicted on him.

The thigh of his left trouser leg was becoming sticky with blood from his earlier tumble into the perimeter ditch – but still he could not stop. He forced himself onward towards the cottages. Perversely, there seemed to be few holes in the fence on this side of the site; it took him several minutes of anxiety and expletives to find a small hole through which he recklessly tore himself. He needed help, so, once through the fence and across the ditch, he headed not for his own cottage but for Rose's cottage further along the row and closer to the entrance to the unmade road that gave access to the rear gardens of the houses. From the road in front of the cottages came once more the sounds and lights of large numbers of heavy vehicles on the move. The cottages themselves were in complete darkness, their inhabitants as Kirk imagined, laying low in fear of the inexplicable events that had unfolded such a short distance away from their homes – places that, until now, they had assumed to be secure.

The injury to his left leg was now forcing itself to the forefront of his attention. With patience that ran counter to his sense of urgency, he unlatched Rose's gate, dragged himself up the garden path and fell against the back door of her house. From an awkward and painful position, he beat against the door with his fist but resisted the temptation to call out. By the time that Rose's flashlight had flickered briefly on his body from above, he was largely oblivious to the world around him. He did not feel himself collapse across Rose's threshold as she quickly unbolted the door and, with some difficulty, dragged him by the scruff of his clothing, into the house. She quickly bolted the door again anxious to shut out the din of military traffic on the road at the front and wondered with further anxiety about just how badly Kirk was injured.

CHAPTER 7

WORMWOOD FALLING

Trying not to think about the blood that was probably oozing onto her carpet, Rose set about examining Kirk's injuries. For a few minutes, he had protested.

"People were fighting... in the woods, Rose. Good God...!"

He sounded slightly hysterical.

"You can tell me about it later."

"But I need to tell you now."

"Alright, you can tell me whilst we do something about the mess you're in."

"Then perhaps I should just bloody well go home."

"You'll do no such thing," was Rose's response. "You need help. Look at the state of you."

"They may decide to search these houses."

"They may," she said, "– but there are other things to worry about at the moment."

She said it in a slightly snappy manner, realising that fatigue was making her impatient but also recognising that he could be right; the houses might well be searched. However, she rationalised, that was all the more reason that she did not want to be alone.

"Come on," she said. "Let's get you up those stairs so that I can clean you up and put you to bed."

She came close to support him and then drew back for a moment.

"Phwaw!" she exclaimed. "What on earth have you been drinking?"

"It was some of my friend's 'Home Brew'. We were trying it out."

"It smells like it… All the same, we need to get you up those stairs."

"Rose, I should go home."

"For the last time, you are not going home – at least not while the British Army is on the loose outside."

She put her arm round his shoulders and began moving him towards the stairs.

Kirk decided to give up the argument. He was able to give her only minimal help as she coaxed him up the stairs and into the bedroom. There, he flopped in her chair as she removed those pieces of his clothing that seemed to be obscuring the sources of bleeding. After only a few moments of this, however, she decided that he might as well remove his clothing completely. She helped him to put on a dressing gown and pushed the dirty and tattered clothes into a large wicker basket in the corner of the room.

In this state, he made a more compliant patient. He jumped involuntarily once or twice as she set about cleaning his wounds, but although they had produced copious amounts of blood, they proved not to be particularly serious. He also managed to tell some of the story of the battle in the woods whilst she finished dealing with his wounds and began wiping away some of the other conspicuous signs of his escapade. Rose listened carefully, surmising that he was lucky to have got away with just cuts and bruises. The extent of the battle came as no surprise since she had already witnessed much of it from the upper storey of her house. Any real astonishment that she still felt derived from the fact that such an event had happened at all.

Somehow she managed to support Kirk as far the bed where she sat him down again and, with a certain amount of heaving and pulling, arranged him so that he was lying fully on the mattress and beneath the duvet. She paused for a few moments, thinking carefully about whether to slip in beside him or not – but then, deciding that she was not likely to get much sleep anyway, sat down in the chair. She felt sure that it would only be a matter of time before the army's response to the battle in the woods would include a search of the houses. Just one look at Kirk would make him a suspect. For a moment she felt miserable, wondering just what was happening all around them and how it was that they had become caught up in it.

***

She must have dozed for a while but woke sharply to the sound of heavy banging on the front door of the house. She pulled her dressing gown tightly around her and went through to the front bedroom and opened the window. Below her, where she was expecting to see soldiers, she could see instead two policemen standing at the door. She called down to them:

"What do you want?"

"We need to speak to you and anyone else who is in the house."

"Alright," said Rose with a sense of resignation, "I'll come down."

Closing the window, Rose glanced along the row of houses and could see similar scenes being enacted at most of them. The street was sealed off at both ends by a large assortment of police vehicles, their baleful lights sweeping the darkness and enhancing Rose's sense that this was really just part of a nightmare that she was having.

Moments later, she was going through the complicated routine required to open the front door.

"Hurry up, hurry up!" came the voice of one of the men outside.

She opened the door. The light was largely blocked from her view by the two large policemen she had seen from the bedroom window. One of them was bending his head lower, seemingly trying to fit into the door space.

Wasting no time on explanations he asked:

"Is there anyone else in the house?"

For a moment she hesitated, wondering about how to account for Kirk's presence in the house then she said, "My partner's in bed upstairs."

"Well go and get him up then," replied the officer.

"And get some clothes on. You'll both be coming with us."

Rose turned and went back up the stairs to where Kirk had begun stirring in the bed. As she went, she could hear the police officers checking through the lower rooms of the house. Whatever protocol should apply on such occasions seemed to have been abandoned. Kirk was slowly propping himself up on one elbow.

"What the hell's going on?" he enquired.

"The police are here. They say we have to go with them. We've got a minute or two to get some clothes on."

Kirk knew that it was pointless to argue. Rose helped him to struggle into a mixture of his own clothes and a pair of Richard's trousers that she took from the wardrobe. She dressed herself quickly in trousers and a top, pulling a thick cardigan around her; it gave her a small feeling of security as well as warding off the night air which by now had become cold.

They both managed to find some shoes and then Rose helped Kirk down the stairs. An officer went past her, taking the stairs two at a time. There was a succession of heavy footsteps from the upper part of the house before he called down:

"No-one else up here."

"OK, Matt, get yourself down here and we'll take these two to the station."

The officer returned down the stairs in a manner similar to the way in which he had gone up them. Despite the dim light of the house and the doorway, he noticed Kirk's difficulty in moving.

"Well," he said. "What happened to you then?"

Kirk was just about to attempt an answer when another voice, rather crisp in its tone, came from just outside the door.

"Save the questions for later. Get these people to the station."

Kirk and Rose were herded ungraciously into the front garden, past a shadowy individual in a senior officer's uniform and were then half led, half pushed along the path to the front gate, where a police car was waiting. They were made to get into the back seat of the car. Rose caught a glimpse of someone trying to resist further along the row.

"Get off me, you fuckin' bastard!" was followed by the sound of someone falling heavily onto gravel. There was the sound of violent scuffling before the person on the ground was seized unceremoniously and bundled out to a waiting police van.

Rose began to reflect that if this was a nightmare it was strangely real. They sat in a daze, huddling together in the back seat of the car and wondering what exactly was going to happen to them next.

"I suppose we have to be grateful that they let us put some clothes on," muttered Kirk. Rose smiled bleakly in the darkness as the car pulled away from the kerb.

*** ✱✱✱ ***

Once they got to the police station, they were immediately separated, and after brief initial processing to do with establishing their identities and addresses, they were taken to rooms deep in the bowels of the building where the only light was provided by dismal strip lights and energy saving bulbs.

Despite the way in which Kirk and Rose had been taken from Rose's house, her interrogators now both introduced themselves as detectives. They seemed strangely formal and polite after the initial treatment that she and Kirk had been given.

She was questioned at length about her work, about Richard's activities and about Kirk, whose presence in the house had caused a slight twitching at the corners of her interrogator's mouth – one of the few facial expressions she had felt able to read during the protracted and repetitious questioning to which she was subjected. She noticed uneasily, however, that information that seemed to her to be insignificant also seemed on several occasions to generate further protracted questioning. After a while, interest in Kirk had dwindled but interest in Richard began to intensify. Again, she was surprised by the general direction of the questions and searched around in her memory for anything that might help her to understand but found the effort in that area was more than she really wanted to make. Besides, she wanted to conserve what energy she had for the strange situation into which she had fallen.

Kirk was initially questioned about why he was in the woods, and the events that had led him to Rose's house. Like Rose, he was questioned by two plain clothes officers; one, thought Kirk, was clearly in middle age. He had spiky grey hair, piercing blue eyes and bore the red cheeked and slightly pinched expression of someone who probably drank a good deal when not on duty. His companion looked to be in his late twenties and almost too slight to be a police officer; tall and thin, his clothes seemed to hang on him. He too had spiky hair but looked, in contrast, like someone who ate a healthy diet and took regular exercise.

Kirk's injuries and description of the events in the woods generated innumerable questions, although, the tell-tale signs of a hangover bore out his story that he had been drinking with a friend until shortly before he had decided to walk home. At one point, he was taken to a lavatory to be sick – probably, as he reflected, out of self-interest on the interviewers' part rather than any concern about his discomfort. He reflected that

David's home-brew had 'staying power' if little else.

The nature of the events he had witnessed was sufficiently dramatic for him to realise that he would be questioned at length. What did he know about the missile? Where had it come from? How had it been transported to the woods? Who were the people in the woods? What had he seen these people doing? Did he know anything about what had happened after the missile had been fired?

He was sure that after a while it would be apparent that he simply did not know the answers to many of their questions. Nevertheless, he had been made to relate over and over again the sequence of events that had eventually led him to Rose's back door; but always they seemed to want something more.

Each time, however, it was his good fortune that he was very obviously nonplussed by the events he had witnessed. The questioning had also widened so that they took him repeatedly through various parts of his life history and particularly events in the last two to three years.

Eventually, he began to feel that he was talking out of a kind of delirium. His interrogators recognised the tell-tale signs that they had reached the limits of their line of questioning. It was at about this time that he was aware of hurried conversations between his interrogators and a third person who had arrived in the dimly lit corridor outside the interview room. He was taken away to a small cell where he was allowed to sleep.

Later, they took him back to the interview room but this time the questioning seemed less intense. Finally, the older officer told him that he was free to go – but that he should not think about leaving the area because they would probably want to see him again.

As he prepared to leave, his first glimpse of daylight in many hours stung his eyes. He collected his belongings from the sergeant on duty at the desk and headed out into the street. As he emerged, he guessed that it was shortly after dawn on the day following his arrest by the police. In previous times, he might have felt some indignation at the way he had been treated, but he was all too aware of the general situation in the country, and it was mainly with a sense of relief that he wandered painfully away from the police station.

Walking, he found, was an effort. His body had not recovered yet from his misadventures in the woods and incarceration in a police station had not helped. As he set out, he tried to ring Rose on her mobile phone but there was no signal. Then he hoped that he might catch sight of a bus. After a while, however, it became apparent that there were no buses running.

Eventually, he managed to find a taxi. The driver must have known something about the events that had taken place near Kirk's house because when Kirk gave his address, he was initially reluctant to take him, saying that there were police checkpoints around the whole area, but business had dwindled almost to nothing and after a little persuasion he agreed to drop him off fairly close to where he needed to be. He tried several more times to phone Rose but to no avail and decided that as he was now approaching the bend in the road at which the driver had agreed to drop him off, there was little point.

As he left the taxi and walked along the road to Rose's house, he soon came within sight of a police checkpoint. The road had been closed off with a barrier and as he approached, a burly armed policeman emerged from a police car parked nearby. Kirk found that his heart was pounding as the policeman checked his identity and then disappeared back into the police car to make a radio call. It was some minutes before he emerged again with the papers Kirk had handed to him. The policeman waved him past the checkpoint barrier, but it was only when Kirk was out of earshot that he gave a sigh of relief.

He arrived at the front of the terrace in which he and Rose lived. A small number of police and army vehicles could still be seen further along the road leading out into the countryside. He walked round to the back door of Rose's house. With relief, he saw her face appear briefly at the window. She gave him a tired smile and then opened the door to let him in.

***

"Come here, you," she said as they folded their arms around each other. Their kiss was a long one but then Rose drew him away to the lounge.

"What happened to you at the police station?" asked Kirk as he followed her.

"I'll tell you all about it later," she replied, "but first I think you'd better see this."

She could access the internet from her television set but selected instead the BBC's 24-hour news channel. They watched the presenters – a man and a woman – seemingly with little emotion – reading a news item about central London. Kirk rarely used the television news services, preferring the internet, but the presenters still seemed vaguely familiar to him. At that moment, it was the man who was speaking.

"We apologise for the continued loss of service from our London centres. We return to our main story, however, which we first reported in the early hours of Wednesday morning. Reliable sources have now confirmed that a terrorist missile, fired from a site near Nottingham, was targeted on central London, specifically Downing Street and the surrounding area. Munitions experts have also confirmed that the missile's warhead carried conventional explosives –and was not a nuclear weapon as had earlier been rumoured. The blast completely destroyed the buildings in Downing Street, including the residences of the Prime Minister, the famous 'Number 10 Downing Street' and the Chancellor of the Exchequer's official residence at number 11. Despite intense searches through the remains of the buildings, no-one has been found alive. It is believed that both the Prime Minister and the Chancellor were in Downing Street when the missile struck.

"We go live now to our correspondent, Sandy Cameron, who is as close to the scene as anyone can get at the present time."

"Sandy, despite the huge importance of these events, we still seem to be getting very little news from within the tight police and army cordon that has been thrown around the scene there."

The camera shot moved into close up, focusing on a balding and bespectacled middle-aged man in an unfashionable raincoat. He spoke directly and earnestly to the camera.

"Well, that's right, David. There is intense frustration here at the way in which this devastating and tragic situation is being handled. It is now nearly 36 hours since the missile struck and yet we have no hard news about the fate of the Prime Minister and the Chancellor. Government sources are still refusing to confirm or deny the widely-held belief that they were both in residence when the explosion occurred."

"Why do you think that there is so little information coming out at the moment?"

"Part of it, David, was revealed by a spokesman from the Ministry of Defence earlier this morning when we learned why no-one is being allowed into that part of the city. It seems that large parts of the area are now heavily contaminated with radioactive material."

"Does that mean that, as some observers suggested yesterday, the terrorists used a tactical nuclear weapon?"

"No, the latest view from sources inside the MoD is that the use of such a nuclear weapon is highly unlikely. The blast damage, devastating though it was, is restricted to Downing Street and the Government buildings in the surrounding streets, strongly indicating that this was a conventional weapon. It's now thought that this was a so-called 'dirty bomb' – a warhead that scattered radioactive materials right across the area where the missile struck."

"When do you think that we will know more about the situation down there in what is, after all, one of the world's major capitals?"

"We all wish we knew the answer to that, David. As you know it isn't just the area immediately around Westminster that's been affected by the radioactivity; it's also a much wider area of the city. Indeed, the whole of the London region has been affected. And as if that was not enough, the Met Office has now forecast that there will be strong winds and heavy rain throughout the south-east today and it's feared that this will spread the effects of the radioactive materials far beyond the point of the immediate impact."

"Is there anything more that you can tell us, Sandy, about the evacuation of the affected areas?"

"Yes, there has, at least, been a lot of information about that. Both the police and the army have been trying to control the exodus, which in the first few hours at least, could have been described as chaos and panic."

"Why is that Sandy? Don't Londoners have a reputation for carrying on with 'business as usual' in the face of such events?"

"You're right, they do have that reputation – but this is something different. The terrorists' use of radioactive materials has spread panic in a way that the Luftwaffe bombs and the various other attacks on London, including more recent ones during the London Olympics, failed to do."

"So, with a single missile, the terrorists have managed to cause a level of disruption in the nation's capital that not even the whole of the Luftwaffe managed to do in World War Two?"

"That's about it, David."

"Well, there we have to leave it for the moment, Sandy. No doubt we shall be returning to you the moment that there is anything to add to this tragic story."

The camera shot from central London withdrew to a corner of the screen and then switched to the studio. This time it was the female presenter who spoke.

"Following that news update, we go now to a panel of experts who have come into our Birmingham studios to consider the implications of the events in London…"

Rose glanced at Kirk. She could see that the news report had shocked him and that he had made the connection with the 'battle in the woods' – as they had now begun to call the firing of the missile and the fighting that followed. It was a little while before he spoke.

"When did you start to find out about all of this?" he finally asked her.

"When I got back here from the police station, late yesterday – I had to get a taxi. I think the bus crews are refusing to operate a service over here. They seem to think that the whole place is still crawling with soldiers and terrorists."

"From what I can see, they're probably right," said Kirk. He mused for a moment.

"You know, Rose, although I was caught in the middle of that fight, I still haven't the faintest idea who those people were. I cannot begin to identify them."

"That's probably just as well for you."

"How do you mean?"

"Come on, Kirk. Do think you'd be sitting here now if the police thought that you had the slightest thing to do with that fiasco in the woods?"

"No," he said, "you're right. The situation in London looks really bad. I can hardly believe that I was a witness to the beginning of all that destruction. I wonder if the PM and the Chancellor are dead. The missile must have killed an awful lot of people. It seems unlikely that they could have escaped."

"Well," said Rose. "Someone seems to be determined that we're not going to be told what's going on until such time as it suits them."

They fell briefly into silence.

Then Kirk looked around. "What do we do now?"

Rose moved from the chair in which she had been sitting and came to sit at his side.

"I know what I want to do," she said. "In fact, it's what I need to do."

She put an arm around him and ran the fingers of her other hand through his hair.

"I can't believe you..." said Kirk. "At a time like this...?"

"Especially at a time like this – we've just had all this in our faces for the last day and a half. I need you to hold me."

Kirk obediently put his arms around her.

"That's very nice – lovely, in fact, but now I need a bit more than that."

She took the fingers of his right hand, drew him to his feet and then towards the staircase. He feigned reluctance but then allowed her to lead him up the stairs and into the bedroom where the duvet and pillows still lay in disarray on the bed. She began unbuttoning his shirt.

"I think you could do with a shower," she said. "But not just now."

With a certain amount of fumbling, they undressed each other, throwing their clothes into the spaces around the bed. Despite his fatigue, Kirk felt a breathless excitement as he lifted Rose's legs and entered her. She gave a small gasp and closed her eyes before opening them again and looking at him.

Their lovemaking was hungry and passionate. When Rose finally lay with Kirk's arm around her shoulders, she held his right hand to keep it still, wanting simply to lie in the afterglow of their lovemaking. Kirk dozed for a while and then fell asleep. Rose also dozed for a few minutes but then slipped out of the bed to make cups of tea for them both though by the time that Kirk awoke to find Rose's side of the bed empty, the tea was cold and the subdued light of an autumn afternoon was falling through the window.

CHAPTER 8

WHITHER?

Although Kirk sometimes felt lonely in the house, there were also times when he valued the solitude; this morning in particular, he wanted time to think about the general direction his life was taking. Familiar cliches ran through his head, telling him this was not a dress rehearsal for 'real life'. In Kirk's mind, the antidote to wondering about the significance of his life lay on his dresser. He walked across and picked up a fossil which he had collected from a beach many years before, when he was still living with Joanne. He turned the fossilised remains over in his hands, wondering how it could be that creatures of such relative simplicity could have this long-lasting memorial when it was extremely unlikely that he would be remembered by anyone beyond a few years after his death – if that long.

The thought did not detain him long – which was, perhaps, a sign that he was recovering from the desolation of his divorce. He might, he reflected, have little control over whether he would be remembered or not, but he could at least enjoy the morning.

He fell to wondering about Joanne – and in particular if she had found anyone else. He hated the thought that by now, she might have slept with someone else – and yet, he thought regretfully, it was none of his business if she had.

It seemed strange to remember now but in his earlier life, Kirk had always felt the need to keep to a semblance of his parents' code of ethics; both of them had been committed Christians and theirs was more than a nominal faith. It had been the foundation of their attitudes towards one another – and to their children. By contrast, when Kirk and Joanne had met, they had lived together for about a year before deciding to get married – a situation that Kirk found easy to conceal from his parents because he lived some distance from them. Meanwhile, he was ambivalent about their moral certainties, partly resenting the unquestioning nature of them whilst simultaneously envying the self-assuredness that their well-defined landmarks in the ethical landscape gave them.

Without such landmarks, he found himself increasingly questioning the conventions of daily life. He had had no qualms about moving in with Joanne when they decided to live together. And, years later, such was his inability to understand the possible consequences, that he fell unthinkingly and to the utmost depths of his emotions into an affair with Sarah – realising only belatedly, that there are some actions in life upon which the clock cannot be turned back.

This was the background to Kirk's attempts to make a new start and, as yet too little time had elapsed for him to feel any significant emotional distance between his present situation and the break-up of his affair with Sarah. Rose, meanwhile, with problems of her own, did not realise the extent to which she was wandering into the wasteland of someone else's life.

Life, though, with a capital 'L' was not waiting for them, reflected Kirk as he tried to wrestle with the events unfolding around him. What should he and Rose do? Then – he stopped to ponder the phrase that was now in his thoughts – 'he and Rose'. Was that indeed how things stood? Had they, after such a brief flirtation with each other, become a couple?

His thoughts played for a while across the choice between going forward alone and exploring whatever lay ahead with Rose. In all honesty, he could not say that he felt about Rose as he had felt about Sarah – or, perhaps, Joanne – but she occupied a warm place in his thoughts. He liked her, was drawn to her and felt comfortable with her. And in the chilliness of his enforced celibacy, he thought that she too would soon be wanting more than a bed left empty by an unfaithful partner. Would he be using her? Answer 'Yes' – but she would also be using him. Could he love her? Answer 'Perhaps' – but he was still feeling that the intensity he had felt with Sarah – and the rawness it had left – were not what he wanted in his life then – or maybe, ever again.

He realised, as so often before, that he was unlikely to reach a clear set of conclusions in his thoughts. He also chided himself for making assumptions about how Rose would feel, and his past record was not one that spoke of emotional intelligence towards women in the private part of his life.

In the bigger picture, however, some of the strands that would go into the making of England's future were already discernible and even if he was unable to see the whole picture, he needed to see enough to know how to live in that future; that, at least, he thought was something he would rather do with Rose than without her.

He paused. There was no detail, no plan – but it was a kind of conclusion and one that he liked. The sourness of his immediate situation, however, began seeping back into his thoughts. He had nothing to do, and a sense of futility was making him listless; there was still no news from the College about his salary and marking the pile of assignments had probably been pointless.

It was now nearly a fortnight since he had last been over to the College site and he needed to know what was happening. The battery in his hybrid car had several hours of charge in it and there was a small amount of petrol in its tank; despite the general chaos, he decided that, for lack of anything else to do, he would be able to drive across to his place of work and find out what, if anything, was happening.

He walked out to his garage at the back of the house, using a small electronic key fob to open the garage door. Next, he opened the large gates onto the shared road at the back of the houses – just as one of the more eccentric of his neighbours, Jim Horton, appeared from the direction of the main road, riding his old bike slowly along towards the gate into his own garden.

It was difficult to tell how old Jim was; Kirk supposed that he was somewhere in his early sixties, but he might well have been older. Jim's face never ceased to startle him, even though he saw him most days; his skin had a worn, sallow appearance and was deeply lined, whilst the lower half of his face was covered with stubbly whiskers. His hair, in similar fashion, was grey and tufted as though someone had hacked at it with a blunt knife and when he opened his mouth, his teeth were decayed with irregular gaps between them, giving his smile a lopsided look. When he spoke, his voice had a gravelly quality that came from the over-consumption of cigarettes and strong alcohol.

"Ah, what a world it is!" he growled as he approached Kirk.

"What do you mean?" Kirk was never quite sure where Jim's opening comments would lead.

"Those young lads from up the road there – all dead. I don't know what the world is coming to."

Although he was on his way out, Kirk felt that he should pay more than his usual amount of attention to Jim's story.

"What's happened?"

"Haven't you heard? Everybody knows about it. Where've you been the last two days?"

"Same place as most of the folks along here," Kirk replied.

Jim looked at him with narrowed eyes but then continued blundering along with his story.

"I was out with the dog looking for rabbits. We had to go over past the woods although they've mostly been sealed off by the army guys and the cops. Well, the dog got excited and dived into the bushes. Next thing I know, he's scrabblin' away this mound of earth. I thought he'd got scent of a rabbit but when I caught'un, there was this foot stickin' outa the ground."

"So what did you do?" It seemed the natural question.

"Whadya' think I did? – Went home and called the cops. Bloody well wish I hadn't though all the shit they put me through."

He paused as if for effect although his listener was already completely engaged with the story; remembering the shots he had heard several days before, Kirk quickly realised that the youths he had thought of as thugs had probably seen something in the copse that would have ruined the plans of the terrorists and that in stumbling across them, they had met far more than their match. As this realisation dawned upon him, it took a concerted effort on Kirk's part not to let his jaw drop.

The look on his face, however, did not entirely escape Jim's notice.

"Whassa matter, mate?" he asked.

Kirk dithered for a moment.

"I was just shocked." He paused briefly. "I wonder if I knew any of them, through College perhaps?"

"Nah, I doubt it. You wouldn't have seen them at the College." He laughed. "No way! They were all NEETS – 'Not in employment, education or training.' You wouldn't have wanted to know them. A lot of people were scared of 'em but I knew 'em. They was OK."

Kirk was very familiar with the term NEETS and was curious about how Jim had got to know so much about a group of youths that most people had probably tried to avoid, but he realised that he might trigger a long conversation that he did not have time for at that moment. He pulled himself back to the present, remembering that he wanted to get to the College.

"Alright, Jim," he said. "Thanks for letting me know but I've got to get going."

Jim looked doubtful. "Where are you off to then?"

"I need to find out if there's anything doing at the College."

"Huh, you' be lucky. Whole bloody country seems to be shuttin' down."

"Well..." said Kirk but left any attempt at explanation hanging in the air. "See you later."

Jim nodded. Kirk climbed into the car, took it out of 'parking' mode and rolled away from the house, making little more noise than the sound of gravel crunching beneath his tyres on the unmade road.

The road that led away from the street in which Kirk lived passed through a large industrial estate; normally busy, the traffic along it that morning was light. He began to wonder where everybody could be, speculating that perhaps they were indoors watching the latest television news updates, searching the internet or perhaps in the pub, drinking and arguing about the events that had taken place. The streets along his route had an eerie, deserted feeling about them and were devoid of traffic or any other signs of activity.

The last part of his journey contrasted with its beginning and passed through a leafy residential area. Turning from a junction onto the main road, he was surprised to see an assortment of debris strewn across the road – stones, pieces of brick, splintered wood and broken glass.

He decided that it would be unwise to take the car any further and pulled into an 'on street' parking space by the kerb, pausing to think about his next move. He was hesitant to get out of the car in a place where there had clearly been recent disorder but then, despite the rubbish in the street, he still felt the need to find out what was happening at the College. As he looked around him, the street continued to be deserted so, deciding to investigate on foot, he began to walk slowly towards the building's entrance.

As he walked, a sense of wonderment slowly enveloped him. Such was the amount of glass, rubble and splintered boards that Kirk guessed that a pitched battle had been fought outside the College. Expecting to see the expanse of green open space that formed the area in front of the College's glass, metal and concrete, instead his view was totally blocked by a huge barrier of plywood boards that had been erected along the front of the building - and across which graffiti had been scrawled. For once, he noted, the slogans could conceivably mean something to someone other than the person who had wielded the spray can. He crossed the street, crunching on broken glass, so that he could stand back from the enormous letters and thereby read them more easily. "Rich Pigs Cost the Earth" he read as he scanned the boards and then, walking a little further along: "England for the English" – a different theme and probably sprayed by a different graffitist.

Feeling distinctly vulnerable, Kirk stood briefly pondering these messages amidst heaps of broken glass, much of which had come from the smashing of nearby shop windows. Whatever had taken place outside the College, it looked as though looters had exploited the situation; packaging lay strewn about in the street whilst clothing and electrical goods had been left hanging out of broken windows. Seemingly the thieves had been disturbed. Kirk pushed sodden card and paper aside with his foot and continued his survey of the wooden barrier.

The wall of plywood curved round to the far end of the site and Kirk could see that some of the panels had been burned away. Scorch marks and broken bottle fragments at the foot of the incinerated barrier suggested that someone had attacked it with Molotov cocktails. The desired effect was no doubt the large hole that was irregularly framed by the charred and blackened remnants of the plywood. Cautiously, Kirk eased himself through the hole.

The ground floor windows had been boarded up but those on the first and second floors had been left unprotected and, like many of the shop windows along the street, had also been smashed. He began making his way along to the building's front entrance, but after just a few paces, concluded that there was little point; the entrance, too, had been boarded up. Thick wooden battens held the boards firmly in place.

Kirk stared up again at the broken windows and as he looked, he was disturbed to see that some of them had not been broken with stones but contained bullet holes. He quickly decided that he had found out enough about the situation at the College and that it was time to leave. The urge to get away was also compounded by his discovery of a single shoe. The shoe – a trainer – would have been white had it not been covered in flies and a red sticky substance which he had little doubt was blood.

He picked his way as quickly as he could back to the hole in the barrier and out to the road. The street was still deserted, reinforcing the deep sense of unease that had been growing in him since he first began to notice the absence of anyone on the streets. What was keeping them at home – assuming, of course, that they were at home? Without knowing why he had not noticed it before, he almost fell over a newsagent's board lying amongst the glass and packaging. Its headline read simply: "More City Riots – Threat to Centre".

Although Hallamton lay out on the edge of the city, he speculated briefly that the urge to riot must have been infectious. Wondering when the rioting had happened, it occurred to him that it had probably taken place during the period that he had been incarcerated in the police station – and that only significant unrest could explain the destruction that he saw all around him.

He looked down the street to the newsagents and convenience shop from which the board had come; it was a shop often used by College staff and students. He walked along towards it and as he approached, he could see that the full expanse of the window had been driven in and the interior gutted by fire. A single piece of burnt timber dangled precariously above the shattered frontage and the blackened cavity of the store. Unsurprisingly, there was no sign of the Asian family who owned the business. His unease now was becoming more akin to fear. Perhaps that was the reason no-one was to be seen on the streets? They had become places of trouble and danger. Fear was keeping people indoors.

It gradually became clear to Kirk that there was little more that he could learn from such devastation, and he began making his way back to the car, wondering as he went how he could have become so out of touch with the events that had taken place. It was true that during the two days that he had been interrogated by the police he had barely seen daylight let alone anything of the outside world. Perhaps it was because national events had taken most of his attention – and he was still feeling the shock of having been an involuntary witness of the missile firing and the battle in the woods.

That, he thought, could partly explain his lack of attention to recent local events, but what perplexed him more was his longer-term failure over the preceding years to read the many signs that must have been there in the news, in the constant stream of books and journals and increasingly in people's conversations. Had he really, in all that time, been so self-absorbed that he had completely failed to understand the seriousness of what was taking place? He could only conclude that he had.

As he drove back to the cottages, he hardly noticed that he was breaking the speed limit. The roads were now so completely deserted that it was possible to believe that another pandemic had swept across the land but once again, it did not register in his innermost consciousness. It was simply something that was passing in front of his eyes – and it was, no doubt, such self-absorption that had led him to push seemingly unconnected events out to the margins of his mind even though he had believed himself to be well informed about what was going on around him.

Perhaps he had relied too much on the kind of news coverage that viewed everything through the lens of 'opinion' – and which had failed to distinguish between the truth of scientific research and the deliberate manipulation of information by powerful, self-serving economic interests? Supposedly, however, he was intelligent; he also bore some of the responsibility for naively believing in the objectivity of the news media.

With a head full of such weighty thoughts, Kirk realised that he needed to pay attention to what he was doing. He had arrived back at his cottage and began manoeuvring his car back onto the garage area. That done, he went in search of Rose. She would help bring him back down to earth. He found her sitting on a chair by the back door of her house, peeling apples from her garden.

"Oh," she said in surprise as he approached. "Thank goodness it's you. I was beginning to wonder if I'd been deserted."

"Not likely, Rose," he said and sat down next to her. "Other than Jim, you're the only person I've spoken to this morning."

"Are you surprised?"

"What do you mean?"

"Everyone's been advised to stay indoors. It's the radiation in London. They say it could be spread by the wind."

"Well that didn't seem to be bothering Jim…"

"He doesn't have a TV."

"Ah," he said.

It had not occurred to Kirk that the radioactive materials scattered in London could be dispersed as far as Hallamton – or that it might be the explanation for the deserted streets.

"So why are we sitting out here then? Let's get inside."

"No, Kirk," she said. "I've been shut up in there since you left yesterday. Anyway, the wind has been blowing from the North for several days now. People in Europe have more reason to worry than we do at the moment." She seemed very calm. It was almost more unsettling than when she was upset.

Nevertheless, after several minutes of silence between them, she decided that discretion was the better part of valour. They retreated into the house where Rose arranged herself in her large, single armchair, leaving Kirk the space to lounge on the settee.

Despite the concerns that they now shared about the radiation it was the destruction at the College that continued to agitate Kirk. His agitation did not escape Rose and she wanted to know what it was that had disturbed him. He related in some detail his wanderings amongst the debris left by the riot and the lifelessness of the College and the adjacent streets. When he had finished, they both sat in silence until Kirk said, "The situation seems to be getting much more serious than I ever thought it would."

Rose looked at him with a frown. "I don't mean this nastily, Kirk, but in the short time we've been together, I have noticed that you're often in a world of your own."

Kirk frowned at her comment but found it hard to deny its truth. He was often preoccupied and sometimes seemingly unaware of what was happening around him, but the terror of the missile incident, his interrogation by the police and now the destruction of the working environment into which he had commuted for the past two years had succeeded in piercing the protective bubble in which he had taken refuge since his divorce. The demands of the present had become overwhelming.

"You may be right about that, Rose," he admitted, "but even I can see that it's becoming very dangerous here."

She nodded in agreement. "Yes, it is – and it isn't going to get any better. At the moment, despite panic buying, there's still food in the shops. But what happens when the food runs out – when there's no more food to be had from anywhere?"

"You're right," agreed Kirk. "But at the moment, there seems to be nothing we can do."

"I'm not so sure."

"What d'you mean?"

"I mean that there may be another choice that's open to us…"

"Really? And what's that?" said Kirk – noticing again that he had become an involuntary half of 'us'.

"Well…I've had a text from my aunt."

Kirk tried not to sigh; Rose's impending narrative sounded none too promising.

"So…is that unusual?"

"Well, yes, actually it is. I hardly ever hear from her. In fact, she's bit of a recluse."

"What's her name?"

"Alison."

"Where does she live?"

Rose shifted in her chair and smiled at him. "What is this? Twenty Questions? She lives in Somerset."

The narrative, thought Kirk, was improving. "Sounds interesting – but if you don't usually hear from her, what does she want now?"

"Ah, well, that's just it – because you see, what she seems to want right now is some company."

"You mean she's suddenly feeling all alone and vulnerable?"

"Yes…except that there's a great deal more to it than that."

Kirk began to look pensive. Rose had yet to say the words, but he knew that what she was going to suggest next was a move to Somerset. Rose's earlier use of 'us' also clearly implied that she wanted Kirk to go with her. He needed, though, to hear her say it aloud – since her suggestion would be important – and would indeed give them another option in a future that was becoming daily more uncertain. Now that he had seen the destruction at the College, moving to rural Somerset could have much to recommend it.

He heard himself saying, "What do you want to do?"

She looked at him quizzically, thinking that, by now, surely he knew what she wanted – but realised that he needed her to tell him plainly:

"I want you to come with me – to Somerset."

At last, she had said it.

There was a pause whilst he gave the appearance of thinking about it but then he said, "Yes, I'll go with you - but I needed to hear you say it! I needed to know that it's what you want."

She drew close and put her arms around him. "Of course it's what I want, Kirk. We've only known each other a short time, but already, being with you feels much better than being with Richard. At least we'll look out for each other rather than trying to do our own thing."

Kirk held her firmly for a moment but then they drew apart and sat side-by-side on the settee.

"So where do we start?" asked Kirk. "I'd happily walk away from the house and the few things I have here, but we can hardly just turn up at Alison's house as refugees."

"I agree with you – but I think we need to have a sense of urgency."

Kirk raised an eyebrow and looked at her. "You're really worried about the situation here, aren't you? There's a lot of unrest but how bad do you think it is?"

"Very bad!" she exclaimed. "The supermarket shelves are almost empty – and what happens when they have nothing, when they close their doors?"

"Well, hopefully, someone at national level is getting a grip on the situation…"

"I wouldn't count on it, Kirk. That missile you saw destroyed more than just a few buildings. It took out most of the government!"

"But they have emergency plans…They must have!" Kirk had begun to feel Rose's level of agitation. "After World War 2, there were contingency plans for nuclear war. Surely, there must be bunkers and emergency food supplies everywhere."

"Are there? Are such things still out there? No one's talked about them for years. But if they are, who will they be for? Who will get them, Kirk? – Not us! Not ordinary people!"

"But we should be 'all in it together'," objected Kirk. "That's how it was in World War 2."

"This isn't World War 2. We're not 'all in it together' and some of us have spent decades denying there's any kind of problem! Now, there are so many 'enemies' we don't know who or what will be out to get us next – or even why. We just know it's constant – that something's being dropped on us all the time." She was white with passion and frustration but had to pause for breath.

Kirk looked at her. She was angry and he did not know how to respond. Then, instinctively, he reached out and put his arms round her. At first, he felt the tension in her body but then, very slowly, she began to relax. He let several long moments go by, holding her gently and waiting until they could talk again.

Eventually they drew apart and Kirk, trying to inject a sense of normality into their conversation asked, "Do we have any cash between us?"

"A little," replied Rose. "I tried to get some more yesterday but the banks are in deep trouble. People have been desperate to get their money out. It was on the TV. The queues in the city centre were round the block."

"Have you tried your card? Can we still shop online?"

"Of course I have – and, no, I haven't been able to shop online."

"So what can we do?"

"I have no idea. The whole banking system is collapsing. They can't even lend to each other, and they've shut their doors to ordinary customers like you and me. They could be the biggest single reason for the riots that have taken place. When you were talking earlier about the College being attacked, it wasn't the College the rioters were out to get; they were just angry and wanted revenge."

"Revenge on who, though? They haven't hurt the banks. All they've done is smash up their own community."

Rose shook her head wearily. "I would have thought you'd understand all this better than I do," she said.

"Oh – yes, I do understand, Rose," Kirk assured her. "But though I see what's happening, I don't really want to believe it."

"Perhaps that's why you had to go to the College – because you couldn't believe that it had simply shut, stopped working, gone offline – whatever you choose to call it?"

"I suppose I was expecting – naively as it turned out – that someone would phone or text – or just send out a simple, good old-fashioned letter – something – anything other than simply disappearing off the scene."

She moved towards him, took his face in her hands and kissed him on the lips. "Kirk, Love," she said, "you may not have noticed but communications around here are not at their best right now..."

* * *

They had now been talking for some time and meanwhile, the light had faded, and gloom had begun to envelop them. He stood and went to look out of the window, wondering if there was a storm on the way, noticing as he did so that a line of cars was slowly approaching from the end of the street. Watching him, Rose commented, "Whilst you're on your feet, Kirk, perhaps you could check the power supply?"

He went to the light switch and checked; gratifyingly, the lights came on. "OK – so at least the power industry hasn't downed tools," he said. "I think all I wanted to know when I went to the College was that, despite everything, we would be able to keep going. It looks as though the power workers feel the same. They're just trying to keep us all going. They deserve a bloody medal."

"Perhaps going to work is what they know how to do," replied Rose. "They're hanging onto it like a security blanket."

Ignoring that she might also be talking about him, he said, "Well, I for one am glad that they are."

By now the line of cars in the street had drawn level with the house and, peering out, Kirk could see that it was a funeral cortege and that it was headed by four large hearses. There was something unearthly, thought, Kirk, about the way in which these black electric vehicles glided slowly forwards, their coffins mounted high inside and bedecked with flowers and football scarves. The coffins, he concluded, could only be those of the four youths whose shooting he had unknowingly witnessed some days before.

Rose came to look over his shoulder. Strangely, he had forgotten to tell her anything about that particular incident.

"What is it?" she asked.

CHAPTER 9

WEST IS PROBABLY BEST

That night, Rose had wanted Kirk to sleep with her. Now he lay awake, thinking about their earlier lovemaking and about the situation in which they found themselves.

He wondered briefly if they were simply seeking comfort with each other but then thought that it was no bad thing if they were. He knew what it was to fall in love. He had fallen in love with Sarah – although he had never been sure if such love was something to celebrate or something that had ultimately proved destructive. Perhaps there was more to be said for loyalty, for constancy even, when daily life together became a little boring. The soaring heights he had experienced with Sarah had been beyond anything he had experienced in the other parts of his life but then there had also been the depths... He did not want to return to such feelings. Gradually he drifted into sleep again.

***

He woke quite early the next morning. Rose's side of the bed was empty and cold. For a few moments, he curled himself tightly up together beneath the duvet, knowing only too well that he should be following Rose and getting on with the day. Then, finally, reluctantly, he threw aside the cover, hauled himself out of bed and pulled on a dressing gown that Rose had found for him. He went down the steep and narrow stairs into the light and warmth of the kitchen – still, they had power – to find Rose seated at the kitchen table and poring over a large sheet of white paper on which she was alternately scribbling furiously and then resting pensively. He seated himself on one of the chairs opposite her.

Kirk guessed that she had been there for some time. He watched her a moment and then asked, "Are you OK?"

"Yes – yes, I'm fine. I couldn't sleep so I decided to get up."

"What are you writing?"

"Just my thoughts at the moment about what we need to do."

Kirk had already had several years' practice in trying to read students' work from the other side of a table and found it quite easy to decipher what she was writing.

It was a list. As he made his first attempt to read it, he thought that it would contain a number of practical items such as a list of the food that they were going to need in the next few days, or perhaps things that they would need to deal with before setting off for Somerset.

His second guess was the better of the two. As he began to make out the words in the list, he could see that she had written several headings – 'House', 'Richard', 'Transport', 'Food'. Underneath each of the headings she had listed a number or items with stars against them.

She gradually became aware of his curiosity.

"It's just my way of clarifying my thoughts. I prefer to write them down rather than let them go endlessly around inside my head."

Kirk thought for a moment and then picked up again on the previous day's discussion.

"You still think this is a good idea – I mean, leaving here and going to Somerset?". It was not that he was getting 'cold feet' but in the cold light of morning, he wondered if he had agreed too easily to Rose's proposal. Had they thought sufficiently about taking such a major step?

For a moment, she looked less than patient.

"Do you have another idea?" she asked.

"Well, we could stay here…Travelling to Somerset could be very risky. Also, you have a house here and I have a house here."

He knew that Rose had already made up her mind and that he was testing her forbearance , but he also knew that there might be difficult times on the road when their determination to travel on would be challenged– so it seemed better to talk about it now rather than simply drift into a potentially hazardous course of action.

"I want to go to Somerset. Having you here has made a big difference – a huge difference – but I still don't feel safe. This place feels as though it's going to explode at any time. If we lock and board up the houses, with any luck, the thugs will choose the easy targets first."

It sounded like a good deal of probably pointless work and right at the last minute.

"What thugs? Who are you talking about?" It was Kirk's turn to feel impatient.

"You can't have listened to anything I said when we talked about it yesterday – the people from up the road here, from Hallamton. If you still haven't noticed, the country is almost at a standstill. No-one's going to work. Soon there'll be no money and no food. People will start to go mad with the anxiety of it all and then they'll be here and everywhere else, grabbing what they can, trying to make sure that they survive even if nobody else does."

For a moment she looked both miserable and exhausted.

Seeing her weariness he said, "You should have stayed in bed a bit longer."

He knew immediately that it was the wrong thing to say.

She looked at him with both sorrow and anger on her face.

"How can I stay in bed at a time like this? How can you? How can you lay up there with all this going on around you?"

Kirk was feeling far from complacent at that moment, but it was not the time to argue with her. He knew that there were no guarantees of safety whichever course of action they took.

They seemed to be headed for a row and they both knew that it could only be deeply unhelpful. They returned to the bedroom, quickly got dressed and then snatched some breakfast. Despite his attempts to test Rose's resolve, Kirk knew that she had persuaded him – at least to the extent that he would rather be doing something rather than simply waiting for events to unfold.

Over breakfast, Rose expanded a little more on her determination to go west.

"I picked up some e-mails before you came down," she said.

Kirk nodded, silently noting that the internet was working again.

"My aunt is almost pleading with us to go down there. I think that she's really worried about our situation here – and about her own."

There was a brief lull before he decided to openly agree with her.

"Okay, okay," he said finally, trying to keep any note of weariness and resignation out of his voice. "You've persuaded me. We can get started after breakfast."

"What are you going to do first?" asked Rose, seizing her opportunity.

"I think that we should just pack up our things and be ready to leave as quickly as possible."

"Right," said Rose, thinking that he had not answered her question but quietly pleased that she was finally making some progress. "I could do the packing. Why don't you concentrate on making the two houses secure?"

Kirk wondered fleetingly and mischievously about political correctness and about suggesting that they should both share in both tasks – but thought better of it. Rose's division of labour seemed like a good plan just at that moment.

Without waiting for him to help, Rose cleared the breakfast table and went in search of bags and suitcases. Having quickly agreed that they needed to be as sure as they could that the cars would be secure, Kirk headed for his garage. They had decided that they would only be able to take one car. Kirk's car was slightly bigger than Rose's and they had agreed that they needed the extra capacity to take at least some of their belongings.

He went to unlock the large gates leading into the garage area. As he drew closer, he saw that Jim Horton was on the patch of ground at the back of his house. He had turned his bike upside down and was working on a puncture. Patience was not his strong point. Kirk winced and tried to creep past as Jim cut his fingers, swore at the bike and then kicked it over in vehement disgust.

"You fuckin' stupid…" He caught a glimpse of Kirk and paused for moment but not for long.

"Oh assholes!" he yelled.

"Having trouble, Jim?" enquired Kirk.

"Whadya think? You as stupid as this fuckin' bike?" He kicked the bike where it lay.

Kirk began to slink away in embarrassment towards his garage door. Jim stalked away in anger towards the back door of his house. His dog, a springer spaniel, crouched to one side, well out of his path; he seemed to have the emotional intelligence that Kirk was lacking that morning.

Having failed miserably with both Rose and Jim, Kirk began to get on with fortifying the garage. At least that was something he felt that he could do competently.

It now seemed fortuitous that when he first moved into the house, the garage had been something of a wreck, and as a consequence, he had already replaced the door and the roof. He decided to board up the windows and plug as many gaps between walls and roof as he could. It would have to do. They needed just one more night there and then they could be on the road. He silently prayed to himself that any troublemakers from Hallamton would not find their way along the road until such time as he and Rose had been able to flee the area.

By mid-morning, he had finished his work on the garage and despite feeling that he had already had enough, he began to cast around for materials with which to board up the windows of the two houses. Then he remembered that the factory that lay just a short distance behind his house was surrounded by high barriers consisting of wire, including barbed wire and large sheets of plywood. A few sheets of plywood were just what he needed, and he felt confident that there was no-one in the factory to worry about them anymore.

Kirk reflected briefly – and whimsically – that in the middle of an environmental crisis perhaps he should be using hand tools, but he was in a particular hurry. He would use power tools; they had been charged with so called 'green electricity' so perhaps that made it alright.

He worked through the rest of the morning and into the early afternoon. Unusually for him, he did not even think about stopping for lunch. He knew that Rose would not stop until she had finished what she had set out to do.

He did pause briefly to make much needed cups of tea for them both and as he was wandering back from Rose's kitchen towards his own house, he saw that Jim was once more working on his bike, this time with more patience. Out of habit, Kirk felt that he should try to make peace.

"Do you fancy a cup of tea?" he asked as he approached his neighbour.

The bike tyre was now back in place, and it looked as though Jim was about to pump it up again.

He looked a little sheepish, scratched the back of his head and then said, "Aw go on then. I ain't 'ad one for some time."

A few minutes later, Kirk returned with a large mug of tea, steaming into the chilly air of the afternoon.

"Thanks, mate." Jim took it appreciatively from Kirk's hands, warming his fingers on the mug and then sipping cautiously at the hot tea.

For a moment, they both stared around in silence, drinking their tea and not rushing to make conversation.

Then Kirk said without alluding to anything specific, "Oh well, perhaps the cavalry will come riding over the hill."

"Cavalry? What you on about?"

"Oh nothing in particular. It's just an expression. I thought maybe someone or other might ride in, tell us everything is OK and that it's back to 'business as usual'."

"You what, mate?" exclaimed Jim incredulously. "There ain't no fucker ridin' in to get us of o' this one!"

Kirk reflected for a moment on Jim's sentence construction and choice of vocabulary whilst Jim warmed to his theme.

"There ain't no 'cavalry' ridin' in this time, least of all the American cavalry."

As usual with Jim, Kirk began to wonder where the conversation was going.

"It's just an expression," he repeated, feeling a little frustrated.

Jim eyed him curiously, with one eyebrow cocked.

"You really don't listen to the news, do you?"

Kirk was puzzled. Rose had said that Jim did not have a television set.

"No, not much," said Kirk weakly, trying to pacify his companion.

Jim continued, "The Americans got troubles o' their own. They ain't gonna be worryin' about us anytime soon."

"What do you mean?"

"You really haven't seen the news then? I saw it lunchtime on that big set in the pub."

Kirk shook his head.

"Four truck bombs been exploded – big ones. They were also these things everybody keeps talking about over here – 'dirty bombs'."

Kirk felt his jaw dropping as he listened.

"Yeah," went on Jim. "They got New York, Washington, Chicago and Los Angeles. There was another in Houston but that one got discovered."

"So when was this? "

"It was about midday our time but day, night in the States – all sorts of different times."

Jim had been watching the television coverage.

"I s'pose I mean they all went off at the same time," continued Jim again, "but y'know with the different time zones and all that. It's a helluva big place, the States."

So it had been a massive, co-ordinated attack.

Jim drifted away into silence, waiting for Kirk to say something. Kirk, however, had no idea what to say. He could only imagine the mayhem and the suffering that the bombs had caused.

Eventually he blurted out in a rather meaningless way, "How on earth did they get past American Intelligence?"

"I dunno – but they keep playing the same shots over and over again. It reminds me of 9/11. It must be great for Al-Qaeda."

"Is that who they think it was? I thought they were history."

"Well, that's who they keep talkin' about. They don't have a clue really. There was one of these weird clips with some ancient bloke in the background, claimin' it was revenge for Osama Bin Laden. He was saying that it was a huge triumph and a victory for the peoples of the world over the 'Great Satan'. You know how those folks go on. I guess they just lay low 'til no-one thought they was comin' anymore. Time ain't the same for them."

Despite Jim's lack of education, Kirk thought that he was probably hearing as much sense as he was likely to hear from any of the media.

"Anyway, mate," said Jim, returning his almost forgotten theme. "I don't think the Americans will be turnin' up for a while yet – they got a bit to do."

Kirk's earlier sense that the known world was collapsing around him returned.

"Sorry, Jim," he said. "I've got to go and talk to Rose."

He had let out a small secret. It was Jim's turn to look surprised – and then amused.

"Oh yeah," he said. "You go and talk to Rose. Good luck to you both."

Kirk rushed away, realising that despite the world-changing events in the news, on an everyday level it was still possible to feel embarrassed.

CHAPTER 10

NO WAY BACK

As he left Jim to his own devices, Kirk was suddenly aware of the fatigue which the preparations of the day had brought upon him. It was with a very conscious effort that he went back into Rose's house in search of the one person who seemed capable of bringing him any cheer at that moment.

The house was now quite dark and almost forbidding. Kirk had boarded all the windows except those in the kitchen. They had decided that if trouble was going to come it would probably arrive late in the night or in the early hours of the morning. Their plan was now to bring forward the time of their departure since they had begun to believe that local people who were bent on exploiting the apparent lack of law enforcement would do so sooner rather than later.

Although by some miracle the power companies were still able to produce electricity, Kirk and Rose had decided to use as little electric light as possible, believing that this would also help to attract the least attention. Kirk could see, however, that as darkness fell, many houses on the hill in Hallamton were brightly lit, suggesting that their inhabitants thought that the crisis would be a short-lived situation or that, for whatever reason, they did not foresee any danger from others around them.

He stood gazing out at the town which was some little distance from them and wondering if somehow, he and Rose had talked themselves into unnecessary pessimism. As he did so, Rose quietly slipped her arms around his waist and kissed him on the neck. He felt the gentle warmth and curves of her body against him. He turned and began kissing her on the mouth, placing his hands lightly on her hips. Their kissing gradually became more urgent until Rose pulled away.

"Not now, Kirk," she said. "We need to eat and then get some sleep."

Kirk sighed but accepted that she was right.

The food was simple, consisting of the last of the vegetables from their respective gardens and some meat that initially was shrouded in mystery but, it subsequently emerged, was a small piece of beef that Rose had frozen months before when she suddenly found herself cooking for one rather than two.

Having worked hard that day, they both cleared their plates. It was their last meal in the house as far as they knew. Unthinkingly, they loaded the plates into the dishwasher and switched it on; as it began its familiar cycle with a series of hums and clicks and swishing of water, Kirk reflected that using it seemed like an extravagant thing to do in view of an anticipated failure in power supply, but he said nothing. They might as well use it while they could, and he knew that they were both behaving out of habit. They left the dishwasher to complete its cycle and Kirk noisily nailed the last of the boards over the kitchen window.

Although there was still power, the internet, radio and television now no longer seemed to be in operation. Rose tried them all in quick succession but was greeted by electronic indications of failure. She found this deeply unnerving. She had been born into an age of television and radio and had never known a previous time when instant news had not been available. The world around them seemed to be going 'offline'; the fuzz on the screens and hissing on the radio was ominous and more heavily message-laden than any news broadcast.

In the darkness, they carried bags and boxes out to Kirk's garage and loaded them into the car until the whole of the boot and back seat area were full. The row of houses remained largely quiet, although glimmers of light could be seen here and there behind drawn curtains.

Two doors further along the terraced row from Rose's cottage, the neighbours had clearly decided to follow a different course. The curtains in every room, upstairs and downstairs, had been left open. Music and light were blasting into the night sky and a hubbub of voices could be heard. If the world as they knew it was coming to an end, they were determined to see it out with a wild party.

Rose and Kirk paused briefly to watch what was happening. As they did so, the back door of the house flew open, and a couple lurched out of the light and into the garden.

They were spectacularly drunk and fell together onto the grass. Then, giggling loudly, they managed each other to their feet again. Staggering off, they made for a car which had been left parked in a pool of darkness by the row of garages. Intruder lights flicked on as they came within range of the sensors, prompting some noisy cursing and laughter from the couple.

Kirk watched as they began hungrily undressing each other in the full glare of the lights. The woman then tried to lie on the bonnet of the car but when her partner launched himself forward on top of her, they both slid to the ground.

The woman began to rummage in a large handbag that she had dragged along with her. A flashing of the car's lights indicated that she had found her keys and together the couple disappeared onto the back seat of the car.

From somewhere in the tangle of limbs an arm was flung out and the car door slammed loudly. Long seconds passed, accompanied by more cursing and laughter, before the car began to rock, firmly and rhythmically. Although the car doors were shut, loud cries and groans could be heard coming from inside. Rose tugged at Kirk's arm, drawing him away towards the house. She was not really sure why. The couple had made no attempt whatsoever to be discreet, but she still felt as though by watching they were intruding on them. There must have been times in the recent days when anyone observing her with Kirk would have seen something very similar – and yet somehow, she clung to the idea that they were different. Had they been as casual as the couple in the car? Had they been driven by love…or lust? She knew that they had felt both.

Inside the car, the man was now grunting loudly whilst the woman's cries were mounting to a crescendo. The car was rocking violently. Then just as suddenly all movement ceased, and noise was replaced by silence.

Kirk and Rose had nearly reached the back door of the house. Going in, they locked the door, climbed the stairs, half undressed but then lay in each other's arms under the covers.

They did not try to emulate the couple in the car. Kirk began to put his hands under Rose's clothing but they both knew that they would have to leave in just a short while and that any sleep that they could snatch in the meanwhile would help them to remain alert as they set out on their journey. Rose gently held Kirk's hands in place as he silently assented to her preference for sleep.

"Eat, drink and be merry for tomorrow we…" he quoted from he knew not which part of the Bible.

"…For tomorrow…we live …and leave," misquoted Rose, cutting short his attempt at humour. Kirk did not make any further reply and instead was soon asleep, this time with his arms innocently around her and his head on her shoulder.

* * *

Kirk had generally found that if he went to sleep with a time for waking fixed in his head, then he would usually wake at that time. It was a curious little trick in which he had a fair amount of confidence. Rose had also set the alarm on her phone. Kirk woke to be accompanied shortly after by the buzzing of the alarm two hours later. He climbed out of bed and went across to the window.

He had left a couple of boards loose in the centre of the shuttering. Taking them down as quietly as he could, he peered out into the darkness. As he looked out, he noticed that every so often lights on the garages at the back of the houses were flicking into life. He told himself that it was probably just a hedgehog or a cat. He listened carefully, thinking that he heard a noise just on the threshold of his hearing. Perhaps the couple he and Rose had seen were still out in the car at the back! He had almost forgotten them.

He began to put on clothes that he had laid out in readiness for their journey. Despite the buzzing of the alarm, Rose still lay in a foetal position, hugging a pillow and continuing to doze. He could leave her for a few minutes longer, but they would need to get away shortly if they were to make the most of the cover afforded by darkness.

Soon, however, Rose had hauled herself awake and, swinging her legs over the side of the bed, began to put on extra clothes that she had put out on her side of the bed. They had left a small amount of food – sandwiches, crisps, the last of the bananas – on the kitchen table ready to snatch up as they left. Now that they were both ready, they picked up the food but at that moment neither of them was hungry, so they pushed it into their pockets.

With a brief tinge of regret, Rose locked the back door of her house and followed Kirk out into the night. Moments later, they were on the unmade road in front of the garages. They were both acutely aware of the intruder lights flicking on as they passed, tracking their path as they headed towards Kirk's garage at the other end of the row. As they passed the car into which they had seen the couple climb some two hours before, they noticed that they were still inside, semi-naked and slumped across each other, presumably asleep.

Away to their right, Kirk could hear loud noise, a hubbub of voices and could see flashlights probing the darkness. A crowd of people was heading down the hill from Hallamton and apparently making for the cottages. Kirk could only guess what they had in mind, but he did not want to wait to find out.

Their hearts beating hard, they both ran the remaining distance to the garage. Together they flung up the garage door and Kirk dived for the driver's seat. It would take only moments to get the car out of the garage, but he cursed himself for not getting them away from the place hours before.

The crowd had now surged a long way down the hill. Some youths had raced ahead and climbed over the fence at the end of the unmade road. Kirk paused as they ran past heading for the first thing they could see – the car in which he and Rose had just seen the sleeping couple.

He could wait no longer. As soon as the crowd arrived they would have no chance of escape. He pressed the button that enabled him to use the car's electric drive. The intruder lights outside were now all fully on and he did not need to use the car's headlights, so he left them switched off. The quietness and the acceleration of the electric motor would give them a small advantage. They felt a desperate pity for the couple in the car, but the crowd approaching the terrace was large and their chances of rescuing them were minimal. Pressing his foot gently on the accelerator, Kirk slid the car out of the garage and out onto the unmade road.

Ahead of them, they could see that the advance group of youths had dragged both the man and woman from the car. The man had been knocked to the ground and lay curled into a ball, trying to protect himself as he was remorselessly kicked. Meanwhile three of the youths had seized the woman and were raping her; the bonnet of the car was again in use but this time with an evil urgency that contrasted sharply with the couple's abandon a few hours before. The woman was screaming and fighting her attackers, trying to get away, but two of them of held her down whilst the third was all too obviously going about his business.

Kirk felt a surge of pity – and then anger. Unnoticed until the last minute, he pushed the accelerator to the floor and the car flew towards the youths. Belatedly aware of its silent approach they began to scatter but not quickly enough. He had not thought that they would be so slow! He stamped on the brake but broad-sided into them. There were several very loud bangs as their bodies made contact and were flung into the air, falling to either side of the car's path.

Seizing her opportunity, the ravaged woman slid from the bonnet on which she had been pinned, gathered the last of her strength and crawled away towards some bushes behind the garage area. Her male companion also made the most of the distraction and followed her, dragging himself bloodily into the darkness.

It was now Kirk and Rose who became the centre of attention. Kirk quickly shoved the car into reverse and lined it up to escape but found his way blocked by the body of one of the youths who lay unconscious in the car's path.

Behind them, some of the crowd had smashed down the fence and had sensed that there was a delay in the car's escape. As Kirk manoeuvred around the body, they began to run forward at great speed. Kirk pushed his right foot down to the floor but there was an agonising moment before the car leapt forward. Rose was wearing a seat belt but still found it necessary to stop herself from being flung about as they rocketed out of the garage area and onto the road. The front runners raced after the car but could not compete with its acceleration. Kirk watched them in his rear view mirror as they fell behind.

The road away from the houses was long and straight. Kirk flew along it at speed, trying to resist the temptation to keep looking back, but Rose twisted around in her seat and gazed out through the back window of the car.

As she continued to watch, she could see flames appearing. In moments the blaze was huge. They must have set fire to a house! She thought that it was probably at Kirk's end of the terrace.

They came to a bend in the road and, finally, Rose could see no more of the scene they had left behind. She twisted back into her seat and said, "They've set fire to the houses."

Kirk nodded grimly, his face dimly lit by the light from the dashboard.

"I wonder if Jim managed to escape?" he said.

"I wonder if any of them have managed to escape?" replied Rose, thinking about the other residents.

"What do you think they were after?" Even though they had anticipated it, Kirk was still puzzled by the attack.

"Just about anything – or anybody – they could lay their hands on!" Rose thought again about the woman who had been raped on the bonnet of her car.

"But why? What do they have to gain by it – especially now that they've set fire to the houses?"

"Oh, I don't know, Kirk. They probably intended something else, but we made them angry. I only knew something of the kind would happen. Everything's breaking down. You could feel it in the air for days – weeks even. The only wonder is it's taken this long to happen."

Kirk agreed but said, "I wish we could have got away with a little less drama."

Rose knew that he was thinking about the youths he had hit as they were trying to escape. "I wouldn't worry about it," she said. "It was us or them. They got what they deserved. Anyway, I think I saw the couple escaping."

Alongside their own escape, it was a straw to cling to now that their houses and everything in them would probably be little more than piles of ash by the time that morning came.

For a while, Rose worried that someone in the crowd might use a mobile phone to send a message ahead of them; there could be more trouble waiting for them just down the road. She pulled out her own phone to check the strength of the signal and was greeted with a message that there was 'No network'. She was still thinking in the 'old' way. There were no systems out there to support either friend or foe. This time, it had worked in their favour, but she realised readily that despite the scorn that she often felt for the technology on which everyone had come to rely, there could be times in the future when they would long for the speed and ease of their receding world.

As they sped through the darkness, lights still glimmered here and there. Rose thought that normally they would have seen orderly rows of streetlights to either side of their route but now, town and countryside alike were enveloped in darkness and the car's headlights were probing forward into a land that was rapidly losing the ability to generate electricity other than by the power of wind and water.

It was by a coincidence that the area in which they had been living had become, in the previous day or so, a small void in the country's communication network. It was one of many such voids that were gradually emerging and expanding, but elsewhere, in general, people were still obeying a government message to 'Stay in the safety of your home' though probably more out of fear than any sense of trust. The message had reached most people in the country but here and there, it was never received.

It was one of the last such messages to emerge. Clinging on by its fingertips, a residual government was trying to preserve a sense of momentum towards a fabled restoration of life as 'normal' but its grip was slowly failing. The radiation in London was eating like a cancer at the ability to govern. Elsewhere, local divisions and communal strife were leading to territorial disputes and the age of the warlord seemed as though it was once again about to dawn.

The hybrid car bore Kirk and Rose on their way. Far out in the night, hydro-electric generators and wind turbines were continuing to churn away at their task, but power stations that relied on regular supplies of coal or oil or complex organisations to maintain and support them, were slowly falling silent. Despite the gradual collapse taking place all around them, most people were still trying to sleep in their own homes – even if they were desperately uncertain as to what the following days would bring. For an hour or two at least, Kirk and Rose would have an uncomplicated journey towards their destination.

PART 2

CHAPTER 11

SOME FOOLS PERHAPS BUT NO ANGELS

In better times the journey to Somerset would have taken just a few hours. Kirk and Rose agreed, however, that they would be unwise to use the motorways. The government would be trying to regain its grip and the motorways would be amongst the routes along which military traffic would flow. They would also be trying to control the movements of civilians and Rose and Kirk had no desire to find themselves being turned back at a police or military checkpoint. Despite the slow progress, they would keep to the minor country roads – or even to lanes and tracks, if necessary.

They were now travelling on an undulating road which took them through woodland. In contrast to their escape from Hallamton, the journey up to that point had been tedious and Kirk felt his concentration waning. They agreed that Rose would take a turn at the wheel.

Kirk had longed to take a break in the passenger seat but found that he could not relieve the tedium by falling asleep. He lay back in his seat watching Rose through half-closed eyelids. Soon, however, Rose was feeling the effects of their lack of sleep. Before their escape, they had managed to doze only for about two hours and now the first light of dawn was just beginning to appear in the sky. She glanced across at Kirk.

"You still awake?" she asked.

Kirk grunted that he was and thought for moment.

"Perhaps there's a track or a clearing just off this road where we could stop for a while."

"Sounds good to me," said Rose.

She slowed down but it was several minutes before they saw a track leading off to the right and away from the road. As she swung the car onto the track, they could see that some hundred yards ahead of them, it expanded into a circle which presumably was used by forestry vehicles or visitors to the woods.

They drove cautiously along, aware that whilst they were on the road they could see clearly, but here in the woods it was much darker. Rose laughed.

"I'm not sure I like this…"

"Well, it's one way I can get you all to myself," said Kirk.

"Perhaps that's what I'm afraid of…"

Her comment teased his thoughts for a moment but then he returned to thinking about their security. It felt as though they would be safe in the clearing and there were no signs of activity in the wood or on the road. It seemed like a reasonable place to rest for a while.

It was cold so neither of them attempted to take off any clothing. From somewhere in the back of the car, Rose had found some blankets. With difficulty, she arranged them over Kirk and herself.

Kirk had tilted back his seat as far as it would go and had also rotated the arm rest out of the way; Rose went through the same sequence with the driver's seat until she lay alongside him. Seeking more warmth, they attempted to put their arms around each other, but the contours of the seats made it distinctly uncomfortable and instead they lay on their sides, facing one another.

"I don't know how much sleep I'm going to get like this," she said.

"You might surprise yourself. It's been a long night."

"It has…" she yawned. Moments later, Kirk could hear the gentle sounds of her breathing but then he too drifted into a sleep that was full of restless and repetitive dreams.

The last of the stars gave way gradually to a bright blue sky. In the subdued light of the woods, Kirk and Rose lay breathing gently beneath the blankets, oblivious to the dawn.

Kirk slept only for a short while before the cold woke him again. Despite his tiredness, he wanted to get on with the day. Stiffly, and with a sense of vulnerability, he climbed out of the car. The radiation blast in central London had left him suspicious of every breath that he drew and of every step that he took in the open air.

His only answer to the paralysis that this implied was to accept fatalistically that eventually everyone would be affected by the tiny, lethal particles that were being carried everywhere in the wind. He mused for a moment on the thought that sometimes the wind was benign. As far as he could tell, at that moment it was blowing from the north, but there would be other times when it would blow from the east. Then the wind would become their enemy. Then they might have something to worry about.

He found that he did not want to think about it. He wanted just to put one foot in front of the other, to deal with today, to love Rose and to share whatever time they had left. There was always another choice, but he knew that neither he nor Rose wanted to think about it, let alone carry it through. They would continue living, whatever that meant for them.

By now, Rose had begun to stir. Like Kirk, she struggled stiffly from the car, hobbled towards him and silently put her arms around him. Although Kirk had not noticed it, a small stream ran just to one side of the clearing. She wandered across to it, squatted down and gingerly dabbed a few splashes of the cold water on her face.

They were both hungry, but rather than go in search of the food they had stored in the boot of the car, they resorted to eating the sandwiches, crisps and bananas they had pushed into their coat pockets as they had left Rose's house; it was all a little the worse for wear, but they were hungry.

Although they had brought something to eat on the journey, they had forgotten that they would not be able to simply pop into a service station. They had but a single, small bottle of water between them. They took it in turns to swig from it, trying to wash down the last fragments of a meal which, if neither of them would remember it for long, would at least keep them going for a while.

"Strange, isn't it..." commented Kirk.

"What is?" asked Rose patiently. She was becoming used to his sudden leaps of thought.

"How we take daily food and drink so much for granted..."

"We won't be able to do that for much longer," she replied. "At Alison's place, we will have to work for it."

"But at least, we'll have the choice – one that people in towns and cities may not have."

"True," she commented tersely.

They shared the last of the water from the bottle in silence. When the bottle was empty, Rose looked at Kirk and asked, "Do you think it would be alright to refill it from the stream?"

"I suppose so," he replied with a glint of mischief in his eye. "But if the radiation doesn't get us, the dead bodies will."

"What do you mean?"

"The dead bodies in the stream... It'll be more like soup than water."

"You are disgusting!" she yelled at him. "Whatever is in the stream, I'm still thirsty! "

She flounced off to the stream, annoyed by his attempts to make light of her concerns, and then kneeling on the bank, reached down until she felt the cold water flowing over her fingers and into the bottle.

She reflected for a moment that the availability of clean water was something to which she hardly ever gave thought. Water came out of a tap – except that in this instance, it did not, and increasingly in the future, it would not.

She walked back to Kirk. "We need to be getting on our way," she said.

Kirk nodded. He wanted to be on the move. Although he had tried to make a joke of it, Rose's concern about the stream had also reminded him of the constant need for clean drinking water. He hoped that Rose's aunt had a reliable well or spring near her cottage.

Rose announced that she wanted Kirk to drive by climbing into the passenger seat. Left to take up the driver's position, he sat for a moment, fiddling with the seat and the mirrors. Then he switched on the engine, put the car into 'drive' and they rolled gently off down the track towards the road.

Despite the problems that surrounded them, the journey still felt a bit like going on holiday. Kirk kept the car purring along at a steady pace although this was partly about conserving its energy rather than simply wishing to begin the day at a gentle pace. It was a consideration that would not last long.

Rose, meanwhile, inspected her face in the mirror on the back of the visor. Her face was slightly smudged with dirt, probably from the bank of the stream when she had gone to refill the water bottle. She opened the glove compartment and pushed aside a can of de-icer and a car owner's manual, searching for some tissues.

Although the roads were devoid of traffic, Kirk's habit of looking in the mirrors had not deserted him. Driving down an empty road was unsettling. What had happened to everyone? Why were they the only people on the road? It made their journey much easier but the thought that no-one else was taking the same course of action made him uncomfortable. It occurred to him that maybe other people knew something that he and Rose did not.

He should, perhaps, have placed a higher value on solitariness. It was to be short-lived. Residents hiding in their homes were not the only people in the area and as Rose and Kirk travelled along the road, they were noticed.

It was Rose whose attention was drawn by a large camping site on the right-hand side of the road. A tree trunk had been dragged across its entrance, barring access to cars, although on either side of the barrier there was still a gap. The camp site, set amongst a swathe of trees, was covered with a motley collection of tents and motorbikes.

The bikers, most of whom were still snoring in their tents, were not people to take government messages seriously whether they were anti-smoking or anti-radiation sickness. After a heavy bout of drinking and fighting, most of them were sleeping off what they regarded as a 'great night'.

Unseen by Kirk and Rose, however, three of the bikers had been placed on guard duty. By contrast, they had spent a very boring night with little to catch their attention other than a few rabbits and foxes. A hybrid car passing through what they now regarded as their territory was a major event, not to mention an event that smacked of a lack of respect. It was the perfect excuse for a little curiosity, even perhaps, a little mischief. Whilst one of them stayed behind still guarding the entrance, two of them set off in pursuit.

At first, Kirk thought that insects were crawling up his rear view mirror – but then the insects seemed to grow in size, and he realized with a small shock that they were being followed.

Kirk glanced cross at Rose. "I think we've got company!" he said. "Look out the back window!"

Rose twisted round in her seat until she could see clearly. He was right.

"I take it you mean the two bikers who are following us." She sounded calmer than she felt.

Before Kirk could reply, he became aware of the heavy thump of a large motorbike engine. One of the riders had drawn alongside them on Kirk's side of the car and was gesturing at them. Rose caught a glimpse of straggly beard and moustache beneath a pudding basin crash helmet.

"I think he wants us to stop" she said, trying to read whatever it was that the rider was mouthing at them.

"No chance!" said Kirk and pushed his foot down further on the accelerator.

In response, the biker roared ahead of them until he had almost disappeared from view. Then suddenly they saw him again, his bike drawn across the road blocking their way.

"What the hell...?" yelled Kirk.

The biker had estimated that Kirk would be forced to stop; it was an estimate in which he was wrong.

"There's a gap!" shouted Rose. "Can you get through?"

"I'm gonna try! "Kirk shouted back.

He pulled the car far over to the right-hand side of the road and pushed his foot down hard again on the accelerator.

If the biker had underestimated Kirk's determination, Kirk in turn had overestimated his own driving ability. His far side tyres mounted the grass verge, and the car shook violently as he got ready to squeeze through the gap left by the biker.

Rose thought she glimpsed a look of incredulity on the biker's face as Kirk lined up the car and floored the accelerator. The car's juddering became almost uncontrollable. Kirk hung onto the steering wheel for dear life but could not avoid a glancing blow to the biker's front wheel. The car rocketed through the gap, and he wrenched it back into the centre of the road.

Rose swung round to see the bike lying at an angle behind them. There was no sign of the rider. Then she saw that far from giving up, the second rider had continued in pursuit. She could only guess that he was angry at what had happened to his companion. Kirk too had seen the second rider in his rear-view mirror. Fear sent a trickle of cold sweat down the middle of his back.

It seemed only moments before the rider had drawn alongside, this time on Rose's side of the car. He wore no crash helmet but instead had tied a red bandanna round his head, so that he bore more than a passing resemblance to a pirate; despite the circumstances, Rose reflected that it was an effect that was slightly spoiled by the goggles he was wearing. Her reflections were brought abruptly to an end when she noticed the holster mounted on the side of his bike and housing a shotgun.

Like his predecessor, the biker seemed to be trying to get ahead of them. Kirk was driving with fierce determination trying to stop him. Every few yards he swerved across his path, forcing him to brake. Rose too had formed a plan and was waiting for her moment.

The biker approached again, manoeuvring to get past. As he did so, Rose bashed the catch on the glove compartment and pulled out the can of de-icer she had seen earlier. She pressed the button to open the window and a gale of cold air blasted into the car.

Kirk was about to yell at her, but the biker was trying to squeeze past again, and he was forced to swerve across his path. As he did so, Rose leaned out of the window gripping the de-icer with both hands, only to find herself staring at the twin barrels of the shotgun.

She reacted by hanging onto the release button of the de-icer. It worked better than she could have dreamed. A strong jet of liquid streamed downwind, plastering de-icer all over the rider's face and goggles.

The gun fell to the road as the biker tried desperately to keep control of himself and his bike. As Rose watched through the rear window, he veered outwards and away from the road, suddenly more preoccupied by a very large oak tree bouncing about in his blurred vision than any thoughts of pursuit or revenge.

More by luck than judgement, he managed to miss the first tree, but it was only to hit the second before he knew it was there. His front wheel thumped into the lower part of its trunk, catapulting him into the air and finally sending him tobogganing through the leaf litter until he came bloodily to rest, face down in the earth. The rear wheel of his bike, smashed from its drive, continued to spin, rapidly at first and then more slowly as it came to a halt and the wood returned to its previous tranquillity.

Rose and Kirk meanwhile made good their escape, not daring to stop or even to speak until they were many miles further on. Then finally, Kirk pulled over to one side, laid a shaking hand on Rose's arm and said, "You just never know when a can of de-icer might come in handy."

***

The pursuit had driven them down the road much further than they had wanted to go. Their long overnight trek on minor roads had brought them down through the Midlands on a south westerly route, through the Vale of Evesham and into Gloucestershire. Like most devices of its kind, the Satnav was not working so Kirk had to resort to using an old and slightly outdated map. Now, however, they found themselves still in woodland which, according to Kirk's map, placed them at the northern end of the Forest of Dean. This was by no means bad because it placed them in an area which was lightly populated and where Kirk still hoped it would be easy to avoid any army checkpoints.

Nevertheless, their position was still problematic. At some time in the night, they had crossed the River Severn. This now placed them on the wrong side of a rapidly widening river. There were also numerous installations connected to the Hinkley Point nuclear power stations, on either side of the Bristol Channel and Kirk surmised that the government would be intent on defending them against any terrorist attackers. Despite Kirk's wishful thinking, there might still be plenty of army activity in the area.

They decided that they would have to travel north again and then east towards Gloucester and skirt round the city and into the Cotswolds. Rose found this a depressing prospect. Whilst they had earlier thought that they would avoid densely populated areas, it now seemed that they would have to go close to Gloucester.

Radio communication was non-existent. Rose tried several times to tune the car radio to any studio that she could find, but for all her efforts was largely rewarded with a persistent hiss. At one point, they caught what they believed to be snatches of Spanish, but the silence of the radio stations left them with a deep sense of unease and still no information about what was happening.

They began a convoluted journey through the outer reaches of the city, meeting along the way an angry farmer who demanded to know what they were trying to do, travelling along 'his' road, crowds of people carrying armfuls of food items that they had stolen from shops and a melee of demonstrators being held back by police. Government exhortations for people to stay in the safety of their own homes had clearly been ignored.

Avoiding the demonstration in itself entailed a long detour and the emotional strain of staying clear of trouble began to tell. Sometimes, they bickered and argued in a way that had not arisen between them before. Once or twice, it seemed likely that they would become trapped and unable to get through to the Cotswolds.

Further east, an exodus from London was underway. Most of the traffic was streaming north, with some people reluctant to become 'trapped' as they saw it in the South West, heading instead for what they thought would be the relative security of northern England and Scotland. Others headed for Wales and for potential conflicts with inhabitants who had no intention that others would be allowed into their territory.

Eventually, Kirk and Rose wore their way round onto roads that once again enabled them to travel south through the Cotswolds and towards Bath and Bristol – although they intended to enter neither of those cities. Sometimes, they would encounter lines of traffic where others had decided, despite the general preference for the north and for Wales, that their holiday homes elsewhere would make a good temporary refuge away from the areas of population. They had also returned now to roads on which small groups of drivers would drive together for many miles but otherwise keep themselves to themselves. Levels of suspicion were high.

It was some time before they found themselves on their own again. After the protracted stress of the morning, the afternoon enabled them to relax a little. They gradually wove their way down through the Vale of Malmesbury, at one point crossing over the M4 on which lines of traffic were at a standstill on the westbound carriageway but where the eastbound route towards London was almost deserted. They were now making their way down towards the Mendips. Rose wondered briefly about her aunt, reflecting grimly that they could hardly have chosen a stranger time to go visiting relatives.

CHAPTER 12

FLOOD WARNINGS

Rose thought that they were nearing the end of their journey. Some of the landscape around them seemed familiar, but she was surprised that much of it lay under a shallow covering of water. Without weather forecasts on the radio and television, it was difficult to know what was happening.

She had always been quite close emotionally to her aunt, but it was now nearly three years since she had been to see her. Rose's relationship with Richard had been all-consuming in the time that they had first been together. Rose's aunt had also found it hard to adapt to the gradual demise of what had deridingly been called 'snail mail'. Rose had always looked forward to the arrival of the letters written in Alison's firm, clear hand in terms of their content.

Kirk and Rose had continued to take it in turns at the wheel of the car. Despite the economic petrol consumption of the car, it was still running low on fuel. They were not too concerned. Kirk's lawnmower had used the same fuel and he had put the mower's petrol can into the back of the car together with other items he had retrieved from his garage.

The flooding was more of a worry. There were many streams and rivers draining the landscape before them, most of them flowing north into the Bristol Channel. Although the rivers were not tidal at this point, the tides in the Channel could affect the rivers' abilities to release their water. Rose could see that, bad though it looked, the scene to either side of the road could be worse.

It seemed unlikely that it was high tide out in the Channel at that point, but she wondered what would happen here when the next high tide began forcing its way up the rapidly narrowing funnel of the estuary. They needed to get up on to the higher ground on the other side of the plain they were crossing. They could see the hills in which Alison's cottage was situated but between them and the higher ground, they might meet a number of obstacles.

Kirk was slowing down. Ahead of them, a culvert had become blocked with debris and water was flowing from right to left across the road. He stopped the car and went to rummage for a pair of boots in the back.

Rose moved round into the driver's seat and called out to him, "Just be careful."

"Of course I will."

He walked towards the flow, hunting along the margins of the road for something to use as he tested the depth of the water. The stream was very swollen and had already swept before it quantities of material from the fields. After some hunting around, he found a suitable branch caught in the metal fence through which the water was flowing. He picked it up, pulling away some of the small twigs by which it had become ensnared in the fence.

The branch made a useful probe. He also needed it to steady himself as he tried to keep his feet in the flow of water. If he lost his footing, he would find himself going no further than the fence on the far side of the road, but it was not an experience that he wanted to try. More important to him at that moment was the depth of the water in relation to the height of the car's exhaust pipe above the road. Probing forward with the branch, he could feel that the water was gradually washing away the margins of the road, but that if they kept to the crown of the road, they might get through. There was also a feature of the car that might help them.

Rose leaned out of the window of the car.

"Why don't we use the electric motor?"

Kirk thought about it for a moment. It was possible to switch the car into electric drive, completely avoiding the need to use the petrol engine.

"So long as the electric motor isn't affected by the water."

"Is there any reason why it should be?"

"Not in this depth of water. It should ensure that we get across although we'll need to use the petrol engine again – we should avoid getting water up the exhaust pipe."

"I know that…" replied Rose patiently. "I hope you're right – about getting across I mean. It's not that far to drive now – but it's quite a long way to walk."

Kirk went round to the passenger side and climbed into the car. Rose pressed the button to override the car's normal system and to move the car forward using the electric motor only.

The hybrid rolled quietly forward into the gliding water. She kept her foot on the pedal although her pulse rate leapt at one point as the front wheel on the driver's side sank into a hole that Kirk had not detected. Fortunately, there was just enough momentum to carry the car through and the rest of the passage through the water was uneventful.

They drove on for a while having switched the car back into its normal mode of operation. The road mounted now to higher ground, and they felt some relief to be getting away from the flooding on the fields below. Before long, however, they were in a fairly narrow lane and the road, which had taken them round the side of a large hill, began heading downwards again. They rounded a bend in the road to be confronted by a stone bridge beneath which a swollen river thundered on its way down a flooded valley. On their side of the bridge, the road was still above the river's surface, but on the far side, the flood was sweeping through a narrow margin of meadow in a gliding mass of sullen brown water.

They were not the first people to arrive at the bridge.

A stout man in a tattered jacket and baggy jeans strode back towards them and rapped on the window. Rose had a vague memory that she had seen him before; he was a farmer, she thought. That was it! He farmed a large area of land not far from Alison's cottage. She remembered now; he was called Andrew.

She lowered the window cautiously to see what he had to say.

"Ain't no way through yer, missus," he said. Although she recognised him, he clearly did not, in turn, recognise her.

"Well, is there a way through anywhere?"

"Depends where yer goin'" was the common-sensical reply. She looked at his reddened outdoor face. He had probably lived there all his life. He would have a good knowledge of the local area.

"We want to get to Isle Tuckett and then on to Hatch End – up on The Ridge."

"Oh yeah," he said. "You can do that, no problem. Just go back to Chilton. The bridge is well above the river there. What's it's like at Isle Tuckett though I wouldn't like to say, but 'tain't usually too bad."

Rose looked towards the bridge. "If you can't cross the river, why are you all waiting here?" she asked.

"Oh we just want to see the river," he said. "We ain't never seen it like this. Mind you, there is one of us reckons he's gonna cross." He gestured towards a tall, strongly built man who Rose guessed was in his early twenties. He had turned up the collar of his jacket, but she could see that he was smoking a flimsily rolled cigarette from one corner of his mouth.

Andrew went back to rejoin two other men who could be heard arguing with their stubborn companion. When he had first spoken, the situation had seemed like a bit of a joke, but now Rose could see that it was more serious than that.

One of the men, a short, dark-haired individual whose jacket was held together with bailer twine, turned to Andrew as he approached and muttered to him out of earshot of the younger man, "I can't make him see sense, Andy. He's a stubborn bugger."

Rose observed, however, that he was not afraid to say his piece. He turned back again and said in a different tone, "Look, Steve, you ain't gonna cross 'ere so why don't you back up and go home."

"Hey Danny boy, I ain't never let it stop me before" was the obstinate reply.

Danny's reply came quickly back. "The river ain't never been like this before."

"So you say. Anyway this thing..." he gestured towards his mud spattered pickup, "can get through anything."

"It can't get through that," said the older man nodding his head towards the flood.

"It can. And it will. Now out o' my fuckin' way." He roughly pushed the older man aside.

At first it looked as though there was going to be a struggle, but Danny had despaired of the argument and turned back towards Andrew and his other younger companion, a man of similar height to Andrew but paler complexion. Danny thought about it for a moment. Of his two friends waiting by the bridge, the younger man, Tim, usually had a reasonably good relationship with Steve. He might be able to have some influence with him. He walked back towards them.

"Hey Tim," he called, "can you have word with him? He won't listen to me."

Tim nodded and moved forwards towards the pickup.

Meanwhile Steve had climbed into his vehicle and was revving the engine.

Tim went to the open window of the truck.

"You don't have to cross here. There is another way round."

"I don't care if there's ten ways round. This is where I'm crossin'. Now just get yer 'ands off my window!"

Tim had placed the fingers of his right hand on the top edge of the vehicle's half open window. He snatched them away as Steve wound up the window, revved his engine again and pushed the vehicle into gear.

"You must be losin' your mind!" he yelled above the noise of the engine.

"At least I got a fuckin' mind to lose," came the muffled reply.

The wheels of the pickup spun on gravel that had been deposited on the road's surface and there was a small puff of blue smoke as the vehicle careered away and across the bridge.

As the group of onlookers watched, the truck crossed the bridge and plunged into the torrent on the other side. At first, it was clearly making headway. The water was not topping the wheels and they could see the vehicle picking its way across but moments later, it came to a point at which the river seemed to have gouged out a channel for itself and through which it raged with greater force and depth. The truck was first knocked sideways by the force of the water and then began to float away downstream. In seconds, it was being swept out into the centre of the swollen river where it was tossed along by the currents before gradually sinking until only the blue roof of the vehicle could be seen.

Silence was the onlookers' first, stunned response, as they watched in horror from the parapet of the bridge. The pickup was being swept ever further from them, but Kirk could still see what was happening. Somehow, despite the torrent, Steve had forced the pickup's door open and was making a desperate attempt to clamber away from the water.

Kirk yelled to the others.

"He's getting out! He's climbing onto the roof."

Steve had begun to have some success and had managed to haul himself onto the only small area of the pickup's metal that remained above water.

A cry that was at once both angry and terrified came floating back to them.

"Help! Help me!"

Andrew thought he had a long coil of rope in his van and went dashing back for it. None of the others could see what possible use it could be by then, but they let him go. Almost anything was better than simply watching someone drown.

Andrew's efforts, however, soon became redundant. The river was carrying along with it a large burden of debris including branches and even the trunks of large trees. Tim pointed from the bridge a short way back up river.

"Hell, look at that!" he yelled.

As they watched a large chicken coop with chickens lined up on its roof came bobbing along in the sliding fury of the river. They could see that the coop was being carried towards the truck which at that moment had caught fast against a rock in the river's bed.

The coop, which was of a shallower draught, bore in upon the truck, finally slamming into it with great force.

Tim was yelling again. "Grab it! Grab it!"

They watched as Steve lunged forward trying to grab hold of the coop as it swung in again, but he mistimed his effort and instead was hit hard in the side of the head by the careering mass of sodden wood. Unconscious, he toppled headfirst into the river.

The onlookers watched impotently from the bridge as Steve's body slowly became separated from the chicken coop and was carried away, face down in the water. A stunned silence returned to the group. Then Danny struck the parapet angrily with the side of his fist.

"The stupid, stupid bugger! What a bloody stupid bugger!"

Tim shook his head. "Thought he could do anything. Never knew his own limits."

"No, nor never will now." Danny shook his head more in sorrow now than anger.

Andrew had remained silent since his dash for the rope but now he turned away muttering to himself. "What a waste! What a bloody waste of a life!"

Whilst events at the bridge had been unfolding, Kirk and Rose had forgotten all about their journey. Rose looked away from the others, tears standing in her eyes.

Eventually Kirk asked, "Is there anything we can do?" He was immediately aware that it seemed like an inane question in the circumstances, but Andrew summoned up the grace to answer him.

"Nah not a lot. I wish there was but" – he shrugged – "you can see how it is. I suppose if there's a phone still workin' at Hatch End you could let the police know."

"If there are still any police left to tell!" interjected Danny.

Andrew decided to ignore him. "That is somethin' you could do – we should all try to do. One of us might get a message through." Kirk was faintly surprised to see a tear rolling down from one corner of the farmer's left eye. Andrew turned away.

"I'm sorry, mate," he said. "I ain't normally like this."

"Well, we'd better get on with it," said Danny after a moment or two.

The three men turned to leave but Andrew turned back again.

"You might see me later," he said to Kirk and Rose. "Steve's mother lives near Hatch End. I expect I'll be the one to tell her."

"Right," said Rose, nodding sympathetically in his direction. "We're sorry about what happened here. I don't envy you."

There was a flicker of acknowledgement in Andrew's eyes and then he turned and walked away.

Once more, Kirk and Rose felt a sense of helplessness. They walked back to the car and climbed in. Around them, there was a general slamming of doors as the others got back into their assorted vehicles. Kirk and Rose waited for them to leave and then followed in their wake, back up the steeply sloping lane.

***

THE RIDGE

The young man's death weighed heavily on their thoughts as they continued on their way, although compared with the events they had just encountered, the rest of the journey proved to be largely uneventful. There was extensive flooding at Isle Tuckett, but it was quite shallow and by using the car's electric motor again, they were able to make their way through to where the lane climbed once more to higher ground. The road was narrow and barely wide enough for two cars to pass. It wound around the hillside amongst thickly wooded slopes, the ground falling away sharply from their route. Eventually, they rounded a bend, and the road began to take a downward turn again towards a long, narrow stone bridge which, as Andrew had described, stood high above the river's torrent. Even so, Rose thought that she could feel the vibration from the water's force as the car made its way between the narrow walls to the other side. The road then climbed again in parallel to the river, rising to a point where it again set off sharply back across the hillside until they came to a point where it made its way onto a heavily wooded plateau that stood well above the watery landscape below.

Travelling along the road amongst the trees they were heavily dependent on Rose's memory and navigation. It was not long, however, before they came to a broad track that swung away from the road. Kirk, who was driving, asked, "Is it much further now?"

"No," replied Rose. "We're nearly there. Local people call this place 'The Ridge'. We've been climbing up the side of it for some while."

A minute or two more elapsed and then Rose exclaimed, "This is it, Kirk!" She pointed to track on their right. "We're here."

Kirk swung the car off the road, and they crunched along a track that was very uneven but serviceable. They had travelled about a further quarter of a mile when the road expanded into a small apron of ground at the front of a detached stone-built cottage. Kirk parked the car by the garden wall, and they climbed out.

The garden at the front of the cottage was in its autumn garb and looked a little drab although shrubs offered some life and colour. A path wound through the garden to a white painted wooden door. Rose led the way, eager to see her aunt again and also pleased to have finished a journey that had been both long and difficult. She rapped smartly on the door using the brass door knocker and a woman's face appeared at the window, her features distorted by dimpling in the glass. She was clearly trying to see who was at the door before answering it. Rose called out:

"Hello Alison! We're here at last!"

There was another slight pause followed by the sound of locks being hurriedly unlocked and a chain being removed. The door opened a crack and then was thrust open wide.

"Rose! I've been expecting you for the last couple of days! Where have you been?"

Rose flung her arms round Alison who responded in kind. For a moment they hugged each other and then Rose drew away and turned towards Kirk, hovering a few paces away.

"Come on, Kirk," said Rose. "Don't wait to be introduced!"

Despite his relationship with Rose, Kirk found it difficult to be immediately informal with Alison. He held out a hand which she grasped but then put both arms around him.

"We're not very formal around here," she said. "You'll soon get used to us."

"Sorry," said Kirk, smiling. "I'm not usually so formal myself – but I am feeling a bit stiff. We've been in the car for the best part of two days. It's great to be here. It's been quite a trip – it really has." He felt foolish. He was babbling.

Overcoming his embarrassment, he took a moment to look more carefully at Alison. She was a little different from the person he had been expecting. She was quite tall and looked to be in her early forties. He had expected someone who looked rather prim, but she had an intelligent, attractive face. She wore a fairly plain dress but one which, nevertheless, revealed a slim shapeliness.

Smiling at Kirk, Alison drew Rose aside. She looked back at Kirk as he gazed around the room, pretending to appraise him then she cocked an eyebrow at Rose.

"So this is the new man! He seems very likeable. You might have made a better choice this time."

Rose looked to see if Kirk was watching them. "Thank you, Alison," she said with a hint of sarcasm. "I'm glad he meets with your approval. I'm sure that you will both get on well together."

Rose had not forgotten that they needed to contact the police about the events at the river. She quickly explained to Alison who listened, shaking her head, a look of sorrow on her face. When Rose told her that they needed to use the phone, however, she said, "Well, you can try, but it's been days since we were last able to use it."

Kirk was sure that she would be right, but he felt an obligation to check. He picked up the receiver and listened. It was silent, useless. He put it back down.

"Andy will tell the boy's mother as soon as he gets back. She knows what Steve was like but it's still a terrible thing to have happened. I'll try to get over to see her tomorrow if I can. Fortunately, she has a younger son. He has plenty of sense. It won't make up for her loss but hopefully, he will help her to cope."

There was a long pause before Alison spoke again. Then she looked more fully at Rose and Kirk and said, "Now, remind me how long you two have known each other?"

"Not long," said Rose, slightly embarrassed. "We live, sorry – 'lived', just a few doors apart but we've only got to know each other in the last few days."

They began to wander away from Kirk. He called across to them. "I'm going to get the bags from the car."

They went a few more steps and Alison drew Rose into a comfortably furnished living room just off to one side of the hall.

"I'm so glad you've come," she said. "It's been a difficult time here."

Rose gave a dry laugh. "I think it's been a difficult time for everyone."

"To be honest, in some ways we haven't really noticed, we've been so busy coping with our own problems – though, I must admit, I'm beginning to miss the phone and the television."

"I know," said Rose. "It makes you wonder what's happening. Most things in the house were still working until shortly before we left. What about the internet?"

"It isn't working. We're missing it – probably more than the telly but we've had so much to do I'd hardly have had time to sit peering at a screen anyway."

Rose went to the window and looked out.

"The Ridge is so isolated," she said over her shoulder. "It's one of the reasons that I wanted to come here" – she hesitated and then laughed again – "that and wanting to see you of course." She nodded her head vaguely in the direction of the world beyond the cottage. "It's going to be sheer hell out there for a long time to come."

Alison looked at Rose." I know. You're right. The world is changing – and not for the better. But we can't change it back. The isolation of this place could have its advantages, but it could also be a problem. If there's further trouble we might find that other people want to move in here. We might not be able to keep it for ourselves."

"Then we'll have to think about that. We'll have to be ready for that possibility."

Alison listened wondering what they would be able to do if a large number of people decided to move in. She was sceptical that they would be able to do anything of significance.

"OK, so what do you have in mind? Do you have some ideas about what we can do if we're invaded?"

"I have one or two," said Rose.

"When are you going to tell us about them?" Alison was gently teasing her, but she would not be drawn.

She laughed instead. "It's not time yet. We've only just arrived, and we had to do some fairly desperate things simply to get here. I'd like a day or two to settle."

Having just arrived after a long and difficult journey, Rose did not feel that it was the time to tell Alison about the incident with the bikers.

Alison decided to try a different tack.

"So how did you meet Kirk?"

"In my local pub."

Rose knew that Alison would want to know about Kirk's background and that she would probably want to know sooner rather than later. There was only so much she could tell her.

"Is he single? Most men of his age are married or at least have a partner."

"He's divorced," replied Rose. "He was divorced about two years ago."

Alison pursed her lips. "He seems very personable – but you can't always rely on first impressions. How well do you know him?"

"Well enough," said Rose. "We may only have known each other a short time but I feel I can trust him. He's been very considerate towards me so far."

"So?" asked Alison. "Are you going to share a room, or will I need to set up two rooms?"

Rose coloured with embarrassment. "No," she said. "We'll be quite happy sharing a room."

Alison smiled and decided to ask her no more about it.

She moved towards the door.

"We're a small, close community up here," she said. "We have to be able to get along together, to rely on each other."

"I know," replied Rose. "I'm sure you can rely on Kirk. He hasn't been an angel in the past but then, neither have I. We've both had some hard experiences. I'm hoping that he's learned his lesson."

She gave a nervous glance out of the window to where Kirk was still trundling bags and boxes from the car to the house.

"Hmmm," said Alison. "But have you learned yours? What happened to Richard?"

Rose looked away. "He's gone off with someone else – up north somewhere." She paused not sure what to say next. "I don't like to think about it."

"Alright," Alison reassured her. "I won't ask you any more about him, but how do you know you've got it right this time? You seemed pretty sure of Richard when you first met him, I seem to remember."

"I might have given that impression, but I don't think I was. Anyway, this feels quite different," said Rose looking directly at her aunt. "Kirk is not necessarily right next to me all the time, but he likes being in my company. With Richard I never knew where he was or what he was up to."

"Well," said Alison, "I'm sorry to give you the 'third degree' but as I said, this is a tight little community up …and for the time being, it's only going to get tighter."

"I'm sure you'll like Kirk when you get to know him. I wouldn't have wanted to make the journey down here without him and he'll be another useful pair of hands. Anyway, we'd better look lively. He's coming to ask for some help, if I'm not much mistaken."

Kirk duly appeared in the doorway, looking a little weary from his efforts.

"I've moved all the bags into the house but I don't know where you'd like us…"

"Oh, I'm sorry Kirk. I was just catching up with Rose. It's been a long time since we've been able to meet. Why don't you just unpack what you need for now and I'll get Jed to help you with the rest of the things in the morning."

Rose raised her eyebrows. "Jed – I hadn't heard you mention him recently? I was beginning to wonder if he was still here with you."

Her aunt gave an ironic smile. "Oh yes, he's very much here…but you'll meet him tomorrow. Rose, why don't you go and have a few minutes to yourself. I still haven't had a proper chance to meet Kirk if you remember and it's not every day that I get to meet a 'strange man'.

"How 'strange' do you like them?"

"Well…I have met a few pretty strange ones in my time."

They laughed.

Kirk, who had been waiting patiently up to this point, also wanted to know more about Alison.

"I could really do with a cup of tea…" he said. "Do you still have such things here?"

"Yes, we do," replied Alison. "Though for how much longer, I couldn't say."

She set off towards the kitchen while Kirk sank into a large armchair by the window.

Rose followed Alison out of the room.

"I thought that you'd probably like a few minutes to yourself – after the journey, I mean," said Alison. "I can look after Kirk for a while."

"Thanks," replied Rose. "I would. It might also be a chance for you to fill in some of the missing pieces and answer some of those questions that you wanted to ask me about Kirk, a few minutes ago."

Alison listened patiently waiting for Rose to leave her alone with Kirk.

"Yes, just what I was thinking…but now off you go. You need that time to yourself."

Rose took the hint and set off towards the staircase, heading for the bedroom that she had always considered as 'hers' and wondering how much it had changed.

***

Kirk went into the living room and flopped in one of Alison's chairs but as soon as he heard Alison approaching with the tea, he shifted into a more upright sitting position.

"Are you alright there?" he asked. "Do you need a hand with the tea?"

"No, it's OK." She set down a tray, on which were mugs, spoons, a small milk jug, a sugar bowl and a pot of tea.

She poured a cup of tea and handed it to him; then after pouring herself a cup she sat opposite him on a settee.

They sat in slightly awkward silence for moment.

Gradually, Alison began to relax, slipped off her shoes and tucked her legs up on the settee, drawing her dress comfortably around them. It reminded Kirk that this was her house. She was at home here – but he had arrived there suddenly in unusual circumstances. She needed to know more about him, and he needed to know more about her.

He said, "It's a lovely house. How long have you lived here?"

"Oh quite a long time – I think that it's about fifteen years."

"Where were you before you came here?"

"Well, I worked briefly for a phone company in Bristol, mapping out cable routes and before that I was student in Sheffield."

"Oh," said Kirk, "what did you study?"

"Geography."

"I haven't been able to make much use of my degree," commented Kirk. "How about you?"

She pursed her lips. "You mean job wise? Yes I have – when I worked for the phone company and then later, when I worked in flood prevention. I needed to make good use of my knowledge in both those jobs. It was whilst I was working for the Environment Agency that I got I married – to Ted. He was an engineer…and he had always wanted to live up here, on The Ridge."

She paused and Kirk waited for her to continue. She had known they would get to this point. Even now it was still sometimes painful to remember.

"He went out one day on a water plant inspection and whilst he was there, he was knocked down by a lorry."

"Oh – I'm sorry!" exclaimed Kirk. The turn of events in her story took him by surprise.

He hardly knew what to say and long seconds went by before he spoke again.

"You must have had a dreadful time," he said at last.

"Yes, it was a bad time...terrible. But these things happen and you either get through them or...well. I did eventually get through it, but it took a long time and a few wrong turnings. In the end I decided to stay. It has helped me over the years – living up here."

She had not meant to say so much. After all, she still knew very little about him. Perhaps it was because she was hardly ever asked about her past life. Most of the people on The Ridge knew her history.

As she continued to think about the past, she found herself fighting down a small upsurge of emotion. It was all so long ago but she had never been able to forget it. Perhaps it was something to do with the fact that Kirk was still a relatively young man – as Ted had been. Perhaps, curiously, it was also something to do with the way that he part-sat, part-lounged in his chair, just as her husband had done in the past. She decided to shift the attention away from herself.

"What about you?" she asked. "Tell me a bit about yourself."

Kirk began to tell her about himself up to that point in time.

Soon she knew that he came from a fairly poor background but that he had eventually managed to get to university. He had not excelled there or been particularly happy but was successful in getting a degree. By contrast, his attempts to become a journalist had been a failure. Eventually, he had found his niche, qualifying to teach adults at a local college and at about the same time, he had also met and married Joanne. Life for them both had then been quite content for several years.

He was hesitant to tell Alison the most recent part of the story, but he knew that he would get off to a bad start with her if she thought that he was being dishonest.

He sketched out his affair with Sarah and subsequent divorce from Joanne. She could probably work out the details for herself. It was the sort of story that she had probably heard a number of times before.

He told her how he had gone to live in Hallamton and then to work at the local college. Finally he told her about the day that he had met Rose and how events had kept them together since then. Alison was particularly interested in his eyewitness account of the missile firing. Before the television and internet had packed up, she had been as shocked as everyone else to hear about it but now, hearing about it from Kirk in her own front room, it had an immediacy that it had not had before.

Kirk told her briefly about their desperate escape from Hallamton and their journey. He included the episode about the bikers although he related only that they had managed to 'shake them off' without telling her how they had done it. Like Rose, he felt that they had done only what they needed to do but he was not proud of it.

Having brought his history up to the present, he sat in silence for a moment.

Then Alison said, "Thanks, Kirk. I appreciate you telling me about yourself – and about your time with Rose. She's very important to me so you can probably understand how I feel. I suppose the other reason that I was asking you about yourself is that Hatch End in particular – and the whole of The Ridge for that matter – is a small community. When people move in here – and it isn't often – we like to know a bit about them. I hope you didn't feel I was prying into your past?"

Kirk shook his head. It was what he had expected. Alison in turn realised that the abridged version of his story that she had heard had also helped him to leave out anything that he did not want to tell her, but she felt that he had told her enough for the time being. He now knew a little about her – and she knew a little about him. Like Rose, she felt that she could trust him and that he would be able make a useful contribution to the small community on The Ridge in whatever way it developed in the uncertain future that lay ahead of them all.

As she sat reflecting on Kirk's story, Alison also found herself thinking about another recent arrival, Janey Capstick. New arrivals were infrequent as she had said, but Janey had moved in just a few weeks before. Alison had formed a favourable impression of her; she was young, attractive it might be said –and, from something Alison had heard, worked as nurse. She hoped that they would all get along together. It was going to be particularly important in the times ahead because they needed to survive not just as individuals but as a community.

She peered at Kirk again over the vestiges of her cup of tea. He was not the most muscular individual she had ever seen but he seemed intelligent and fairly practical. Perhaps Jed, her partner, could help her to see that Kirk was given a good introduction to their way of life – and to helping out with all the work that needed to be done each day.

Kirk was also peering back over the rim of his own mug. He guessed that Alison was making up her mind about him. He could not guess at everything that she was thinking but he knew that she wanted Rose to be there. Rose in turn wanted him to be there. It was all probably immaterial because the world outside was becoming more dangerous by the day and he and Rose now had nowhere else to go and no thoughts of leaving.

They talked for a while longer. As they listened to each other they both felt that they were going to get along well together. Alison felt reassured by the fact that Kirk had wanted to be with Rose during the recent problems and dangers that they had shared. Kirk was happy to dispel from his mind the image of primness that had conjured itself up in his mind for no clear reason when Rose had first spoken about her 'aunt'. Alison seemed completely approachable. He liked her already.

When they had finished, they cleared away and Kirk went outside to spend five minutes by himself. Some yards from Alison's fence there was a large tree stump. He walked over to it and sat on it, ruminating about some of the feelings that had surfaced during his conversation with Alison.

He thought again that he had not resented being 'interviewed'. She was having to take a great deal on trust. Would she be right to trust him, he wondered? His thoughts returned unbidden again to Joanne. He wondered what she was doing whilst also realising that whatever it was, they were no longer part of each other's lives.

The situation in which everyone now found themselves was bad, but he could do nothing to help her. It was the biggest part of his betrayal – even if it was occurring long after their divorce. When he last heard, she was still living by herself. Despite the feelings that he had developed for Rose, he regretted the consequences of his disloyalty to Joanne.

He thought back to his affair with Sarah – to the details that he had not related to Alison. Where did Sarah fit into it all? She was beautiful… and mad …and probably bad as well, but so much fun to be with. When he was with her, he had been able to forget himself. When they were together, he had felt that for a while any sense of time or place receded.

For his part, he had wanted her from the first, but she had constantly played with his emotions. Looking back on it now, it was her propensity for playing games that had eventually destroyed their relationship. He could not stand the roller coaster of emotions that she caused in him – or the duplicity that their affair had dragged them into. He had still loved Joanne so what had led him to betray her? He could not explain it to himself other than by believing that he had allowed himself to be ruled by his desire for Sarah.

So, he reflected ironically, he had 'loved' Joanne. Then he had 'loved' Sarah – and loved her in a way that he had not experienced before, but it was an insane, dangerous, destructive love and of a kind that people should be warned about rather than hearing it eulogised in poetry and song.

Would it make any difference anyway? Now he 'loved' Rose and this 'love' was different again, but was his love any deeper than the mattress they would share that night? He knew that it was unnecessary to reproach himself about his feelings for Rose, but part of the damage done by Sarah was that he found it hard to trust himself and felt that he needed to spend this time questioning himself and agonising over the ebb and flow of his emotions.

He reflected, not for the first time, that he might have done better to have conformed to all the ill-informed nonsense that was incessantly talked about men; he should have cultivated an obsession with cars and football.

If he was going to show his loyalty to Rose, however, then this time it would need to be different. Dire though the general situation was, it might at least enable him to make another and better start.

***

Dusk was gathering when Rose called him back into the house. Since there was no longer any electricity, Alison had placed candles in one or two windows and several more in the kitchen where they were going to share their evening meal. As Kirk came into the house from his seat on the tree stump, his sense of smell was assailed by the delicious smells of cooking food which by now was almost ready for them to eat.

Alison was retrieving a well-used casserole from an oven heated by a large wood burning stove. She removed the lid to reveal a bubbling stew of vegetables and a small quantity of meat. She ladled it onto the plates whilst Kirk and Rose waited with as much patience as they could muster but moments later they found it hard not to gobble down the hot food; they had eaten very little during their journey and they were both very hungry. Eventually their pace of eating slowed to one at which conversation was also possible. Alison smiled wryly to herself. Their appetites told her a little bit more about their escape.

Rose was the first to speak.

"This is absolutely delicious!" she exclaimed between mouthfuls.

"Mmmm," agreed Kirk." You could hardly have cooked anything better."

"We aim to please. There's plenty more if you want it, although I need to save some for Jed."

Alison had already placed a good-sized portion of the stew to one side in a large, covered dish.

"When will we meet Jed?" asked Kirk.

"Oh, it'll be in the morning now." Alison glanced briefly at him as she ladled a little more food onto her own plate. "We've been having trouble with foxes, so he's gone out with the gun."

"How many people are there in Hatch End now?" It was Rose's turn to pick up the conversation.

"There were just 20 of us although with your arrival, we've achieved the handsome total of 22."

"Is it going to be possible to provide for us all up here?" Kirk knew that it was rather late to be asking the question, but it had been in his mind ever since Rose had first said that she wanted to come to Hatch End.

"I would think so." Alison looked at them confidently. "Everyone will need to contribute up here but there is enough land and more work than we can really manage now that we can't use machinery anymore."

"It might be just a short time before we can get access to petrol and diesel again," said Kirk.

Alison looked sceptical. "Do you really think so? I think it will be a very long time before they're available again – if ever. What you have in your car at the moment is probably some of the last."

Rose shook her head. "I can't believe how quickly everything's happened. How have we gone from a society, that was working much as it had done for nearly a hundred years, to this breakdown?"

"The signs were there, Rose. We all knew that we were living in a way that wasn't sustainable." Kirk remembered that they had talked about it before.

"Did we all know that though?" A hint of vehemence had crept into her voice. "A lot of the people I knew didn't believe it. They were busily scoffing at me just days before we left."

"There are just too many of us in one small island. In the last ten years, we've completely lost control of numbers." Alison carried on mopping up gravy with a piece of bread as she spoke. "There were pressures even ten years ago but the heat and the droughts in Africa, the Far East, the Middle East – even Southern Europe, have made people head north."

Kirk agreed. "It's the only thing they can do. They just want the basics – food, water, a roof over their heads – the things that we all need to survive."

"True," said Rose. "But no-one here is simply going to hand those things over to them. We have our own problems."

"You're right," said Alison. "We do have our own problems, but they're not on the same scale. Anyway, people have stopped asking if they can come into the country. We have a lot of coastline and there's always someone with a boat who will get them in, if they can offer enough money."

Rose was not content simply to hear familiar stories rehearsed again.

"I know that immigration is a major problem but it's so frustrating that we never look below the surface. Drought in East Africa is hardly new but we've all played our part in making it worse."

Neither Kirk nor Alison disagreed with her although they knew that elsewhere, despite everything that was happening, Rose's viewpoint would still have been regarded as controversial.

There was something of a pause before Rose spoke again.

"Alison, how safe do you think we will be here?" she asked eventually.

Alison had now thought about it many times. "Safer than in most other parts of the country," she replied.

"There's not much to prevent people from getting up here if they want to," said Kirk.

Alison nodded. "Yes, you're right, but we can make it more difficult if we put our minds to it."

"We can also hide." Alison and Kirk glanced quizzically at each other as Rose made her remark.

"I certainly agree that one of our best defences is the obscurity of this place," said Alison.

"I mean more than that," said Rose.

"I had a feeling that you did," said Alison. "Still, I think that it would be better to talk about this when Jed is here. He knows this place better than any of us."

Rose and Kirk wanted to talk about it then and there and were a little reluctant to agree but they knew that she was right.

Having spent the previous night in the discomfort of the car, they were also looking forward to sleeping in a warm and comfortable bed.

The table was quickly cleared, and Alison began extinguishing the candles.

"What about Jed?" asked Kirk.

"He'll be alright," said Alison. "He knows where to find everything."

She handed Kirk a candle. The light fell on their faces as she did so, and her fingers brushed Kirk's as he took the candle from her. A faint look of surprise flickered briefly across her face' and she smiled fleetingly at him. Kirk read the expressions on her face, smiling his 'thank you' at her, in return.

Rose had groped her way ahead of them and had managed to light another candle in the bedroom. Kirk followed her in time to see that she had taken off her clothes and had put on a white nightdress which hung fairly loosely around her and yet still managed to show off her shape to advantage. The strings intended to fasten the nightdress across her breasts still hung loose. Kirk's heart beat a little faster when he saw them.

"I thought we'd be little old fashioned tonight," she said. "I put yours over there."

A pair of blue striped pyjamas was waiting on a chair. Kirk laughed but obediently took off his clothes and, putting on the pyjamas, fumbled ever so slightly with the cord of the pyjama bottoms. Rose watched him with a faint but slightly impatient smile. He slid under the covers and put his arms around her, grateful for her warmth after the chill of the bedroom.

"I thought you were never going to get here. What took you so long?"

Kirk did not reply but instead kissed her on the mouth, then on the neck, then on those parts of her breasts that his lips could reach when he pulled back the fabric of her nightdress. She smiled at him, bathing in the candlelight and the pleasure of his kisses.

He slid one hand down to her waist and pulled her gently closer. She winced a little as the coolness of his hands slid down to the hem of the nightdress and then onto her skin. He kept them there for several long moments allowing them to warm then he watched her through half closed eyelids as he finally moved his right hand into the warmth between her thighs.

Neither the nightdress nor the pyjamas lasted very long after that. She gave a gasp as Kirk entered her, and pleasure began to overwhelm the last of her inhibitions. He ravished her thoroughly, letting his hands range freely over her body until he could hold on no longer, struggling not to bite her fingers as she put them into his mouth; even in that moment, she did not want Alison to hear them on this or any other night.

She wanted him to caress her again with his fingers. He held her close, stimulating her with his fingers until eventually she pulled his hand away. They lay with their arms around each other until finally they both drifted off to sleep.

It was some time later that Kirk woke and heard the door of the house quietly open – and shut again. Candlelight flickered for a while on the landing beyond the bedroom door. Kirk listened as muffled voices held a brief conversation; Alison's voice could just be distinguished and then a deeper voice – presumably that of Jed. He heard Alison's quick, light footsteps on the stairs and then some while later, heavier, slower steps.

The house fell into darkness again as the last of the candles was extinguished and the noise of creaking wood announced that someone was getting into bed. A further short interval followed before the bed could be heard again, creaking rhythmically this time; Alison's involuntary cries and moans came to his ears despite the thick walls of the old house.

Kirk tried not to listen but instead still found himself focusing intently on the sounds from her bedroom. She had not explained her relationship with Jed but it was now largely apparent. He tried to push away his thoughts.

Rose had satisfied him; he had slept afterwards – a peaceful sleep after the passionate exertion of their lovemaking. He was pleased for Alison that she had someone to love in this isolated place, but another feeling stirred almost below his consciousness.

Somewhere beneath his conscious thoughts there was a familiar, perennial sense of restlessness. In the dim light that was available in the room, he looked at Rose's face, tranquilly full of the gentleness of sleep. He despaired of himself; she had satisfied him beyond the expression of words, certainly beyond anything that he had a right to expect; and yet… and yet, was he envying Jed?

He pushed away his thoughts again, wanting his feelings and his appetites to leave him alone. He wanted peace. He wanted contentment that outlasted the afterglow of lovemaking.

***

Kirk slept most of the night. Sometimes he lay softly touching Rose and at other times, he lay in his own space on the other side of the bed. In the early hours of the morning he heard the wind mounting and the tiles rattling on the roof. Rain followed. It was not a faltering rain but a prolonged and sullen downpour that did not slacken in any part of the hour for which Kirk was aware of it.

The rain stimulated his thoughts as he lay sleepless, this time not allowing images of Rose or Alison to stop him from thinking about the course events were taking.

He had no great vision and could not see very far forward. Like Rose and Alison, he thought that their best hope of survival lay in their obscurity and that the parcel of land on the plateau, or The Ridge as it was called locally, would be below the threshold of covetousness for most potential settlers.

He hovered over the idea of 'settlers' coming into the area. The area was, of course, already 'settled' but by a relatively stable population of a few farmers, smallholders and local commuters. Here on the plateau, he and Rose were the only newcomers of whom he was aware; everyone else had lived there for many years. In the morning, weather permitting, they would be able to explore the area around the cottage and form a clearer picture of their situation.

Visions of the drowning at the bridge began involuntarily to trouble him. Images of the man's desperate attempts to get onto the roof of his vehicle and the subsequent sweeping away of his body down the river invaded his thoughts with an intensity that had been absent until then.

For a while he wrestled with the unwanted images, tossing and turning in the bed and running the risk of disturbing Rose.

The pain of recent years, however, had taught Kirk not to dwell on such experiences. Instead, he chose another compelling direction for his thoughts by reflecting on the flooding that they had seen and the idea that in the future, the area that they had managed to cross in the last part of their journey might become a huge 'moat' cutting off that part of Somerset from the surrounding approaches.

It was not much of a deterrent at that moment, but if the changing climate brought severe flooding from the Bristol Channel, the rivers along its coastline would all be affected. It might deter people from venturing into the area unless they had a commanding reason for being there. The rivers of North Devon lay to the west of them and were prone to flooding; the Tone and the Parrett also ran in complicated loops to the east and in their present swollen state were a further deterrent to would-be travellers. In the future they might once again become considerable barriers.

Kirk knew, however, that he could only half-convince himself. There were many roads old and new which breached the 'moat' on which the inhabitants of Somerset had sometimes relied in the past. In times of greater security and trust, communication with other parts of the country had been a lifeline for the prosperity of the area – or so it had been believed, but then like so many other regions of the country, much of its identity had been lost and it had come simply to manifest a rather sluggish, impoverished version of the homogenized 'culture' that had remorselessly become all-pervasive.

Kirk had begun now to sink into sleep but, despite the fact that they had uprooted themselves from the Midlands and survived several ordeals to get to Alison's cottage, the insecurity of their situation was still troubling him. Smug feelings of safety were far from the troubled drifting of his mind as fatigue gradually overcame his consciousness.

Outside, the wind and torrential downpour thundered across the landscape with a vehemence that was orders of magnitude greater than any turbulence in the dreams of sleepers beneath the path of the storm.

***

Rose heard Jed and Alison moving about the house well before Kirk showed any signs of stirring. Trying not to disturb him, she put on a dressing gown and made her way down the stairs to the kitchen.

Jed was sitting at the kitchen table, his head of dark curly hair bent over the scrambled eggs that he was eating. He beamed as she entered and got up quickly from the table.

"Rose! Come on, let's have a look at you!" he said. "It's been a long time since you were last here!"

He was a tall, strongly built man. His tanned face, full of character, reminded her that he was one of those individuals who somehow managed to combine an active outdoor life with a keen, intelligent interest in the world beyond the local community in which he worked.

He had been Alison's partner for a number of years and on previous visits, he and Rose had become good friends. She was drawn by his good humour and knowledge of the countryside but knew from hints dropped by Alison that he also had a darker side.

They hugged in the middle of the kitchen, Rose gasping a little as his powerful arms enfolded her. They held each other until Alison reappeared from a small utility room to one side of the kitchen.

"Now, Jed," she said, "you can just put her down!"

Jed smiled. "I'm not sure I want to. I haven't seen her in years."

He held onto Rose for a second or two longer and then let her go.

Alison looked patiently past him and said, "Now that you're here, Rose, would you like some breakfast!"

"Oh yes please. I'm famished!"

"OK," said Alison, "there's some cereal in the cupboard. We also have some eggs – if you fancy an egg for breakfast?"

"I wouldn't mind some cereal, if that's alright?"

"Of course it's alright. It's in the cupboard just over there."

Rose found herself a bowl and went to find the cereal. Alison had two or three assorted boxes in her cupboard. Rose opted for the cornflakes, discovering that there was not much left in any of the boxes and then went to look for some milk.

Alison looked at Rose's meagre portion of cornflakes. "I'm sorry there's not much left," she said. "It's been about a fortnight since they had any in the local shop. At the moment there are no deliveries getting through. Most of the food we have is what we produce here."

Jed had listened solemnly, whilst Alison was explaining. He shook his head. "Unfortunately, it can only get worse. In the future, we will almost certainly be relying entirely on the farm. At the moment, we have plenty to eat but we're just going into the winter. By the time we get to next February or March, it could be a different story."

Alison thought that the conversation was getting a little sombre. "Don't let it spoil your cornflakes, Rose," she said. "We'll all get through somehow. Some foods have been in short supply for a long time, haven't they? We've just got used to it."

Jed agreed. "Yes," he said, "I can still remember being able to buy rice in the village shop."

They laughed. Rose had another thought. "Well, there's plenty of water in Somerset. Perhaps we could start growing our own rice?"

"The temperature might be rising but it's still not quite warm enough yet." Jed looked thoughtful as if he was quietly entertaining the notion.

"There is something that we do have in ever increasing amounts."

Rose and Alison looked at him curiously, wondering if this was going to be one of Jed's slightly offbeat little jokes but he was perfectly serious.

"The fish population in these parts is certainly increasing and it'll probably increase enormously if the fish are left alone."

Rose made a wry face. "Are you kidding?" she exclaimed. "I hate fish."

"Well you may have to learn to love it," said Alison. "Besides, we know some pretty good ways to cook it."

"Mmm," agreed Jed. "The water quality was getting better around here but the flooding and the loss of power at the water treatment plants has meant that there's been a lot of pollution again recently. Still, 'needs must'. We catch and eat a lot more fish that we used to."

Impressed though she was by such self-sufficiency, Rose wanted to make another wry face but decided that it would not be a tactful thing to do. Meanwhile, she had found the milk and sat down at the table to eat her cornflakes. Kirk had still not appeared so she said to Alison, "Shall I go and wake Kirk? He hasn't had a chance to meet Jed yet."

"Oh don't worry about that!" exclaimed Jed. "He could probably do with the extra sleep. I was hoping that we could all go for a walk along The Ridge and that I could meet him then. I also want to see if last night's storm did any serious damage. It was a pretty bad one – even by the standards of recent years."

Rose had plenty of questions but so far she had made only slow progress with her breakfast and was still feeling hungry. She decided that the questions could wait. She helped herself to a portion of scrambled eggs. A few minutes later, Jed had donned his hat, coat and boots and was on his way out through the door. He gave Alison a kiss and waved to Rose.

"See you later," he said. "I'm looking forward to meeting Kirk but make sure that you both wear your walking gear."

"He's not kidding," said Alison. "You'll need it."

Waking to find himself alone, Kirk briefly rubbed his eyes and then scrambled out of bed. He peered out of the front window and saw that Rose had already gone out into the front garden. He dressed quickly, putting on old clothes in anticipation of a muddy walk later in the morning.

Alison was pottering about in the kitchen as he came down the stairs.

"I suppose you'll be needing some breakfast," she said with mock severity.

Kirk looked at her as she spoke. Despite her words, there was a smile hovering around her lips. A ray of sunshine had penetrated the gloomy November sky and briefly illuminated the kitchen. Kirk tried to be unobtrusive as he looked at Alison, but she seemed to radiate good qualities as naturally as the sun breaking through the clouds. He saw wisdom, calmness and kindness flickering through her smile; then he pulled himself back to earth, inwardly reproving himself for his flights of thought as he did so.

"Well, do you or don't you?" said Alison.

"Oh – oh yes." He faltered lamely realising that he had not allowed himself adequate time to wake up.

"Well," went on Alison, "the rest of us have had scrambled eggs this morning. Would you like some?"

Kirk agreed that he would, feeling at that moment that half-awake though he was, he would nevertheless be quite happy to eat as much as Alison cared to provide. Fortunately, although cereal was running low, there were no other shortages that morning and he was able to eat a breakfast that, together with the previous night's meal, went some way towards compensating for the lack of food on the journey south.

Alison made them both some coffee, pouring it from a cafetiere into two good sized mugs. She put down a mug next to Kirk and then sat down with her own drink on the opposite side of the table. A lock of hair fell across her face, and she brushed it unselfconsciously to one side.

"I don't suppose we'll be able to drink this stuff for much longer," she said, ruefully sipping at her coffee.

"Not unless we can grow it along with rice and some of the other things we haven't had for years," said Kirk.

Alison smiled. Kirk looked up. "What?" he asked.

This time she laughed. "Oh it's only that I've already had this conversation with Rose and Jed."

"That's just like me," said Kirk, "saying what others have said long ago."

"Whatever any of us said about food shortages," said Alison, "none of us said it forcefully enough."

Kirk could see now that her mood had become more sombre.

He nodded. "We've talked about it endlessly. It's been in the news for years, but we did nothing. Now here we are."

Alison thought about what he had said for a moment.

"I partly agree with you," she said. "Climate change has been in the news but much of the time it's been pushed to the bottom of the agenda. On the occasions that it was in the news it was often shoved away on websites. Anyway, in the media we only got reports about what was happening. We never seemed to hear about why it was happening."

"Yes," said Kirk. "It was superficial. Apart from a few brave individuals, many people backed away from the hard truths about climate change and for that matter, about world population and food shortages."

Alison nodded but she was curious about his use of the word 'brave'.

"Why do you say, 'brave individuals'? What's brave about them?"

"I suppose that I'm talking about a kind of 'social bravery'," he replied. "The willingness to think for yourself, not to run with the herd just for the sake of it and not to be deflected by mockery – because there's always plenty of that about."

"Yes," said Alison. "I've been surprised at the savage treatment meted out to ordinary people – and to politicians – almost anyone who's tried to lead us towards better ways of doing things."

Kirk sat thinking about what she had said, remembering the many times in recent years that he had felt his anger rising as globally important issues were omitted from the news in favour of those that were purely domestic or ephemeral.

They had lingered for some time over their coffee. Without really thinking about it, Alison laid her right hand on Kirk's arm, gently spreading her fingers.

"Come and help me clear away," she said. "We should be out with the others. We need to see what damage was done by the storm last night."

Reluctantly, Kirk agreed. Their conversation, brief though it had been, had met a need in him for serious conversation about serious issues. It was an opportunity that had rarely arisen in his everyday life.

By now they were standing next to each other, washing up and drying plates and cutlery. She sensed his disappointment that their conversation had come to an end. She looked sideways at him. "I've got to go over to the vegetable garden a bit later today. Why don't you come with me?"

He looked a little surprised. "I thought that this was the only garden that you have," he said, looking out through the window towards the back garden of the house.

"Oh no," said Alison. "That's a useful bit of ground but it would never keep us all going in fruit and vegetables right through the year. No, we've got a bigger piece of ground over by the edge of the wood."

"Okay, sounds like a good idea to me – but what about Rose and Jed? What will they be doing?"

"I think Jed wanted to take Rose over to the other side of the wood to see the sheep. She's helped him with the sheep in the past and I think she would be interested to see what sort of flock we have now."

"Alright then," he said. "So we'll do a swap."

She raised an eyebrow and looked him.

"You'll need to get your walking boots and a coat. It's fairly mild out there but it is November – and the storm left plenty of mess behind."

"Don't worry – I'll be ready before you."

"We'll see about that!" she said with a laugh and went off to change into some suitable outdoor clothes.

***

Kirk and Alison left the house by way of the garden path at the front. As they left, Kirk glanced briefly at his car. There was barely any petrol left in its tank, just a small amount left in the petrol can – and after that had been used, no more that could be bought from anywhere. The car would then effectively be an almost worthless aggregation of metal, plastic and rubber.

A short while later they were walking along the edge of the wood towards the spot where Alison had earlier agreed with Rose and Jed that they would meet.

Kirk was faintly aware of a roaring sound away to his right, but at that moment, it was at the limit of his hearing, so he said nothing about it. Alison was focused on meeting up with Jed and Rose.

As they approached, Jed spotted them and came towards Kirk, hand outstretched. "It's good to meet you," he said.

"And you too," replied Kirk, shaking Jed's hand vigorously.

"I've heard a lot about you from Rose here."

"Oh dear!" exclaimed Kirk.

"No, no, it's alright," Jed added with a laugh. "She's had only good things to say about you."

"Well, that's a relief then," said Kirk, looking at Rose with a smile.

The two men stood back, quietly sizing each other up, trying to form clear first impressions.

Alison, wanting to draw them all together said, "What did you see at the end there?" She gestured towards the point where the path on which they were walking seemed to disappear and where the tree line gave way to a steep slope down into the valley below.

Her question brought an instant response from Rose.

"You'd better come and see for yourselves," she said.

Kirk thought that he caught a hint of something serious in her voice.

They walked solemnly along the path to a promontory at the terminal point of The Ridge. A fence had been placed across the end of the path to prevent visitors from falling inadvertently over the edge. Alison and Kirk both gave involuntary gasps as they looked down.

Far below them, a river was gliding in a wide, sliding torrent around the contours of The Ridge. The height and the motion of the river below made Kirk feel slightly giddy and he looked away to steady himself. Alison, however, continued to stare down at the swirling waters.

"Whoa!" she said. "That is some flood! I've never seen the river like that before."

Jed looked rather grim. "No, I haven't either. But that's not the only thing I haven't seen before. Just keep looking."

They did as he said and after some moments, they could see the trunks of trees, broken pieces of wood, clothing and a huge mass of assorted flotsam and jetsam borne along in the river's surging flood. Kirk was not surprised. He and Rose had seen similar sights the day before.

He looked quizzically across at Jed whilst Alison and Rose continued staring down at the river.

Jed was aware of Kirk's gaze, but he had seen something that had gone unnoticed by the others.

"Just keep watching!" he yelled. He had to raise his voice to be heard above the roaring of the water.

Kirk turned his gaze downward again – and then began gradually to make out what it was that was now holding the attention of the others. At first he could see what appeared to be no more than sodden clothing being swept along by current; but then he saw a face and the whiteness of a pair of hands.

His attention became riveted to the water's churning surface. There were bodies in the river, dozens of them. At first he could barely pick them out amongst all the materials being swept along in the river's muddy brown, but then he began to make out different colours of clothing and then to recognise the bodies of men and women, and finally, the smaller bodies of children. The sight of the children brought an immediate and involuntary lump to his throat and tears sprang into his eyes. At that moment, he did not care what the others thought. Instinctively, he put his hands to his face.

The others were stunned into silence but Kirk, unable to restrain himself said, "What on Earth? Little kids...those poor little kids." His voiced tailed away into nothingness.

Jed and Kirk avoided each other's eyes and looked away. Rose and Alison held each other, shaken by what they had seen in the river.

For a long while, nobody spoke, then Rose said through tears, "We didn't see that before. I wonder what happened? There are so many of them – so many people."

Jed stood, continuing to watch and reflecting grimly that some dreadful event upstream must have swept all these unfortunate people – adults and children alike – into the river's merciless flood. They could only guess at what had happened, but there were some clues. Every so often a car roof could be seen bobbing along amongst the debris, and after a while, it became apparent that there were many cars in the river although in such a breadth and depth of water, it was sometimes hard to identify what they were seeing. The huge size of some of the objects being swept along by the river also made them gasp; giant rocks and lumps of concrete were tumbled long as though they were of little consequence although their enormity suggested that they weighed many tonnes.

At last Alison exclaimed, "I can't stand this anymore! I can't stand here gazing down at all that death and destruction!"

She had previously leaned far over the fence at the end of the promontory in her efforts to see what the river held in its pitiless torrent, but now she turned away and set off striding angrily back along the path. Jed let her go for a moment and then went after her. A few yards further on, he caught her in his arms and held her as she sobbed into his coat.

Rose and Kirk followed a few yards behind. They too were deeply moved by what they had seen. The previous day's sense of frustration returned to them. There was nothing they could do or say that would make any difference to the situation. For both of them it was also the second demonstration of the river's power – though one that was far more devastating than the sights of the day before.

They had enjoyed the walk out to the far end of The Ridge. Now, the return journey seemed like a wake, a grim trudge into the darkness of an uncertain future

CHAPTER 13

IT'S THAT MAN AGAIN

Freddie Bolton was too young to remember the Second World War. His father had also been just a little too young to get caught up in its lethal tentacles. His grandfather, however, had fought in North Africa and Italy.

Bolton's father had been a sixties 'hippie', a rebel who was viewed with scepticism by the rest of the family, most of whom had served in the armed forces. Bolton's mother shared some of her husband's ideas, but in her, they were more securely based; she worked for a publisher and tried to encourage him to take an interest in books, as a result of which, he had done well at school and subsequently went on to university. However, there had always seemed to be something inevitable about his gravitation towards the army. As children sometimes do, he had reacted against, rather than followed, the model represented by his father and in so doing, found himself swimming against the tide of the times – although in this, ironically, he became something of a rebel just as his father had been.

Freddie Bolton was not given to introspection, but he sometimes wondered how a love of being outdoors had eventually led him into the dangers of Iraq and Afghanistan. He found excitement in active service, but it was eventually scarred with scenes of brutality and cruelty that had left their marks on him as they had on almost everyone around him. He became 'desensitized' to a large degree, trying to keep the barbarism that he witnessed out of his head and out of the decisions that he had to make, often in split seconds; the effort was probably only sustainable because he was at the peak of his abilities.

His work, however, often brought him into contact with the world of the intelligence services, and it was into this world that he eventually went.

If the military background of his family had dominated his life, his mother had always shown a strong interest in the theatre. She had played a variety of amateur roles, and in his childhood, Bolton had been taken to see some of her performances. Later, when he had more of a choice in the matter, he still went to watch her, and he sometimes wondered if he had inherited her facility for 'role playing'. He found it easy to slip into the aliases that were often required of him. Becoming Mark Ridgeway had not been difficult for him on the day that he went to meet Kirk Hallam.

He had been lucky to survive the beating handed out to him on the night that Kirk Hallam had found him lying in the street. He could not explain to himself why his attackers had not simply shot him. Perhaps he had survived only because they had wanted to make the attack look like an ordinary street crime – of which there was plenty – and could not afford to draw attention to their imminent activities by shooting an intelligence officer. The local police were fooled because they had only superficial information. His colleagues were not fooled but lacked the information that Bolton had only pieced together on the evening that he was attacked.

Bolton generally specialised in maintaining a low profile, but when he had been assigned to the group responsible for the surveillance of the missile terrorists, he found himself playing a much more significant role than he had anticipated; at first, neither he nor his colleagues had understood the size of the game that was being played out. The links between the terrorists and their sponsors were nebulous, tenuous, reached back a long way, and were supported by plenty of technical expertise and capital.

Sympathetic dissidents inside the UK had eventually been the instruments of the challenge. Fuelled by a vision of a world in which the United States and her allies had been overthrown, they had been manipulated by a long and complex set of strings from the Far East.

British and American intelligence had struggled with the complexities of the terrorists' plans, and it had taken a great deal of work to piece together the picture that had emerged. The picture, however, was still largely descriptive. The motivations of the terrorists and the shifting alliances between the various groups involved were still poorly understood.

With hindsight, the tactics of Bolton's assailants had been very effective. They had bought just enough time to put the final pieces of their plan in place. As a further result of the attack, however, he had unwillingly obliged them by suffering from amnesia.

The visit to Kirk Hallam's house had helped. The house had been used in the past by a terrorist cell that Bolton was investigating, and he had thought that the terrorists might have left some signs of their activities there, but it was now some time since they had left and there were no immediate clues that Bolton could find during his brief visit. Fortunately, the view from Hallam's window was more helpful in stimulating his battered memory. This, together with the passage of time, led him to remember that on the evening of the attack, he had just come into the possession of some vital information.

Whatever the information was, he had managed to remember that it had been passed to him by a contact. He had not met the contact but resorted instead to a time-honoured technique; they had used a so-called 'dead letter box' located in an old iron works near Kirk Hallam's house. It had seemed rather bizarre, a throwback to the days of the Cold War, but surveillance of electronic communication was intense and the 'letter box' lay outside the sweep of the pervasive security cameras. At the time, it had seemed like the least risky option.

Despite his constant wariness, he must have been tailed and the subsequent injury to his professional pride was scarcely less than the physical injuries inflicted on him by his assailants. Meanwhile, the nature of the terrorists' plans returned piecemeal to his memory and back into place as a full-scale emergency.

Unfortunately, by that time, their activities could not be forestalled. Bolton had been forced into the attack on the terrorists in the woods just as they were bringing their plans to fruition and although his unit had killed a number of the missile crew, the enemy had always held the initiative. He had been forced into an operation that lacked both planning and resources. Some of the terrorists had simply been able to melt away into the woods, particularly following the destruction of the helicopter and the resultant loss of two of Bolton's men. The whole thing, he thought, had been a classic British 'cock up'.

After the battle, the police had taken a number of local residents for questioning. They knew that it was unlikely that any of them was involved or that the terrorists would have tried to hide there, but they were reaching round for somewhere to begin. Although Bolton suspected that the police had been infiltrated, the decision was made to warn them that they were wasting their time. Kirk, Rose and several of their neighbours had then been released.

Meanwhile, the missile had done its work – and a general sense of failure had followed. There was no time, however, for any inquisition, and in the event, many of the London staff who might otherwise have been held accountable were now the victims of acute radiation sickness. There had been a huge failure of intelligence well beyond Bolton's sphere of operation.

There was great uncertainty as to where the next attacks would come. His contact had told him that wind farms were a secondary target. It was thought that their destruction would have less immediate effect than the destruction of some of the primary targets – coal-fired power plants and nuclear power stations that might shortly add to the woes of people fleeing from London.

However, 'the terrorists' as they were still being called, had identified wind farms as a source of energy that would be difficult to destroy and some of them might keep going even after an assault. They could therefore enable resistance to continue. On this last point, Bolton was determined that, should the need arise, the terrorists would be proved right.

For the time being, the contingency chain of command operating from the West Midlands had ordered him to the Welsh side of the Bristol Channel. There was still no news of an expected attack on the Hinckley Point nuclear power station – an event that Bolton privately thought was certain to come before assaults were made elsewhere.

The initial attack, the 'dirty bomb' on London, had been enough to cause an immediate civil emergency across the whole country, but Bolton was perplexed that he had still had no news of others that were known to have been planned. For the moment, the main explanation seemed to be that communications everywhere had been disabled.

There was another puzzle. Radiation counters carried by his unit indicated that radiation in the area had not significantly increased. The explanation in this instance was that the wind was still blowing from the north and that the airflow was carrying the contamination away from them. He knew that it could not last. Weather patterns were changing, and it could only be assumed that at some point, the wind would move round to blow from the east.

Bolton's small detachment of men had camped briefly to the west of Gloucester, near to the place where Kirk and Rose had paused to snatch some sleep. Whilst the detachment was there, a motorbike messenger had arrived from WMC – the West Midlands Centre – a messenger, he noted, who had nearly been prevented from getting through by a group of bikers who were camping in the area. There seemed to be no means of communication that was infallible.

The message he had received directed him and his detachment back to the English side of the Bristol Channel. There was, at last, the news he had expected – news of an impending attack on Hinkley Point. They had moved as a matter of urgency to join up with an Army unit that was already in the area.

That evening, as a result, he sat ruminating with an Army colleague, Greg Thorndike. In terms of the Army's usual working relationships, the temporary arrangements they had quickly established between them might not otherwise have existed. Bolton's senior officers at the WMC knew, however, that they were all involved in a struggle for survival and had left it to his experience and discretion as to how he developed his working relationship with Thorndike, who had only been assigned to North Somerset shortly before the missile had struck central London.

Between themselves, they were on first name terms and their conversation was informal – but purposeful. At that moment they were ruminating about their position and the steps that would be needed to protect the installations further along the English side of the estuary. They had made an open fire and sat before it, the light dancing on their faces.

"Communication should be back up in a day or two," speculated Thorndike.

"I certainly hope so," said Bolton. To him, two days in the present circumstances seemed an unconscionable amount of time. "I wonder what's happened at WMC?"

Thorndike could offer only limited information. "It's hard to say. They have various sources of power. The grid seems to be out everywhere we've been, but they have access to solar and wind generators. They also have diesel generators."

Bolton briefly continued to puzzle over the situation but then said, "Well, radio or no radio, decisions need to be made about the installations at Hinkley."

Bolton nodded. "I've heard we're getting some help."

"WMC have sent their specialist unit down there. Wendy Collingwood has been drafted in for advice."

Bolton had worked with the unit before.

"Why Collingwood?"

"She has the best knowledge of the people – and the tactics – likely to be involved in an attack. Her unit has previous experience in defending large installations."

"Uh hum," said Thorndike. He and Bolton both knew that the unit in question had been involved in defending oil installations overseas. Bolton privately surmised that an attack on a nuclear power station with its attendant radiation risks was something else again. It was also the first time that Collingwood's unit had been ordered to use their expertise inside Britain.

Meanwhile, Bolton had continued talking.

"The Navy has quite a large presence in the estuary and is available to assist at Hinkley. There's serious flooding in the area at the moment. It will give Collingwood plenty of problems. As far as I can gather, most of the population have taken to living on boats – or on hilltops."

Almost unwittingly, Thorndike went into 'lecture mode'.

"I thought that was how the place first got its name? It was always flooded in winter and people could only graze their cattle on the lower ground in summer – so they became known as the 'Summer Set'. History seems to be repeating itself."

Bolton looked at Thorndike with a look of quiet amusement on his face. He was momentarily tempted to make a derogatory comment about being a 'mine of useless information' but was restrained in the end by the need to get on with the discussion.

"That may be so, but just now the inhabitants of North Somerset who are still there are wanting life to return to 'normal' – whatever that is."

"Do they realise that this is the new 'normal'?"

"Probably not – that could take a while. For the moment, Hinkley Point – whatever the problems there at the moment – is a source of power."

"That's not my information," said Greg. "The reactors are being shut down – on orders from WMC."

Bolton nodded, wondering why he had not been told such an important thing before, although he knew that shutting down the nuclear power plant was an obvious step and one that was a fully planned part of emergency procedures. He would have to overlook any blunders in communication. For the time being, his task was to help protect the facilities at Hinkley – should it prove to be a target.

The events of recent days made it necessary for them to pool information and to draw heavily on each other's knowledge and experience. The whole assemblage of military personnel in the area needed to work as a team – albeit a large one. They moved from the fire to a trestle table inside an adjacent tent, pulling towards them maps, laptops and other materials needed for their planning. The fire outside was guttering low before they had done enough to pack it all away again and head for their sleeping bags. Bolton was briefly disturbed by the roar of a motorbike as a messenger was dispatched for the West Midlands. He hoped to hell that radio communications were soon up and running again.

CHAPTER 14

NOT THE FUTURE WE WERE CHOOSING

Jed went off to do some of his jobs. Kirk had hoped to keep him company that morning but after the visit to The Ridge and the sights they had seen, no-one felt like talking very much – so they kept their own company. Alison went back along the path, but this time, branching off on a different path after she had travelled a few yards. Kirk guessed that she would be going to the vegetable garden.

When she got back to the house, Rose felt in need of distraction and found a book of puzzles to occupy her mind. Kirk dithered for a while. They had made love the previous night, but they had not talked to each other much since their arrival. This was not the time to approach her, Kirk thought, but he wanted to spend more time in her company. After the forced pace of their introduction, there were many ways in which they were still getting to know each other but he wanted to be loyal to her. After his miserable failure to be loyal to his wife, he wanted to prove to himself that he could be loyal to Rose.

He drifted about in the back garden for a while and then went into the house. Rose was still engrossed in her puzzles, so he did not disturb her. Instead, he wandered out onto the front path of the house and then onto the path that ran along the edge of the wood. He decided to find out where Alison had gone. She had, after all, suggested that they could meet later in the day.

The wood had a dank, sombre air to it as he made his way along the path. It was late November and fallen leaves lay in a thick carpet underfoot but as he looked up at the trees, a great many leaves still clung to the branches, despite the storm of the previous night. The weather seemed unseasonably mild. It was not the way he remembered autumn woods in his childhood when he would have expected by now that the trees would be largely bare of leaves and that the wood be a lighter and more open place despite the gloominess of the weather.

After he had been walking for several minutes, it occurred to him that he might not have taken the right path. He had only a vague notion of the path that Alison had taken and there seemed to be a good many tracks criss-crossing the woodland. He guessed, however, that the vegetable garden would not be too far from the cottage.

The path he was following was gradually bending around to his right. It had brought him a short distance into the wood but now it led him back to its edge and into a large clearing. As he came out from amongst the trees, before him was an area that looked like a collection of allotments. Narrow paths ran between rectangular plots of land, dividing the space into clearly delineated strips, each with its own small shed. There was plenty of bare earth to be seen since autumn was well advanced. Kirk saw a plume of smoke rising silently from the far side of the clearing and he headed towards it, guessing that it was where he would find Alison.

She was heaping weeds on to a fire as he approached. She smiled and said, "I wondered if you would find your way over here."

Kirk came closer to where she was standing.

"It wasn't that difficult," he said.

It was a mild day for autumn, but the warmth of the fire was still welcome. They both stood close to it warming their hands and in doing so, standing close to each other.

"Where's Rose?" asked Alison.

"Back at the house," he replied. "She was doing puzzles when last I saw her. Where did Jed go?"

"He'll have gone to help Andrew – one of the farmers up here on The Ridge. I think you met him yesterday."

"Yes, he was there...at the bridge." Involuntarily, Kirk's thoughts returned to the scene of the drowning at the river.

Alison looked at him, sensing that he was not yet ready to talk about it.

She returned to loading weeds onto the bonfire. It had proved to be hot work and she had taken off her waterproof jacket despite the autumn chill in the air. Her cheeks had healthy roses in them, and she was just a little out of breath from the exertion of her work. Her breasts rose and fell perceptibly with her breathing.

He watched her for a moment then, as she became conscious of his gaze, he said, "Can I help? Is there another fork here somewhere?"

"Yes, over there." She nodded towards the open door of a small shed at the end of the plot. He wandered over to it. After a moment of searching about inside, he found a garden fork and returned to help her.

They worked together until the vagaries of the smoke from the fire caused them to stand back. Kirk looked sideways at Alison, wondering if she had recovered from their experience that morning.

"Awful, wasn't it?" he said. She knew immediately that he was talking about the bodies they had seen washed along in the river's flood. She had thought about nothing else.

"Yes, it was," she replied. "I don't know what I expected to see, but it wasn't that. It was such a shock!"

"Mmm," murmured Kirk in agreement, "especially the children."

She looked at him. For a moment he thought that she was going to burst into tears, and he moved to put an arm around her but she motioned him away.

"No, no," she said, "I'll be alright. Just give me a minute."

He stood back while she turned away from him. He watched from a short distance away as she sobbed to herself until finally, she pulled a small handkerchief from her pocket, dabbed at her eyes and then turned red-eyed back towards him.

"I'm sorry," she said. "It's just that children are so..." Kirk thought that she was going to cry again but she managed to say, "They're so innocent. It was such a terrible thing to have happened."

She could not find the words to describe her feelings and she faded into silence.

Kirk said, "I thought I'd come and find you but perhaps you would have preferred some time on your own?"

"I did come out here to be on my own," she replied. "But now that you're here, I'm glad to see you. Besides, you and Rose – and Jed for that matter – must all have felt the same."

He moved close to her and then put his arms around her, gently holding her close to him. This time, she did not resist but stood resting her head upon his chest.

Eventually, she said, "I did say to you and Rose that I would go and see Steve's mother."

He nodded but then asked, "Do you think that's a good idea – after this morning, I mean?"

She appeared to think momentarily about what he had said but then said, "It's something I must do. I'll be alright. She's been a good neighbour for many years. I really must go and see her."

She moved gently in his arms, and he let her go. She picked up her jacket and put it on.

"I'll see you back at the house then," he said.

She gave him a small parting wave and then turned along the path that would take her towards the cottage that Steve had shared with his mother.

Kirk watched her go before heaving a final forkful of weeds onto the bonfire and then returning the garden forks to the shed. Closing the door, he saw that there was no lock. It seemed a little careless but then it was unlikely that anyone would want to steal Alison's garden tools. It was only his second day on The Ridge. He was still thinking like a town dweller rather than a member of a small, rarely visited community in which everyone knew everyone else. With the smoke of the bonfire billowing behind him, he turned back towards the path leading to Alison's cottage.

* * *

When he got back to the house, Kirk unlatched the front gate and went to the front door. It was not locked. He sat on the front doorstep and with something of an effort, took off his boots before going in.

Then he went through to the small utility room just beyond the kitchen. The walk back had made him feel hot and he wanted to splash his face with water before going further into the warmth of the house. A log fire was burning in the front room overlooking the garden. It seemed something of a waste for there was no-one using the room. Rose's puzzle book lay discarded on one side together with her pencil.

Kirk's slippers had not been a priority when they had been doing the packing. He went up the stairs in his walking socks and went into the bedroom. Rose lay on the bed outside the covers but seemingly fast asleep. He sat down on the edge of the bed but then felt her turning towards him.

"Where have you been? I've been waiting for you."

"Oh, just out for a walk," he said.

"Where to?"

"Along the path at the edge of the woods and then a little way into the wood itself."

Sleepily, she pulled him towards her.

"Mmm," she said. "You smell fresh." Then she changed her mind. "No you don't. You smell of fires – bonfires. Where have you been?"

"I went out to the vegetable garden. I saw Alison there. She had a bonfire and was burning up garden rubbish."

"Oh," said Rose. "Did she come back with you?"

"No," said Kirk.

"Where is she now?"

"She's gone across to see Steve's mother."

"Oh – she'll be gone for a while then?"

"I expect so," he replied.

"You're still not really holding me closely," complained Rose. Once again, she pulled him towards her and then changed her mind.

"Phwaw, you really do smell! If you're going to get any closer to me, you can take those clothes off now!"

The bedroom was quite cool, and Kirk felt reluctant to take off any of his clothes but decided that he had better do it since he had never been known to show a lack of passion for Rose before. He looked at the way she was lying on the bed with her eyes half open, watching him. Perhaps it was not such a bad idea after all.

Moments later, he had left his clothes in a pile and was padding towards the bed.

"Mmm, you look much better now," said Rose, noticing that Kirk's mood was showing signs of becoming more amenable. He lay down next to her on the bed. "This doesn't quite seem right," she said. "You now have no clothes on at all whilst I'm still wearing all of mine. Why don't you take my clothes off as well?"

Kirk heard himself say that it sounded like a good idea. He kissed her and began working on the various catches and buttons that held her clothes together. Soon he had her down to her underwear. He kissed her and felt his desire for her take over. He took off the last of her clothing. Her body was warm, but her hands were cool. She ran them over Kirk's chest and stomach.

"I think that it would be better if we got under the covers," she said.

Later, Rose lay basking in the afterglow of their lovemaking and feeling drowsy in the warmth of the bed. Usually, it was Kirk who fell asleep but soon she slipped into a gentle doze whilst he continued to lie awake.

He too felt contented, but he had done very little work that day other than heave a few weeds onto Alison's bonfire. By comparison, Jed had been out for some hours now, working on a neighbour's farm. Kirk knew that he would need to make himself more useful in the days ahead if he was to be fully accepted into the life of the household.

Alison returned from her visit to see Steve's mum. The poor woman was still beside herself and had clearly not slept at all the previous night. Had it not been for the presence of Steve's younger brother, Alison would have felt reluctant to leave her, but she felt sure as she left, that she was in safe hands. She could only imagine how Steve's brother, Jonathan, was feeling, but he seemed to be in control of his own emotions and able to take care of his mother for the time being.

She had paused in the garden to do a few minor jobs but eventually decided that she wanted to be indoors. She went in through the back door and then up the stairs to her bedroom. She quickly changed out of the clothes she had put on that morning and then went towards the top of the stairs. The landing was rather gloomy, but she noticed that the door of Kirk and Rose's bedroom was open. She tended to keep it shut because her cats liked to sleep on the bed if the opportunity came their way. She looked in briefly to check that they were not already in there but saw instead Kirk's head and naked shoulder. Beyond him, she could see Rose sleeping peacefully in his arms.

She pulled the door gently towards her and quietly turned away, feeling slightly guilty as if she had been spying on them. It would be many hours before Jed came back from his work and it would be longer still before there would be any sort of tenderness between them. He would have done almost a full day's physical work but would still want to make love to her before going to sleep. He was big and physically strong. She never felt able to resist him and yet she was finding it increasingly difficult to respond to him in the way that he expected.

She dismissed her thoughts from her head and went downstairs where she set about preparing a meal. Some while later, Kirk and Rose both appeared, offering to help. It felt a little awkward at first, but she accepted their offers because it might have seemed odd to do otherwise. They were all competent cooks and between them, they had soon put together an evening meal which looked and smelled delicious.

Since it was late autumn, the light had faded, and they lit candles. It was now several days since the electricity supply to the cottage had failed, but the charm of eating by candlelight had not yet worn off.

As the meal was approaching readiness, Jed returned from his work and after kissing Rose lightly on the head, went upstairs to wash and change. Soon, they were all seated round the table, ladling food onto their plates and eating heartily.

Alison felt happy and was pleased that they were all together. Kirk, however, felt a certain amount of tension. He was still the newcomer amongst a group of people who had known each other for many years.

Jed was tucking into his food with a vigour that the others could not match. They found themselves watching him eat and wondering where he put it all. They tried to be discreet, but he gradually became aware of their eyes upon him.

"What?" he said at last. "What's the matter?"

Kirk laughed. "Oh nothing," he said." Nothing at all. It's just that we can tell who's been doing the work around here."

There was vigorous coughing from Alison. "Excuse me!" she said loudly. "I'll have you know that I've also been working hard today."

Jed looked sympathetic and silently offered her another ladle of food. She accepted a little of it but then got him to give the rest to the others.

Kirk began to feel more a little more relaxed. Sharing food helped to ease any tensions that there might have been, and they all had to be able to live and work together in the times ahead. After their journey south, he and Rose both realised that in the world outside their immediate surroundings, enormous danger lurked for everyone. At the time, it had seemed like something of an adventure, but the scale of events weighed upon them as they set about adapting to a new way of life.

"Is there any news from elsewhere?" asked Kirk as they began to ease back from the earnest business of eating.

Jed looked up at them. "There is some news," he confirmed. "I did get to talk to Andrew this morning. He's been out to one or two of the local villages. Things are not looking good."

Kirk hesitated for a moment, wanting to know more but not quite knowing where to start. "I thought that it was almost impossible get in and out of here now. I thought that there was no petrol or diesel to be had?"

Jed looked at him steadily for a moment. "There isn't," he said, "but some of those people over at Hatch End can ride horses. Andrew and his son have always lived here. They know this area better than anyone else and they were able to pick their way through the flooding on horseback."

"So, if there are no communications, how are they managing to get news?" asked Kirk impatiently.

"Well, it's not completely true to say that there are 'no communications.' There are some. A few people still have the use of amateur radio and there's even a crude kind of newspaper going the rounds – a one or two page affair, though it costs plenty of money to get your hands on a copy."

"What about the internet?" asked Rose.

"Seems to have gone completely," answered Jed. "No-one really knows why but I've heard it said that it was subjected to some kind of massive electronic attack."

Rose knew that such a thing could happen, but the thought of such destructiveness brought to bear on what she thought was one of the better things to come out of the twentieth century, induced in her a mixture of anguish and incomprehension.

"But why?" she asked. "Why would anyone do such a thing?"

Alison had sat patiently until now. "Western Europe and the US have always had plenty of enemies," she said. "There are many people who hate so-called 'globalisation' and the 'one size fits all' approach to civilisation."

"Hmm, civilisation!" snorted Kirk.

"Well, there you are!" said Alison. "Even in the UK, plenty of people have hated the kind of society that has grown up around us."

Jed wanted to return the conversation to a level that was a little closer to home.

"Does anybody want to know how news is travelling at the moment?" he asked.

They looked at him, smiling faintly. They had almost forgotten the beginning of the conversation.

"I have a feeling that you're going to tell us," said Kirk.

Jed raised an eyebrow. "It's just travelling by word of mouth from village to village, farm to farm."

"So it's subject to all the usual problems of verbal communication," said Alison.

"Of course," agreed Jed. "But for the moment, it's the only news we have. The big news, the bad news is that someone has made a major attempt to weaken the country and to destroy the Government."

"That's hardly news," commented Kirk. "What views are there about who's responsible?"

"Unfortunately, there are almost too many candidates to count. But whoever it is, has also been manipulating oil supplies."

"So we're talking about Muslim countries in the Middle East?"

"It would be easy to suppose that." Jed seemed to know far more than the others would previously have imagined. "But the consensus seems to be that they're from a number of countries, not just from the Middle East. They draw their inspiration from some sort of successor network to Al Qaeda."

"What do you mean – a successor network? What happened to the old one?" Rose felt she was losing track of the conversation.

"Nothing has really happened to them. They've rolled with the punches and have kept moving on and changing locations and personnel. They had to change their personnel because so many of them have been killed."

Kirk's focus had always been on the environmental issues but here they seemed to be at an intersection with terrorism.

"So you're saying that this network has been manipulating the West's dependency on oil to weaken the West and make it more susceptible to religious and political manipulation?"

"Yes," replied Jed. "That's about it."

"But don't they need the West's money?" asked Alison.

"They did do – and to some extent, they still do, but since the Chinese have become serious rivals to the Americans, the oil has begun to flow much more to the East than the West."

"That all makes sense," commented Rose, "but why haven't the Americans reacted more strongly to all of this?"

"They have reacted strongly – but in many cases, also wrongly."

"How do you mean?" asked Kirk.

"What I mean," replied Jed, "...is that the terrorists have committed outrageous acts and subverted major aspects of the American's economy, but the Americans have not really been able to hit back. The terrorists know that the Americans are heavily dependent on technology, but they can't hit back hard when the terrorists are operating from scattered places within the territory of sovereign states."

"Hmm," said Kirk. "Asymmetric warfare."

"Exactly," replied Jed.

Rose got up to make them all a drink.

"All right," said Alison, "I'm amazed that such a 'big picture' can come through such restricted channels as the ones around here – but what I really want to know is how much danger are we in?"

"I will answer that, but first, the person I got all this from is someone who told me that we are all in a lot of danger from terrorists."

"That also is not news" said Kirk. "But who is this person you've been talking to?"

"He calls himself Robert Lawson – but I don't suppose that's his real name. He says he's civilian, but my guess is that he's in some branch of the intelligence services."

"So how did he turn up, bearing in mind that the rest of us are finding it impossible to get around?" asked Alison.

"On horseback – I was out with Andrew, and we met him."

"So were you riding as well?" Kirk was curious.

"Of course – it's the only way we've been able to get around."

"I didn't know you could ride," said Alison.

"I can't – well not really – but I'm having to learn quickly."

"And all this time we thought you were working," laughed Kirk.

"Ah yes, but we've been looking at the defence of this place and he's given us a lot of ideas. We've got a lot of work to do."

"Will we get to meet this 'Robert'?" asked Rose, returning with the drinks she had gone to make.

"You might do. Good bloke – Robert. Tough as old boots but seems to know what he's talking about."

They talked for while longer, sipping their drinks before agreeing that tomorrow they would begin in earnest with their attempts to make the place more defensible. Soon Rose and Kirk and then Alison and Jed climbed the stairs to bed. Rose was soon asleep, but Kirk lay listening –

and feeling guilty for listening.

* * *

Alison and Jed lay looking at each other. Alison said, "I really admired you this evening. I had no idea that you knew so much about the situation. Why didn't you tell me all this when we were here on our own?"

"I didn't want to trouble you," he said. "I also wanted to wait until Rose and Kirk were here because we're going to need their help. Anyway, you never seem very keen to talk about big events. You always want to focus on what's going on in the neighbourhood."

"That's right," replied Alison, "because it's what affects us most."

"But you can't understand the 'small picture' without looking at the 'big picture'."

He paused and then said, "Anyway, I'm tired. I've been working and I just want a bit of pleasure before I go to sleep. I need some comfort."

"Oh Jed!" Alison kept her voice low, but he could still tell that she was angry. "You know what I think about you using me just to comfort yourself!"

"Ok, ok!" he said. "But all the same...Anyway, you like it too."

He rolled into a more active position and placed a large and rather cold hand between her knees.

"Jed!" she pleaded, but he wasn't listening. It had been a hard day and he needed the sheer pleasure of her body. They always wore night clothes although Alison forever wondered why they bothered. She felt her nightdress being pushed up past her bottom and nearly beyond her breasts and then felt her legs being pushed irresistibly apart. He was large, strong man. She did not want him at that moment, but neither could she physically resist him. She lay with her legs thrust wide to accommodate him and then felt him entering her.

"No, no, Jed!" Please." She pleaded with him again, but it seemed simply to make him angry. He could not understand why she had a problem about it all. His thrusts became even harder.

She gave up and clung to him, eventually losing herself in the savage pleasure of having him inside her.

However, when she later lay by his side as he slept, deep resentment built up in her again. She thought, "How dare he? He didn't care what I

142

thought! He didn't care what I wanted! It was all about him!"

She had sometimes tried to tell him how different being penetrated was from being the penetrator – but for all his ability to understand the political 'big picture', he could not or would not understand her feelings.

A flow of hot tears began to moisten her pillow. Jed slept on but in the other bedroom Kirk had heard the bed creaking again and now could just make out Alison's tearful snuffles. After this evening, he had a certain admiration for Jed. He was clearly much more than just the local 'hired help' – which was what Kirk had initially assumed – but the situation with Alison was much more complicated. He felt powerless and therefore frustrated.

He also felt a certain amount of anger with himself. Moonlight fell through a gap between the curtains, illuminating Rose's face. She was a lovely woman. What more could he want? Why did he not feel content? He lay watching Rose for a while before drifting off into a fitful sleep.

* * *

A good many miles away, Robert Lawson's horse was cropping the grass around the post to which his owner had tethered him. 'Robert Lawson' was the name under which Bolton was currently working, although another alias that he had used recently whilst working in the Midlands was 'Mark Ridgeway.' False names provided a very limited level of disguise but they often helped prevent people from making immediate connections between one set of events and another, and kept others at arm's length from Bolton's true identity and role.

Bolton was sharing the results of a visit to 'The Ridge' with Greg Thorndike, the officer he had been assigned to work with. Just at that moment Thorndike was unhappy with a problem that they were jointly facing and with Bolton's suggestions for dealing with it.

"It's no good!" Bolton was saying. "We have to take them into our confidence. We do not have sufficient numbers to defend every last part of this area."

Thorndike mused for a moment on what he had said. "So if I understand you correctly, you want to include these people in the plans to hold back the attack on Hinkley Point? You want to use them as a sort of citizen defence force, a latter day 'Home Guard'."

"That's right," replied Bolton. "I don't see that we have a choice – unless of course we simply leave them out of the plans and fight all around them – or put them in boats and ship them out."

Thorndike stood thinking for a moment. An attack was coming very soon. They both knew it. There were not enough boats or even horses to get the inhabitants of The Ridge down from their perch in time.

There was another more basic flaw in Bolton's argument. Thorndike felt a duty to tackle it head on.

"So why 'Hatch End'?" he asked. "Of what possible advantage could it be to the enemy to capture Hatch End? We both know that as backwaters go, it's a pretty good one. Why would anyone in their right mind want to be bothered about Hatch End?"

Bolton had to remind himself that he preferred working with someone who would put alternative ways of thinking to him. He did not need someone who simply endorsed his ideas and plans. He needed someone who was not afraid to test his thinking in an argument – however vehemently they did it – rather than to have his plans found wanting in some operation that went off at half cock.

"For no reason to do with the village of Hatch End," said Bolton. "But it does have every reason to do with the fact that The Ridge is the highest point for some distance around and also the driest point. There are large areas of level ground up there. It would make an excellent base from which to operate helicopters."

Thorndike's ears pricked up at the entry of the word 'helicopter' into the conversation.

"As far as I'm aware, the enemy doesn't have access to helicopters," he said flatly.

Bolton gave a barely audible sigh. "I'm afraid that they do have access to them now, Greg," he said.

"What?" Thorndike could hardly believe it. "How has that come about? Where on Earth did they get helicopters from?"

"From us," said Bolton resignedly. "They stole them from us. From Middle Wallop I believe. Classic military cock up. Everything was on the ground, and everybody was farting about with radiation suits and the like."

Thorndike did not want to believe such a sorry story but knew that Bolton would not be joking about something as serious as the matter of helicopters. There was another objection that he had to Bolton's account.

"What about them? They can die of radiation sickness just as readily as we can."

"Of course," agreed Bolton. "But remember the people in this 'Martyrs Brigade' are all ready to die for the cause."

"And what cause is that?" asked Thorndike acerbically.

"You know the answer to that as well as anyone," replied Bolton. "It's your lot who've been sweating the prisoner we took at the camp site yesterday. What has he had to say?"

"Not much – or at least, not much of a military nature. At first he stuck to his story about being here to fight 'The Infidels'. Then after a while, he said he'd come here to avenge his family. He's from southern Afghanistan. He says that his family – in fact, his entire village – was wiped out during a British operation that went wrong."

Bolton briefly searched his memory trying to recall if he had had any involvement with the British operation in question. It was quite possible. There again, it was possible that the prisoner was lying.

Thorndike was perplexed by the whole set of events. "This is a hell of a long way north for them. Since when have people from southern Asia taken to invading the UK? Where did they get the training, the weapons, not to mention the capital to finance it all? It seems as though we must have been looking away."

"You're right," replied Bolton. "You're exactly right!" There was a strong hint of exasperation in his voice. "You know the story already. They fool us for years. They keep us busy with small scale terrorist scares in towns and cities all over the West. They threaten to bomb the London Olympics in 2012 and again in Rio in 2016. Then, just when we think they've given up and gone home, they shoot down a European A380. Aircraft wreckage and over five hundred people falling out of the sky. But you know all that, Greg. They've kept us with our heads stuck firmly up our own arses for just long enough to be able to mount a serious attack on the West."

Thorndike nodded. "Yes," he said. "But we've always had them on the back foot."

"No," said Bolton firmly. "We've never had them on the back foot. From the time that they began to control the flow of oil and from the time that the American economy went seriously into recession, we were always the ones who were retreating."

Thorndike understood that they were simply rehearsing information that they already knew because despite being in possession of a great deal of data, they were still struggling to understand how it was that they were fighting an army of international combatants from the Far East, the Middle East and Africa on UK home territory.

Bolton understood Thorndike's difficulty in understanding the course that events had taken. Thorndike, however, had begun to puzzle about another point.

"I don't believe that they could mount anything on this scale without state sponsorship from somewhere."

"You're right," replied Bolton. "Previously, they didn't have the finance, the resources or the level of organisation required to mount an operation of the kind that we're seeing. But this time, they're being sponsored by several states – countries that want to bring about a complete shift in global power. However, there is one state in particular, one that in the past we armed and whose soldiers we trained..."

"The connection between oil and power is easy enough to understand," observed Thorndike. "What's less easy to understand is why we're dealing with an insurgency and an invasion. There must be more involved than simply a desire for revenge – and they don't need to invade us to control the flow of oil."

Bolton agreed with Thorndike's reference to an insurgency, although he did not believe that a full scale invasion was taking place.

"Don't underestimate the desire for revenge," he said. "But this is not an invasion, at least, not from the information that I have. It's more of a probing attack – an attempt to destabilise us, to soften us up. The invasion, if it ever takes place, will come later. If you're asking why they've come here instead of staying at home, it's because they need land, they need water – things that we have, and they don't. Some parts of Africa and Asia have become so hot that they're almost uninhabitable and people are moving north in vast numbers – because they have to."

What Bolton had said was not new to Thorndike, but it was useful to hear it rehearsed. They had to understand the motivations of the people they were fighting. He knew, as well, that the balance of power was shifting, just as the conspirators had planned. Presumably some form of counterattack was being prepared – but with communications as bad as they were, it was impossible to know what was happening.

The UK seemed to be drifting on the western fringes of Europe like an aircraft carrier that had lost its steering. There was no information at that moment as to what was happening in other parts of Europe or in the United States. Bolton had some knowledge of the 'bigger picture' but, as he had said to Thorndike, he was being told just enough to enable him to fight and to motivate others to do the same.

The conversation had taken them away from the initial planning that they were putting together.

"So that's the background but we need to get on," said Thorndike. "These plans have to be ready by tomorrow."

They pored over their maps of North Somerset, North Devon, the Welsh coast and the Bristol Channel. However, Bolton had one more major piece of information to impart. He waited, letting Thorndike work through the processes that he had already explored.

After a moment or two, he looked up and said, "They're not going for renewables – wind farms and the like, are they?"

"No," said Bolton. "This lot really mean business. The moves towards some of the installations on the Welsh side were a feint."

"Right," said Thorndike, with an intake of breath. "So we are talking about Hinkley Point – the nuclear power station."

"We are," agreed Bolton. "It's not an easy target. But if they can destroy it or even simply damage it, they'll have knocked out a major power supply. They may also have caused a massive release of radioactive materials. There's a further advantage for them as well..."

"And that is...?" asked Thorndike.

"It's on the Western side of the country," replied Bolton.

Thorndike finished the remark for him, "And the prevailing winds blow from the West."

"Just so," said Bolton.

None of this was really a surprise to Thorndike. He had always known which target he would choose. Headquarters had never been in any doubt either, despite the large contingent of combatants that now appeared to be heading towards the Barrage. At least this time they had not "had their heads up their own arses," as Bolton had put it. The Navy, including the Special Boat Squadron, had a large presence in the Bristol Channel.

"So what's the form?" asked Thorndike.

Bolton began to explain. "Collingwood's liaising with the Navy. SBS are going to operate a pincer movement from the Channel. The units under her direct command will be defending the power station. Their plan is basically to attack before the enemy can get any of his missiles into use."

Thorndike knew that on land, it would be his task to organise a running battle of attrition but that a strike against the missile batteries would be needed at the earliest opportunity.

"A concerted missile attack would be enough to achieve their purpose. Do they have a large reserve of missiles?"

"Our information is that they have four batteries, each with four launchers."

"And what's the strength of the force?"

"They have about 10,000 soldiers in the country and that 2000 of those have been deployed into the area around the Barrage and Hinkley Point."

Thorndike drew a sharp breath. "This information seems to be coming forward rather late in the day," he said. "Initially I was given to believe that we would be dealing with a few groups of armed insurgents. Now I find we're dealing with a well-armed force intent on knocking out a nuclear power station!"

Bolton looked a little weary. He had the greatest sympathy with Thorndike's predicament.

"I'm sorry, Greg," he said. "You know that we're only told what WMC believe we need to know. This is a substantial force. We think that they've deployed a total of about 4000 men into the Bristol area."

Trying to conceal his irritation, Thorndike asked, "How did that little lot get here?"

"In disguised container ships – they landed in Pembrokeshire on the night of the London missile attack and dispersed whilst everyone was trying to find out whether we still had a government or not."

"Mmm," murmured Thorndike, "I remember. I was constantly getting reports of troop movements that we knew nothing about, but as far as I'm aware the only uniforms to be seen were British Army – which came as no surprise after the events in London."

"Exactly," grunted Bolton. "Every other bloody thing we've ever produced has been faked in the Far East. British Army uniforms must have been a doddle."

Thorndike ruminated for a moment thinking about what Bolton had said. "They have enough to take Hinkley. The bigger total – 10,000 – isn't enough for an invasion though."

"No, but 4000 is enough to tie us down here for the next few days – and if they do manage to damage the reactors, then God help us all."

"If it's not an invasion force, they're still here in appreciable numbers. To put it simply, why go to so much trouble?"

"Depends on how you look at it," replied Bolton. "It's not a lot of trouble if you control the oil in a world that's running out of it. Not if you are religious fanatics bent on creating a new world order – and certainly not if you have nowhere to live and remember your village being blown to bits by the British or the Americans."

Thorndike returned to an earlier point in the conversation. "So if this is not an invasion, why are they risking men and materials?"

"The consensus is," said Bolton, "that this time they're just here to hit us hard and run. They can always come back when they're ready. It's a strategy that was used on a smaller scale many times in Afghanistan."

"We're going to be at full stretch," said Thorndike. "You've convinced me that The Ridge is important, but we can only send a detachment over there."

"I understand," replied Bolton. "That's why I'm proposing that we need the help of the people who live up there. We have very little time to get them organised, but it's the best we can do."

Thorndike nodded. There was, he thought, little else that he could do other than agree to Bolton's proposal even though he was very reluctant to involve civilians in such an operation.

He broke off from the conversation but then remembered a piece of conversation with Bolton. "Do I recall," he said, "that there was a biker's camp near the route to Hinkley?"

"There was," said Bolton, "but it's not there now. The bikers had a visit – though not from us. The invaders beat us to it. The bikers were a bunch of thugs, but knives, axes, a few handguns and motorbikes without petrol are no match for a small army of fanatics armed with automatic weapons. What made it worse was that the invaders seem to have regarded them as some sort of satanic cult."

Thorndike turned away feeling that he needed to ask no more. There was, he thought gratefully, at least one small distraction that had now been dealt with.

***

For the second night in a row, Kirk was finding it hard to sleep. He was no longer thinking about Rose or Alison. Jed had said during the evening meal that they would all be called upon to play their part in the defence of The Ridge and the village. He knew that Jed was right, if only because there was nowhere to run.

A further thought was also troubling Kirk. Even if they were able to defend themselves against human marauders, they might still succumb to a much older and more powerful adversary; without power and with inadequate supplies of food and water, the winter might finish what the enemy had started – and what had so far seemed like something of an adventure could turn into a nightmare.

He decided that he needed a drink of water. He crept quietly out of bed, down the stairs and into the kitchen. The moon had not set, and its light slanted eerily into the kitchen. He cautiously made his way towards the tap but was startled by somebody who was already standing there in the shadows, someone in a long white nightdress.

Kirk's heart began to thud and then Alison stepped forwards into the moonlight. He could see her body silhouetted beneath the nightdress.

"I'm sorry, Kirk. I didn't mean to startle you," she said in a whisper. "I couldn't sleep. I was just looking at the garden in the moonlight."

"I came down to get a drink," explained Kirk.

"Oh, let me get you a glass." She went to a kitchen cabinet, took out a glass and then filled it with water from a spring water tap that they had resorted to using in recent days. She handed the glass to him, watching him drink with a faint smile on her lips, seemingly unconscious that he could see the shapely outline of her body, in the moonlight.

She returned to gazing out at the garden bathed in the ghostly, mysterious light of the moon. "It's such a beautiful night..." her voice trailed away. After a few moments, she turned back to face him. "I should go back to bed. It's getting cold."

She began to move past him, but he gently caught her in his arms, kissing her lightly on the cheek and feeling the warmth of her body against his.

She did not resist him and as he slowly withdrew, she turned her head so that when he kissed her again, it was on the fullness of her lips.

She placed a hand on the arm that he had placed around her waist. "You should go back to bed as well," she whispered.

He did not reply but waited as she went out of the kitchen and up the stairs and listened from below as she went into the bedroom that she shared with Jed, softly closing the door behind her.

A few moments later, he followed up the stairs in Alison's footsteps. He crept into bed but had hardly settled when he heard Rose ask, "Where have you been? I thought I heard noises downstairs."

"I just went to get a glass of water." He was aware that he was being economical with the truth.

Rose put her arms around him. He loved her in both the passionate moments and in the everyday things that Alison had spoken about. How strange that just a few moments before, he had found himself putting his arms around Alison. He responded to Rose and held her gently, resolving that in future, he would make every effort to be loyal to her. Rose appeared to fall asleep and soon Kirk followed her, his head lolling on her shoulder.

She was still awake, however, and lay awake puzzling for a while about the noises downstairs or more specifically voices she thought she had heard... but then, she had hardly been awake and before that she had been dreaming vividly.

★★★

CHAPTER 15

PREPARATIONS

The pace of life at Hatch End had seemed leisurely when they first arrived, but Kirk and Rose knew that events in the outside world would once again be having an impact on them.

They ate breakfast quickly because Jed had told them that they needed to meet Robert Lawson at Andrew's farm. The farm lay on the other side of the wood, but it was not far to walk. Kirk noted from the calendar in the kitchen that it was the first of December. Following the recent storm, it was a crisp, bright day. The air was cold. They needed thick coats, hats and even gloves. Kirk could barely remember when he had last worn gloves. Jed stuffed his hands into his pockets and stalked along the path. Rose thought that he and Alison seemed a little distant with each other. She wondered briefly what had happened between them.

Kirk had more than a little idea as to what had happened, but he could say nothing. He was also resentful of the turn that events were now taking. Up to that point, he had felt that they had managed to retain a measure of control over their own destiny. Now it was being taken away from them. They would have to do someone else's bidding. Rose could see that he was brooding and made an accurate guess as to the cause.

"This is for everyone's good," she said, answering his unspoken thoughts. "We don't know anything about fighting. Presumably this 'Robert Lawson' is a soldier. He will tell us what we need to do."

"You're right," agreed Kirk ruefully. "I suppose he wouldn't be here unless it was important – but I was just beginning to look forward to a quiet life in the countryside." He joked about it although he hardly felt like doing so. Every day now, they would be reminded of the perilous situation of which they were a part.

Forgetting for once to foster his manly image, Jed had linked arms with Alison. She still felt cold and aloof towards him but did not resist and gradually became drawn along by his obvious mood of anticipation. She glanced at the four of them heading along the path; it was as though they were off to some social meeting rather than heading towards conflict with an enemy as yet unseen and unknown. Of all of them Jed looked the part. Rose did not look like anyone's idea of a soldier, but Alison knew that she had an inner toughness that would probably serve her well in whatever was to come. She and Kirk, she thought, were the most vulnerable – but somehow they would just have to get through whatever experiences were about to come their way.

They gathered not in Andrew's farmhouse but in an adjacent barn. Kirk thought that the farmhouse told its own story of former, prosperous times. It was large and rambling but spoke of the wealth and energy of its owners. Everywhere he looked, the farm seemed to be tidy and well organised. Despite the numerous disasters that had befallen the country in recent days, it was still too early for any of them to have had an impact on the farm – which, in any event, Andrew was now steering towards self-sufficiency.

They sat on bales of hay which had been pulled into a semi-circle for the purpose. In the space that faced towards the semi-circle there was a further bale, which, for that moment, was vacant.

They heard not the clopping of horses in the outer courtyard but the roaring of two motorbikes. Feeling a little resentful of those who still had access to oil, they sat studying one another whilst they were waiting. The air of quiet expectation was punctuated every now and again by the bellowing of an animal in an adjoining building. Feeling faintly ridiculous but nevertheless in need of an introduction or two, Kirk stood and went across to shake hands with the other men who were also there waiting for their anticipated visitor. Andrew or 'Andy' as he had become known to Kirk when they were at the bridge, reached over and shook Kirk's hand with a crushing grip.

"Pleased to see you again," he said. He smiled. "This is Jim, my eldest lad."

Jim was a tall, broad shouldered, fair haired man with an open intelligent face. He looked every inch the farmer.

He winced at his father's introduction. "I'm a bit more than a 'lad'," he said. "Anyway, this is my wife Wendy, my son Tom and my daughter Tabitha." The children looked shyly towards Kirk who was more used to the boisterous self-importance of urban children.

Just then, there was a certain amount of bustle at the entrance to the barn. Rose was calling to him to sit down. He sat down on a bale that had been left vacant for him between Alison and Rose. Jed sat between Alison and a man that Kirk recognised as Danny, another of the witnesses to the events at the bridge. Rose put her arm through Kirk's arm, but it was Alison who whispered in his ear, "That's Steve's mum just over there". She nodded to a small, plump, grey-haired woman who sat with a deeply sad expression lining her face. A young man whom Kirk assumed to be the son Alison had referred to shortly after he and Rose had arrived, sat with his arm around her shoulder. Kirk could see in him some resemblance to Steve, the impetuous older brother who had been drowned at the river. To their right sat a young woman with an attractive face. Her jacket and boots were not fully successful in concealing the rest of her appearance, but Kirk thought that she seemed oddly detached from the families who were gathered for the meeting. He leaned towards Alison and whispered in her ear.

"Who's that?"

She followed his gaze without difficulty.

"I wondered how long it would be before you noticed her," she said with a smile – and a certain amount of emphasis on the word 'her'.

"She's Janey Capstick…"

"Does she live on The Ridge?" asked Kirk.

"Yes," said Alison. "Her husband's a farmer. Their farm is next door to this one."

They were interrupted by Rose, who was tugging at Kirk's arm. "Shush, you two!" she hissed. "The main act is here."

A tall, very upright figure strode into the space in front of the bales. Kirk looked at him in a fairly nonchalant way – but then looked again, fighting hard not to give away his astonishment. He had last seen this person, known to him as 'Mark Ridgeway', walking away from his house in Hallamton and towards a car parked a little way down the road. Momentarily, it seemed a long time ago, but then a great deal had happened; he reminded himself that it was barely a month ago.

Freddie Bolton immediately recognised Kirk. He had made an almost full recovery from the amnesia brought about by the attack made on him in Hallamton. His memory for faces seemed to have returned, unimpaired. However, he allowed no flicker of recognition to cross his face.

On his part, Kirk reluctantly supposed that he had better remain complicit. He let his gaze fall and listened in silence. As he did so, however, he also registered that another person, more obviously an army officer, had accompanied him into the barn. This officer was not quite so tall, had a round almost boyish face, but nevertheless gave an immediate impression of mature competence. The meeting had barely started before Kirk felt that the two visitors had imposed their joint presence upon it.

Looking for the briefest moment at Kirk, Freddie Bolton introduced himself as 'Robert Lawson'. Most of those in the meeting had already heard this name and some of those present, such as Jed and Andrew, had met him before. Freddie introduced his companion as Lieutenant Colonel Thorndike. Brief introductions over, he immediately began to tell the meeting as much as he was prepared to reveal about the plans that they had made for the fate of Hatch End.

The villagers watched and listened in rapt silence. It had been a while for some of them since their last geography lesson, but they readily recognised the maps and aerial photographs that Freddie Bolton and Greg Thorndike produced between them.

Freddie was used to handling meetings that were potentially difficult. Like Thorndike he would have preferred to evacuate the civilians from The Ridge and then to re-populate it with army personnel, but time was very short and, in any event, the flooding and general crises all around them determined that such an operation would be time consuming, resource intensive and unnecessarily hazardous. He and Thorndike had decided that, on balance, it would be better to let these few beleaguered individuals play a part in defending themselves. He was not in the smallest part sentimental, but he tried to avoid looking at the children; he did not want to become in any way emotionally engaged with any of the people there. Somewhere, however, in some of the further recesses of his mind, the phrase, "lambs to the slaughter" kept flashing like a morbid and ominous neon sign.

Thorndike was in a similar frame of mind. He was striving to push the resemblance between Andrew's grandchildren and his own children, who were now in the north of Scotland, to the back of his mind. They had a job to do, and they could not afford to fail. Between them they outlined that part of the plan that they wanted the villagers to know about.

They drew on the villagers' local knowledge to confirm, rather than identify, those places that the invaders would be most likely to attack. The army would do the fighting, but the villagers would be provided with the means to defend themselves. Freddie Bolton knew that if it came to such a pass, the villagers would stand little chance, but one or two of them knew how to shoot and they might just divert the invaders for long enough to allow the defending soldiers to press home their attack on the invaders.

Thorndike and Bolton had decided the night before that the defence of The Ridge was more important than any immediate concerns they might have about civilian casualties. To both the east and west, towns and cities were falling into chaos and civil strife. The invaders had taken advantage of natural disasters to help them in their invasion – and they had oil, a commodity of which the British had very little. He could not afford to expend scarce resources defending a few civilians who happened to be sitting on an important military objective.

Thorndike was fully aware of the parameters of the plan. The villagers were told that they would be supplied with enough diesel oil to power their farm machinery in bolstering the natural defences of the hill. A chill ran through the small gathering as he told them that they would probably have to endure a helicopter attack which might render the outer ground defences irrelevant, but they could not assume that this would happen. There was no mobile phone network in operation, although they would set up a basic telephone system so that the villagers could communicate with each other.

Kirk surmised that the plan seemed paper thin, wondering what else was planned and what was being kept from them. Meanwhile Bolton and Thorndike both knew that time was short and now that they had paid their brief visit to The Ridge, they would need to get away. They planned to weaken the invading force by as many means as they could and then to counter-attack. They did not want to lose control of The Ridge at any point, however, since it would take an enormous effort in terms of personnel and other resources, to get it back again. They now had to move on to the next part of the plan. Other officers and a number of soldiers would be arriving shortly to work with the civilians on the practicalities of the plan.

At the end of the meeting, the two officers were 'matter-of-fact' in their approach to the villagers. Questions were not allowed. The soldiers arriving shortly would lead the effort to prepare for the defence of The Ridge.

Rose reflected that it seemed strange to be talking about helicopters when, other than farm machinery, motorised transport of any kind was not available to the villagers or the rest of the population in the surrounding area. Like Kirk, she was depressed that the way of life they had hoped to adopt should now be so rapidly overtaken by some brutal, external military battle.

The sound of motorbikes could be heard from the yard again and then the villagers were left to their own devices for a few brief minutes. There was a rather angry and anxious discussion, mainly amongst the men but also including Rose, Alison and Janey Capstick.

Rose had once seen a television programme in which Jewish fugitives had hidden in an underground network of tiny dwellings. They had survived the snows of winter. Perhaps such a construction could help them now since houses above ground would be obvious targets. The farmers knew, however, that they were so short of time that any such constructions would be overly ambitious. The most that they might manage would be some small underground shelters in which they could hide until the invaders left or were driven out. Alison found herself wishing that the rather paltry leaf fall of that winter so far had been more substantial – but there would be sufficient to hide their 'fox-holes' if such concealment became necessary.

Events proved to be such that they had just two days before the attack came. To the east, there were many signs of war. The persistent rattle of helicopters and burr of automatic weapons told them that the engagements in the marshes had begun. With binoculars, inflatable raiding craft could be seen working their way along the water courses and attacking enemy detachments as they found them. A hovercraft was also being used and excited a certain amount of admiration from observers on The Ridge until it was hit by an aerial missile attack and fell burning into the waters of Sedgemoor, disappearing beneath a column of thick, black, oily smoke. Flashes from guns and missiles winked across the watery wastes of the marshy landscape below and every so often the earth shook with the thud of an enormous explosion. Further north, somewhere along the Bristol Channel, much larger columns of oily smoke were beginning to blot out the sunlight, imparting a nightmare quality to the embattled landscape before them. Kirk was at the edge of the wood with Jed when they first saw the smoke.

"Where's that?" asked Kirk.

"Avonmouth, I expect." Jed raised a grimy face and gazed at the vast plumes of smoke that were filling the sky. "Whatever oil we had before, we now have less."

The engagements in the marshes were sporadic but continued round the clock.

Jed and Andrew were both strong and fit. Together they formed the backbone of the villagers' contribution to the preparations. Around them, although the detachment was small in relation to the size of the task, soldiers seemed to be everywhere, preparing camouflaged emplacements, setting up traps of various kinds and laying mines. A missile battery was set up and camouflaged. It represented the most serious hardware to be found, although two tracked armoured vehicles had been brought in to give fire support and armour, whenever it was needed. Jed and Andrew did not underestimate the enemy but thought that the defenders on The Ridge would be able to resist strongly, if an attack came.

The soldiers, both male and female, were young; in the eyes of Kirk and Rose, they had a fresh 'baby-faced' look. Janey Capstick and Sam, the daughter of one of the farming families on The Ridge, found themselves watching the young men as they worked and enjoying what they could see, in the winter weather, of their physiques.

Sam was barely 17. Amongst her friends she was considered tall, had light brown hair and the slimness of an active young woman. A cheeky boyfriend at college had told her that she had 'nice tits'. He had not lasted long although she was not prudish and smiled to herself at the clumsy compliment he had intended to pay. She was the daughter of a farmer with a comfortable living but knew that they would be lucky if any of them survived beyond the next two or three days. She had her eye on a dark haired, well-muscled young soldier, who had been helping to move supplies into her father's farm. She made it her business to find out his name; it was James Ligo – Private James Ligo.

At the back of the large barn, he had seemed remarkably slow at first to understand what she wanted, but once realisation had dawned, proved very effective in helping her to achieve her wish. There was barely time to relish the afterglow, and she wondered if either of them would make it through to the days and weeks beyond tomorrow. He left her, covered with her own wax jacket; she lay for a few moments longer musing on the pleasures of his body. She was glad she had not missed the experience.

***

Most of the people on The Ridge shared the same mixture of anticipation and dread.

Jed, Alison, Kirk and Rose had all worked themselves to a standstill, helping to set up gun emplacements, dig out the shelters and bolt holes that they had discussed at the meeting but finally reaching the point where they thought that rest would be the best form of preparation that they could make.

Earlier, they had all been given a crash course in basic firearms training. The details of it swirled around in Rose's head as she lay trying to sleep. She had worried about whether weapons would turn them into targets but was told by an instructor that they were all targets anyway and that the weapons were for their defence.

Unlike the younger women, her feelings about the soldiers were mixed. She found it hard to adjust to the coarse, staccato manner in which they spoke, and she could not decide if she was attracted or repelled by the raw physicality that they had brought with them. She also reproached herself for her own churlishness; she had no social pretensions and knew that the young men and women around them would be expected to sacrifice their lives if necessary in the savagery that almost certainly lay ahead of them. The people attacking them would all be the brothers, sons, fiancés and fathers of someone, somewhere. There would, however, be no women amongst them.

She believed, however, that if women across the world had been able to influence the course of events, such conflict as that which was about to take place, would have been avoided.

Day faded rapidly into night. The mood in the cottage that evening was surly and tense, not least because they were all very tired from the day's work. They managed to co-operate sufficiently to put together a meal which they ate by the flickering light of a few stubs of candle. There was no power supply from the grid now, but the house had some energy supplies of its own; there were solar panels on the roof and a wind generator at the bottom of the garden. Together with the other resources of the house – the wood burning stove and the huge stock of candles that Alison had been able to assemble, they would be able to get through the winter – if they survived the expected attack.

The civilians had all been assigned specific roles. As far as possible, Thorndike had planned to keep them away from the action but since evacuation was now impossible, he knew that at some point they would almost certainly be involved. Geographically, The Ridge was too small a place for them to be protected from the expected onslaught.

Together with the other householders on The Ridge, Alison, Jed, Kirk and Rose had all been assigned the task of picking off any of the enemy who managed to get through the outer defences manned by the Army. The geography of The Ridge was such that their attackers would have to come through specific 'gateways' – points at which there was natural access to small areas of strategic ground that they would want to occupy. During the brief span of time in which the Army had led the preparations, the flooding and the steepness of the contours on the western side of The Ridge had been reinforced with a variety of defences such as explosives and gun emplacements. However, it was anticipated that the main brunt of any attack would come from the north-east and it was on this side of The Ridge that the army had focussed its heavier firepower.

Kirk and Rose had decided to keep most of their clothes on in readiness for news of an attack. They lay on the bed with a light cover drawn over them, dozing fitfully. Alison too lay on her bed trying to sleep. Jed, however, had decided to sleep on a couch downstairs.

This was largely because the idea of getting the phones to work had been abandoned. The rest of the preparations had absorbed all the time and resources that they had. Instead, it had been decided that a soldier on a track bike would be the most effective means of providing a warning.

In the event, Jed was awake before the warning came. The bike could be heard snarling its way along the track at the edge of the wood. For a few brief seconds, Jed listened to its approach but then scrambled from the couch and began hauling on his outdoor clothes. The first light was just appearing in the sky as he felt the cold air of a winter morning on his face. He was at the gate when the soldier arrived.

The track bike braked rapidly and turned around since the cottage represented one end of its brief journey. Although the bike's headlight was dimmed, it still dazzled Jed as he was briefly caught in its beam. The soldier drew level with Jed at the gate, throttled back the engine and yelled, "Balloon's up, mate! An attack's expected within minutes. You need to get your people out and off to their posts. You have very little time. Good luck!"

He nodded at Jed and then was gone. The stink of petrol fumes hung on the air and the slowly fading snarl of the bike's engine could be heard as he headed back towards the cottage.

Once inside, however, there was no need to rouse the others. In the dim light of the cottage, they were scrambling into their outdoor clothes. Kirk sat looking strangely incongruous in the homely surroundings of the kitchen; the rifle with which he had been issued lay on the table in front of him and a small backpack lay at his feet. To Jed's disbelief, he was sipping nervously at a cup of tea from one of the thermos flasks they had prepared just before going to bed.

"Come on, Kirk!" exclaimed Jed. "You don't have time for that now. The attack's expected any minute."

Kirk nodded in mute assent. He had almost finished the tea and threw the small amount remaining down the sink. Rose and Alison somehow managed to smile grimly as they gave each other a hug. Then they were off.

Although the so-called 'gate' to which Kirk and Rose had been assigned was just a short distance from the gate assigned to Alison and Jed, they had to walk along diverging paths to reach them. The paths plunged directly into the woods and, in the gloom, the two couples soon lost sight of each other. Kirk and Rose had previously explored their way along the track and were familiar with the area they would be defending.

They had been assigned to guard a gateway through a large stone wall that ran through the woods. The army had barred the gateway and put razor wire along the wall on both sides, but the intention was that the enemy would not be allowed to get past the outer defences.

Kirk and Rose lay concealed on opposite sides of the track. Had it been possible, Rose guessed that the Army would have preferred to evacuate them. She wondered briefly if they were more of a liability than an asset here but knew that they were now committed to doing the best that they could. If they could avoid shooting each other, it would be something of an achievement.

They had not long to wait. A large explosion ripped through the trees, shaking the ground and sending clods of earth flying into the air. Kirk kept his head down behind a large rock just in front of him, listening to the patter of falling fragments of soil. He wanted to call out to Rose but knew that they should do nothing to give away their presence.

Now they had begun to hear the repeated chatter of weapons. There was a swoosh of missiles which went over the positions in which they lay. Almost immediately, large explosions could be heard from the other side of the wood where some of the Army's emplacements were located. The noise of weapons now seemed to be coming from all around them. A determined attempt to seize The Ridge was being made.

A sound that filled Kirk with dread could be heard just ahead of them. It was a helicopter although to which side it belonged, he had no idea. It passed low over the wood and Kirk thought that he could make out British markings, but it disappeared in the direction of the missile explosions. He counted three more, coming in behind the first and sweeping swiftly across the wood. If they were enemy helicopters, they were taking a great risk. They could soften up the defences, but they too were very vulnerable to attack. It would depend on how effectively the Army would be able to respond. He wondered briefly how a force that they had been told consisted of 'terrorists' was able to gain access to helicopters in a country that was far from any friendly base. The deep ominous throb of a troop-carrying helicopter came just behind the initial wave. It passed rapidly over them, following its predecessors towards the far side of the wood. Unless it was a British helicopter, the outer defences would now become largely irrelevant.

It took little imagination to see that if a helicopter-based attack was taking place on the far side of The Ridge, the plan that had been developed would become a shambles. He called across to Rose. They crawled towards each other and met on Rose's side of the path.

"Whose helicopters are those?" asked Rose as soon as she could make herself heard.

"I've no idea," replied Kirk, "but they seem to be attacking the defences on the other side of The Ridge – so I guess that they must be enemy helicopters, no matter what the markings say."

Rose nodded. "So where does that leave us?" she asked. "It looks as though they've completely by-passed the outer defences."

Kirk agreed. "They'll be landing over at Andrew's farm, behind the main defences."

"What shall we do?" Rose stared anxiously into Kirk's face.

"Well, we can't escape from The Ridge," said Kirk. "We could try to find out what's going on."

Rose thought about it for a moment. "We know what's happening," she said. "There's a battle taking place. We're not soldiers."

"No – but we either hide or we try to help our own people." Kirk said it with little conviction other than that he would find it hard to live with himself if he skulked in the woods without trying to help the people who were defending them.

"Okay," said Rose. "We'd better do what we can – but we also need to know what's happened to Jed and Alison."

It seemed like the right decision even though it meant leaving the gate they had been told to defend. At that moment, however, events took another turn. From ahead of them there came the sound of people approaching the gateway. Alarmed, Rose and Kirk rolled in separate directions, away from the path and into better cover behind the rocks that poked up through the woodland soil.

Hardly had they done so when a group of four soldiers appeared warily probing forward towards the gateway. Kirk thought that they could not be aware of his presence or that of Rose. Two of the soldiers began to work at the razor wire with wire cutters whilst the rest crouched, waiting to get through the gap in the wall. One of them covered the others with his rifle. Kirk watched as Rose took aim and shot him in the side of the head. Kirk felt his heart thudding in his chest. It had taken until that moment for the reality of the situation to fully dawn on him.

There were angry shouts from the remaining soldiers who dived to the ground and wriggled forward, clearly intending to target Rose. Kirk had a good view of one of them as he crawled across his line of vision. He fired.

It was not a clean shot. He had intended to hit the soldier in the head, but the bullet passed instead through his upper arm and torso. He lay yelling in agony and bleeding profusely into the leaf litter of the woodland floor.

There was a brief stalemate in which no-one moved but then one of the two remaining soldiers seemed to be reaching for a radio device of some kind. Once again it was Rose who reacted first. She managed to get off several shots, smashing the device and shooting the soldier in the neck.

The remaining soldier did not retreat but instead fired a number of shots in the direction of the rock behind which Rose was crouching. He crawled rapidly forward. Kirk could not get clear view of him; for several moments he disappeared but then there was the sound of a ricochet and Kirk found himself clutching his left ear. He could feel blood running down the side of his head but fought off the temptation to panic. The imminent danger to Rose helped him to re-focus. He tried to get a view of his enemy but without success. Then, from somewhere behind both Rose and Kirk, there came the successive sound of shots being fired. For a few brief moments, an eerie silence fell upon the wood. The shots had not found their target. Kirk caught a fleeting glimpse of Jed and Alison crawling through the undergrowth. Meanwhile, concealed from view until the last moment, the remaining soldier crawled back between the trees and made his escape. Kirk caught a brief glimpse of him but decided that he would not pursue him.

The brief silence was broken by ground-shaking explosions and the cackle of weapons in the general direction of Andrew's farm. Kirk crawled across to where Rose still lay concealed behind the rock. She had begun to shake violently.

"Bloody hell! Bloody, bloody hell! Do you just realise? I've just killed someone. I deliberately shot two people!"

Kirk began to worry that she was going into a state of shock.

Kirk momentarily remembered the two bikers they had met on their journey. It was possible that they had brought about the death of at least one of them although the incident on the road had not involved the same deliberate intention to kill as the one that has just taken place. He put his arm around her, trying to calm her but also trying to suppress similar feelings of his own. Rose sobbed into his coat. Neither of them had wanted to take the life of another human being. He voiced the obvious thought.

"We had to do it, Rose. If we had not killed them, they would have killed us. We had no choice."

"That doesn't make it any better though, does it? Is that supposed to make it better?"

She was angry and almost shouted at him but continued to hold onto his coat.

Jed and Alison finally arrived through the undergrowth and joined them behind the rock.

"Where is he?" asked Jed. "Did I get him?"

"No, I'm afraid not," said Kirk. "He escaped back through the gate. What happened where you were?"

"There were just too many of them," he said resignedly. "They were pouring in. Someone has messed up."

"Jed's right," agreed Alison. "We were supposed to pick off the ones who had been missed by the outer ring, but large numbers of them have got through. We have very little ammunition left."

At that point, she caught sight of the blood on the side of Kirk's head.

"What's happened to you?" she asked.

"It was a ricochet off one of the rocks. It caught the top of my ear."

Rose had not realised that Kirk had been hit. She peered anxiously at the damage.

"Here, let me see to that," she said, reaching into her pack for something to deal with the wound. She found some wipes and proceeded to clean the blood away from the site of the injury.

Kirk jumped as he felt the sting of the antiseptic in the wipe but then forced himself to sit still.

"It's not done much damage," said Alison, peering closely. "You were lucky."

"We were very lucky," agreed Rose. "But I don't want to keep pushing my luck."

"We don't have a choice." Jed looked across at the three of them. "We had a narrow escape at the other gate – but now we need to decide what we do next."

Kirk spoke reluctantly. "We need to know what's happening at the Farm."

For a moment, the others looked at him intently then Rose said, "I agree. There's little more that we can do here. We may be some use at the

Farm, and we need to know what's happened."

They knew that by travelling towards the farm they would be placing themselves in greater danger, but they also realised that there was now nowhere on The Ridge that was safe. Their best chance of survival seemed to lie in finding the soldiers who had been brought in to defend them.

The others nodded their agreement with Rose's assessment, and they began to move off through the wood and back in the general direction of the path from the cottage. Jed led the way, following the line of the track but staying inside the cover of the tree line. Soon they were nearer again to the cottage but, having ascertained that it had not yet been taken over by enemy soldiers, they continued to move on towards the farm.

The sounds of the combat were growing ever louder as they picked their way through the trees but then as they edged their way through the final stages of the journey, they could see soldiers in British uniforms slipping away in the opposite direction. They looked at one another and were close enough to see the anxious expressions on each other's faces.

Alison wanted to stop, but Kirk and Rose reluctantly followed in Jed's wake, and she had little option but to stay close behind them. They were now very close to the farm and an ominous quiet had fallen on the landscape.

Jed finally halted just inside the deep shadow of the trees at the edge of the farm. The others lay in the undergrowth just a short distance from him. Ahead of them they could see the shattered remnants of the fence which had previously formed the boundary between the wood and the yard on this side of the house. For the moment, there was no sign of the helicopters.

Suddenly Jed motioned to them to stay down. Soldiers were deploying into the yard.

The watchers in the wood had only a short time to wonder about what was happening. Kirk crawled forward so that he lay next to Jed's position in the undergrowth but from where they had a clear view of the Farm.

"What the hell are they doing?"

"I think they're taking the family hostage!" Kirk thought that he could see Andrew, Jim, Wendy and the children being hustled into the yard.

"Why are they doing that?"

"Perhaps in an attempt to blunt a counter-attack – maybe by using them as human shields."

"Huh," scoffed Jed. "They're under-estimating Thorndike and Lawson. That won't stop them. They'll attack anyway."

"We're the only chance they have."

"What?" Jed could not hear what Kirk was saying.

"We're the only people who can get Andrew and his family out!"

This time Jed heard him. "I think you're right," he agreed. "But we don't have much time." He pointed towards a jeep-like vehicle that had drawn up at the edge of the tree line adjacent to the farm.

The family were being led across the farmyard towards the vehicle, but then something delayed the group. One of the soldiers had spotted something at the edge of the wood. Jed could see that Andrew's son Jim had begun to struggle with his captors.

As they watched, Rose crawled up next to Jed, and Alison slid into a space next to Kirk.

"What's happening?" asked Rose.

"Looks like they're taking Andrew and his family hostage," replied Jed. "But something's holding them up."

The soldiers guarding the family had raised their rifles and were using the butts to club the children's father to the ground. Andrew attempted to go to the aid of his son but met with the same fate. The children clung to their mother Wendy who could be heard screaming at the soldiers, "You bastards! You barbaric bastards!"

Jed motioned to the others gathered around him.

"Kirk, you and Alison try to take out the guards on your side. Rose and I will go the other side and try to take out the two over by the house."

He crawled forward beneath a damaged section of fence into some rough ground on the other side. Rose followed.

Kirk and Alison followed them but then moved away to the left until they could peer through the grass at the soldiers who now lay in their line of sight. For the moment, the guards were distracted. Wendy was putting up a struggle and was being beaten by the guards. The children were attempting to help her but were also coming under the blows from the guards.

Jed raised his rifle and fired but never knew if he had hit the target because simultaneously, there was a burst of automatic gunfire and those unable to run for cover were shot as they ran or lay on the ground. The guard closest to Wendy spun away, dropping his rifle.

Kirk watched as three of the soldiers turned and tried to retreat into the farmhouse.

They managed to run just a few strides before they were cut down by gunfire from the edge of the wood. Andrew had initially been overcome by shock and horror at the unfolding of events, but now his chief thought was to find Jim and get him away from his captors.

Seeing that Wendy was free of the guards who had been beating her, he yelled at her to get the children into the woods, then he seized the rifle that had fallen to the ground and went in pursuit of the guards who were dragging Jim towards the farmhouse. Whilst he went after them, the machine gunfire from the woods was being carefully controlled to give Wendy and the children a chance to escape into the trees.

Decisions being made some distance away, however, were now overtaking the events in and around the farm. The initial burst of gunfire had signalled more general fighting along The Ridge. Jed called to the rest of the group to work around to where Wendy and the children were headed. They just had time to hear his words before all other sounds were drowned out by the sound of a jet aircraft screeching at treetop level across The Ridge. From the far side of the farm came the loudest bang that Kirk and the others had ever heard. Flames and oily black smoke leapt into the sky from behind the farm. Through the general din of the foreground, however, they also heard the deep throb of engines and the whine of helicopter rotor blades.

"It's the troop carrier. They're trying to get out!" yelled Kirk, to no-one in particular.

He crawled forward. Despite the undergrowth, he could see past the farm and out to where the ridge curved its way above the river's course. A moving speck far out in the distance caught his eye and then he found himself squinting at a seemingly silent aircraft approaching at prodigious speed along the course of the river.

The troop carrier had just begun to climb above the roof of the farm. A point of light winked from beneath the aircraft's wing and a missile accelerated towards the helicopter, which erupted in a descending ball of flame over the farmyard. The jet pulled up and over the destruction, turning away in ghostly silence to make another run.

Moments later the shock wave from the aircraft slammed into the farm and the roar of jet engines shook the countryside. Kirk was briefly enthralled by the attack but then became aware that Wendy and her children were pinned down at the edge of the yard and were in imminent danger from the blazing debris that was being showered all around. The stretch of trees towards which they had been running had also now caught fire.

Without thinking, he scrambled over the remnants of the farmyard fence and began running towards them. Jed followed, intending to provide any necessary cover. Rose and Alison headed directly towards Wendy and her children.

In their focus on the intended rescue, they did not see the jet complete its turn and begin its second run towards the farm. Then Kirk, who was a little ahead of the others, became aware that the jet's second run was much slower than the first. A bomb could be seen falling from beneath the aircraft and then a series of explosions progressed towards them along the flight path of the jet.

The word 'bombs' had barely formed in his brain when he was briefly aware of an explosion that lifted him up as though he was little more than a toy and then...nothing.

CHAPTER 16

REMNANTS

Something was intruding into the pain that disturbed his sleep. Slowly, he became able to identify what it was. Someone was touching his face. It was not unpleasant. The touching was not unpleasant – but then the background pain became the foreground. He stirred, trying to open his eyes.

Someone was trying to speak to him. The words seemed muffled at first and were coming through a constant swooshing which was almost certainly the sound of his own pulse, but then he began to make them out.

"Lay still, Kirk. Don't try to move."

Gradually, painfully he managed to get his right eye open and then his left eye.

A woman's face was hovering above him. He lay staring up at her. Beyond her he could see the branches of trees and here, close to his face, the steady motion of tall grasses.

The woman's voice, he thought, was very beautiful – but it sounded sad, anxious and sad. She had an interesting and attractive face. He thought he had seen it before but could not remember who she was.

She was wielding a grossly inadequate piece of material with which she was attempting to wipe his face. Then suddenly he felt sick.

He gave her no warning as he jerked to one side and vomited into the grass. Then he lay on his side, his face just above his own vomit before jerking away again to lie on his back.

The woman waited and then returned to his side. As he looked up this time, he could see that her face bore a map of cuts and bruises. Tell-tale lines of tears ran through the grime that covered her cheeks and disappeared somewhere along the edge of her jaw.

It had taken all of Alison's strength to drag Kirk back to the edge of the wood. She had no reason to suppose that they would be any safer there; unexploded munitions probably lay all around them but out there in the yard... Her mind recoiled from the devastation, from the battlefield that the farmyard had become with its debris of corpses, body parts and the moans of the dying. There had been no further fighting on The Ridge, but she could still hear gunfire in the marshes below and every so often an explosion would light up the darkness and send its waves of sound rolling across the landscape. She could only speculate as to why no-one had arrived to give medical assistance to the wounded and her first course of action was to search for those she knew and loved.

In the intervening hours, darkness had fallen. An eerie winter moon had enabled her to find, in the blue shadows that slanted across the yard, the bodies of Rose and Jed. Wendy and her two children were just recognisable, but she could not bring herself to approach their corpses. They lay in a heap, with Wendy on top of the two children as if in death, she was still trying to protect them.

For a long time, she had cradled first Rose and then Jed, weeping bitterly and lamenting over them and rocking their inert bodies in her arms. She had not found Kirk until later. Somehow the explosions had flung him free of the devastation.

A thunderous throbbing in her temples and the sandpaper soreness of a parched tongue had made her realise that she was becoming dehydrated. Although she was still feeling concussed by the multiple explosions, she remembered that she had left her pack at the edge of the wood. She headed for the broken section of fence through which she had earlier set out in the vain attempt to rescue Wendy and the children. It was then that she had stumbled across Kirk. He had been flung many yards and dumped on the ground like an unwanted doll. Carefully, she prised him over towards her, until at last she managed to get him into a recovery position. His face was a mass of minor cuts and bruises, but although his breathing was rather slow, it was not difficult to tell that he was still alive. Before she had thought about it, she had seized him in her arms and wept...and wept.

Eventually coming to herself again, she remembered that if he had any internal injuries or broken bones, she needed to keep him as still as possible. She left him temporarily and picked her way through the broken fence and into the edge of the wood. After a certain amount of searching, she found her pack; it lay undisturbed, despite all that had happened, in the place that she had left it.

She rummaged in the pack and found her water bottle and a small first aid kit which she had only had the foresight to slip into her bag moments before leaving the cottage. She made her way back to Kirk and began trying to clean some of the dirt away from the cuts and bruises that marked every part of his face. Then she checked as systematically as she could for any signs of broken bones but after some moments she came to the conclusion that there were no obvious signs of damage.

It was then that she had heard a series of small noises. Her heart began to beat faster, and she looked about her with a heightened sense of their vulnerability. She looked around, but for that moment, could not identify the source of the sounds.

She decided that somehow she needed to get him into the cover of the wood, but she could not lift him and as yet, he was exhibiting no signs of consciousness. She decided to drag him across to the edge of the trees.

Despite the coldness of the night, she was sweating profusely by the time that she managed to get Kirk to a position in which she considered that they would both be safe. He was not a big man but moving him had been difficult and she had also had to manoeuvre him past a corpse and pieces of debris from the destruction of the helicopter.

The grass at the edge of the wood was long and the outer branches of the trees reached overhead, giving a sense of shelter and security. Kirk seemed to be breathing more easily now, but still he did not stir into consciousness. Then, suddenly, he began to open his eyes. For a moment, he lay on his back looking up at her but then, alarmingly, he rolled away from her and was sick.

She waited and then, when he had finished being sick, waited again for him to come back to her. For some moments after that he lay on his back with his eyes closed and letting her continue with the task of cleaning his face. Eventually, he opened his eyes again, slowly breathing her name.

"Alison."

She smiled at him – but it was a sad, weary smile – a smile to acknowledge that, after the loss of memory that she had detected in his eyes, he had remembered her name. Painfully, he put out his arm and gently ran his fingers from her lips down to the tip of her chin. Gently, she took his fingers and kissed them.

Moments later, he struggled to sit up. She moved to help him, but his strength was now returning, and despite a certain giddiness, he stood up, steadying himself against the remnants of the farmyard fence. For a little while, he looked about him. Alison looked on, watching the signs of recognition return to his eyes and tensely anticipated the inevitable questions.

Realisation was dawning on him. Rose was not with them – and neither was Jed.

"Where are Rose and Jed? Where are they?"

Despite her own grief, she prepared him. She placed her hand on his arm and looked directly into his face.

"It's bad news, Kirk. In fact, it's the worst. They're both dead. They were killed when the bomb was dropped on the farm."

Her voice was flat, detached as though it was not her own voice but someone else's.

Gently, carefully, she put her arms around him and held him. He, too, realising that she would be trying to deal with her own grief, held her against him and tried for the moment to hold onto his own emotions.

They continued to hold each other for some moments before he said, "Did you find them?"

With her hand to her mouth and struggling not to weep, she nodded.

"Can you show me?" he asked.

She nodded again but turned her face away from him, not wanting him to see her tears.

She moved towards the shattered fence and stepped again into the moonlit arena, making her way towards the place in which she had found the bodies. She watched as Kirk went to look at Rose. He was shocked. Her eyes were closed but there seemed to be little wrong with her. He believed for a moment that like him she was simply unconscious, knocked out by the blast. He moved to hold her but then, in horror, realised that a large shard of metal was projecting from her back.

Gently, tenderly, he took her in his arms but holding her like this, he could no longer restrain his tears. "Rose, Rose my darling. You're cold. So cold. Why are you so cold?" He knew that it made no sense to ask the question but in that moment he did not care and he did not care if

Alison saw his grief. He and Rose had loved each other. They had been together just a short time and now she had been taken from him. He wept, controllably at first but then he could suppress his emotions no longer.

Alison waited. Eventually Kirk stood up and stepped carefully and respectfully back from Rose's body then, taking off his coat, he stepped forward again and placed it over her.

He stood like this for some minutes but then Alison drew him away and towards the second body that lay just a short distance from that of Rose. Kirk did not investigate but he could see from where he was standing that Jed had a huge open wound in the right side of his head. As he drew closer, the extent of the wound became clearer. Even if he had been given immediate medical help, Kirk could not imagine that he would have survived.

Grim faced, Alison stood at Kirk's side but then turned away. Kirk stood for moment or two longer, reflecting that Jed had never shown any signs of fear. He had led the little group in its brief encounter with a savage enemy, but both he and Rose had finally been killed by their own side.

Kirk turned away and caught up with Alison. She was waiting by the fence. He drew close and she looked into his eyes.

"I can't spend any more time here. I need to go back to the cottage."

He nodded. They started towards the path at the edge of the wood but then they both become aware of a noise – a snuffling, restless noise – coming from the farmyard. It was the same noise that Alison had heard some time before. Kirk went to investigate. In the moonlight, he could see a fox tugging at one of the corpses. He stooped, picked up a stone and aimed it at the fox's ribs. He missed his target, but the fox veered away and scampered back a few yards, staring defiantly back at him, its tongue lolling from the side of its mouth as it panted into the night air.

Alison arrived at his side.

"Come on, Kirk," she said. "There's nothing we can do here. Even if you drive that one away there'll be others to take his place. I want you to take me back to the cottage."

Kirk silently assented and together they set off along the path at the edge of the woods.

***

It seemed faintly ridiculous to Kirk that Alison had to fumble about in her pack for the keys to the house. The walk back had taken them a little time and after the devastation they had left behind they were surprised to find that the cottage had survived unscathed. Kirk reflected briefly that there was after all no particular reason why it should have been damaged. It was well away from the area in which the fighting had taken place and the wood had provided it with protection.

***

Once inside the house, forgetfully returning to a lifelong habit, Alison flicked on the light, but the room remained in darkness. She disappeared into the utility room and came back with a torch. Wearily, they sat at the foot of the stairs, tugging off their boots and leaving them by the door before flopping onto a nearby couch.

They dozed leaning against each other. Eventually Kirk said, "I need to go to bed. She hesitated for a moment before saying, "I need to go to bed as well, but I don't want to be on my own."

Kirk looked at her, understanding how she felt.

"And I won't be able to sleep up there," he said, raising his eyes towards the room that he had shared with Rose.

"There is another bedroom," she said. "We could sleep in there."

"That sounds good to me," he replied.

A short time later, they lay together under a thick blanket but still wearing most of their clothing, wanting not to be alone but each silently grieving for the partners they had lost.

They held each other and fell asleep, dreaming turbulent dreams from which they awoke in endless feverish repetition. Eventually as morning approached they both fell into a deeper sleep and despite intentions to the contrary, they remained asleep until the morning was well advanced. It was Kirk who eventually woke first, for a few brief moments silently admiring the beauty of Alison's face but then remembering the heaviness of Rose's death and returning again to the bitter feelings of the night before. He slipped out from beneath the blanket, leaving Alison to sleep.

His conscience was pricking him hard. They had left the dead lying in the farmyard because they had been exhausted, but now they needed to bury them. His stomach was reminding him that it was many hours since he had last eaten. The refrigerator was no longer working, but Kirk picked through what food there was, finding some scraps of meat and some cheese. It seemed like a strange breakfast, but he knew that digging graves for Rose and Jed would take most of the energy that he had.

He sat at the kitchen table briefly pondering the various imperatives that tugged at him. As he did so a bleary-eyed Alison came and flopped onto the chair beside him. Her hair flowed over the table as she laid down her head, still struggling with sleepiness.

Without thinking, Kirk reached out his hand and stroked her hair. It seemed only a little thing. They had spent the night huddled together but after a moment or two, Alison carefully withdrew from him and went to search in the refrigerator for herself. She returned a very short time later with a similar mixture of food, although she had also managed to find some bread and butter to eke out their slender meal.

Seemingly out of context, Kirk said, "We'll have to go back to the farmyard."

Alison, who had a mouthful of food, nodded and eventually managed to say "Yes, I know".

Kirk returned to his silence. After their sullen breakfast, they found two spades in the garden shed and trudged wearily back along the path they had followed only a few hours before. The noise of army vehicles reached their ears before they could see the farmyard. Work had begun on the far side of the site where bodies were being loaded into lorries and ambulances. Kirk and Alison went to speak to the officer in charge of the work and asked permission to remove the bodies of Rose and Jed.

At first, because it was at odds with the details of his instructions, he was reluctant to agree, but when they told him more of their story, he finally nodded, reassuring them as well that the bodies of Andrew and his family would be carefully removed and respectfully buried. Some minutes later, he watched, seemingly without emotion, as Kirk and Alison carried first Rose and then, with much greater effort, Jed to the edge of the woodland.

There at the edge of the wood, the soil was deep and easy to dig. They were grateful for this small mercy. Working together, they had soon dug a hole which was a little deeper than Kirk's height. Carefully, they laid Rose in a sheet and a thick blanket that they had brought from the house. They did not know what else to do. Then they lowered her into the grave, weeping over her as they did so.

They turned then to Jed. Alison brushed away tears but did not brush away Kirk's arms as he held her before they began the arduous task of digging his grave. It had to be substantially larger than the grave that they had dug for Rose and their fatigue was beginning to tell. Eventually, however, they had done their work and the sides of the grave stood higher than their heads so that it was with some effort that they scrambled up and out again.

Solemnly, they shovelled the earth into Rose's grave. Kirk worked hard to hide his distress, shovelling with anger and determination and trying not to think about his brief flirtation with Alison. Soon, the earth had been returned to the hole from which it came, and they stood, heads bowed, sunk in a very modern confusion about praying or not praying, but perhaps still managing to show their respect for someone who had died trying to save others.

Alison seemed more thoughtful as she helped Kirk to shovel the earth into Jed's grave. He had loved her, she was sure and yet he had rarely sought her true consent when taking his pleasure with her; but for all that, he had been their indisputable leader and had also died bravely, trying to rescue members of Andrew's family. Again, they hung their heads in the solemnity of silence. She also thought briefly about her kiss with Kirk but was less inclined to feel guilty.

Together, they found two large stones from amongst the many that littered the woodland floor and placed one at the head of each grave before finally setting off together back to the cottage. Soldiers were still clearing the farmyard of the remnants of war, and they watched for a short while before returning to the wood and then the cottage. Neither of them felt much like talking, and they communicated with each other only as their needs dictated.

When they reached the house, they both felt hungry after their exertions but sat together again on Alison's settee. Without really realising what was happening, they fell asleep side by side and continued that way until the daylight had begun to fade.

They eventually solved the problem of food when they realised that the freezer was only slowly defrosting and that it contained a small quantity of frozen chicken. Alison also found an assortment of vegetables which they were able to use with the chicken to make a stew.

When they had eaten, they cleared away the dishes and went to sit again in the front room of the cottage. Alison lit just enough candles to enable them to see and Kirk locked the doors. They thought that after the conflict there were very few survivors on The Ridge, but until they could find out who was left, they did not want to attract unwanted attention.

Kirk sat apart from Alison, feeling a huge emptiness. He struggled to believe that Rose was not simply somewhere else in the house. Although he and Alison had buried her, in his thoughts he was waiting for her to come into the room and for them both to hear her voice, to hear the inner optimism of its tone, whatever the content had to say.

Similar thoughts were passing through Alison's head. Jed had not always treated her well, but she still ached to see him walk into the room, if for no other reason than that it would bring her reassurance that, despite events in the outer world, events in her inner world would continue to follow much the same pattern. Now, Jed's rock-like presence would no longer be there. Every moment of their continuing existence would be dogged by uncertainty.

When she spoke, it was almost as though her mind was speaking directly into the silence that lay between her and Kirk.

"How did we get to this moment?" Her thought was articulated in pain but even at this point, was a part of trying to continue rather than coming to an end. Kirk knew that Alison was trying to understand why Rose and Jed had died and that grief needed to take its own time.

The question was left hanging between them. They were entering into a time when the most basic aspects of existence would become a daily struggle and their willpower to continue with their existence would be tested many times over.

***

They slept apart. The cottage was quite large and there were two bedrooms besides those in which Kirk and Alison had slept with their previous partners. They were dependent on each other but for some while, they came and went on parallel but separate courses, speaking when they felt the need of another human voice, but otherwise drifting about, bent on the tasks that needed doing and which required only minimal discussion because their necessity was obvious; these included such things as collecting firewood, topping up stocks of food and fetching water.

They were both aware that the amount of physical labour in their lives had undergone a huge increase. Unsurprisingly, their clothes began to hang loose upon them. At first, they were discouraged because at the end of each day, they had just enough energy to put together a meal and then to drag themselves off to their rooms, but after a while, their stamina began gradually to increase again, and they found that they were better able to continue working into the evening.

The calendar in the kitchen hung neglected on the wall, but Alison attempted to mark the passage of the days by crossing off the dates on the calendar in the room that she had previously kept as her office. Then one morning, as she and Kirk were eating what was usually a rudimentary breakfast, Kirk was surprised to find a few thin slices of meat on his plate. He looked across at Alison who was already tucking into her own small portion of meat.

"What's the occasion?" he asked.

"Don't you know? You've obviously forgotten about such things as calendars."

He continued to look mystified, so she slid across the table towards him a small package.

Enlightenment began to dawn on his face as he recognised that the mysterious item was parcelled in Christmas wrapping paper. He felt himself grinning foolishly. He felt foolish again as he voiced a lame and all too familiar excuse.

"But I didn't remember at all. I haven't got you anything."

"I didn't really expect that you would. I only realised because I've got a calendar in my office."

Kirk nodded. Strangely, although there were now just two of them in the house, there were still places that they implicitly recognised as being the territory of the other person. Kirk had not given the smallest thought to entering Alison's office. In a similar way, Kirk had now occasionally taken to going into the room where he and Rose had previously slept, but Alison decided that, for the time being at least, she would stay out of the room and leave it as a space in which Kirk could be by himself, if he so wished.

"Well," she said. "Aren't you going to open it?"

"Oh yes, of course," he said, fumbling with the paper and then tearing it away to reveal a small, plain cardboard box – and within the box, a knife; he recognised it immediately as a Swiss Army knife. He looked at it admiringly and then began to pull out some of the blades and tools that were ingeniously packed away within it.

She had become good at reading the questions that formed on his face before he ever spoke them, so now she said, "It belonged to my husband. I saw you the other day hacking at some wood with a kitchen knife, so I thought that you might find it easier with that."

"Yes...yes of course, I would," said Kirk. "But it must have huge value for you..."

"It's one of those things that was designed to be used," she said. "Besides, I have plenty of other things that remind me of him."

She was pleased to see Kirk's obvious delight, but there was no fire in the room or, indeed, in the house. Instinctively, she stood up, intending to busy herself with something that would help her to stay warm. Kirk also stood up and moved to her side of the table. There was a small patch of skin at the base of her neck that was not covered by the thick pullover that she was wearing, and it was here that he kissed her.

She turned towards him. This time, he kissed her on the lips.

"Thank you" he said.

She returned his kiss but then went to move away. For a moment, however, he continued to hold her and was surprised to see a look of annoyance cross her face. He let her go.

"We're not ready," she said.

Feeling frustrated and angry he retorted, "We'll never be ready!"

"We will," she said. "Of course we will."

"Then why not now?"

There was a pause in which she faced him angrily. "It's not now because I don't want you trying to force me! That's what Jed always did! I want us to be different."

Kirk already knew what she was telling him and being reminded of it helped him to understand. His feelings of disappointment began to recede.

He reached down his coat from a nearby set of coat pegs.

"I'm sorry – I understand," he said. "But I could do with a bit of time to myself."

She let him put on his coat and then him caught by one of his sleeves, putting her arms around him.

"Don't be cross with me," she said. "I want us to be together, but I still spend most of every day thinking about Jed, not to mention Rose. Surely you're the same?"

It was true. He spent much of his time feeling profoundly empty and missing Rose. It was a piece of foolishness on his part that he had needed Alison to remind him.

She could see that her remark had struck home. He would go and have some time to himself – in the garden or in the woods nearby. She would also have some time on her own.

She let him go but as he made his way to the door, she called after him, "We both need some time, but I don't want to spend the whole day on my own! It is Christmas Day after all!"

By way of reply, she heard the door close behind him.

Outside, it was a chilly day but nothing like as cold as the December days that Kirk remembered from his childhood. He set off down the path that they had taken on the day of the battle. A short way into the woods, there was a clearing in which he had found an old tree stump on which he could sit and pull his thoughts together.

At first his thoughts wandered over the immediate situation in the house, but he had spent time on it already that morning and felt a little weary of it. It took him a while to identify the feeling that was swimming about in his head but then he made himself bring it to the forefront of his mind. Somehow – and he was still not altogether sure how – the civilization around him was slipping away. The army had fought back against an invading force – and had won for the time-being, but what would follow? Would other invaders follow in the path of those who had been so expensively repulsed?

He wondered, not for the first time, about events in the rest of the country. There was no news and, for the time being at least, he felt sure that there would be none. In his own mind, he was certain that the breakdown that he and his companions had witnessed close at hand was also happening everywhere around them. Financial chaos, triggered by energy shortages, had been the first sign of the disorder that was to come. Then terrorist groups had struck at the government and decapitated it just ahead of a carefully planned attack.

For a while, he thought about the attack. It seemed strange that although it had severely tested the defence forces, it had not overcome them, even though they must have been weakened by the loss of central government and by the civil disorder that had broken out all around them.

He speculated that the invading force had not, after all, been intended to make any permanent gains but that, instead, it had been an initial expeditionary force, the task of which was to probe the country's defences to find out if they had sufficient resilience to defeat a further concerted invasion.

What particularly troubled Kirk was the highly organised nature of the attack. Nothing in the news before the breakdown had prepared him for the idea that Britain and Western Europe had resources that people from further south and east were desperate to find, that they might fight to obtain – resources such as water, a relatively cool climate and land that could still be farmed.

There were too many questions within this for him to answer. He found his mind drifting to different but connected issues. The major storm that had ravaged Southampton, for example, was not an isolated event. A previous storm in the North Sea had recently caused extensive flooding on the East Coast and in London. Such storms had happened throughout British history but what was different now was the frequency with which they occurred and the ferocity of them when they did so.

From his seat in the woods, he could not see the flooded lowlands in which many of the previous days' battles had been fought. Before the conflict, he thought that there had still been many people managing to hang on in the area, but now it seemed most likely that few had survived the fighting and the floods. Those who had survived had probably fled to the four points of the compass, travelling on foot, bike or horseback or possibly using the last vestiges of petrol or diesel oil in their cars.

He and Alison would need to discover if they were the only survivors on The Ridge. He had deliberately stayed away from the area around Andrew's farm where he knew that the Army still had a presence. There were people at the other end of The Ridge, whom he and Rose had not had time to meet. Perhaps they had also survived the onslaught.

For the time being, he was alone with Alison. For both of them, the days since the deaths of Rose and Jed had been a misery. He felt the usual pang of guilt about having flirted with Alison before Rose's death. He could not explain to himself why he had done it. He loved Rose and felt loyal to her, but still he had felt attracted to the older woman. He pondered the fact that she was Rose's aunt; it seemed strange that, having been drawn to Rose's relative youth and optimism, he should now feel a desire for Alison. The fact that she was older than him did not seem to matter very much. She was not so very much older than him. Her additional years also lent her a certain air of mystery that he found himself wanting to explore.

He wondered if anyone had ever successfully penetrated the mysteries of attraction. He felt drawn to her perceptiveness, her ability to cut to the heart of anything that they were discussing. In the aftermath of the battle, she had also shown a certain resilience and toughness – qualities that would be needed in the mounting scrapyard of the civilisation that was now collapsing all around them.

Yet, he wondered if it was any of these things – important though they were. If he thought about her, what did he remember; was it not perhaps the smile that only showed in certain moments or the turn of her shoulder or the way in which she would brush away an intrusive lock of hair?

The chill of the wood seemed now to be gradually penetrating his bones. He decided to walk back to the cottage. Inside his head, he was only a little way further forward, but the fresh air had invigorated him, and he had been glad to get away from the sad and introverted atmosphere that had pervaded the cottage whilst he and Alison had found themselves alone together there.

It seemed as though Alison too had felt the need for a change of mental wallpaper. As he approached the cottage, he could see a plume of smoke rising from the chimney and smelled the smell of apple wood. He recalled the logs that he had seen in the back yard. He closed the door and felt at once both the slight chill of the house and the warmth emanating from the freshly lit fire.

He wandered through to the kitchen. Alison appeared just a few moments later. He could immediately tell that this morning she felt in need of a change of heart and a change of mood.

"Did you enjoy your walk?" she asked with a smile.

"Yes, I did indeed," he replied. He looked at her more closely, pleased that her mood seemed to have changed since he had set out for his walk. "What happened to the trousers and top?"

She was wearing a dress that showed a generous portion of shoulder and neckline. The hemline was below the knee but still showed her legs and a strappy pair of shoes that had nothing to do with practicality.

"I'm afraid that I've had enough of trailing about here in the same old clothes and with the same old miserable faces..."

Kirk too was fed up with the sad routines and the dreary days that they had endured since the deaths of Jed and Rose but thought that they would grieve for a long time to come. Perhaps they would be grieving for the rest of their lives...

"It's not surprising that we feel the way we do. Rose and Jed have been taken away from us. We have only ourselves to rely on amongst all the chaos and destruction that must be going on out there and we don't yet know if we have enough food and fuel to see us through the winter."

"Listen, Kirk, we've survived! Remember, we've survived – and we're going to carry on surviving! We also have each other. It could have been even worse than it is. One of us could have been left here to survive alone!"

For a moment her words seemed almost blasphemous, sacrilegious. There had been many times when he had wondered why he had been spared, why he had not died with Rose and Jed. There had been hours, days when he would have welcomed oblivion.

He did not want to be angry with her. He placed one hand gently on her shoulder. There had been very little deliberate physical contact between them since they had spent the aftermath of the battle slumped against each other. She moved closer to him, and he moved his hand so that it lay lightly on her neck. They kissed but then she moved a little away from him and said, "We both need some food. We haven't eaten much for days and I'm seriously hungry." She looked at him. "Do you mind if it's chicken?"

"No," he said. "Chicken for Christmas – it sounds really good to me!"

The chicken was fresh. She had killed and plucked one of the hens the previous day, but cooking it was going to be a problem. It could not easily be done in the oven of the big wood burner in the kitchen, so she had decided to spit roast it over the fire in the front room. They were gradually adapting to cooking over the fire, but as with almost everything they did now, they had to adjust to the time and effort that it took. Alison had already improvised a spit on which the chicken could be cooked. Kirk prepared the vegetables in the kitchen and when the chicken was partly cooked, placed them alongside it, over the fire. With a certain amount of ingenuity and the juices from the meat, Alison managed to make some thick gravy to pour over their food.

Kirk, meanwhile, went in search of wine but some minutes later, he had managed only to find two bottles of sloe gin. After Alison's heroic efforts with the gravy, he felt rather apologetic, but she seemed pleased that he had found anything at all. They allowed themselves a single glass whilst they finished cooking the meal; it had a slightly syrupy texture and, at first, something of a medicinal flavour, but after a few sips they found themselves enjoying it. Soon they both had red cheeks, though whether this was caused by the sloe gin or the heat from the fire was open to question.

Soon the food was ready. They briefly debated whether they should eat in the kitchen or there, in the front room by the fire – and then agreed that since the civilization of which they had until recently been a part, was now collapsing around them, this was a ridiculous discussion. The warmth of the fire was very inviting, and they decided to stay where they were.

If they had felt hungry before, by the time the meal was cooked, they were feeling ravenous, and Alison filled their plates with food. They both knew that they would struggle to find sufficient to eat throughout the rest of the winter and early spring, but they had decided they were going to enjoy the day and that they would have plenty of time to worry about their problems later. They sat a little distance apart, Alison on the settee and Kirk in the armchair, bending forward at slightly uncomfortable angles to reach their plates, which they had placed on their laps.

Perhaps Kirk's thoughts about the food were affected by his hunger, but it seemed to him that Alison's cooking had rekindled in him memories of all the best meals he had ever had. The food was delicious. Fortunately, there was enough chicken and vegetables to satisfy both their appetites. Alison had chosen well from amongst the chickens, and the meat would last them for further meals to come. He glanced sideways at her and could see that she was enjoying her own cooking.

They cleared and then refilled their plates until, finally, they could eat no more. Kirk was feeling sleepy but made a determined effort to clear away the remains of the meal. He wondered briefly why he should worry about tidiness on such an occasion but decided that some lifelong habits were worth keeping no matter what was happening elsewhere. Small, daily things were something to cling to. He placed sufficient wood on the fire to keep it burning for a while. He did not want to be disturbed for some time. Drowsiness overwhelmed him and he fell asleep in his chair.

Eventually, the fire guttered low and the returning chill of the room slowly brought him back. He turned in his chair, trying to find a position in which he could keep warm. Finally he gave up and went in search of another big log to place on the fire. Returning, he placed it on the fire and then looked across at Alison. She had curled herself into a foetal position on the settee. He padded across and slid onto the settee beside her, placing an arm over her and tucking into the warmth of her body. The fire filled the room once more with the warmth of its glow and they slept until, sometime later, Alison said, "I'm going to bed. Are you staying here?"

"No," replied Kirk. "I think I'll go up as well."

He checked that the fire was safe to leave and then followed her out of the room and up the staircase, their paths illuminated by a candle that she had lit. She paused on the landing at the top of the stairs, so that he could see his way. He was about to turn into the room that he now thought of as his own when she said, "No, Kirk, not in there. I want you to sleep with me – but not in there." She drew him along to another landing that lay at a right angle to the one that their bedrooms adjoined. She opened the door of a bedroom on her left and then went in, leaving the door open. Kirk followed her into the flickering candlelit room, drawing the curtains to shut out the blackness of the night.

CHAPTER 17

BUBBLE WORLDS

Somehow – Kirk wondered afterwards exactly how – they struggled back from the pleasures of their small personal world. He reflected that they had not been away long – but this new world around them would be, he knew, an unforgiving one in which they would always struggle to survive. He had slept for a short while after making love to Alison, but then on waking again had felt hungry and decided to go in search of some breakfast. As he climbed out of bed, the air seemed cold in a way that he had rarely experienced it before. It was now many weeks since anywhere in the house other than the kitchen and the lounge had been heated. His breath dissipated before him in a plume of vapour.

He dressed quickly but then went to wash his face and hands in cold water. A shower, let alone a bath, was out of the question. He bustled down the stairs towards the kitchen. The house was still in semi-darkness. As he went about his tasks, he fell into a world of his own, a world in which he mused on the solitariness of their new existence. He wondered vaguely if they could be watched by a satellite – and then decided that he did not care about the answer. Twelve months before, he would have been worrying about speed cameras. Now his main concern was about where the next meal was coming from.

He went to the kitchen cupboard and looked through the boxes of cereal that, according to their labelling, were now all out of date. He took down a box of porridge oats and sniffed at the oats, wondering how they would taste if he made the porridge with a mixture of water and goat's milk. He would need to get the milk from outside; he pulled on a jacket and went out through the backdoor to the deep well at the side of the house.

It was not a round, brick built well with a small, pitched roof over it of the kind so beloved of nursery rhyme illustrators; instead, its entrance was at ground level and was set against the kitchen wall. To reach it, he had to stand on the flagstones that covered the top of the well and which formed a kind of grey plinth behind the kitchen. The entrance was covered by a single, heavy flagstone. With some effort, he pushed back the stone, revealing a dark, cavernous space. A small stone that he accidentally dislodged with his foot seemed to take an appreciable time to produce the expected plop in the dark waters below. A rope, tethered to a bracket on the house wall reached down into the darkness. He hauled on the rope and by slow degrees, brought up the basket in which he and Alison now kept many of the items that they would previously have kept in the refrigerator. The plastic bottle looked much the same as if it had just come from a supermarket – and the milk would be fresh and cold.

He looked up momentarily from his small world, gazing out towards the trees. Dawn was gradually breaking in a clear, wintery sky. Perhaps it was a matter of fancy, but it seemed to him that the air they breathed was gradually becoming fresher. Beyond the trees, he knew that there would be no early morning traffic jams. No-one would be commuting to work. The speed cameras would be quietly corroding away, part of a now useless road network reaching out its slowly deteriorating web of tarmac, concrete and steel across the country's soil.

He lowered the basket back into the depths of the well, tethered the rope and laboriously pushed the flagstone back into place. The rays of the morning sun were beginning to illuminate the clear blue of the sky. It was a sky beneath which he felt very small and insignificant, but also one under which it seemed good to be alive.

A little reluctantly, he went back into the gloom of the house, wondering if the embers in the kitchen stove could be breathed back into life so that breakfast could be made.

***

Above him, still in the bedroom, Alison stirred in her sleep, the smell of food tempting her from the warmth of the bed and the lingering glow of their early morning lovemaking.

Smelling the food and seizing a moment of impulse, she scrambled from the bed, quickly pulling on her clothes in an effort to keep out the numbing cold of the room. She made her way down the stairs to the kitchen, where Kirk had slowly won his battle with the stove and where there was now a saucepan of porridge bubbling away on the hob.

He seemed preoccupied with the food, but as she approached, he caught her round the waist and began to reach his hands beneath the warmth of her pullover. She pulled vigorously away from him, retorting as she did so, "You can warm your hands before you do that!"

She moved away from the stove but was still in search of warmth and, in her dishevelled state, was also feeling in need of a wash. A hot shower would have been wonderful, but without a supply of gas the boiler in the utility room was now useless. Reluctantly, she climbed the stairs once more to the bathroom where she carefully removed the clothing she had put on a few minutes before, one article at a time and progressively washed and dried herself, gradually putting on each item again until she was able once more to warm herself in her underwear, pullover, trousers, socks and shoes.

Returning to the kitchen, she found Kirk at the kitchen table, spooning mouthfuls of hot porridge into his mouth. She ladled some porridge into a bowl and then went to sit at his side.

For a few minutes they ate in silence until she said, "So what are we doing today?" It was a deceptively simple question but behind it they both knew that there lay a gradually unfolding way of life that would be very different from the one on which they had based all their previous assumptions.

Breakfast was perhaps the simplest meal of the day but, as he donned his coat and made for the door, Kirk found himself reflecting that they would need to change their eating and drinking habits. It would not be long now before they ran out of breakfast cereal completely. The tea and coffee they had taken for granted almost throughout their lives would also run out very soon unless they could find somewhere nearby from which they could replenish their supplies.

He kicked at the leaves that had piled up around the gate. He was already embarked on the first answer to Alison's question. They needed wood to fuel the fires in the lounge and kitchen. Fortunately, it was one of the few resources that was not in short supply, and he had become used to scavenging around the margins of the trees. The strong winds of recent weeks had blown down a good many branches and had proved to be a blessing in terms of the quantity of wood that he was able to pick up from ground close to the house. Soon, he would be in the backyard peeling off his coat as he sawed and chopped the branches into logs before stacking them in the log store that Jed had built at the side of the house.

For a short while, Alison had remained in the house, thumbing through her cookery books. Most of them were now useless to her since the recipes relied largely on ingredients that came from distant places which were now inaccessible to them. She had just two books in which she could find useful ideas; both had been passed on to her by her grandmother and had been published shortly after the Second World War. For a few moments longer, she carefully turned the pages, brown with age, before replacing the elastic bands that she used to prevent the books from falling apart. One of the books had given her an idea. She put on an anorak and went to see what she could find in the vegetable store.

She had stored a good supply of fruit and vegetables in a well-ventilated outhouse at the side of the house. Learning how to store fruit and vegetables had grown out of her gardening activities and now as she entered the outhouse, she was met by a cool autumnal smell of apples, pears, potatoes and a variety of root crops. It had seemed like a fascinating hobby when she had first begun to experiment with it all; now she knew that they would be depending on her skills to see them through the winter.

***

Kirk felt rather foolish and wondered if Alison would later reproach him for wasting his time. He had found and cut a straight piece of wood from an ash tree. When he stood it on the ground, its length roughly matched his height. He took it back to the house and after some hunting around, had found some string. He cut a notch in one end of the ash pole and tied the string into place as firmly as he could. He cut another notch in the other end of the pole and after some considerable effort, managed to bend the ash sufficiently to make a bow and then tie the string's other end into the notch and around the remaining end of the wood. The curve of the bow was not quite uniform, but he decided that it would be good enough for his first experiments.

He then went in search of some straight lengths of holly with which to make the arrows. Eventually, he managed to find six thin straight branches from which he stripped the leaves. Into one end of each arrow, he carved a small V-shaped notch which would fit onto the bow string. The other end of the arrow he carved into a sharp point. He was not satisfied that the points would be hard enough, so he returned to the house and carefully hardened them in the fire that they kept burning in the front room of the house. Fletching would increase the accuracy of the arrows, but for the moment, he did not know of a way to do it.

He briefly looked around for Alison but there was no sign of her. He wondered where she was but decided that if he was going achieve anything before nightfall he would have to stick to his task.

He spent a short while getting used to the bow and loosed off a number of practice shots at a cardboard target that he set up against a tree. With such a bow and with so little practice, he could hardly hope to be very accurate – but he might be lucky. He had to start somewhere.

He set out along the edge of the wood, heading for a spot where a few days before, he had seen a cock pheasant paying court to some hens. He thought that he might be lucky and find them in the same spot again.

As he walked, he hunted along the ground before him, in search of a piece of wood that would serve as a club. It needed to have a certain amount of weight but also to fit neatly into his hand so that he would be able swing it with the force needed to stun and then to kill his prey. It took him some time, but finally, amongst the leaf litter he came across a piece of oak about the length of his forearm and the thickness of his fist at one end, but which then tapered to a width that enabled him to grasp it firmly and comfortably in the palm of his hand. He swung it experimentally to left and right. It felt perfect and he felt a sense of satisfaction in having found it.

He looked up past the tops of the trees to the sky. At the start of the day, it had been a clear blue; now there was a thin high layer of cloud, and it had a certain milky whiteness to it. He judged from the light, however, that it was probably early afternoon.

The spot in which he had seen the pheasants was bounded by large, overgrown holly bushes. With some excitement, he saw that just as on the previous occasion, there was a cock pheasant straight ahead of him and strutting to and fro in front of the bushes. To the right-hand side there were three hens and then away to the left there was another cock pheasant. Kirk knew that his accuracy was negligible and that his best chance would be to get in close and then to wound one of the birds. He might then be able to finish it off with the club.

The cock pheasant was altogether larger than the hen birds. His red wattles and iridescent feathers stood out strongly against the foliage of the bushes behind him. The mottled brown of the females made them much harder to see and they appeared to be grouped together so that it was difficult for Kirk to distinguish one from another.

The cock pheasant seemed to present an obvious target. Kirk stealthily placed an arrow on the string of his bow and with painstaking slowness began to draw back the string. The cock seemed at first not to notice him but then caught sight of him and watched him with a sidelong inclination of its head. The hen pheasants crouched in the grass and, from where Kirk was squatting, were almost invisible. He was still some yards away and it must have seemed to the cock bird that he was not an immediate threat. After a moment or two, Kirk thought that he had a clear view of the cock bird's chest and drew back the string until the tail of the arrow was level with his ear. For a moment, he strained to keep the bow steady whilst at full stretch, then he let fly the arrow.

Both the cock bird and the hen pheasants immediately rose in the air with a tremendous clatter of wings, cackling loudly as they went. The explosive reaction of the pheasants caught him unawares and he sprang to his feet, his heart pounding in sudden alarm.

The pheasants disappeared over the hedge, and he rose from his position feeling both awkward and a little stupid. Then to his right, he noticed a movement in the grass. He walked rapidly across to the spot and saw that although he had been a long way off his target, his arrow had gone instead through the wing and ribs of one of the hen pheasants. She lay barely conscious but was trying lopsidedly to flap and scrabble away from him towards the hedge. Quickly he fetched his club and after two sharp blows to the back of the head, she lay dead on the grass, and he was able to pick her up.

He cradled the bird in his hands. A small bubble of blood had formed on one side of her beak, and she felt warm to his touch. He felt humble, a little shocked and slightly guilty. He had never killed a wild creature before, but now he had somehow managed to wound and kill a bird that had seemed almost certain to escape.

The bird's head and neck hung limply down from his fingers. Although from a distance she had seemed to be a drab brown in colour, now that he was so close to her, he could not but marvel at the natural perfection of the markings in her feathers. For all that human beings were so skilled at making wonderful objects, he could think of nothing from the human world that would match the complex patterns and shading of colours within the pheasant's plumage.

A more experienced hunter would, no doubt, have taken the bird by the neck or feet and carried it casually back home; Kirk, however, clutched the bird to him as though he was afraid that someone or something was about to take it away from him. His bow, arrows and club lay on the grass. With his free hand, he picked them up and began making his way back towards the house.

The trees now lay on his right and although his pheasant hunting had lasted quite a short time, the light was beginning to fade in the sky. Winter afternoons are short, and he knew that he had other tasks to do before darkness once more descended on the landscape. He scurried along, glancing only now and again to left or right.

Then, to his left, he thought he caught a glimpse of movement; he thought he had glimpsed the movement of a head, a momentary bobbing of fair hair somewhere over towards the wrecked farmhouse, the grim remains of which could be seen against the gathering gloom of the sky. He looked hard again, wondering if his eyes were playing tricks on him. He knew from previous experience that it was easy for the mind to misinterpret the interplay of light and shape. For a few moments longer, he stared hard towards the spot in which he thought he had seen movement; but all seemed still and silent and the fading of the light drew him once more back to his journey home.

The cottage flickered with light, providing him with a welcoming beacon on the final part of his trudge along the path. Alison, bent on some task of her own, appeared in the front doorway and was surprised to see him approaching with the dead pheasant and small armoury of bow, arrows and club.

"Well, what have you got there?" she asked. She could see that he was holding some sort of dead creature in his hands, but she had just come out of the light of the cottage and her eyesight had not adjusted to the gloom.

"Just a little something I brought you for tea," he said, wondering how she would react.

As her eyesight enabled her to see the pheasant, her eyes grew round, and her face lit up with surprise.

"Wow!" she exclaimed. "You have been busy! But I'm afraid that we won't be able to eat it for tonight's tea."

Kirk was puzzled. "Why not?" he asked.

"Because pheasants need to hang. Sometimes they need just four or five days but in this weather, it could be two weeks."

"So I went to all that trouble and still we can't eat." He sounded petulant, almost childish.

"We can eat but pheasant can be quite tough, and it does need to hang for a while. Since you shot a hen bird – and it looks as though it's a fairly young one – she should be quite tender and juicy."

"Ah well," he said resignedly. "All we have to do is to survive for two weeks."

Alison laughed. "It isn't quite as bad as that," she said. "I had some pieces of rabbit meat and I've put them together with some vegetables to make a stew."

"Rabbit!" exclaimed Kirk.

"Well, there are plenty of them around. There are always so many here that the farmers regard them as pests."

"How do you catch them? Catching a pheasant was hard enough!"

"You'll be pleased to know that it's a lot easier than your effort with a bow."

He thought for a moment that she might be mocking him. A slight smile seemed to be hovering around the corners of her mouth.

"So what d'you do? Hide behind a bush with a big net?"

"That might be possible," she laughed. "But Jed showed me how to make and use a snare. We've got dozens of them out in the shed."

"Ah," he said. "I still have a problem."

"Just one! You do surprise me."

He ignored the mild sarcasm in her voice and continued, "I don't know anything about snares. I wouldn't know one if you held it up and waved it in front of me."

"Don't worry. I'll show you tomorrow. For tonight, we have plenty of food."

She disappeared into the kitchen to hang the pheasant and to check the stew. When she returned, Kirk had begun lighting some of the candles.

He gestured towards them as she approached. "We'll need some more of these soon," he said. She said nothing but reflected that catching rabbits might be easier than finding more candles.

As she came closer, he caught her by the waist and drew her to him. "Do we have long to wait?" he asked.

"Depends what you have in mind. The stew will be a little while. We could do some other things."

He smiled and looked towards the stairs.

She followed his gaze but said, "No, Kirk. It'll be pretty cold up there. I'd rather go in the front room."

She drew him by the hand towards the front room door.

"It'll be pretty cold in here too," he objected.

"No it won't," she said.

"How do you know?" he asked.

"Full of questions, aren't you," she said. "Anyway, I put another log on the fire, just before you got back."

She sat down on the settee and laid gently back, lifting her legs and raising her feet onto the settee cushion.

Kirk sat down beside her. He did not think that she would object to his next move.

They were, for the time being, existing in their own wintry world of alternating discomfort and secret pleasure. For the time being they were loath to go looking for the harsher realities that lay beyond them.

Bolton's world, by contrast, was one of almost continuous discomfort and harsh reality. Not far away in a geographical sense but, increasingly, a world away from Kirk and Alison in terms of accessibility, Bolton lay in his sleeping bag musing about how long it would be before he saw his wife again. He ached to be with her.

It was a grim time. The mysterious expeditionary force of invaders had been repulsed for the time being. Bolton had no idea if they would have the resources to return, but it was clear that the terrorists who had been responsible for firing the 'dirty bomb' into central London had struck a bigger blow than they had probably thought possible. Civil government had all but ceased; but it was the fate of military government that was preoccupying him most at that moment. The flow of intelligence and commands had been fairly steady until very recently. Now communications seemed to be faltering.

He and Thorndike had some very practical problems to contend with. It was some time since the soldiers had been paid – and besides, there was nothing for them to spend their money on. Most of them knew very little about the fate of their families. Unsurprisingly, it was becoming hard to motivate them. There was no longer any central direction to their activity, and it was becoming difficult to believe that only a short time before, they had fought an engagement with well-armed and well-trained soldiers and had overcome them.

He climbed out of his sleeping bag. He needed to talk to Thorndike, but it would have to wait until he had washed and dressed. The cold of the air in the tent sent him reaching in the semi-darkness for additional clothing. Although he had awoken early and therefore had been able to spend time thinking generally about his lot, he now had to give thought to the most daily and pressing problems; how to ensure, together with Thorndike, that those around him would continue to be fed and clothed, how he would continue to identify for them their 'mission' and how he would maintain all those aspects that enabled them to be coherent and effective as a unit of military organisation.

Although it was an English February, still thinly clad he made his way past the tents in which other soldiers were still sleeping. A camp guard briefly flashed light from a wind-up torch in his face and then saluted and apologised in a single set of loud and slightly clumsy gestures. He discounted the black spots in the middle of his vision with the comforting thought that there were, after all, some signs that organisation and discipline within the camp were still holding up well. The question which nagged at him daily now, however, was that of how long this situation could be sustained and under what circumstances this body of people around him would continue – or should continue – to operate in its present form.

Soldiers, he reflected, lived with discomfort. He knelt on the grass bank of the nearby stream to wash himself in the icy water.

Coffee was becoming scarce. Somehow they had found some. Thorndike cradled a cup of the valuable liquid in his hands, warming them without otherwise admitting to the cold of the air around them.

"The problem is acute," he was saying. "We've heard nothing from WMC in days."

They were in Bolton's tent. Outside, it was now a cold but sunny morning.

"Yes," replied Bolton. "It's mystifying. Our problem is, though, what do we do next? Our task, the task of the people out in the Channel, is to maintain the security of this area even though it's already been wrecked by the events of the last few weeks."

"That is a rather dramatic way of putting it," responded Thorndike.

"Then how the bloody hell would you put it?" asked Bolton, puzzled.

"I'm only paid to think up to a certain point – and not beyond. When WMC get back to us, I'm sure that most of this will already have been resolved."

"Do you have a time limit in mind for WMC to get through to us – or do we just wait around here for ever and a day just to prove our loyalty? I think that they're gone, caput, wiped off the map."

Thorndike was surprised by both Bolton's words and his vehemence. "We don't know that, and we can't assume it. As far as I'm concerned, we have to wait until there is some real evidence that WMC is out of action before we start making irreversible moves with this unit."

Bolton knew that Thorndike was mistaking his intentions. "I realise that some of this represents the 'unthinkable' as far as we are concerned, but we are already in a situation about which nobody seems to have thought before it occurred."

"Unlikely."

"What do you mean?"

"It's unlikely that nobody foresaw something like the present situation."

"Well, if they did," rejoined Bolton, "they didn't tell us about it. Meanwhile, we've had no orders, instructions or communication of any kind for four days. Have Davis and his team kept up the effort to contact WMC?"

"Of course they have," sighed Thorndike.

Bolton hesitated for a moment. He knew that the conversation had taken an entirely wrong course, but he excused himself with the thought that he needed to know how Thorndike was thinking. That at least was not so unpredictable; as usual, it was stolidly on the middle ground. He realised that there was a problem, but he was not going to see it as anything outside their normal mode of operation.

Bolton reflected for a moment that he was wasting energy. He did not need to convince Thorndike about the situation. Events in the next few days would almost certainly do that for him. He just needed to ensure that he and Thorndike put together a coherent plan – but also a plan that would ensure the continued loyalty of their soldiers, not all of whom had the same unwavering and somewhat unimaginative temperament that Thorndike was displaying. He decided to try a different tack.

"So what do you think should be our course of action?"

"I think that we wait some more – at least for the next few days. It may well be that some serious problem has occurred at WMC, but if they have survived, I think that we can expect to hear from them in the next four to five days."

"Meanwhile?"

"Meanwhile we keep up our state of readiness. We continue with the training and daily work routines, and we keep everybody ready to move at short notice. We also have a more immediate problem. Food supplies here are dwindling very rapidly. We can requisition what we need from the area under our control, but it will need to be achieved in the next two days."

Bolton nodded. Other than replenishing the food supplies, it was largely a recipe for marking time, but perhaps that was appropriate. He had no idea what was happening at the West Midlands Centre but whatever it was, it could well be something on a significant scale that would require them to simply wait out the gestation period. All the same, the lack of communication was inexplicable and very unusual.

"Good," said Bolton, "I agree – but we also need to be thinking about the situation that will prevail if we still haven't heard from WMC in that time."

Thorndike's face remained impassive, but inwardly he felt a sense of relief. There were problems of which Bolton was aware, but which thrust themselves upon Thorndike much more frequently: there were seriously wounded soldiers within the camp, and, like food, medical supplies were a dwindling resource; they had also taken a number of prisoners during the battle at The Ridge and interrogation was proving to be a long, slow process. Only now were the first pieces of information beginning to produce a coherent picture. Moving on now would not be helpful to the intelligence effort.

Thorndike paused for a moment; Bolton had been to The Ridge gathering intelligence before the battle. After the battle, the clearing up operation had been limited because their resources were stretched. They needed more information and now that satellite intelligence and electronic surveillance had largely ceased to exist, it was back to traditional methods.

Thorndike continued. "We need information from the Ridge again. If we have to move quickly, we don't want to find that we've left hostiles behind us."

Bolton nodded. "You may have to move before I get back, but you can send someone to fetch me."

They agreed. The intelligence was vital. Sending Bolton was risky, but his insights had been critical both before and during the recent battle and his forays into the area had provided him with knowledge that no-one else had. He would be gone for three weeks.

Later that day, he set out on horseback. He would meet other travellers on horseback along the way, but potential danger and mutual suspicion would limit the contact between them. He had his favourite horse – a big chestnut stallion with a strong, steady temperament. Bolton patted the horse's neck affectionately.

"Hey, King!" he said quietly. "It's you and me. We're a team again."

They had debated sending a companion with him, but Bolton wanted to draw as little attention to himself as possible – and, despite being seated on King, he would look like a great many other travellers who had been displaced in local disruption and who, for reasons best known to themselves, now traversed the wide area between the two coasts of the peninsula. Most to be ready for were those individuals whose enterprise, as ever, had led them to murder and steal their way into situations in which they had access to vehicles and weapons that only the army could match. Neither Bolton nor Thorndike wanted to readily give away information about the unit's position and strength to those it might have to combat in the near future.

Bolton rode until after dusk. He was forced to keep to the roads for some of the journey. The flooding of the landscape was worse than he had known it before. For a while, he had ridden along the hard shoulder of the now abandoned and deserted M5. To either side of him he could see wide expanses of flooded fields. The landscape was taking on a wild aspect that Bolton had never seen before in the many years that he had previously travelled along the motorway. Wildfowl had been quick to take advantage of the increase in the watery expanse to which they had access.

It was something of a relief to find the bridle track that he had been looking for and to head away from the reminders of civilisation's demise. In the dusk, there was a cottage light burning across the intermittently dry and flooded fields. It seemed a little rash to have such a light attracting attention, but he turned the horse towards it, checking as he did so that he had his gun within easy reach.

The lamp by the cottage door was powered by batteries which in turn, Bolton supposed, were replenished by some form of renewable energy – probably solar. The light went out as he approached the cottage. It had not been there for his benefit.

He knocked loudly on the cottage door. At first there was no answer. From the corner of his eye, he saw a curtain twitch. Light within the cottage flickered, lit no doubt by the fire, the smoke of which he had seen rising against the red and yellow sky of nightfall. A window above his head opened and a woman's voice – clear and determined – called down to him.

"My gun is aimed at the top of your head. Put down any weapons you have."

Bolton, meanwhile, found himself covered by another gun from a window to one side of the front door. Behind the gun, he thought he could make out the head and shoulders of a young male – probably a teenager. Despite the possible danger of his situation, he could not help noticing that the boy's hair was long and unkempt. It was obviously a while since anyone had given him a haircut.

It seemed a long time before the door opened by the smallest crack and he could hear the same female voice as before saying rather angrily, "Cover me from the window. If he does anything suspicious, just shoot."

Bolton had already worked out his options. The boy would have his work cut out to hit him, but in a play to ease the tension, he put down a handgun and a knife on the cottage's 'Welcome' mat and stood back.

He heard the boy call back to his mother, "Be careful, Mum, he's well-armed!"

"Okay, okay!" Tension was still making the woman angry, but the boy was right, Bolton reflected. The woman's irritated reply was incautious.

The door opened a little more widely. A woman in boots, trousers and a roll neck pullover was pointing a shotgun at his head. Bolton remained confident that he could kill both the woman and the boy, if he had to, before they had moved more than a few inches from where they stood – but there seemed to be no need to do so.

As Bolton had supposed, the woman was not as cautious as she should have been.

"What do you want?" she asked.

Bolton did not reply. She came closer but only as close as he would allow her. He stepped slowly back.

"Stand still!" she yelled at him angrily.

He did so but stood at a slight angle to her. He did not allow her to see the machine pistol in the left sleeve of his coat until it was too late. He could see her tightening her finger on the trigger of the gun. She did not see the pistol until he allowed light from the doorway to glint on its muzzle. He was perilously close to squeezing off the rounds that would tear her apart. He knew that they were approaching the moment of decision. He decided to answer her earlier question.

"I need food for my horse and shelter for the night."

The delayed and slightly casual response to her earlier question seemed to take her by surprise. It was not what he wanted her to feel. Bolton assumed that, for the moment at least, she was on her own with the boy. She appeared to think for a moment.

"If we give you those things, how do we know we can trust you?"

He was surprised by the reply. He had assumed that she would send him away into the darkness at the point of her gun – but now that she had seen him, the woman knew that she either had to be able trust him or she had to kill him there and then. She did not want an armed stranger wandering around outside the cottage in the darkness. If he could be trusted, she would rather have him where she could see him.

She called over her shoulder into the house. "Chris, put the light on in the barn."

There was a pause while the gun at the window was withdrawn, and a light appeared in a small barn over to the right of the cottage.

"Now walk ahead of me," she said.

This time Bolton said, "That will give you the advantage. I suggest that we walk together but ten yards apart until we reach the barn. Then we can talk."

She thought about it before saying, "Alright, but don't forget. No stupid moves. I've had plenty of practice with this thing."

He doubted it. Her grip on the gun was wrong. She could fire it but not without risk to herself. As they approached the light of the barn, he also thought that he detected movements of the shotgun that suggested nervousness. He did not want to put it to the test and regretted having come to the cottage. The last thing he needed was a jumpy householder behind the barrels of a shotgun. It reminded him sharply of how the world around him had changed.

Now that they stood in the light of the barn, he could see that she was clearly nervous. She looked at him carefully, undecided about what she was seeing.

"Who are you?" she asked. He resorted to his familiar strategy; he would tell her some of the truth but not all of it.

"I'm an army officer," he said. "I was north of here about two months ago but have to go back."

She looked at him carefully. "Supposing that is true, do you have any ID with you?"

He nodded. Keeping her carefully within his sight at every moment, he fished for the false identity card that he kept in his jacket.

"Hmm, 'Robert Lawson' it says here if anyone can believe that."

He noticed, however, that she had stopped trembling. She did not believe his identity card, but her own experience was picking up that he was what he said he was – an army officer. His body language was saying that he was alert but not likely to use the pistol that had appeared in his left hand.

"I suggest we both sit down," he said. She sat down on an old garden seat recently removed from the garden, keeping her eyes firmly fixed on him. He sat on a piece of farm machinery opposite her.

As they both began to sense that they were not in the company of a psychopath, the tension between them began gradually to subside, although Bolton's training told him that this was a time in which he needed to be particularly alert.

"So that's me," he said casually. "Who are you?"

"Charlotte," she replied, "Charlotte Walters. I'm a farmer's wife – or at least I was until six months ago when my husband drowned – trying to rescue his sheep."

"I'm sorry to hear that," he replied.

Although his role in life necessitated deceit, Bolton was not essentially dishonest, and she sensed this.

"It's alright," she said. "I'll probably never get over it. But I'm beginning to get used to the idea. If you're going to kill me you'd better get on with it. You might be doing me a favour." He noticed that she muttered her last remark half to herself. He made no comment but continued listening to her.

His silence became a long, awkward pause before she said, "Don't give much away, do you?"

He smiled at her faintly. "I could do with getting my horse," he said. "I left him tethered by the gate."

"Seems like you'd better bring him in then. Have you eaten? I can offer you something, but food is getting scarce around here."

"I think I can help," he said. "I have some food with me, but I need to fetch my horse. It's in one of the saddle bags."

Decision point had been reached. They both knew it. They had both had plenty of opportunities already to kill the other but had not done so and it would be to their advantage if they could trust each other.

They shook hands rather formally then after a moment's hesitation decided that it was safe to hug one another, their English reserve at last giving way to hospitality.

She stood back from him, seemingly a little surprised. "Well, Robert – or is it 'Bob' – if we've decided that we can trust each other, once you've sorted out the horse, you'd better come into the house. Chris doesn't get much male company these days."

"'Bob' will do fine," he said. He too began to relax. He fetched King and found the food that would be his contribution to the meal that evening. Feeding and watering the horse took a while, but eventually he presented himself at the cottage door. At first the boy seemed both curious and tentative, watching him from across the room and not saying very much. Bolton noticed a static model of an RAF transport plane on top of a bookcase. He guessed that the boy had built it from a kit.

"Is this yours?" he asked. Chris nodded, a lock of his long dark hair falling across his face. "I've flown in these," added Bolton. "Quite a few times."

Chris tried still to be cautious but was interested. Bolton regretted always having to be on guard, but he told him a little about his experiences and could see that the boy was taking it in. He was an alert and intelligent individual – and was having to grow up more quickly than might have been anticipated.

Charlotte came in. Bolton had anticipated giving some help in the kitchen but instead she asked, "Do you want to wash? The sink is through here. The food will be ready in just a few minutes."

He found the sink lit by candlelight and, finding also a bar of soap and a flannel, took off his shirt and began to wash his face, arms and torso. The water was cold but nothing like as cold as water from the stream had been that morning. Charlotte, feeling a little guilty, stood back watching the light play on her visitor's muscled body. A scar on his right shoulder seemed to confirm that he was who he said he was. It looked like an old bullet wound. She felt a little foolish about her earlier attempt to intimidate him with the shotgun and began to understand something of the risk that she had taken.

"Sorry," she said, "I forgot this." He turned towards her, and she handed him a towel. He was a big man, she noticed – a big man with firm muscles. He filled the tiny room in which the sink was situated. There was a scar on his upper chest corresponding to the scar on his back. She turned away, trying not to linger. Bolton dried himself and put on his shirt, appreciating the chance to feel clean again.

A short while later, the three of them sat down to eat. It was a simple meal. Tinned meat from Bolton's saddle bag had somehow been spun out with a quantity of vegetables, but they ate with gusto and were reluctant to finish. Then they sat for a while at the table, talking. Chris and Charlotte told Bolton about the farm and about problems they were having with the encroaching waters around them. He told them what he could about his mission to find out about the aftermath of the battle. He could see that their curiosity had been stimulated. It would have been impossible for them not to have seen or heard the battle.

Bolton was pleased that Chris took a good part in the conversation. He appeared to have an inner confidence that Bolton found attractive – and yet, he had enough self-possession to contribute to the conversation without wanting to be the centre of attention. He seemed remarkably mature for his age.

They were all, in their own ways, watching each other. Charlotte watched with quiet pleasure to see Chris respond to Bolton and to see that her son did not make a fool of himself as he was being paid attention by this experienced and attractive man. She guessed that he was not who he said he was – and noticed too, that he had a wedding ring. Bolton watched her when he could. She had a smile that belied the aggression that he had seen earlier. It seemed to be behind them now. She was a young woman and a widow – something she had never expected to be.

Chris also had to make a judgement but felt sure within himself that the stranger could be trusted and that his mother was safe. After they had cleared the table, he said, "Mum, do you mind if I go on up? I've got a really early start tomorrow."

She smiled. "No, you go on up. See you in the morning."

"Goodnight then," said Chris.

After the difficult introduction, Bolton had assumed that he would be spending the night in the barn with the horse. He helped Charlotte clear away the remains of the meal and then moved towards the door.

Charlotte looked surprised. "Where are you going?" she asked. "I thought that you'd already seen to the horse..."

"I have," he said "but..."

She started to laugh. "You surely didn't think that I was going to ask you to sleep in the barn?"

"I didn't think anything of it," he said. "I've made a career out of sleeping in such places."

"Well tonight at least you can sleep inside, in a warm, comfortable bed."

Bolton smiled." Sounds good to me," he said.

"Come on. I'll show you your room."

He followed her up the stairs to a fairly large bedroom above the lounge. "I hope you'll be comfortable," she said.

The bed looked very large. She tried to read the slightly bemused expression on his face.

"It used to be our guest room, but it hasn't been used for a while. That's hardly a surprise I suppose with everything that's been going on."

He smiled at her. "It's very good of you," he said. "What time will Chris need to be up in the morning?"

She paused for a moment before replying.

"He has to be out at about five o'clock. He looks after the animals. He won't disturb us. His bedroom is on the other landing, and he goes out very quietly. I usually get going at about seven."

Bolton sat down on the bed and tested the springs. "This is going to seem like heaven," he said.

"Mmm, I hope so," she replied. Then she turned and went down the landing to her own room. She called back over her shoulder, "I hope you sleep well."

Bolton called back to her that he would but reflected that it had only been about three hours before that she had held him at the point of a gun.

He pulled off his shirt, trousers and socks and pulled back the covers. From somewhere she had found him a pair of pyjamas. He put on the bottoms but could not be bothered with the jacket. Having spent much of the day riding, he could hardly wait to be between the sheets; in gratitude, he slid between them and was almost instantly asleep.

His sleep, however, was restless. His muscles ached from the ride, and he struggled to find a comfortable position in the bed. Eventually he drifted into a deeper sleep in which he dreamed that he was riding endlessly through watery wilderness. In his view ahead, a single hill stood out above the cold wastes of the fens that stretched into the distance on both sides of the causeway along which he was riding.

As he continued on his journey he drew level with someone standing on one side of the causeway next to the water's edge – someone in a long cloak, someone fairly small; this together with the style of the cloak led him to guess that the person waiting for him was a woman – a woman in a cloak with its hood drawn about her head and clasped at the throat with an intricate silver brooch. She beckoned to him to come down. She wanted him to come down from his horse. He hesitated for a moment, not sure about giving up the advantage afforded by the horse, but then slid from the saddle. He caught a tantalising glimpse of her face hidden within the dark folds of a cloak. She was smiling, mysteriously. Was there something sinister in that smile?

He was woken by someone shaking him – gently but insistently. He had learned long ago the habit of being instantly awake and alert. He sat up with a start, ready for whatever was happening.

"Hey! Take it easy."

Charlotte's voice helped to pull him into the reality of the room but now the hand on his shoulder was gently restraining him.

Blearily he looked at her. She had on an old dressing gown which she held together around her with her free hand.

"You seemed to be incredibly restless in here," she said. "I came to see if you were alright."

He reached out a big hand and put it on her shoulder. Her bones felt small – almost delicate – beneath his exploratory touch. She tilted her head to one side so that her hair fell across his fingers but then straightened up again.

"Well," she said, "since you are alright, I'm going to see if there's any food in the house for breakfast."

Fleetingly, he wanted to pull her into the bed with him but then he let her go. It would be a breach of the trust they had established and besides, he could not stay there or own any obligations to anyone. How long had he known her? It was still barely more than a few hours. In moments, he was scrambling from the bed and pulling on his clothes.

He poked at the large living room fire until he had exposed enough hot embers to toast some of the bread that Charlotte had piled onto a plate. "Should we wait for Chris?" asked Bolton, wondering what had happened to the lad.

"No, he's still feeding the animals – but he'll be in shortly when he's finished."

It was still early so Bolton did not need to rush. He munched his way through the toast. The light was not yet good enough for him to clearly see his way.

Charlotte busied herself with jobs in the kitchen and Bolton began to look for his riding gear. As the light outside began to improve, he briefly bustled about, getting ready to leave.

Perhaps it was simply a reaction to being in a domestic situation – a situation from which he had long been absent, and which was no longer one in which he reacted appropriately. When she came close to pull back the heavy curtain over the front door, he forgot who she was and pulled her to him. Her dressing gown fell open and he slid his arms around her, feeling the contours and warmth of her body. He had kissed her before he had really thought about it.

Then, he stepped away from her, slightly taken aback by his own presumption. She smiled at him – and to herself. Only slowly did she draw the dressing gown around her again and pull back the curtain from the door.

He felt foolish and, for once, in a situation of which he had little experience. "I forgot. I... It was a time from the past."

She was slightly amused at this big, tough man bumbling away before her but decided to spare him. She placed a hand on his upper arm.

"Chris will be back in minute," she said. "But it's alright. Don't apologise. Besides, I wouldn't have minded being 'Mrs Lawson' even if it was only for a short while."

He was about to remind her that she did not know him well enough to make such a remark, but then remembered that it was he who had made the first move. He looked briefly into her eyes and, seeing an unsatisfied hunger there, he made no spoken reply but moved towards the door.

Then he was out into the yard, wondering at himself. Chris was in the barn and Bolton's horse seemed to be waiting for him, listlessly moving about as if to hint that he wanted to make a start.

Chris helped to saddle up. He had little experience of horses but proved to be a willing helper. Bolton showed him what to do, pleased for his part to be back on familiar territory. Chris felt a little tense at first in the company of this older and experienced man, but soon settled into their mutual task.

Now that he was saddled up, King stood snorting into the cold air.

"Think he's trying to tell us something?" asked Bolton with a grin.

Chris was a little in awe of the big chestnut stallion. "What's his name?" he asked.

"King," replied Bolton.

"Seems like the right name for him," said Chris, nodding in approval.

Bolton smiled, seeing no reason why he should not have a bit of a joke with the lad. He leaned in a conspiratorial way towards him. "There is another part to his name – which not everyone gets to know."

Chris was unsure about what was coming next but decided to play along with it.

"Oh, what's that?" he asked, rather tentatively.

"Arthur," said Bolton. "The other part of his name is 'Arthur'."

Chris was not quite sure how to respond but said, "He's in the right place then. 'King Arthur' returns – in our time of need."

Bolton laughed, wondering how much Chris knew about the area in which he lived.

"Some would quibble about the place – though I'm not one of them," he said with a faint smile. "But the time of need is certainly here. You be sure and look after your mum. She's a good lady."

Chris nodded. He did not need a visitor to tell him that, but he watched as Bolton swung into the saddle and King shifted slightly to take his weight.

Reaching down to Chris, Bolton shook the boy's hand.

"Good luck," he said and steered King away. Chris watched attentively for a moment and then gave a final wave before turning towards the house. Inside, Charlotte was standing silently by the front room window watching as Bolton rode back onto the road.

"I don't know who you really are, but I think I could trust you..." She muttered the remark to herself, but Chris put his head around the doorway.

"Are you alright, Mum? Robert's gone. That's some horse he's got there – 'King' – good name – right name for a horse like that."

"I'm sure it is," she replied. "Now do you want some breakfast? You must be famished."

She wanted to busy herself. Somehow she felt disloyal to her late husband and wanted to put thoughts about 'Robert' out of her mind. Chris seemed a little slower than usual going about his routine in the kitchen; she surmised that he might be having similar feelings.

Bolton too was musing briefly on how he had somehow mistaken Charlotte for someone he knew, someone with whom he thought he could be more than a little familiar. Had memories of his wife been haunting him again? In retrospect, he felt embarrassed. It emphasised to him once more that it was a long time since he had seen any of his family – but then that was true for many other people – including most of the soldiers in his unit. He brought his attention back to the road and to his horse, trying hard not to let the brief glimpse of Charlotte's nakedness into his thoughts again.

King might have a certain majesty about him but for some while, his task consisted of trudging through the pools and puddles along the causeway ahead of them. Eventually, when they had travelled several miles north of the cottage, the terrain began to take on a familiar look. Bolton had kept in his view the long ridge of elevated land that lay across his view to the north-west. Now he began to hear the sound of a large volume of running water. Trees, bushes and tall grasses obscured the river that lay ahead but Bolton wanted to persevere until his course intersected with the path that ran along the river's bank. The heavy rain that had fallen recently, however, had turned the fields either side of him into a quagmire. The causeway along which they had been travelling had been washed out by the flooding of the river and left him well short of the elevated track that ran along by the river. Bolton had to decide whether to attempt to reach the path, or to try to find an alternative route which was possibly safer, but which would almost certainly add considerably to the length of the journey.

He tried to gain some clues about the ground between where they were and the intersection with the path. At the furthest point, if they managed to get there, they would be close to the river. King hesitated, sensing before his rider that the ground before them was boggy and unable to take their weight. Then, almost before they could react, they had slid into mud that came up to King's knees and Bolton could feel his horse's uncertainty. Calmly, he steered him to an island of firmer ground and then began to look for a way through to the path. By looking carefully at the vegetation, he could begin to recognise the places where the water lay in dips and hollows. Although it was a cold, grey day, he could see water glinting here and there between the tussocks of grass and reeds. Every so often, King would plunge into a hole that caused him to labour and struggle to keep his footing; Bolton hung on, gripping the horse tightly with his knees and encouraging him whenever he could; not that King needed much encouragement – he was a strong, courageous horse. After some plunging and scrambling, they began to approach the path when – at the last moment – King was once again plunged deep into an area of boggy ground.

Despite his self-control, Bolton found his heart pounding as the horse struggled to find solid ground with his hooves. With an almighty effort, King managed to gain some purchase with his hind legs and then finally to push himself and his rider up on to the path. For such a large horse, he was very nimble, and snorted his relief to be free again of the clinging restraint of the mud.

Bolton turned King's head in the direction of the path. The varying width and depth of the river determined that in some places it was wide but fairly shallow. In such places the flow was still rapid and powerful, but he thought that they might be able to find a point at which where they could ford across to the opposite bank. In other places, the water was deep and glided along in ominous silence beneath the steep, frowning slopes of The Ridge. If horse and rider found themselves in such places at this time of the year, their chances of survival might be minimal. Looking at the dark winter woods brooding over the sullen river, he found himself wondering briefly if at any time in the distant past Arthur and his knights had ridden along the route on which he was now set. Had the world changed so much and, anyway, what kind of world was it now? Arthur's world had been one of violence and savage combat between armed men. Women were variously portrayed as beautiful, mysterious, seductive, cunning and, sometimes, murderous. This now was a world of scientific certainties where Arthur's realm had been one of strange legends and belief in magic. Looking at the river and landscape around him, Bolton found it easy to understand how people had believed in mysterious forces of good and evil and strange spirits that seemed to arise from nature quite as much as from the imaginations of human beings.

"But where now, was all that 'scientific certainty'?" he wondered. Was it collapsing with the society around him? He thought briefly about his wife and family again; he was the Army's servant but with communication becoming ever more tenuous, his concern about them was becoming ever more pressing. Was there anymore 'Army' with a capital 'A'? His thoughts strayed again to Charlotte. He was trying not to think about her, but she and Chris were vulnerable. He tried again to dismiss her from his thoughts. How would she and the boy defend themselves if the need arose? It was not, could not be, his concern.

The day was advancing and the daylight diminishing. It would not be so long now before he and the horse would need food and shelter again.

Whilst Bolton had been deep in thought, King had continued faithfully trudging along the track. Now, however, they had come to a place where the river was wide and where the current was likely to be quite strong, but where they would stand a reasonable chance of being able to cross.

Bolton twitched King's reins and coaxed him down to the water's edge. The water looked reassuringly clear, and the bottom, firm and stony. It was a chance they had to take. King stood for a moment and snorted into the cold air but then began to pick his way into the water...

* * *

As Bolton and his horse forded the river, miles back along the route he had travelled, Charlotte stood at the kitchen window of her farmhouse, watching her son work in the yard. Robert Lawson's arrival had reminded her of their vulnerability. The Ridge – the place he had gone to – would probably be safer. They would have to leave the farm behind – the land over which her late husband had toiled – and take just enough animals with them, to enable them to survive. Even the thought of such a decision made her stomach churn, but it might be the only place within a short travelling distance in which they could be safe.

She thought about it for a moment. Perhaps they would meet Robert Lawson again – and perhaps he would be able to tell them how safe – or how dangerous – The Ridge had become. Then again, almost anywhere would be safer than this place, constantly subject to flood and far removed from any source of help. She went to the back door, opened it and shouted across to her son.

"Chris! Chris! Come here! There's something I want to discuss with you!"

CHAPTER 18

WINTER'S CHILDREN

Janey Capstick was thinking about her husband, Will. In many ways, she could hardly have asked for better. She knew, they both knew, that the battle on The Ridge was probably just the first of many desperate events that lay ahead of them. His skills were vital. He could turn his hand to almost anything on the farm and so far – despite the loss of fuel for vehicles and machinery, despite the loss of electrical power other than the small amount that they were able to generate themselves – he had not baulked at any of the challenges that had faced them. The mixed farm that Will had run for some years now, he was slowly turning over to the kind of production that would ensure self-sufficiency for himself, for Janey and for the family that they hoped to have.

Janey's parents were out there still living in the South Midlands she supposed, but she had not heard from them for weeks. She missed them greatly but was at a loss to know how she could find out what had happened to them. Her brother lived close to her parents, so she hoped that he had managed to see that they were safe. Other than these anxieties, however, the situation on The Ridge left her with little opportunity to brood about the lack of contact. Daily survival, daily work were their preoccupations dawn till dusk – and often before dawn and after dusk.

She and Will had been married for about two years. They wanted children and yet, despite the last two years of married life she was still not pregnant. She had trained as a nurse before the onset of the 'troubles' as she sometimes referred to the breakdown that was taking place all around them. She had skills as a midwife and knew that they were in a good position to manage the birth of any child that she conceived – but as yet, the conception of their first child still eluded them.

It was a cold, grey afternoon. Will was busy in one of the barns. She had come out to the furthest part of her husband's farm to a point where it bordered the land that had belonged to Andrew, and she was carrying an old hurricane lamp. She thought briefly about the battle that had been fought on Andrew's farm; many of the buildings were now wrecked and the family had been killed in the fighting – though whether by the invaders or by the RAF, it was impossible to know. The Army had cleared the invaders from their vantage point and from the wetland areas below, but no members of Andrew's family had reappeared. So now the farm lay empty, devoid of life except for Andrew's animals, which Janey and her husband were still endeavouring to feed. Fortunately, the fighting had not wiped out all the winter feed that Andrew had stored away, so she felt sure that they would be able to see the animals through to the spring.

She felt awkward coming here. 'Ghosts' of the recent past seemed to haunt the old barn which lay just ahead of her, and it felt wrong to be walking on land that had not belonged to her and Will. As she approached, the warm stone of the old barn began to feel more welcoming. There was no lock on the huge wooden doors. She should get one. There might be very few people about, but the times were profoundly unpredictable.

She found a nail in a beam above a part of the floor that contained no straw, wood or anything else that could burn if there was any kind of accident and hung from it the battered old hurricane lamp that she had brought with her. Despite its appearance she knew that she could rely on it and that it would give her a steady light.

The barn had a deep, frowzy smell imparted to it by straw and the sheep that she had brought in because they were in need of temporary shelter during lambing. Lambs could be heard bleating, a sound that was punctuated at intervals by the deeper bleating of ewes.

She had not left them for long because she knew that one of the ewes was almost ready to give birth and she might need some help when she did. The ewe had already found a quiet corner away from the other sheep and lay on her side by a straw bale, clearly in the late stages of her labour. Janey prepared to help mother and lamb, but it was to prove unnecessary. The lamb's head appeared. As a precaution, she took its legs between the fingers of her left hand whilst supporting the lamb's head with her right hand. Shortly, the lamb's full head and shoulders appeared and then the lamb came all the way out in a rush. Janey placed the lamb in front of its mother, leaving her to lick clean her new offspring.

She knew that she could leave her now. The ewe's second lamb would be born very shortly but the first birth had gone much more smoothly than anticipated, and it seemed unlikely that there would be any problems with the second. She wiped her hands and moved to ensure that everything was well with the other sheep, but as she did so, she was startled to hear a loud snort. It sounded like the snorting of a horse, but she had not brought a horse into the barn. She spun around trying to see where the noise had come from.

She caught just the briefest glimpse of a large horse tethered in a far corner of the barn – a corner that in her concentration on the sheep she had ignored. Some attempt had also been made to conceal the horse, although its large size made it very difficult to hide. She began to move towards the horse, but with a shock, found a very large hand being clamped over her mouth and a deep, very precise male voice saying in her right ear, "No harm is going to come to you. Make no sudden noises or movements – and then I can release you."

Fear and anger brimmed in equal proportions in Janey's head. The size and strength of the hand told her, however, that in any contest of strength, there would only be one winner. She needed to buy time.

She nodded her muffled agreement and found herself pushed gently away from her assailant into a position where he could see her. She turned to look at him, angry and defiant, but then as she did so, her eyes widened.

"I know you!" she said. "You're Robert. You were here before the battle!"

He nodded in acknowledgement, but she spat at him angrily in a lower voice, "What the hell were you thinking of! You didn't need to surprise me like that!"

Keeping his eyes fixed on her he said, "I'm sorry, but I need a little help – and I also need to know that I can rely on your discretion."

Janey's heart was still pounding hard. She looked carefully at Robert as if refreshing her memory of him. He was not dissimilar to Will in height and build but there was a cool, determined air about him that made her feel a little afraid of him – something that she never felt with Will.

The careful look that she had been giving him took on a superficial air of contempt.

"And why would someone like you need help from someone like me?"

He stood watching her for a moment. She was not to be underestimated. A direct approach seemed best.

"I need to rest my horse and find him some food. I also need to check on the situation up here in general."

She nodded, unsure as to how to reply. After all, it was this man who had organised the defence of The Ridge. She wanted to help him if she could – but, somehow, she felt vulnerable and wondered if she was taking a risk. She was alone with someone she barely knew – a soldier, someone used to violence.

Robert had continued talking. "I'll be here a few days. It would be a big help to me if you didn't tell anyone that I'm here."

She looked at him. "My husband may find out for himself. He sometimes comes over this way. He could easily see you – and a horse like that one over there is not exactly easy to hide."

In spite of herself, Janey began to smile.

"Well, I suppose I could disguise him as...?" He paused as if trying to think of something suitable but then laughed at the ridiculousness of such a thought.

The sound of his laughter seemed to break the ice. She felt herself beginning to mellow.

"I can help you. I don't mind if it helps people up here."

"It will," he said. "We need to know that we've succeeded in clearing the enemy out of here. I want to look around for a day or two and my horse could do with being rested. He's had two days of fairly hard riding."

"I can find him some forage," replied Janey. "We're not short this winter. How about you? Have you got enough food?"

"I always carry enough with me, but it does get rather boring. If you have anything you can spare, it would be welcome – always assuming that it doesn't cause suspicion?"

She shook her head. She could easily bring him a little extra food without it causing problems at home, but she was still puzzled by the secrecy. If he wanted her help, surely he could take her and Will into his confidence?

"Perhaps we should simply tell my husband? He's hardly likely to tell anyone and he spends most days out and about on The Ridge. He could tell you if he saw anything suspicious."

Robert appeared to think about it for a moment but then shook his head.

"The fewer people who know I'm here, the better. Some of the enemy may still be hiding out. There's no lack of places. The less you know about what I'm doing the less you can give away."

He turned away from her briefly. After the searches that had been carried out several weeks before, the chance that remnants of the enemy could still be in hiding were small, but they had to be sure. There was still the risk of sabotage or that survivors could find their way back to join enemy forces still at Hinkley Point. Thorndike's resources were thinly spread, and he could ill afford the distraction of further problems from enemy survivors on The Ridge.

Janey realised that she would get no more information out of Robert. She would give him the help that he needed, but she would have to conceal it from Will. She would have to return later but Will would not think that anything was amiss; the sheep always took a lot of her attention at that time of the year. She would return with fodder for King and food for Robert.

It was the first evening of a routine that she would follow for the next week. It caused very little remark from Will who was busy trying to repair a plough and was grateful that she had work of her own to pursue.

Over the days that followed, she returned to her longing to be pregnant. She and Will had made love throughout the two years of their marriage and for some time before that... There must be a problem with one of them or possibly both. If the problem lay with her, in the absence of medical tests she would never know but if there was a problem with Will there might be a way to find out. This thought had allied itself with her awareness that, when she was helping Robert, feelings that had already faded in just two short years of marriage had begun to stir again. Robert was big, muscular, with something of a raw hunger about him...

So it was that one evening, she approached the barn with a feeling of anticipation in her heart. Already, the hurricane lamp swung very slightly in a draught from the big doors of the barn. Robert's sleeping bag lay unzipped along its length and lay open on a comfortable pile of straw. Janey had come with the things that he and King needed. All was as usual. But this evening, she also brought with her a decision. There was something that she needed, that she desperately wanted, something that Robert might be willing to supply.

Freddie, or Robert as Janey knew him, was a shrewd man. He did not need Janey to provide him with an explanation. Like her, he had also come to a decision. The woman who had given him shelter at the farm a day or so before his arrival at The Ridge had stirred his instincts – reminding him of pleasures that had lain almost forgotten for a long time. His family was far away, and God alone knew when he would see them again. Now here was Janey, bringing him food, taking care of his horse. Perhaps there was something more that she could bring him – and something that he could give her in return. Involuntarily, his hand strayed to his temple. He had fallen from his horse just before he had arrived at The Ridge. There were still one or two after-effects that troubled him. He was aware that sometimes his vision became blurred. He hoped that his judgement was not becoming similarly affected as well...

Janey sat by him, nibbling at a little of the food but not really feeling hungry. She did not now suspect this big man at her side but instead felt comfortable in his presence. She put out a hand and put it very carefully, tentatively on his knee. He did not take it away but let it rest there – and then ran his left hand around her neck and shoulders.

King munched away at his fodder, ignoring the play of the light and darkness on the wall of the barn as separate shadows became close and then closer still until they blended into one another. Small sounds punctuated the flickering twilight – perhaps a sigh or a kiss or small cry of pleasure – or perhaps just the noises of the sheep and of the many small creatures to whom the barn was home.

***

Janey stood before the window, looking across the garden and the fields next to the farmhouse. Will was happy and had gone in search of something they could drink. The flowers in the garden and the leaves on the trees and bushes marked the onset of spring. She had come back early from a visit to the barn. Freddie, or Robert as far as she had known him, had left weeks before – gone to check around the woods and then on to rejoin his unit. Had she known him too briefly to miss him? The barn now seemed a rather dreary place and in the growing light of the spring evenings, less mysterious than it had by the light of the moon, the stars and the hurricane lamp. One or two new ghosts now jostled about there, the most recent having precipitated out of the air that very evening, imparting a chill to what could otherwise have been a small time of unadulterated joy.

Will had returned with a glass of cider for himself and a glass of apple juice for Janey.

He shambled into the room, stooping slightly to get his tall frame through the doorway. He had a fresh, jovial face reddened by the winds of hilltop farming and long hours of working outdoors, day by day in winter weather.

"Sorry dear," he said, "it's not champagne but there again, this is a Somerset baby!"

She tried to look cheerful because she knew that it was expected of her.

He was not usually very sensitive to her moods but noticed that she seemed less than overjoyed.

He put one of the glasses into her hand.

"C'mon, Janey. This is just what we've both wanted for a long time. You must be happy?"

She flickered a brief smile at him, not wanting to distract him or to make him suspect that she had any regrets or that she was anything less than joyful about her pregnancy.

For a moment, he looked uncertain. "You are sure about this, aren't you? I mean, it couldn't be that you've just made a mistake?"

She managed to look suitably exasperated. "Of course not!" she said. "I am a nurse or rather was – but I haven't quite forgotten everything I was taught. Anyway, I don't need to be a nurse to know I'm pregnant. Being a woman is quite sufficient for that!"

"Wowee!" he yelled childishly and began to waltz her around the room.

"Hey, hey!" she yelled at him as he tried to drag her along in his prancing. "I'm a pregnant woman – remember? I need to be treated with care!"

He stopped. "I'm sorry! Sorry!" he exclaimed and placed a gentle but slightly irreverent hand on her stomach.

"God, why did I marry you?" she asked. "You're such a turnip!"

"Ah, but I'm a very nice turnip. That's why you love me."

"Do I?" she asked.

"Do I what?"

"Love you, you stupid turnip!"

His face took on an expression of mock solemnity.

"Turnip, maybe. Stupid – no."

She turned away from him, smirking into the fading light outside the window. Then she frowned as a thought as jagged as a piece of broken glass stabbed at her memory again. It had been the thought that had been nagging at her before the first heady sips of cider and before Will's light heartedness had distracted them both.

She tried to sound casual, offhand almost.

"Did you say that you'd found a horse? Sounds quite extraordinary."

"It is extraordinary!" he exclaimed. "It's a really fine horse and I found him just wandering about, cropping the grass at the edge of the wood. There was no sign of his owner anywhere – and I spent a long time looking. The saddle and reins were still on him. At first I wondered why – until I tried to get near him, that is."

"Why? Was he difficult to get near?"

"You could say that. Just spooked I suppose, having lost his owner, but it took me a long time to get his confidence. From the state of his coat, I think that he must have been wandering around for some time, weeks even."

"Wouldn't you have noticed him before?"

"Not necessarily. It would have been easy for him to keep out of the way. He must be used to being around people and perhaps he just finally wanted to be found. How do I know? If he'd been in the woods, none of us from this side of the hill want to go too far in there."

"What do you mean?"

"Well, the army guys thought that they'd weeded out the last of the enemy, but I'm not so sure."

"You think there's still someone hiding in there?"

"I think so. We gave them plenty of places to hide. Do you remember all those bolt holes and shelters that we dug?"

She nodded. She remembered it well.

A deep feeling of sadness was coming over her, but she had not quite finished with her questions.

"So what's he like – this horse? You still haven't really told me."

"Oh no, I haven't, have I? He's a big horse, chestnut, beautifully proportioned – powerful. Looks as though he was meant to carry a big rider."

"Well," said Janey thoughtfully, "he's going to need a name. We can't just keep referring to him as 'the horse'.

Will agreed.

"Hmm, I thought that you might like to name him. Perhaps we could go over to the barn together in the morning. You could have a look at him and see what you can come up with."

"I will come with you, of course, but now that you have described him, I think that I can picture him very clearly – and probably think of a name for him as well."

"What, without even having seen him? You need to see him really."

"Ok," she replied, certain that she would have no difficulty in naming the horse. She wondered briefly how difficult it would be to gaze at King again without knowing what had happened to his rider.

***

Kirk was looking out of the kitchen window. From his vantage point, he could see new leaves beginning to open on the trees. Along the hedgerows bordering the garden, celandines had begun to appear. Alison came alongside him to see what he was looking at.

"We're well on the way," she said. "We've nearly seen our first winter through."

Kirk thought that this was tempting fate, but both of them were inclined to believe that the worst of the winter weather had now passed. Alison had made a new calendar using the one from the previous year to help her work out the new days and dates.

Kirk felt relieved that their stocks of food had lasted them well. "We still seem to have plenty of food left," he remarked.

Alison nodded her agreement, but he could tell that she was going to add a note of caution.

"We have – and we've managed to come through one of the leanest times of year – but we still have some time and a lot of hard work to go before we can begin to harvest this year's fruit and vegetables."

"We can forage though." He did not want to start feeling pessimistic just after he had noticed one of the first signs of spring. "There's always plenty of food around if you know where to look for it."

"Oh is there now?" She came closer and although the winter had been hard for both of them, he could see that there was amusement in her eyes. "A few months in the countryside and suddenly you're an expert."

"Yes, I know," he agreed. "You're quite right – but I've always felt myself to be something of an expert in country matters."

It was a moment or two before she understood his joke but then she said, "Oh very funny. Ha bloody ha. Would you like to know something that will take the smile off your face?"

"Not really," he said. "But I have a feeling that you're going to come out with it anyway."

She hesitated. "I've missed a period."

Alison's prediction had been right; the smile disappeared immediately from his face.

"Are you sure?"

"Of course I'm sure. They're always very regular. I'm now two weeks overdue."

"It could be something else. We're not exactly living in the lap of luxury here. Perhaps it's something to do with diet – or long hours of work?"

He seemed anxious to find some explanation other than that she was pregnant.

"You're right. There could be some other explanation – but I'm pretty sure... You don't seem very pleased...?"

He was frowning slightly but his frown dissolved into a smile "No! No!" he protested. "It's nothing like that. I knew that you might become pregnant. It's just that...I haven't been a father before..."

She came closer and put her arms around him. "I know that..." she said. "But don't act as though you're surprised. There isn't a contraceptive for miles around – not of the old medical variety – so I haven't been able to take any precautions and I'm not sure that I would have wanted to anyway. I want to be pregnant by you. I thought it was what we both wanted."

He looked at her with just a hint of the frown that she had seen previously. "Of course it is," he said. "I love you and I want you to have our children. You know that."

She laughed at him. "I know how you feel about me," she said, but then continued, "All the same, I still sense a 'but' in your voice."

"How d'you mean?"

"I mean that you seem to have mixed feelings now about me becoming pregnant!"

He had not really wanted to tell her how he felt but how could he explain? He was by no means sure of the explanation himself. His attempt was a little stumbling but went some way towards the truth.

"I'm just anxious, I suppose. Neither of us is really young and, well, I've never delivered a baby before."

She had thought about this already but now that he said it to her, she was reminded of the risk that she was taking.

"I can understand that," she said. "But how do you think I feel? As far as I know, medical services are almost non-existent. It will be even more of a risk for me than it was for my grandmother. Still, we're not completely without help."

"How do you mean?" he asked. The news was something of a surprise to him. "I thought that we were the only ones still surviving up here."

"No, no," said Alison. "I don't think you're right. I think there are some other people who escaped. They live round at the other end of the Ridge."

"Who are they?"

"Well, if I'm right, I think that I've seen signs of the Capsticks – Janey and Will. Their farmhouse is right over the other side of Andrew's land – or at least, what used to be Andrew's land."

"You haven't mentioned them before."

"In a way I have," she replied. "I did say that we should investigate to find out if there was still anybody else up here." She hesitated for a moment. "Anyway, I think I've seen signs of Janey in the last few weeks."

He remembered Janey from the meeting in the barn, but he was a little puzzled that Alison had not specifically mentioned seeing her since then. He remembered, however, that he thought he had caught a glimpse of a young woman on the afternoon he had killed his first pheasant – but had subsequently dismissed it as the sort of illusion that is commonplace in the countryside at dusk.

When he returned from his reverie he said, "I haven't heard you mention anything about seeing Janey – at least, not recently."

Alison, who had been having similar thoughts to his own replied, "No – you're right, I don't think I did mention it, but then I was never one hundred percent sure that I had seen her. It's easy to be deceived when you're wandering around on your own up here."

He thought about what she had said for a moment but then went on, "Alright, supposing you are right, supposing you did see Janey. Is it likely that she'd be able to help us?"

She was guarded but hopeful in her response. "Oh yes," she said. "Definitely – if it was her I saw, she's a nurse – or was. I'm sure she would help."

Alison hesitated. Finding other survivors was suddenly becoming of great importance but she wondered why they had not tried to seek them out before. "We should have tried to make contact with the neighbours before now," she said.

"Remember, though, we don't know who's survived!" replied Kirk, a little more forcefully than he intended. "It could just as easily be some of the enemy as any of the people who were living up here before the battle. I think we need to be very cautious until we know much, much more about who's still out there."

She agreed with him, but she had lived on The Ridge for many years and felt more confident about the general situation than Kirk.

"You may be right, but we won't find out by hiding in here – or by poking around just a short distance from the house. We have to get out there and find out who's alive and what's happening!"

Kirk did not respond other than to nod his agreement. He knew that they would need help and that the only way that they would get it would be to co-operate with whatever neighbours they still had left. Their period of isolation was coming an end. If nothing else, there would be another mouth to feed, another small being to shelter, protect and clothe.

Despite Alison's thoughts about her pregnancy, he began to feel that they had been very careless about it all. Now they had added to the very problem that in his heart he felt was at the bottom of humanity's difficulties with Planet Earth. There were just too many people. It might not be very obvious in such an isolated place, but it was nonetheless true.

Alison looked at him, as if trying to read his thoughts. "Whatever we think about our situation here, we have to make this child feel welcome. It needs all our love, right from the very start."

Again, he nodded his agreement, this time looking very solemnly at her. "Of course I will love our child," he replied. "You know I will." He paused for a moment. She was still holding him. He kissed her on the mouth and looked into her eyes.

"Why do I always want you? Why can't I just leave you alone?" He knew as he asked that it was a stupid question, but he also knew that in the answer lay the root of the Earth's problems.

She smiled at him, knowing that he was serious but also, again, wanting to make the most of what would probably be their last time of solitary freedom.

"Because you can't," she said. "Because you just can't."

* * *

CHAPTER 19

TOPOGRAPHY OF A DISASTER

Thorndike was having to acknowledge to himself that his problems were mounting by the day if not by the hour. It was now six days since Bolton had been due to reappear. He had tried to radio WMC in Birmingham but there had been no response. He had speculated about the possible reasons, but they all amounted to the same thing: he was receiving neither orders nor intelligence.

Two days after Freddie Bolton's failure to reappear, Thorndike had decided to use a small amount of their precious petrol reserve by sending a despatch rider north to WMC. The rider should have been back the next day, but he had also now failed to reappear.

Meanwhile, out in the Bristol Channel, the Navy was faring only a little better. Ship to shore communication was good, but although there was regular scanning of the frequencies, there was no communication from elsewhere. A sense of grimness and awesome isolation had begun to fall upon both Navy and Army personnel alike; prior to the catastrophe, they could hardly have imagined a situation in which both terrestrial and satellite communication would virtually cease.

It was afternoon and the loneliness of command was making itself felt. Thorndike was struggling to understand why the 'civilized' country around him was falling apart and why it was failing to function in a manner that was broadly similar to the way in which it had functioned for many decades before. Central government seemed to have entirely collapsed and there had been no signs of any kind of assistance coming from Europe or North America. It had to be assumed, he thought, that a fate similar to that of the UK had befallen both continents.

After the missile strike in London, there had initially been a huge increase in both official communication and the global 'chatter' on which it had generally been possible to eavesdrop. Initially, mobile phones had continued to be useable and despite the mayhem around them, radio amateurs were still finding it possible to broadcast their messages around the globe. Slowly, however, they had fallen silent, and it was this 'silence' that was exercising Thorndike's thoughts.

In an attempt to gather intelligence about the situation, the Navy had sent one of its aircrews on a succession of missions. Although the battle in Somerset had consumed a large quantity of the Navy's oil reserves, a helicopter from the contingent in the Channel had been ordered to fly a number of sorties over Wales, the South West Peninsula, the Midlands and the South of England. Wherever they flew, whether they used video and photographic evidence or their own direct reporting of what they saw, the picture being assembled by the aircrew was the same.

At first sight, the expanses of countryside across these extensive areas looked much as they had before the disaster. By flying low, however, by making use of infra-red equipment, occasionally by landing and, more generally, by making full use of resources such as binoculars, the crew began to piece together the changes that were taking place along the corridors of territory that they were able to explore.

Often, as they flew over the countryside, there were very few immediate signs of human activity. Then as they continued their flight, they would gradually spot individuals or small groups of travellers making use of every kind of road and track, although it was rare to see people openly walking or riding on the major roads or motorways. Invariably, these travellers would be seen on foot, bike or horseback, but vehicles relying on oil were parked everywhere in redundant ranks and lines outside shops, offices and factories, or along residential streets. Many cars, lorries and vans had been abandoned on roads and motorways where their drivers had tried to get as far as they could before the petrol ran out.

There were many indications that organised medical and veterinary services had ceased to function. Amongst the signs of this breakdown were the numerous corpses – of both human beings and domestic animals – in every conceivable stage of decay. It was not, however, always easy to see them from the air. When for any reason the dying found themselves in the open, they often seemed to crawl away to hidden places in a last attempt to seek shelter.

From all that they saw, though, the helicopter crew could tell that starvation, disease and conflict were making a vast, swathing cull of the population and that, if the whole country was suffering on the same scale, the number of deaths would be apocalyptic.

It was part of the crew's mission to make close-up examinations of situations on the ground – although, in practice, it was often unsafe to land. On one of the first sorties, a large crowd of people made a rush towards the helicopter as if to prevent it from taking off again. The pilot had pulled it back into the sky with just seconds to spare.

After that, they landed only following very thorough reconnaissance of the area below and always where they could see clearly in all directions. Occasionally, however, they would land to make close up examinations of corpses. Often, the bodies that they found bore signs of violence or the tell-tale emaciation of famine and disease. Domestic dogs could be seen roaming in packs and it seemed likely that together with wild animals such as foxes, it was they who were sometimes savaging the bodies of the dead and dying.

The villages, towns and cities were hazardous places to visit. On several occasions, the aircrew had witnessed savage fighting on the ground. Once they had flown low enough to see that swords, axes and knives were being used. Those who were fighting seemed mostly to be young men who, when injured, lay where they fell or were seen being dragged back behind some invisible line by other combatants.

The aircrew were wary of going too close to such conflicts. Reactions to the helicopter varied enormously. Some people waved whilst the first instincts of others seemed to be to hide. Occasionally, clenched fists greeted them, and weapons appeared. Twice on their missions, they had met with arms fire directed at them from the ground.

Fire too was something that ravaged large areas of the towns and cities. The aircrew saw a large fire at a timber yard in Gloucester burning out of control and beginning to move through the riverside area of the city. In Bristol, they had seen another enormous blaze around which people were engaged in a running battle with each other. The noise of the helicopter made it impossible to hear weapons being used on the ground, but some of those fighting below could be seen to be in possession of rifles. It was during this incident that the aircrew were suddenly aware of the helicopter being struck by several rounds of small arms fire, causing the pilot to veer sharply up and away. A short while later, when they landed back on board ship, they found minor damage to a rotor blade and to the nose wheel assembly.

After this, they had sufficient fuel for just two more flights. On these last journeys, they had been able to clearly see the gradual flooding of a vast area east of Taunton, bounded by the Quantock and Blackdown Hills on its western edge and by the Mendips to the east. The numerous rivers that flow across the landscape between Crewkerne and Yeovil and the Bristol Channel were becoming indistinguishable from the general inundation that was taking place. The quantity of water below them was breath-taking and had now begun to resemble a small inland sea which was gradually cutting off the northern part of Somerset and the South West peninsula from the rest of England. Wherever they looked, water glittered back at them, reflecting the moods of the sky and remorselessly covering over the once-familiar topography of the Somerset Levels. Only to the south through Cranborne Chase and along the Dorset Downs would it still be possible to find a relatively dry route into the Axminster area.

The helicopter returned from its final sortie to the destroyer from which it had come. Thorndike returned, pondering the whereabouts of Freddie Bolton and wondering what had happened to him. Some hours later, the Navy's report came into his hands and, at last, he had some information – even though as he read it, the news was grim, much worse than he had anticipated.

Then he had a short time to reflect and in his own mind became almost certain that Freddie Bolton must have had an accident or met with an enemy he had not been able to avoid or overcome.

Thorndike was not given to self-criticism, but he began to think again about the decision to send Bolton back to The Ridge on his own. He knew the reasons for the decision already, of course; Bolton's role often necessitated working alone – very few of the soldiers in the camp had the skills that would enable them to keep up with and live alongside him and no-one could be spared from the continuing operations against the enemy in the Hinkley Point area. Information from The Ridge shortly after the battle led him to believe that enemy attempts to capture it and use it as a vantage point had failed – but without news from Bolton, doubts about security on his western flank continued to trouble him.

***

Kirk's curiosity had been drawn by the behaviour of two crows that he could see hopping about on the woodland floor. He walked closer to investigate. As he did so, he began to realise that he was looking at a body lying partly concealed amongst the undergrowth.

He wondered, as he went closer, if he had been the first to discover it. There were signs amongst the leaves and the foliage that someone had been there before him. Recently, it had become less common for him to leave the path that skirted the woods, but that morning, he had decided to investigate one of the many paths that ran beneath the canopy of the trees. The leaves were already appearing and were reducing the light that filtered down to the woodland floor, but Kirk's recent experiences told him, well before he knew for certain, that the bodily shape partly concealed amongst the undergrowth was that of a human being.

Despite his recent familiarity with death, Kirk was circumspect in approaching the body. He did not know for certain that the person on the ground ahead of him was dead. If the body was a corpse, then when had the death occurred? If it had occurred as the result of an attack, then the assailants might still be close by. There was a strange sense of déjà vu.

He looked all around but there seemed to be no immediate threat. Despite his circumspection, it was important to find out what had happened to the person he could see lying on the ground before him.

If this was just some poor itinerant who had fallen into an exhausted sleep on the woodland floor, he would not welcome a rude awakening. If it was a corpse that Kirk was looking at, then it had all eternity to sleep – but if he was looking at someone who was injured or sick, then he would have to do what he could to help. This time, there would be no emergency services to appear out of the darkness.

***

Freddie's courage had not deserted him. There was, though, within him, a sense that time was short. His attackers had mistakenly left him for dead.

He could not feel his feet or the lower parts of his legs. His assailants had assumed the victim's wounds would lead him immediately into the next world. However, he had fallen in such a position that for a short time, the blood loss from his body was limited and he was also able to continue breathing.

He had caught only a glimpse of his attackers; the sallow skin of their faces suggested that they were from the Middle East or perhaps from one of the war-torn countries of the Far East. People in those places had borne the brunt of war for so long now.

In a strange calm that floated through his brain in the moments of dying, he wondered what hubris had led him into such a careless death. How many faces could he see? There were three, perhaps four peering in at him. There were heads with dark hair, different shapes and sizes, floating before him. There had been no strategy, no tactics, no game of chess; in carelessness and complacency, he had walked into an opportunist trap. There was no chance now to fight back. Where was his spirit; where was his desire to live?

He had left his spirit inside Janey. His wife was far away; dead or alive, he did not know but he had betrayed her. Of the new life that Janey was carrying, he knew nothing. His death was deserved. He had always thought that he would fight to the last fibre of his strength, but now he had failed, not by being defeated in a fight but by walking blindly into a trap. All his previous victories counted for nothing now, his time had come – and would shortly be gone. His attackers occasionally wandered closer. They were not afraid of him but instead were careless of his presence. He could not recognise the language that they spoke. One of them spat in his direction before wandering off to light a cigarette.

Then the group was disturbed by a noise – someone was walking through the woods. Whoever it was, they would avoid conflict if it was unanticipated. They melted away into the bushes and the shadows. Besides, the intruder was carrying a gun.

Will Capstick moved cautiously forward, pushing the butt of his rifle into his shoulder. The killers of the man lying on the ground were just a short distance away. He had seen them move back amongst the trees.

He went just close enough to see what had happened. He recognised the man lying on the ground as Robert Lawson, the man who had accompanied Thorndike at the public meeting in Andrew's barn. Will's eyes roved back and forth, keeping an eye on the middle distance but also taking in the small crater in the ground a few yards in front of where Lawson lay. Lawson himself was lying on his back as if gazing up at the trees, but as Will moved closer to get a better look, he suddenly realised with a shock that Lawson's feet and the lower parts of his legs were missing.

It all made a kind of grim sense. Will had heard an explosion, a dull thud that sent the rooks cawing into the winter sky. He had decided to investigate, thinking that perhaps an animal had triggered some of the munitions left behind after the battle on the Ridge. Now here was Robert Lawson, dead or dying, he was not sure which.

He moved closer, searching for signs of life but could see none. A large sticky pool of blood had soaked the ground where the lower portions of Lawson's legs should have been. Ahead of him there was flickering of the light amongst the trees. Someone was hiding. The explosion began to look less like an accident and more like a booby trap. He decided to get out. There was no point in becoming the second victim of whoever was lurking amongst the trees.

He lingered for a few moments more, but he could see nothing further – and he could do nothing. As far as he could tell, Lawson was already dead. He owed it to Janey and to any children that they might have in the future not to play the vain hero.

It was perhaps to Kirk's credit that he disregarded his fear and stayed long enough by Lawson's body to think that it deserved a proper burial. He felt that if he had no respect for the dead, he could have no respect for the living. Whatever this man now before him had done in his lifetime, he should have a decent burial. Kirk determined that he would return to the house for his spade, and he decided that he would do it that morning whilst he could still see what he was doing in the twilight amongst the trees.

He explained to Alison when he got back. At first, she worried about the danger posed by the invaders who still remained in the woods, but then she decided that Kirk was right and that despite any small risk that there might be, Robert Lawson deserved a proper burial. She would help Kirk to bury the stranger they had met so briefly but whose planning had previously helped to preserve the few people who still remained on The Ridge.

In a short while, Kirk had returned with Alison to the place where the body lay. He had left it covered with leaves. In the previous year, he had left the same body lying in the street whilst he phoned for the ambulance and police. It had, it seemed, all been a wasted labour – except that it had kept the mysterious stranger alive long enough to protect at least some of the small population on the Ridge.

They toiled away with spades until at last they had made a deep rectangular hole in the ground. He was a big man, but the soil was not hard to dig, and they soon had a grave that was large enough to accommodate the corpse. Eventually, they had finished. Piles of soil lay to either side of the hole, but they had left enough space to allow them to place the body in a large sheet which they had brought with them for the purpose.

Kirk had closed the corpse's eyes. Their work was difficult enough without them having a sense that 'Robert' was watching them from beyond the grave. Alison helped in getting the body onto the sheet and, with great difficulty, they lowered it into the hole. The weight was such that they too were nearly pulled into the grave. Then, after much heaving and sweating, they stood back. The sheet with its heavy load lay in the bottom of the hole ready to be covered with the soil of the woodland floor.

Alison stood back, her spade still in one hand but her head lowered in respect for the man whose body now lay below them. Kirk followed suit, feeling rather numb, feeling selfish that he was aware of his backache and wanting now to finish the job and get back to the house and clean up.

He took his spade and showered down the earth onto the rounded whiteness of the sheet. A moment of decision had passed and now they vigorously shovelled the earth down into the hole, wanting to get the job finished. The earth went back into the hole more easily than it had come out, but it was still an appreciable time before the ground was level again and they were ready to mark the head of the grave with a large grey stone that they found nearby. They stood briefly by the finished grave. Kirk wondered what name should go on the headstone had they been able to carve it. Would it be 'Robert Lawson' or 'Mark Ridgeway' – or perhaps some other name, unknown to anyone except those most closely connected with the dead man? After a moment or two of further silence, they shouldered their spades and moved off down the path towards the cottage.

The wooden door behind Kirk and Alison was not readily visible but then it had always been intended that it should be concealed. Kirk and his companions had not worked on that part of the woodland fortifications and so did not know that a refuge had been dug back into the hillside at this point. From behind the door, which was being held ever so slightly ajar, a pair of eyes watched the couple on their route back to the cottage.

The people within the refuge had a sense of having settled a debt – but they were also uneasy. They had survived the battle but once they emerged into the surroundings, they would be only too visible.

If they had been in what was left of urban Britain, they might have been subsumed in the general population, but here, in the prevailing situation, their presence was incongruous, out of place. They had seen the farmer carrying a gun shortly after they had murdered the soldier. It was not unreasonable to suppose that there were still plenty of weapons all around them. In the battle, they had momentarily been the majority but here – they were probably surrounded by people who would return violence with violence. They could not kill everyone they saw. This alien woodland place seemed more ominous even than the terrors that probably lurked in the towns and cities. Here, they could be picked off one by one; elsewhere, if need be, they might just be able to survive amongst the petty thugs or the ranks of the local warlords.

In a few more hours, darkness would fall. They would be heading out of the area. If after the weeks of winter, anything was left of the force that had been designated to attack Hinkley Point, they needed to rejoin them. They would leave these locals to their wilderness and their solitude and take their chances with the ever-increasing expanses of river and wetland. Then they would head for whatever was left of nearby towns and villages, of streets, houses and shops. Out here, there was food to be had but it was hard won. They were half starving, but they were tired of rabbit and pheasant, of a few, paltry stolen vegetables. Somewhere they might be able to find real food in the tins and bottles littered around the shelves of derelict supermarkets.

Had he been aware of it, their reasoning might have seemed strange to Kirk but then he would also readily have understood the lure of the familiar. The invaders had grown up in the slums of the Far East but had been brainwashed into believing that in 'The North', there were still places that were cool, where there was still food and water available, where they

234

would not be noticed in the general chaos created as millions migrated across Asia and Europe. They had even been told that the women were 'loose' and given the right inducements would go with anyone. They no longer needed any brainwashing or 'reasons'. They would eventually become just a part of the mass of peoples moving from the hot middle places of the Earth towards the relative coolness of the poles.

The devil, however, was in the detail. Somehow, the military contingent of which they were a part, had ended up in a junction, a dead end, a geographical cul-de-sac on the margins of the Atlantic Ocean. Now, they were intent on finding their way out, back to the people they had come with and back into the remains of a civilization which, however bloody and chaotic the situation, was preferable to life in the wilderness. Out here there was only solitude and, lurking in the backs of their minds, anxieties about the possibility of madness.

Back in the cottage, the spring water tap poured its cold water onto Kirk's hands. A stream of earthy water swirled its way down the plug hole. He turned away, dried his hands and made for the hallway. Alison had already changed out of her muddy clothes and had washed her hands in the sink upstairs. Placing her hands on her own face, she could feel that they were still cold. It was a spring day, and the house was a little warmer than it had been through the weeks of winter. She decided to change into a dress.

Then she felt restless. She wanted to forget about the death that had been all around them for so long. She wanted life around her and within her. She splashed a small amount of the perfume that she still had on her dressing table around her neckline – and then went in search of Kirk. She found him in the lounge. He had also changed into some cleaner clothes. She went closer to him, slowly placing the fingers of the right hand on his neck.

He reached out to her and drew her in. They kissed and he held her close as they sank onto the settee. She felt his hand reach down to the hem of her dress. She did not try to stop him. In that moment it was what she wanted, and his movements were quick and decisive.

Minutes later, she lay back in his arms, a warm glow suffusing her body. She lay looking past him out through the front window into the brightness of the day. Even if they had taken such rudimentary precautions as were available to them, the moments for such considerations had passed. She did not care now about that side of things. She wanted to have their baby – but she also wondered if such a world was one into which she wanted to bring a child, a child that would always be hers and that would be, until its death, always vulnerable.

She pushed her thoughts aside and returned her attention to Kirk, kissing him on the cheek. It was, she thought, probably too late already for such reflections.

* * *

Thorndike was now presuming that Bolton was missing – and, in all probability, dead. He had been due back at the camp many days before and Thorndike knew that he would have to proceed without him – and without the intelligence that he should have brought with him.

On a personal level, Thorndike regretted the loss of someone with whom he had a good working relationship. He might even have said it was a 'friendly' relationship other than that part of its value lay in their ability to challenge each other when necessary. The situation in which they worked did not encourage anything more than professional duty, but he would have said to himself, if to no-one else, that he preferred Bolton's company to that of most other officers in the camp.

The challenge of the situation as it had developed was the kind that had probably been planned for somewhere in the country but if so, news of it had never filtered down to him. Meanwhile, he busied himself with the tasks of sustaining the morale of the soldiers in the camp and of maintaining readiness in case they should receive any orders. The prevention of disorder in the area was a further task that would fall to him, but up to that point, he had been entirely preoccupied with such actions as the defence of Hinkley Point. In any event, as far as he knew from the information available to him, most civilians with the means and common sense to flee the area had done so. Occasionally, he found himself asking what Bolton would have done and missing the person who, in the winter months, had provided much of the intelligence underlying the area strategy.

It was a source of relief to him that the attempts to attack Hinkley Point had been thwarted, but earlier that morning, he had been in discussion with some of his fellow officers about a marauding gang that, in the vacuum left by the ongoing depopulation of the area, had established itself some miles to the north of his encampment. A small group of traumatised and half-starved individuals had been brought in at around dawn the previous day by the soldiers on perimeter patrol. After they had been allowed time to rest and to revive themselves with some of the Army's food, the survivors had painted a vivid picture of the violence and lawlessness that was developing in some of the areas around them.

It confirmed what Thorndike had heard from the Navy's reports. He had the capacity, with the people and the resources under his command, to enforce a rudimentary peace in the area around the Army's encampment but it was not the first priority of the mission on which they had been sent into the region, and at that moment, he was in limbo.

For the time being, without Bolton's information, he had only scraps of intelligence as to how much of the armed incursion had survived in the fastnesses of Somerset. There was also no intelligence coming from WMC – a situation that he found bewildering. He could not imagine what it was that could have befallen an organisation the size of the Army's centre in the West Midlands that had prevented them from communicating with him. Within the remit of his original orders, he had sufficient scope to proceed, but had anyone asked him prior to his present predicament if it was a possibility that he envisaged, he would have discounted it as being very unlikely.

The Navy's resources, too, seemed to be rapidly dwindling. At least, though, he still heard from them. On the seaward side, they continued to act as eyes and ears for themselves and the Army units ashore. The news coming from the ships bobbing about in the Bristol Channel at that moment, however, was not news of a human adversary; it was, instead, news of an enemy that had existed long before the evolution of human beings – that of the weather and more immediately, in this instance, a storm that was rapidly blowing its way into the area.

A depression of great depth had formed off the Atlantic coast of Spain and was moving north-east through the western side of the Bay of Biscay and into the Celtic Sea. The faxes came in. Thorndike scanned them but regarded them as another factor to be taken into account. Bad weather was always a concern, but his rudimentary knowledge of isobars and their significance was not uppermost in his thoughts at that moment. Better meteorologists than he had missed the significance of depressions in the Bay of Biscay.

The meeting with his officers had taken place in the late afternoon. They had decided that, despite the prioritising of Hinkley Point, the information brought to them was of sufficient concern to warrant an armed investigation of the problems of lawlessness and disorder in the area and that they would send a contingent north on a fact-finding mission before launching any significant action. Reflecting on their decision, he was happy with it. It fell within the bounds that he could defend if required to do so and also helped to keep his soldiers focused and in a state of preparedness.

In contrast to disorder breaking out to the north of their position, the weather was a perennial English topic of conversation. Education and social habit would not have predisposed Thorndike or any of his officers to be overly concerned about it except that, in other circumstances at that time of year, he would have been ruminating about its likely impact on the forthcoming cricket season.

The Navy personnel, however, had a much closer association with the weather and at least a few of them were looking with concern at the depression moving towards them. There was also some discussion of the possible impact of a very high tide driven before winds that were now getting close to hurricane speeds. With the estuary at their backs, the funnelling of such a huge volume of water into the confines of the Bristol Channel looked likely to have an impact similar to a tsunami in its proportions.

Whilst decisions were being made about the disposition of the ships in the Bristol Channel, Thorndike had also begun to think about preparations for the approaching storm.

The unit's trucks had to be kept within the camp compound, but it was sensible to move vehicles away from the vicinity of the stream unlikely though it seemed that even in flood it could amount to anything significant. Soldiers were instructed to check on tents to see that they were fully secured and any equipment likely to be picked up by excessive amounts of wind or water was stored away in some old farm buildings that were currently being used as a camp storage area. Everyone anticipated a noisy night and perhaps a drenching if they had to turn out for any reason. The storm warnings had come late in the afternoon when most people in the camp had already done a substantial amount of work. Soldiers went about the preparations in a spirit of duty rather than with any belief that they could be important to them whilst the cold and discomfort of it all were simply accepted as their constant companions.

Thorndike returned to his tent and peered again at the local maps he had spread out on a table. He looked carefully at the narrowing of the contours in the valley upstream from the camp site. Then he looked more carefully again, surmising to himself that the geography of the valley was not unlike a funnel, the upper end of which was inserted into the hills behind them and the lower section of which was the flat expanse on which they had camped, and which opened out into a wide, triangular area where the valley emerged from the hills.

From the entrance to his tent, he looked at the sky and estimated that he had just minutes to make the decision as to what he should do next. The terrain was such that there was a possibility that a flash flood could cause severe damage in the camp; but then, the storm was already gathering and, if they were going to move to higher ground, they would have to do so quickly. There was very little time in which to act. There would be, he knew, reluctance to move but the danger was imminent.

He was momentarily angry with himself that he had not understood the immediacy of the situation before, but then he dismissed the feeling. There was too much to be done – and too little time in which to do it.

***

It was Alison who woke first. The noise from the house was phenomenal. Every part of it seemed to be rattling or creaking and groaning. From outside came occasional unidentified crashes and sounds of destruction.

She reached out in the darkness towards a box of matches. Finding it, she moved to sitting on the edge of the bed and then struck a match and lit a candle. She noticed that there was a strong movement of air in the room which caused the candle's flame to wander disconcertingly. She looked briefly across at Kirk where he lay with just the lower half of his body beneath the covers.

The light of the candle illuminated the smoothness of his back. For a moment she was distracted but then the noise of the storm intruded on her thoughts again. The house seemed secure. There might be some damage but with only candlelight available and with just the two of them there, she felt rather helpless to do anything for the moment. Shivering with the cold, she crawled back into bed, not worrying about whether or not she disturbed Kirk as he lay, apparently oblivious to her movements. She felt sure that the storm would soon disturb him anyway.

She waited, listening to the winds whistling around the chimneys. She thought that she could hear glass smashing and pots in the back yard being flung about. Eventually, she could stand it no more and shook him urgently, at first calling to him in little more than a loud whisper, but then realising that anything less than a shout would not be heard above the noise around them. In a final loss of patience, she yelled "Kirk!" almost straight into his ear.

Unlike her previous efforts, this seemed to galvanise him into wakefulness.

"What is it? What's the matter?" His tone was fractious, bad-tempered.

"Don't you hear it?"

"Hear what? What's going on?" he asked, but then she put a finger on his lips and said, "Listen".

Despite his irritation, he paused and did as she bid him. The crashing and the destruction that was taking place around them could clearly be heard. Out of past habit, he wondered briefly if his car was safe, standing where he and Rose had parked it, at the front of the house – but, more significantly, close to the edge of the woods.

Alison had shifted position and had propped herself up on one elbow.

"You hear it now?" she asked, her voice full of tension and urgency.

Belatedly, he was beginning to realise why Alison was so anxious. They were powerless to prevent what was happening outside and yet they were enormously dependent on the security that the house gave them.

He lay looking at her in the amber glow of the candlelight. There had been signs of the oncoming storm earlier in the evening, but they had ignored them. He moved closer to her, putting an arm around her shoulders and drawing her closer. She put her head on his chest, briefly reassured but still alert to the fury of the storm and to an overwhelming sense that the house was straining to maintain its grip on the earth. She dozed for a moment or two but then they were both startled by a roar that rose above the incessant din.

"The roof's coming off." Kirk was suddenly aware of what was happening. He muttered the realization to himself but then an instant later yelled the message to Alison, "The roof's coming off! We need to get out of here!"

Barely conscious of their actions, they leapt out of bed. Out of habit, Kirk grabbed his dressing gown from the back of the door and threw Alison's to her. She pulled it round her quickly and picked up the candle she had lit earlier. Miraculously, it was still alight, despite the air currents that were now eddying round the room. She sheltered it with her hand and guided them both through the door and onto the landing. Immediately, they found themselves yelling and cursing with pain as their bare feet came into contact with the debris that had rained down from above. Pieces of smashed tile, ceiling plaster and roof insulation littered the floor where the storm, in the blindness of its force, had simply ripped away a jagged section of roof and distributed its wreckage into the house and the garden below. The damage was much worse than above the bedroom. Alison forced herself to look up. Far above her head, clouds and fleeting patches of starry sky could be seen jaggedly framed in the wreckage of the roof.

She attempted to see a way through the rubbish littering the floor. By the flickering candle, she grabbed Kirk by the elbow and did her best to steer him towards the stairs. She could see that he was still yelling with pain but in the din from above them, she could not hear him.

Moments later, they were picking their way down the stairs. She guided them into the front room where, in the darkness, she reached for the light switch and then felt momentarily foolish as she remembered that there had been no electricity for weeks.

For some reason, this simple mistake caught the raw edge of her feelings, sensitised as they already were by the damage to her house. When Kirk stumbled into the room moments later, she flung her arms around him and wept into his chest. He was taken by surprise but then held her in his arms, doing his best to reassure her. He drew her onto the settee.

For the moment, she had had enough of their situation.

"Why is everything so bloody, bloody awful..."

Her fear and sadness were mingled with frustration. They had survived all this time after the battle and the continuing downward spiral of life around them, but now this stupid, mindless storm was wrecking her house and heaping even more hardships upon them than those they had already endured.

As she sobbed, she realised that her crying was futile. For a few brief moments, she had felt overwhelmed. There was after all so much to cry about – her husband, Jed and Rose, her family. If she began to cry for everything that had happened, when would she stop? They needed all their energy just to survive. She could not afford the luxury of tears.

Kirk was murmuring something to her. She strained to hear, lifting her head to do so.

"Don't cry, love. There's nothing we can do now. We'll have to wait until morning."

His words drew her thoughts away from the sombre litany of woes that had rehearsed itself so rapidly in her head moments before she had begun to sob. Slowly, she brought her feelings under control again.

They had made love earlier in the day, immersed in pleasure and oblivious to what was happening in the world outside. She wondered again how they would manage when the time came for her baby to be born. There would be no hospital staff standing by, no anaesthetics to dull the pain. She wondered if it would be more than she could endure.

She knew, though, as she lay thinking, that life had to continue and that she was part of its persistence. She pushed herself closer to Kirk, who had already fallen asleep. There was foolishness, perhaps even a kind of egotism, in supposing that they had any kind of control over what was happening to them. Tomorrow would have to take care of itself – until there were no more tomorrows.

***

The trucks growled their way through ever increasing amounts of mud. Thorndike had decided to move food, oil and other essential supplies away from the stream which, even now, looked deceptively innocent. To many of his men it seemed crazy that they should be moving so much equipment simply because of a remote possibility that the piddle of water flowing along one side of the site might flood during the oncoming storm.

It began with a few large spots of rain followed by a brief lull. Then the rain began to fall again with increased intensity and the wind blew with a force that seemed intent on smashing away everything in its path.

There was now so much happening that Thorndike's critics forgot their grumbling and stepped up the tempo with which they were carrying out their orders. It had begun to look as though there might be some flooding after all – and they could ill afford to lose any of their supplies. A trio of food trucks had begun travelling across the site toward higher ground when the middle truck, which had been forced by the contours to follow in the path of the truck in front, began to wallow in the mud churned up by the leader.

The huge wheels on the truck made it almost impossible for soldiers to help by pushing. A towing chain was found from somewhere and anchored between the front truck, now on firmer ground, and the second, the driver of which waited patiently to be towed out of the worsening mire.

The rain had become torrential and, backed by a roaring wind, was quickly drenching anyone forced to venture into its driving downpour. Those who did, soon found it almost impossible to keep their feet and involuntarily slipped and slid like drunkards into the rapidly extending puddles of water that were accumulating in the dips and hollows around them.

Thorndike had found some waterproof clothing and stood on a small rise of ground, trying to assess the scene around him. The front truck would almost certainly make it and might just manage to tow the following truck out of trouble, but the third truck had an almost impossible task unless, like its predecessor, it could be hitched to another powerful vehicle on firmer ground.

He quickly scanned the rest of the site, sweeping his eyes steadily from the lower end where the stream descended through a dense cover of trees, up towards the point at which it emerged from the 'V' of the steep-sided valley behind him.

He was struggling in the incessant wind and rain to keep his footing, and although he had excellent eyesight, observation was becoming very difficult. Despite this, he noted with momentary satisfaction that the tents had remained firmly anchored in their positions although they were clearly taking a battering. There was just one small tent at the top of the site that seemed to be in trouble and was about to lift off in the wind's onslaught; gradually, the ropes and pegs tore loose until it resembled a large, camouflaged flag flapping furiously in the wind and straining to disappear over a neighbouring hedge.

The stream by now was brimming the banks and tumbling down its course in a turmoil of muddy water, carrying with it branches and other debris from the trees in the valley. With a certain amount of alarm, Thorndike could see that the volume of water was increasing by the minute and that it would very shortly be over the banks and swilling its way across the site. It was clear that anchoring the tents against the wind had become an irrelevance. Instead, it was the protection of his soldiers' lives that was now becoming an issue.

He had barely had time to register this thought when he became aware of slight trembling of the ground beneath his feet which steadily increased in a crescendo of movement until he could plainly feel it as a pronounced vibration rising up through the soles of his boots. Then all sensations were overwhelmed by unfettered amazement and dismay as a vast towering wall of water roared out of the valley in an all-obliterating flood of destruction. Thorndike was tumbled over and over in the cascading torrent of disaster, propelled with a force that would not allow him to get his head above the water.

Then, with a slam, he stopped. Something had blocked his path. Concussed and winded, he desperately tried to maintain his grip on the trunk of the tree against which the water had plastered him, whilst at the same time striving to get his head above the surface.

He finally succeeded, making use of the water's force to pin himself against the tree whilst also managing to get just enough freedom to surface and begin gulping down desperately needed air. For what seemed a long time but was in reality just seconds, he lay pinned upright against the tree, grateful for its huge girth but battling against the surging mass of water to force air down into his lungs.

Eventually, shaking with exertion and shock, he forced his head around until he could see the part of the torrent that lay behind his left shoulder. Some yards back, he could see a vehicle jammed athwart two trees. The vehicle lay on its side with its wheels towards the spate and its camouflaged roof just visible against the black of the pine trunks against which it had lodged.

The current from that side of the torrent swept not in a straight course but instead across towards the tree where Thorndike was pinned in sodden desperation. At the moment where his straining glance was returning to the fissures of the tree bark in front of him, he suddenly caught the briefest glimpse of army clothing being swept along in the flood. It was riding rapidly in the current towards him. Instinctively he forced out an arm and clenched his fingers into a steel grip on the sodden material. A broad pair of shoulders bobbed to the surface then a mass of black, matted hair. He recognised the individual; it was Williams – Corporal Williams.

Aided by a brief slackening in the current, Thorndike edged a little further round to the right of the tree trunk, drawing Williams after him. Involuntarily, William's head struck the trunk a glancing blow. It had a salutary effect and instead of knocking him out, caused him to rear up his head with a yell of pain. Spitting leaves and other debris from his mouth, he surfaced into painful, white-faced consciousness against the trunk of the tree.

The two men lay gasping, unable to move any further from the precarious positions in which they were pinned by the numbing flood. Thorndike tried to yell encouragement to Williams, but against the incessant din of the water, he was unable to make himself heard.

For what seemed an interminable time, they hung on, their hands devoid of all sensation, until an increase in the flow of water and a slight shift in the currents arbitrarily peeled them away from the trunk and out into the main course of the flood. Here, alternately bowled over and over in both the depths and the shallows of the cataract, they were first drowned and then tumbled around in an eddying pool that captured them in its ceaseless motion, but which would not then release them again into the torrent that had swept them into their restless grave.

Few survived the outpouring of the water from the hills. Soldiers, civilians, animals, machines, vegetation, even rocks and boulders caught in the water's irresistible might were swept on and on until, very gradually, the driving downpour began to slacken and then, eventually, to cease. Hours later, the flow of water slowly ebbed in volume until the flood became a sullen, gliding mass making its way to the sea. Darkness came and there was bitter chill in the slowly subsiding howl of the wind.

When daylight came, it looked down upon a landscape that was inundated with water. Huddled where they could find a refuge from the storm, birds waited out the weather's fury, until at last they could fly again and begin once more their ceaseless hunt for food.

In natural succession, the water birds preceded those who could only survive at the water's edge until islands slowly emerged on which all could take rest and where some could find a meal.

Darkness and daylight came and went again before the carrion birds found that they could pick and tear at the many corpses, big and small, strewn across the landscape – and not excluding those which bore the shredded remains of army uniforms.

***

A little further inland, the weather confined Kirk and Alison to the house for two days. They were forced to pick away at the clearing up and to make gloomy decisions about which parts of the house they could still use as living space.

Then, jointly, after a great deal of peering through the windows, they decided that they could stand their confinement no longer and ventured outside. For lack of practical alternatives, they plodded along the path around the periphery of the wood. They had travelled some way when they saw further along the path another couple gazing towards the imposing exterior of Andrew's farmhouse. As they drew closer, Kirk thought that he remembered them from the meeting in Andrew's barn, but Alison recognised them immediately.

"It's Janey and her husband Will!" she exclaimed excitedly.

By now, the couple had noticed them approaching and Alison yelled to them.

"Hey, Janey, Will!"

The two couples now gradually converged until the two women finally hurried towards each other, Alison at something approaching a run and Janey, although she was the younger woman, at a more measured pace. Kirk and Will also approached one another, eventually grasping outstretched hands in a handshake that managed to be at once both tentative in its beginning and strong in its subsequent grasp. Then they stood back as slightly bemused bystanders whilst the two women continued to hug and kiss each other.

Alison was uncharacteristically extrovert in her greeting.

"Janey, how you doing? How are you?"

Janey, slightly overwhelmed, finally managed to say, "I'm fine, Allie! Really good! How about you?"

Kirk had never heard anyone call Alison "Allie" but since formality was clearly pointless, he let it go unremarked, and anyway, the two women appeared to have forgotten that the men were there.

Alison drew closer to Janey, her mouth slightly open in excited surprise. She gave her friend a gentle hug and then stood back in surprise.

"Hey Janey, what's this?" she exclaimed and then, extending her hand towards her friend, ran her fingers very gently over the roundedness that was just perceptible beneath Janey's coat.

Janey did not try to draw back but patiently let her friend continue running her hand over the slight roundedness of her abdomen.

"Is this what I think it is...or are you just putting on weight?"

Janey's reply was coy, teasing out the guessing game a little longer.

"Well, I haven't stopped eating carefully, if that's what you mean."

"You know that's not what I mean. You're pregnant, aren't you? You're expecting!"

There seemed little point in denying it so with a large smile, Janey replied, "Yes I am."

Alison took Janey by the arm and drew her to one side – for by now, the two men were engaged in a conversation of their own.

"When's the baby due?" asked Alison.

"Mid-November – should be about the 20th," replied Janey. "I worked it out on the calendar in Will's office – probably one of the few still in existence."

Alison grinned. "That's great news – although I'd have said it might be sooner than that. How are you feeling?"

"Not bad – well, good generally although I had a lot of morning sickness a few weeks back. I suppose that's only to be expected. It could be a few more weeks yet before I'm free of it."

Alison laughed. "You seem very philosophical about it all. I'm not sure that I would be."

"What do you mean?" retorted Janey. "You've already had two. You know all about it."

Alison was not so sure. "It was a long time ago."

Janey could see that the subject of Alison's children was going to be a sensitive topic. She looked across at Will and Kirk. They were still deep in conversation. She decided to try a different approach.

"I've thought about you. I've been wondering about you for months – ever since the meeting in Andrew's barn – and then the battle... What happened to Jed...and Rose?" Her voice trailed away.

Alison looked sadly at her younger friend and explained about Andrew's family then about Jed and Rose. Janey could see at several points that she was close to tears but thought it best to let her continue. Finally, Alison told her about Kirk. There was another long and difficult pause.

Then Janey said, "We were on the other side of The Ridge. I saw the jet go over and I heard the bomb. I didn't know what had happened. Will and I had talked about it and were sure that Andrew's family must have been killed. It's terrible. I'm so sorry...I don't know what to say... But I'm pleased that you and Kirk are together. I'm sure that's better for both of you."

Alison looked away but then, feeling the need to talk about something happier than the events she had just related, she began to think about something of which she had only recently told Kirk. She rapidly pondered the wisdom of the sentence that was forming in her head. In the circumstances, Janey might be shocked. Then, in the end, she simply blurted it out.

"I'm pretty sure that I'm pregnant as well!"

Janey wondered if she had heard correctly. For a moment, she could manage only a puzzled, quizzical look.

Seeing her expression, Alison said, "It's not so strange you know!" Her exclamation was indignant and just a little too loud; the two men looked briefly in their direction. She waited before turning back to her friend. Janey looked anxious.

"I know that! I know you can get pregnant!" she spluttered.

What had begun as a piece of clumsily presented news then seemed likely to dissolve into a fit of embarrassed, slightly hysterical giggling.

"How do you know?" she began, looking a little red in the face. "I mean what signs have you had?"

Alison's embarrassed look became one of bemused incredulity.

"What?" she exclaimed. "Call yourself a nurse? The usual signs of course, sickness, wanting strange mixtures of food – the whole – the whole shooting match." It was the wrong phrase entirely but then, seeing Janey's initial reaction and feeling mildly embarrassed anyway, she was struggling to retain any sense of seriousness.

"Does Kirk...?" began Janey. "I mean, does he..." She was spluttering again.

Alison looked at her friend with a knowing look. "Oh yes," she said, deliberately misunderstanding the question. "Quite frequently. In fact,

I'd say that was the trouble...really."

They dissolved into mutual laughter.

The sounds of amusement from the two women caused a slight pause in the conversation between Will and Kirk. Will, who often tended to be taciturn, was, for the moment, a willing partner in conversation.

"No, Kirk," he was saying. "You don't need to worry. We can all feed ourselves here – very well. We've got everything we need."

Kirk agreed but needed the conversation. The last time he had spoken to another male was when he had spoken to a soldier who had been given the task of removing bodies, after the battle on The Ridge.

"It'll take a lot of hard work."

Will smiled. "Of course – it always does."

Kirk had already related to Will an edited version of the episode with the pheasant and the bow and arrow. Will had laughed but managed to stay on the right side of tactfulness.

"There's lots of ammunition at the farm," he said, meaning the place that they still referred to as 'Andrew's Farm'.

"But don't you feel...well, a bit strange, going in there?" asked Kirk.

"I do," confirmed Will, "but I need what's there. I mean, since we were talking about guns and ammunition, there's enough there to last me – probably both of us – a lifetime."

"We won't be able to depend for ever on what's left of the past," responded Kirk.

Will agreed. "No we won't. I'm sure you're right – but we can buy ourselves some time. It will take us a while to make tools and weapons that we don't have at the moment."

The four of them had now been there for some while. Eventually Will said first to Kirk and then to the two women, "Janey and I need to get back. After that storm there's a huge amount to do – but we must meet up again!"

Kirk nodded. "We must," he agreed. "We can help each other a lot."

Alison and Janey had already agreed to help one another and gained as much reassurance as they could from each other about a situation in which they were both expecting to give birth but in which the only medical expertise available would be Janey's.

Alison said, "We've all got huge amounts of work to do but let's make a definite arrangement. Why don't we meet up here again, a week from now at, say, ten o'clock?"

Janey thought that it was an excellent idea but commented incredulously, "You mean you still have a calendar – and clocks that work?"

Relieved to have at least found two other survivors, Kirk wondered why they were being so formal about their arrangements with each other. He said, "That's great as a definite arrangement, but I think now that we've rediscovered each other as neighbours, we should be able to call on each other whenever we need to."

Janey agreed. "Will and I haven't come across any other survivors up here yet – so we need to help each other. For the moment, there is no-one else. We're all there is!"

The others nodded, smiling in recognition that she was right, but both couples were deeply relieved that they had found each other. The prospect of companionship and mutual help was enormously reassuring after the isolation they had endured in the aftermath of the battle. A small but very significant step had been taken.

It was the beginning of what proved to be a long and supportive friendship that was ended only by the natural processes of life.

* * *

Many years later, however, in old age, Kirk reflected that for all their apparent openness and pleasure in each other's company, beneath their friendship there had been secrets and tensions between Janey and Will that he had only gradually been able to understand. His thoughts had gone back to when Janey's baby was born. At first, Will had seemed every inch the attentive husband and father but then, as the child began to grow and develop, the picture had changed.

There had also been the question of the mysterious 'Robert' – the individual who had first introduced himself to Kirk as 'Mark Ridgeway' so long ago. Years later, in a conversation with Will, Kirk had referred to the enigmatic 'Robert' and noticed that he bristled at the mere mention of his name. He decided, out of tact, not to talk about him again and learned only later, what had happened to bring about such a reaction.

Alison, too, when she had recovered from the considerable risk and pain of childbirth, had pondered the relationship that Janey had with her child and, for that matter, the changing relationship that Janey had with her ceaselessly working husband.

As the time passed, matters subtly changed, memories faded. Mutual reliance and friendship had increased – but the shadows of the past had never quite dissipated and, over the years, had gradually borne out their consequences.

Meanwhile, the children had grown and played together, aware only of those points of personal history that their parents chose to tell them about – and their world had expanded – though only a little because very few – so very few – had been fortunate enough to survive the great collapse, the catastrophe that had infested all but the obscure places, the hidden backwaters, the places where the sparse remnants of the human race could hardly be bothered to go without good reason.

To Kirk, in retrospect, it had seemed only a few short years before he and Alison, Janey and Will had passed into old age and their children in turn had grown into adulthood, producing grandchildren for them all to adore and endlessly fuss over whilst they had continued the struggle to survive in the small island of existence that was theirs.

* * *

PART 3

CHAPTER 20

NORTH BY SOUTH-WEST

Joel stood still for a moment and held the compass steady, waiting patiently until the needle had ceased swinging to and fro. It confirmed that they were heading South-west. He was tall, well built from years of work on his parents' farm and had a good head of thick curly brown hair. A blend of both seriousness and good humour ran through his family so that his companions found him an easy person to travel with. His parents and grandparents between them had also ensured that he had an education which, by the standards of the times, ensured that he took an informed and intelligent interest in the world around him.

The journey had already taken them nearly a week and although it was proving arduous, Dobbs, their horse, was untroubled by it. He was a black shire with a white blaze running down between his eyes and over his nose. Long, white hair fell in 'feathers' from below his knees down to his hooves. At over 18 hands and with the strength to match, he was both an asset and a companionable friend. It was his steady stride that set the rhythm and tempo of their journey. For him, the journey was little more than regular exercise with meals thrown in. The large panniers that were mounted on either side of his back, carried not only food and equipment needed for the journey but also four valuable fleeces that Joel and the others would use to trade for their needs whilst they were in Falmouth – the destination for which they were heading.

Unlike Dobbs, Joel found that there was a certain tedium in the combination of incessant physical effort and discomfort; a tedium from which he escaped into a world of his own for long stretches of time. At first, he had thought about the farm a great deal. His parents would be having to work extra hard there now because they had come to depend on him, but then, after he and his companions had been trudging along their route for several days, he realised that for a while at least, he needed to forget about The Ridge and Somerland and concentrate instead on the task that they had been given.

They were close to midsummer and the evenings were long. They continued on their way for a while before deciding to set up camp for the night, next to a river that flowed down from the moor over which they would travel on the following day. Sam and Berta put up the first of the two tents that they were carrying, leaving Joel to put up the smaller of the two for himself. He had eaten already. The meal had taken a while to prepare but they were still able to get hold of vegetables along the way and Joel had skinned a rabbit that he had snared at a previous site. It smelled good as they roasted it – and tasted even better.

He watched Berta and felt a little sick with envy. Soon she would go into the tent with Sam, and everything around would seem to fall silent. He felt jealous, left out. Perhaps she preferred Sam's steady, patient character? He was just slightly younger than both Joel and Berta, and on occasions they took advantage of his relative youth by teasing him.

Fortunately, his good nature determined that he never became resentful about it. He was a little shorter than Joel but had a wiry toughness well suited to the journey they were making. His youthful, outdoor face alternated between the frown of someone concentrating on the task before him, and the infectious grin and enthusiasm that he brought to conversations with his two friends. Like Joel, he was well accustomed to physical activity, and he strode about the camp site they had made for themselves with long, easy strides.

Joel watched Berta for a moment or two, letting his eyes rest on her and knowing that she was aware of his gaze. She was several inches less than his height and, this evening, she was wearing a dark blue dress that fell to about the middle of her calves. It had been a hot day and one which had yet to really cool down, so she wore nothing around her arms or shoulders. Her fair hair had been bleached by the sun and she had tied it back in a ponytail. Her fair skin, already tanned from the outdoor life that she led on her parents' farm, had become a deeper golden colour during the journey; they had now spent several days on the road and the weather had been hot.

At first, when they had set out on the journey, Berta had seemed detached, aloof from both him and Sam. She needed to share accommodation with one of them because there were only two tents and Dobb's panniers could not carry more. They should have discussed it before the journey began but had put it off because they had felt that it was an awkward topic. Then on the first evening, Berta had come to his tent saying that she wanted to talk. The conversation was not a success. She lay turned towards him, on his blanket, showing enough of her neck and shoulders to make him want her quite badly.

Returning from his reverie, he gazed at her again. Her dress was not completely shapeless; it showed the curve of her bottom, her straight back and the beautiful roundedness of her breasts. She turned to look briefly in his direction, giving him a fleeting smile and registering that she had known that he was gazing at her.

Then she ducked into the tent. In a moment or two he would have to get out of his own tent and find a way to keep himself cool on what promised to be a very warm night. He remembered that first evening again when he had wanted so much to reach out and touch her skin, but he could not do it. He could not put out his fingers towards her even once. Instead, he had sat awkwardly, unusually tongue-tied and clasping his hands together. As much as he wanted her, foremost in his mind was the journey on which their parents had sent them, and besides, he knew very little about women. He was a little bit afraid of her and frightened that if he touched her, she would be offended and that he had been wrong all the time about the signals that he thought she was sending him.

Sam had joined them a little while later. Joel had chosen to put up the smaller of the two tents and with three of them in it, they were quite cramped. Between them, they had then decided that Sam and Berta would share the larger tent for the duration of the journey. Now Joel lay on his back, gazing out and up at the warm summer sky and the swifts and swallows swooping about above the landscape of the moor over which they were travelling, feeling excluded and wondering what sort of relationship it was that Berta shared with Sam in the confines of the double tent.

As the three of them settled down, the evening fell silent and a kind of breathing peace fell over their small encampment, leaving the world to the creatures of the night and the slowly appearing stars.

***

For some time, Joel was unable to sleep. Instead, although it had been a long and active day, he lay drowsing. The field in which they had camped was fairly rough, so he had to keep shifting position in order to avoid outright discomfort. The heat of the day still lingered on. Eventually, he began to drift away from thoughts and sensations of where they were, and instead, started to think about his family.

As usual, his first and longest thoughts were about his grandfather. To most people it would probably have seemed strange that he often spent more time thinking about his grandfather than he did his father. Joel thought that this was because in his childhood he had spent a great deal of time in his grandfather's company.

He did not blame his parents for their apparent lack of attentiveness. It had always been like that and as soon as he was old enough to help on the farm, he began to understand that since they kept both crops and animals, they were kept busy in every part of the year.

The first time he had seen his grandfather's name was on a note written by his grandmother. He knew that she must have written it for some special purpose because paper was very precious. The paper had been folded in two and on the front of the folded note was a drawing – a picture of an eagle soaring over the landscape. Inside, his grandmother had written simply "Happy Birthday, Kirk. With all my love, A."

It had taken Joel a while to discover that his grandmother's name was 'Alison' but then one day, she had taken him out with her on one of his first visits to her friend whom he had always known as 'Janey' and she had called out as they approached her farm, "Hey, Alison, we're over here."

Janey was out in her garden with Sam in tow, weeding between the vegetables.

His earliest memories of Janey were of the times that she came to visit his grandmother's house. She would sit and gossip with his grandmother in the kitchen. Grandfather Kirk would occasionally stop as well during the day but generally he was too preoccupied with his work – with which

Joel was often enlisted to help.

Some of Kirk's time was spent working on the garden and the other land that his family had started to cultivate, but a fair part of it was devoted to repairing the house. He once told Joel that this was because the house was a 'wreck' and he did not want the damp to get in and spoil his books, but if it had ever been in a state of disrepair, there was little sign of it in the years that Joel was growing up. His grandfather had spent a great deal of time hauling materials from one derelict building after another and using them to remedy the damage inflicted at various times by the numerous storms that had become both more frequent and more severe, so that during Joel's youth and childhood, the house had always seemed to be in good order.

Despite his general preoccupation with work, Joel's grandfather still found time to pore over his books – which was something else in which he would sometimes include Joel. His grandmother would mock his concern about his 'old books' or perhaps, his 'precious books', but it was never more than a joke, if only because she too could sometimes be found browsing her way along the shelves in the room that had become their library.

It was largely thanks to his grandparents that he first learned to read, both spending time with him as he tried to get to grips with the small number of children's books that they still had in their collection. In the years that he had spent on his parents' farm he was never short of teachers. His father James had inherited Grandfather Kirk's love of books – and of learning.

Joel did not think that the two things were necessarily identical because his father also taught him a great many things that could not be found in a book – at least, not the books in his grandfather's collection. He liked to learn practical things from his father. Grandfather Kirk was never truly a farmer although he had not shirked the constant round of activity needed to look after the cottage and the smallholding that he and Joel's grandmother had gradually developed.

Joel's father was no taller than his grandfather but was tough and wiry and always ambitious in a very practical way. Despite Grandfather Kirk's concerns, he had wanted to take in more and more land so that eventually, after a big argument with his father, he had left and set up home for himself in one of the semi-derelict cottages on what had been Andrew's

Farm. There, he was closer to Farmer Will, Janey's first husband, for whom he was already something of an apprentice and who taught him all that he could about farming and the many craft skills that went with it.

Joel's mother, Emma, was the daughter of an 'incomer' as the people of The Ridge called the few people from elsewhere that they allowed to settle amongst them. She had brown hair, a kind, homely face and a slightly plump figure that seemed at odds with her constant activity around the house and farm. Emma's mother, Charlotte, had moved to seek refuge on The Ridge shortly after the Great Collapse. Little was known about her other than that she had moved from a farm on the 'Levels' when her husband had died and that she had settled near Hatch End with a son from her first marriage. From her mother, Emma had inherited determination and warm heartedness but also an occasional tendency to melancholy.

She knew little of her father other than that he had been a hardworking farmer. There were no photographs of him since the science – and art – of photography had become consigned to history. A pencil sketch done by her mother showed an alert, rather good-looking man with dark hair and a moustache. Emma's mother had told her many times that she owed her love of being busy to her father. He had died whilst Charlotte was still a young child of an illness that had remained undiagnosed because medical expertise was in short supply on The Levels at that time.

Now the family mantle had fallen on Joel's shoulders. Together with Sam and Berta, he had been chosen to travel to Falmouth. From there they had to bring back a badly needed part for the wind turbine on which their tiny community depended for its electricity. The part had been imported because the ability to manufacture it in Britain no longer existed. Outside the three families whose young people were undertaking the journey, there was also a great deal of interest in their adventures. People from The Ridge rarely ventured away from their hilltop domain, but despite their caution, they were curious about the world outside and hoped that Joel, Sam and Berta would bring back a wealth of news.

The decision to send them had not been an easy one. Their families were loath to part with them and had agonised about the situations into which they might be going, but it was gradually recognised that they were the ones best suited to make the journey. The decision to send Berta had particularly caused both anxieties on the part of some and a raising of eyebrows on the part of others. In the end it was her grandmother, Janey, who insisted that she was the equal of any of the young males on The Ridge and that since her family would particularly benefit from the electricity the wind turbine would produce, she should be sent.

Joel gazed out through the open entrance of the tent, hoping that the night sky would distract him. He lay for some time with his head at that end of the tent trying to pick out the constellations that his grandfather had shown him. It was also much cooler to lie that way round and despite his attempts to keep track of the many falling stars that burned out their fleeting lives in the sky above him, neither the slowly receding heat of the day nor the unending spectacle of the night, could finally keep him from sleep.

He was woken by the buzzing of a fly which had become trapped in the tent. The sun was already making it too hot to stay wrapped inside his blanket. He crawled out to see what the day would hold.

The first thing that he did then was to rummage in his pack for the old towel and the ever-diminishing piece of home-made soap that his mother had given him just before he left. Next to the cloth in which he had wrapped the soap was a leather sheath containing a knife. Out of habit, he slid it out to look at the blade, which remained, through constant attention, keen and bright.

He put on just enough clothing – a shirt, the trousers he had now worn for several days, and his shoes – and walked across to a small river that ran down between steep banks of rock and soil. The water had a distinct brown colour which came from the peat through which the river flowed, further out on the moor. It took him several minutes to find a place where he could wash because the bed of the river was very uneven and was strewn with rocks and pebbles of various sizes. Finally, he found a place where the bed shelved into a curve of the river and where he could wade until he was knee-deep in water. He took off his clothes and laid them on the bank, placing next to them his towel and the sheath knife.

Despite the steadily increasing heat of the sun, the water was still initially cold as he began splashing himself. He moved a little further out onto a tongue of pebbles that reached across towards the opposite bank, knowing that at some point the water would become much deeper. Soon the water was just beneath his chin and his toes were only just touching the pebbles on the bottom. Then, briefly, he found himself swimming.

He turned himself around so that he faced back in the direction from which he had come and swam a few vigorous strokes to regain his footing on the pebbles. As he stood up, he was still waist deep in water and, cupping his hands, he scooped it up to splash his face.

Aware that his morning ritual was not yet complete, he waded and walked across to where he had left his knife, towel and clothes. His clothes, which had warmed in the sun, were covered in dust and other signs of their journey. Patiently, he washed both his shirt and trousers in turn and laid them on a large and rapidly warming rock to dry. They would not be fully dry when he put them on again, but the growing heat of the sun was such that a little dampness would be welcome.

Returning to his ritual, he softened the stubble on his chin with soap and water and then shaved away the whiskers with the razor-sharp blade of the knife. He ran his fingers repeatedly over his skin until finally he was satisfied with his efforts, washed the knife clean and dried it on the towel.

By now, he thought that Sam and Berta might have emerged from their tent; he made his way tentatively over the rocks and pebbles to peer over the top of the bank but as yet there was no sign of them. Turning back, he managed to find a grassy hollow in which he could sit and warm himself whilst he waited for his clothes to dry and his friends to wake.

Joel was usually patient and methodical – habits he had learned from both his parents – but this morning, he wanted to be on the move. Fortunately, sounds of Sam and Berta stirring in their tent were soon to be heard. He went to check his clothes. As expected, they were still quite damp, but he put them on and then walked barefoot across the coarse grass, carrying his shoes and everything else in his hands.

"Hey Joel, how you doing?" Sam had emerged from the tent and called across to him as he approached. His hair was tousled, and his clothes looked as though he had quickly thrown them on.

"I'm OK," replied Joel. "Is Berta awake?"

By way of reply, Berta's head appeared between the flaps of the tent. Her eyes were still partly shut, and her face had the slightly pinched appearance of someone who had only just emerged from sleep.

"Of course I'm awake," she said indignantly but then gave a huge yawn which she was unable to stifle because she was using both hands to clutch the material of the tent around her.

A few minutes later, she emerged dressed in a long shirt that looked as though it had been given to her by her father, and walked with her towel, down to the river. Sam busied himself, trying to put together some breakfast; that morning; it would largely consist of fruit they had managed to barter for or find along the route. They needed to eat because the latest stage would be a long one, and all three of them hoped that it would be the last full day of their journey.

Having found the fruit, Sam set it out in the battered wooden bowls that they had used throughout the journey. Then he walked across to check on Dobbs who was grazing on the grass below a nearby tree. Dobbs tossed his head and gave a welcoming whinny as he approached.

Berta meanwhile had finished bathing in the river and crested the top of the bank, still towelling her hair which, now that it was released from the ponytail in which she generally kept it, was quite long. Small patches of dampness spotted the shirt she was wearing as she came in from the sun and tried to find a convenient rock under the trees.

Sam had drifted away from Dobbs and had gone into the tent, after which he headed for the river, as the others had done. It would be a good day on which to start out by feeling clean and fresh.

Berta found a rock just out of the sun and sat cross legged with her bowl of fruit. Joel went to join her, finding a rock of his own and stretching out his long legs before him.

"Phew, it's hot!" commented Berta. "Did you find it hard to sleep last night, Jo?"

"Yes," said Joel. "It took me a long time to get off, but I stuck my head out of the entrance of the tent – and that made it lot cooler."

Berta smiled. "Yeah, we had the flaps of the tent open as well but somehow I was still hot."

"Do you think it's any hotter than when we were really young – you know, when we were still little kids running around on the farm?"

"Yeah, I think so," she said. "I've got used to the summers being like this, but it still seems to get hotter every year. Just look at this place. It's all shrivelled up. One spark and the whole moor would be alight."

"You're right," agreed Joel.

Berta had seen countryside burst into flames before. Her father's farm was still littered with remnants of the past including glass from broken bottles which would sometimes act as a lens and focus the sun's heat on the tinder-like remains of plants.

Berta tried not to think about it. So far, they had always managed to damp the fires down and they had never had a problem close to the house.

"We'll need our hats today," continued Joel. "And around the middle of the day, Dobbs will need a break, preferably in a place where there's water."

"Huh," said Berta. "Not just Dobbs. We'll need a break too."

She looked up. Sam was making his way back from the river. He came and slumped down beside them and began munching away at the fruit.

"What I wouldn't do for a nice piece of meat," he commented.

"I could make a guess," said Joel.

"Oh yeah, Jo, and what would that be?"

Joel ignored him but then said, "We were just talking about the heat. We may have quite a long trek across this moorland. Once we get away from here, there'll be very few trees, but by midday, we'll need some shelter from the sun."

Sam forgot about his joking and listened intently. "So what does the map tell us?" he asked. "When will we get there?"

"Well, not today," replied Joel but then, seeing the frowns on their faces, he added, "But we should be there in no more than two days. Here, have a look for yourselves." He waited as they came to look at the map. It was an old map from his grandfather's library, and, in many respects, it was woefully out of date, but it was all that they had.

He set the map down on a tree stump and traced out the route that he hoped they would be able to follow.

"When we leave the moor behind, I want us to head for Mitchell and then drop down towards this little place here – Shortlanesend."

"If it still exists," commented Berta.

"There may well be little left of it," agreed Joel. "But we need to head just to the west of Truro and then turn south towards Penryn and Falmouth."

"Wouldn't it be quicker to go just to the east of Truro – or even through Truro itself?" asked Sam.

"I agree it looks as though it would be quicker," replied Joel, "but when we get closer to Truro, I don't think that we'll be able to cross the Truro River."

"So why don't we simply go through Truro?" persisted Sam.

"It's possible that we could," said Joel appearing to agree, "but we've avoided the towns so far and, for all we know, Truro is ruled by gangs just as much as any of the other towns we've heard about. I don't want to risk it – at least, not before we have to."

"And I'd rather not take the chance either," said Berta. "We'll have enough problems when we get to Falmouth."

"Which at this rate, could be sometime never!" exclaimed Sam impatiently.

Joel and Berta looked at him, understanding his frustration. Then Berta said, "Joel's right. We have to succeed and going into Truro or going east of it is too big a risk."

Sam scowled, looking past them into the distance.

Seeking to lighten the mood, Berta said, "It isn't just you, Sam. I can't wait to have a proper meal and some clean clothes, perhaps even a bath."

"Hmm," said Sam. "A proper bath would be great, but it could depend on what the water situation's like."

"It's by the sea!" laughed Berta. "There's water everywhere!"

"Unfortunately, not the kind that you can drink and I'm not sure that I want to take a bath in salt water," said Joel.

"Just joking," said Berta. "No need to be so serious. Anyway, a salt bath would be a big improvement for you, Sam. You've begun to smell absolutely dis... gusting!"

Sam gave a snort of indignation and launched himself at her, but she was too quick for him and skipped out of the way before running towards the tent. Joel watched with a smile, quietly wishing that they would include him in their pranks. Sam chased Berta twice around the tent before she finally dived into it. Joel was surprised to see that Sam did not follow her but stood awkwardly at the entrance to the tent before making a show of moving off to pick up the bowls that they had used for breakfast.

Joel stood up and walked across to his tent and belongings. Although it was a well-practised routine, breaking camp was a bit of a chore and he wanted to get on with it.

It took them just a short time to pack up their few belongings. Some they put into the packs that each of them carried, whilst larger items such as the tents were put into panniers strapped on either side of Dobbs' back. Dobbs tossed his head and swished his tail, trying to ward off the flies.

Although it was hot, they were looking forward to the journey. As soon as they were ready, they left the shade of the trees, crossing the river by means of an old clapper bridge and striking out along a rough and undulating track that would take them further out onto the moor.

The heat shimmered over the heather and butterflies fluttered across the face of those moorland plants that were able to survive the baking temperature. A lark had risen into the sky and the liquid notes of its song cascaded down to them.

It was Sam's turn to ride on Dobbs. Joel and Berta struggled along, trying to stay close to Dobbs and, despite the heat, chatting to one another, reassured by the familiarity of each other's voices. The wide brims of their hats cast shadows such that in the glare, the whites of their eyes were the most visible parts of their faces.

From his elevated position on Dobbs' back, Sam sympathised with the two walkers.

"We could do with that old car outside your grandad's house," he commented.

"I don't think so," replied Joel. "There's not much of it left."

"Why's that then?" asked Sam.

"You know as well as I do, Sam. It's been there nearly 50 years. It's rotting away and it's got plants growing in it. Anyway, he stripped everything useful off it long ago."

Sam looked thoughtful. "Seems strange to think about it though," he said. "Something that wasn't alive but that could move along by itself."

"People knew how to make such things when my grandfather was young," observed Joel.

"We could do it now if we really wanted to," said Berta. "My dad says we could make 'fuel' from the crops we grow."

"Ooh – 'fuel'!" exclaimed Sam, mockingly. The other two took no notice of him.

"Not without using up valuable land that we use for growing food," replied Joel. "It takes every inch to grow what we need for our families, let alone trying to grow a surplus for trade in the village."

"All the same," said Berta wistfully, "it must have been rather special to ride around in one of those things."

"You have to remember that it was 'the People Before' who wrecked the world with their machines. My parents say that we don't want to go back to that way of living." Joel had resorted to the strange phrase – 'the People Before' – that he had heard his parents use so many times, when talking about the society of which now only his grandparents had direct memories.

"Huh," said Berta. "Do we have a choice? I've heard that those people were so greedy and selfish that they were like locusts. They stripped the world of everything that they could find."

Sam agreed. "Yeah, they left us nothing," he said.

Joel took a different view. "I like things the way they are. At least we have a good place to live and plenty of food."

"But we have to work for all of it," complained Berta. "My mum says that in my grandmother's time, you could just go into a giant shop – a 'supermarket' – and buy anything that you needed straight off the shelf."

"Some people could do that, but I don't think it was true for everyone – not even for people in this country," replied Joel. "My grandfather says that millions of people were starving."

"I know," said Berta. "We've all heard the same things, but I like to imagine sometimes how good it would be, even if it was just for a short while, to live in the kind of luxury that my grandparents lived in, back in the twentieth century."

"I think that there are probably still millions of people out there starving to death," said Sam, momentarily ignoring Berta's comments.

"You're probably right," agreed Joel. "But we don't really know much about the outside world because we don't encourage visitors."

"OK," said Sam, "But every so often, we get someone in the village begging for food, and sometimes, they've travelled quite a distance before they get to us."

"Yeah," said Berta. "The last visitor we had brought quite a lot of news. My dad seemed to know him already."

"He wasn't begging though," objected Sam.

"No, he wasn't." Joel had met the visitor. "He'd been to the Ridge before. He sometimes acts as a messenger. He took a letter about the part for the wind turbine down to Falmouth and came back again about three weeks later, with the reply."

"I remember all that." Sam seemed a little indignant. "Sometimes we have to talk to people from outside to get what we need... but it's hard to know if we can trust them."

"I know what you mean," agreed Joel. "We're quite lucky to be living on the Ridge. We have most of what we need but now and again we need to trade with people from outside for the things we don't have."

"All the same," said Sam, "we don't want strangers nosing around up there and knowing about everything we've got."

"I guess you're right," replied Joel. "But sometimes when we have plenty and others around us are starving, it feels to me as though we're being selfish."

"Huh," snorted Berta impatiently. "Selfish my..." Sam wagged his finger at her, stopping her momentarily. "Self-protection is more like it," she continued. "We've largely survived on The Ridge because we keep ourselves to ourselves."

"Well, perhaps, but really, we're almost as selfish as 'The People Before'." Joel seemed determined to have the last word on the subject.

Berta was indignant. "I wish you wouldn't use that stupid phrase. And anyway, I don't think so. Nobody could be that selfish."

Sam was getting tired of the conversation. "What's the name of this place we're going to? What's it called? Foulmouth?"

"Falmouth," corrected Joel, laughing. All three of them knew why they were travelling, but Sam liked to rehearse the reason every so often in order to justify to himself their present level of discomfort.

"You know the name of the place as well as we do," sighed Berta. "Your parents were there, just like mine and Joel's when it was all agreed. Why d'you have to keep asking?"

"I know! I know! We need the parts for the turbine. Too bad we don't make them on the Ridge."

"Yeah," replied Berta impatiently. "But we don't. We have to go to Falmouth. Nobody makes parts in Falmouth either, but they do have plenty of ships there. They bring them in on the ships."

Sam eased himself in Dobbs' saddle. "It still doesn't make complete sense to me," he persisted. "Why are we three travelling all this way? Why didn't our parents come themselves? It's not exactly safe – and as for sending a girl..." He let his voice trail away in obvious provocation.

Berta was not slow in rising to the bait. "I can look after myself!" she snorted. "And usually I end up looking after you as well!"

"OK," said Joel. "There's more than one reason. Our parents thought that we're the ones who can best be spared to make the journey. They're also expecting us to show that we can look after ourselves and take our share of responsibility." He gave Sam a meaningful sideways glance.

"Oh yeah," laughed Sam, "such as by staying home and having babies."

Berta's face became red with indignation. By way of reply she punched him hard in the leg.

"Ow!" he yelled, still laughing.

Joel frowned, irritated by Sam but also wondering why Berta's parents had sent her on the journey. Sam had been joking and it was true Berta was well able to take care of herself, but they knew that Falmouth was likely to have its share of roughnecks who would see her as 'fair game'.

Despite his misgivings, Joel decided to say nothing about that aspect of the journey and, turning instead to Sam, he commented: "I think for that, you can get down off the horse and let Berta ride for a while."

There was no immediate response from Sam, but Berta scowled at him. It was not the moment for her to show any kind of inclination to ride on Dobbs.

"Ride him yourself!" she said sideways to Joel, clearly angry with what she saw as his condescension.

Joel gave a silent, inward shrug. There were times when, as far as his two friends were concerned, it seemed impossible to 'get it right'.

Sam belatedly decided to scramble down from Dobbs, but Berta refused to take his place, walking instead by the horse's side as he clopped his way along the rough track.

They had now been travelling for some time. Although their hats shielded their heads from the sun, they also prevented the loss of body heat. Sam's face was beaded with perspiration.

"Anyone want some water?" he asked, proffering the water canteen. They took it in turns to swig from its contents, taking care to preserve some for later. Eventually Berta decided to forget her annoyance and swung herself into Dobbs' saddle.

"Changed your mind then?" asked Sam.

"Just be careful," she said. "I can spit on you from up here."

Sam grinned but decided that discretion was the better part of valour. Joel looked about them. The sun was still burning down upon the rolling moorland; they needed a rest and Dobbs needed water. He pulled his map from the side pocket of his pack and tried to study the route, but unless they stopped, it would be difficult to look at it in detail.

Fortunately, Berta from her elevated position on Dobb's back spotted one of the few clumps of trees to be found in this part of their route.

"Hey, up ahead!" she called down to Sam and Joel. "I can see some trees. A copse, I think!"

"Trees!" thought Joel with relief. They would be glad to rest in the shade for a while. It was also several hours since Dobbs had last had a drink and they needed to find him some water.

Joel need not have worried. As they drew in from the dust of the road and under the shade of the trees, he could hear the sound of running water. Berta dismounted from Dobbs, who, without any further prompting, found his own way over to the stream that ran through the copse. There was a shallow pool that he could reach, and he lapped noisily at the water, his large and surprisingly pink tongue lolling from his mouth as he did so. Whilst he was drinking, Berta fastened him with a long tether to a nearby tree.

Since they had now been travelling for a number of days, this was another part of their waking hours for which they had a routine. Berta dug in her pack for the bread and meat that she had put there earlier that morning. Silently she handed Sam and Joel the 'sandwiches' that they had made shortly before they had set off.

Sam had managed to slice the remnants of rabbit meat into very thin pieces. They still tasted of the herbs that they had used to add flavour to the slices of rabbit. Joel savoured the meat but could only chew slowly at the bread – which was far from the best that he had ever tasted. It reminded him of the cardboard that Grandfather Kirk kept in his study. Fortunately, the apples that they had brought helped to take away the taste of the bread.

Having eaten, they gradually began to feel drowsy. Dobbs stood sentinel, patiently waiting amongst the trees and swishing his tail. Sam was the first to fall asleep. He lay on his side, his back towards the other two, and was soon quietly puffing his way into sleep. Berta had found a comfortable spot between them and propped against an old tree stump, began to doze so that her eyelids fluttered and her head lolled to one side.

For a while, Joel studied the map that his grandfather had given him. Although it was hopelessly out of date, it was a prized possession – and at least it gave them some idea of where they were going. Joel had found himself using large amounts of 'interpretation' as they travelled along, but so far, enough of the old routes remained for him to be able to make general sense of where they were going.

As he had thought, they would not get into Falmouth by nightfall; it would be some time the next day. He felt his concentration beginning to slide. In an attempt to stay awake, he propped himself against the tree trunk that Berta had also used as a support. Sleepily, he looked sideways at her. She seemed to be completely oblivious to the world. He decided that since he would have to give in to the irresistible somnolence that was enveloping his senses, he might as well be comfortable. He put out his legs and arranged himself as best he could against the tree trunk.

He was very close to sleep when he became aware of sweet-smelling fair hair tickling his cheek and lips. He opened his left eye just enough to see that Berta's head was slowly slumping onto his shoulder. He should have woken her perhaps – but then he did not want to offend her – or Sam. Her breath was now warm on his cheek. He did not mind. It was in some way comforting. His arm, however, was suffering from 'pins and needles' so he put it around her shoulders. She stirred slightly but did not wake. He too then slept, dreaming rather fitfully of a dark shape silhouetted against a pale sky and of Dobbs tugging against his tether and shifting restively amongst the twilit trees.

***

It was a shock to wake! Dobbs had reared on his hind legs, whinnying loudly. A stranger's voice could be heard saying, "Easy there! Easy!"

Joel was first to open his eyes. A bat-like silhouette loomed before him. Involuntarily, the words "What the hell...?" burst from his lips.

"No trouble, stranger! Just passing through. Don't stir yourself!"

Joel, though, was already awake and his heart was pumping hard. He wanted to know who the stranger was and why he had come close enough to intrude upon their sleep.

Joel got carefully to his feet, peering at the stranger in the twilight beneath the trees. Warily, he edged his way forward, trying to get a better view of their 'visitor'.

"That'll do, boy." The stranger spoke again and something in the tone of his voice ensured that Joel did as he was told.

Joel ceased his slow movement forwards. There was tension between them, and he decided to offer some information, hoping that it would ease the way into conversation.

"We're travellers and we're headed for Falmouth."

The stranger looked at him carefully. Joel could now see that he was wearing glasses; they were wire framed and had small lenses. After a moment or two, the stranger spoke again.

"That's not telling me much, is it?" he said. "I can see you're travellers – and this is the road that leads down to Falmouth – although it's a little way yet. What's your name – assuming it's not a secret, that is?"

"Oh, yes of course – I'm Joel. My friends are Sam and Berta." He turned, gesturing towards his two companions and giving himself the opportunity to check that they were now awake. He was reassured to see that they were, though neither of them had yet scrambled to their feet.

The stranger peered towards them. "Which one's which?" he asked.

Joel was surprised by the question but said, just a little impatiently, "Berta's the girl, Sam's the boy."

"She looks a bit more than a 'girl'," commented the stranger. Joel noted that he said nothing about Sam. "But no matter. You've told me who you are so I should do the same the same for you. Alistair McLennan at your service!" He swept his black cloak round in front of him and bowed in a manner that Joel thought was quite excessive.

"Pleased to meet you," said Joel, stepping forward to shake the stranger's hand.

McLennan, as he had now named himself, studied Joel for a moment longer and then put out his own hand, accompanying the gesture with a slightly lop-sided smile.

"Ay, I guess I can trust you. Pleased to meet you!"

By now, Sam and Berta had also come forward to shake McLennan's hand. He shook their hands in turn – vigorously – smiling as he did so, clearly not worried that he was alone with three of them.

Joel was surprised to see that, despite the heat, their new-found acquaintance was dressed all in black. For the moment, he did not remark on it, letting it pass so that he could register the rest of their visitor's appearance. He was not tall by any means – all three of them were taller than him. He was slightly built, it seemed to Joel but there was something about their acquaintance that warned him to take things slowly.

McLennan now stood back, letting his gaze wander across each of them in turn. Finally, he asked, "So what are you all doing here, miles from anywhere? Travelling to Falmouth, you say. What's in Falmouth that would tempt you away from home and hearth?"

His turn of phrase had a slightly archaic quality. This time it was Sam who took it upon himself to reply.

"We're on business for our parents," he explained. "We have to fetch something that they need – from Falmouth."

"Ah," nodded McLennan. "So that's it! And where are you from? Nowhere close, I bet."

"We're from Somerland," volunteered Berta.

"From 'Somerland', eh? Well I've travelled all over – and I've never heard of 'Somerland'.

His voice slowed and he repeated the name 'Somerland' as though he was chewing a tasty morsel that he wanted to savour.

"Well then," said Berta, ignoring his last remark. "Where are you from, Mr McLennan, and what are you doing out here – 'miles from anywhere'?"

"Oh!" said McLennan, rolling his eyes and seemingly delighted that she had spoken to him. "It's Alistair, plee…ase. I see that you are satirical, young lady, and so comely – surely you are."

Berta was not sure what any of this meant but McLennan was now launched on his own kind of explanation.

"Where am I from?" he savoured the question as he had the word 'Somerland'. "Well," he said after a moment, "immediately, I am from this place –" he turned and gestured towards the road … "this 'Falmouth' but then, really, I'm from all over – everywhere – and nowhere in particular."

During their brief conversation they had slowly drifted out from beneath the trees and towards a road that lay beyond; as they looked at it now, the three friends were both curious and a little taken aback. McLennan laughed to see their surprise.

"There now!" he chuckled. "There's a thing! Our three musketeers have never seen a road like this one. Well, my dears, we really haven't seen much, have we!"

They were all, with one voice, about to protest when he looked away from them along the road to what Joel judged must be the North. Together they followed McLennan's gaze to where a cloud of dust seemed to be approaching them at a considerable speed.

Abruptly, McLennan's voice changed and instantly, he became more business-like. He turned towards Berta but then to all three of them.

"This is what I am doing here!" he announced. "I am waiting to catch the 'Flying Packet'."

The 'Flying Packet' to which he had referred now drew clearly into view, slowing as it did so. Joel, Berta and Sam nearly bumped heads as they craned their necks to see this strange horse-drawn vehicle which was now coming to a halt just a short distance from where they stood.

Berta guessed that it had been built specially to travel quickly on roads such as the one in front of them. As she stared at it, she could see that wooden planking formed a platform on which four passengers could be seated, facing each other in two pairs. The platform was mounted on four, large diameter wheels. These looked a little heavy to Berta, but she was surprised and curious to see that a strange black material ran around the circumference of each wheel. She surmised that it was like the rubber that formed the tyres on the old car belonging to Joel's grandfather. The 'tyres' on the Packet also explained why they had heard very little noise as it approached.

Providing a certain amount of protection from the sun and heat was a white canopy, securely mounted on a strong metal frame but partly fastened back at the sides so that the breeze created by the passage of the vehicle could help to cool the three passengers who were already aboard.

At the front of the Packet was a driver, mounted on a driver's seat. The driver's feet, in turn, were a little up in front of him and planted firmly on another board that enabled him to tug on the reins without being dragged onto the road behind the two magnificent horses providing the motive power. Berta ran her eye over them. They could be twins, she decided. Both had magnificent dark brown coats and handsome, well-groomed tails. A white blaze ran down from between the ears of each horse to their noses. They were hot and steamed in the heat, but she fancied that they still had plenty of running left in them.

McLennan stepped decisively forward.

"This is me!" he called back rather quaintly, waving a cane which, until that moment he had held unnoticed in the folds of his cloak. Sam and Joel noted it as another little surprise amongst the collection of surprises that they had already connected with Mr McLennan.

He climbed aboard and then, leaning out of the vehicle, he called back to them. "Nice meeting you! Hope we meet again – in Falmouth!"

With that, the driver gave a gentle slap on the reins and the Packet drew away. It travelled slowly at first but as it approached a bend, Joel, Berta and Sam could see that the horses were moving at a fast trot, raising a cloud of dust that followed the vehicle beyond the point at which it was visible between the banks that bordered the road on its southward passage.

One by one, the three friends peeled away from the road and returned to where they had left Dobbs impatiently tugging at his tether, clearly excited to see other horses.

"Sorry, Dobbs old fellow," said Sam. "They've gone now."

"We should be going as well," commented Joel.

"So much for our nap! And I was sleeping so comfortably." Berta gave Joel a sly little sideways smile that went unnoticed by Sam. Joel smiled back, pleased that she now seemed much more relaxed in his company than she had ever seemed before they had set out on the journey.

Sam had gathered up the cups and plates that they had used for their lunch and was rinsing them in the stream that ran through the copse. When he had finished, Dobbs lowered his head to drink once more before Sam packed away the utensils, unfastened the tether and led the horse over to where Berta and Joel were waiting.

"According to Alistair," said Joel, "we would have to travel fast to reach Falmouth before nightfall."

"Do we need to?" asked Sam.

They both looked at Berta who shrugged and said, "I've waited this long for a decent bed, what's one more night? Besides, I don't feel as though I want to travel much further today."

The other two agreed. They set off in the same direction as the 'Flying Packet' but at a more sedate pace and vowing to find somewhere comfortable to stay for the night.

It took them a little while to settle back into the rhythm of their journey. The smooth surface of the road was very welcome, but it also seemed to hold the heat. To either side of the road, large rocks which had been moved aside when the road was built, lay strewn about, adding to the rugged appearance of the landscape.

It was now Sam's turn again to ride on Dobbs. As soon as he had clambered onto the horse's back, they all began to trudge along once more, accompanied only by the sounds of their own movements. The landscape around them was largely brown and seemingly dead, although small patches of greenness could be seen where the remnants of streams trickled their way amongst the rocks.

The road ahead shimmered in the heat, sloping steadily upwards towards a point where it formed a small u-shaped nick in the horizon. All of them were sweating and measuring out the effort needed to reach the crest of the road. Berta lowered her eyes, trying to see how long she could go before looking again at the point at which Truro might be visible to them.

They were not to be disappointed. From the hill on which they stood, they could see the old city stretching away to the south and east. Almost immediately, Sam pointed to three large towers reaching far above the rest of the town.

"What on earth are those?" he asked excitedly.

Joel already had an idea from Kirk's description before their journey had begun, but he checked the map before speaking.

"I think they're the towers of a cathedral," he said. "Look!" He pointed to where a cathedral was indicated on the map.

"We don't have those in Somerland," said Berta. "What's a cathedral?"

"It's like a huge church – and we do have churches in Somerland," Joel replied. "Not that they're used much anymore."

"So you're saying it's a big church?"

"Yes, that's right – a very big church – much bigger than the one in the village."

"It must have been some building," said Sam. He peered into the distance, trying to see it as best as he could. After a pause, he spoke again. "It looks rather green from here."

"That could be because it's become overgrown," said Berta.

In an earlier time, Berta's comment would have seemed laughable, but Joel and Sam readily accepted her explanation.

Berta spoke again a short while later. "The place is obviously inhabited," she said, and pointed to plumes of smokes rising into the air from a number of points across the city.

"Yes," said Joel. "I've been watching those. I think we're right to stay out of the place."

"We don't know that it's ruled by gangs." Sam was the least willing of the three of them to keep to their policy of avoiding the various settlements along their route.

"No, we don't," said Joel. "But Falmouth is where we're headed – and it's not worth the risk to go exploring down there." He nodded towards the city. In his heart, he was much more reluctant than he sounded, but he knew that if they became ensnared in any way in the old city, it would add both time and cost to their journey. There was also the risk that they would never escape.

After they had spent some further minutes looking down towards Truro, Joel set out just ahead of Dobbs and the other two, heading just a little south of west along a farm track that took them away from the road and along the foot of a steep escarpment. Further up, dark woods towered above them, giving a sombre feel to a day that was otherwise still bright with sunshine and heat.

For the next few hours, they toiled on, keeping to tracks and minor roads, only too aware that the routes they were using were only passable because people still used them. It was tiring countryside to travel through. Having chosen to keep to the byways, the roads and tracks took them over steep hills and down into deep valleys, but, as they had hoped, they saw no-one.

Eventually, they found themselves behind the remains of an old industrial area and to the west of a very large set of buildings indicated on Joel's map as a hospital. They stared in silence through the evening sunlight at what must once have been an extensive group of factory units and hospital buildings, but which was now a wilderness of trees and shrubs, many of which sprouted from window spaces, shattered walls, roofs, and former road surfaces. Slowly, the whole area was disappearing beneath a jungle of vegetation with just an occasional glint of glass or hint of brick, metal or plastic to suggest that the area had ever been anything other than scrub and woodland.

Joel carefully steered them between two settlements which now appeared completely derelict and overgrown, across what must have been a substantial road and which, according to his map, had once been known as the A390. Their path now lay downwards for a little distance until, having crossed a stream, they came to some abandoned farm buildings near a place which had apparently been known as 'Mount Prickle'. It was here that they decided to spend the night, although Berta decided at an early stage that however the place had first got its name, it was now particularly appropriate.

They managed to make a meal of sorts, cobbling together a stew of vegetables from their rapidly diminishing stock. Then, after a tired but careful inspection of the abandoned buildings, they found a small stone outbuilding that still retained part of its roof, and which offered a dry floor on which they could sleep. They tethered Dobbs outside in a place where he could crop away at the grass to his heart's content. Then between them, they gathered together some bracken and having heaped it on the floor, improvised with their bedding until finally they lay in a huddle, wrapped in their blankets against the chill which unusually had overtaken the warmth of the day. Welcoming each other's presence, though otherwise seemingly unaware of one another and separately wrapped in their own cocoons, they slept until the first rays of sunlight came slanting in through the many gaps and cracks in the walls and roof of the old building.

Unusually, it was Sam who was first to wake, although the others were also soon awake once he began to stir. Their routine was well established, although on this particular morning, fetching water involved a rather difficult trek across the overgrown course of an old railway line to the nearest stream.

It was a fairly cheerless breakfast. By now they were running low on both fruit and vegetables, and they had another day's travelling before they were likely to arrive in Falmouth. In the event, they ate a small amount of the fruit, knowing that by mid-morning they would be feeling hungry again.

The start of the day's walk did little to improve their collective mood. At first, they had to climb out of the valley that contained the stream from which they had drawn their water.

After looking at the map together, they decided that it would be best to travel east towards the Truro to Falmouth road. Initially, their route was very overgrown, but eventually they found a lane which was relatively free of vegetation, and which ran downhill towards the route that they were seeking. Soon they were standing at the junction of the lane and the main road into Falmouth.

Having tried to keep clear of other people, they now felt exposed and conspicuous, but they agreed that in this last part of their journey, they needed to travel quickly if only because they had very little food left and were now looking for someone with whom they could barter for vegetables. Joel and Berta agreed that Sam could ride on Dobbs again, although it was not his turn. On his way out of the valley that morning, he had put his foot into a hidden rabbit hole and wrenched his ankle. By the time that they reached the main road he was limping badly and Joel, whose turn it was to ride, concluded that walking would be preferable to listening to him complain all the way into Falmouth.

The road surface was good and something to be appreciated after the rough tracks and lanes that they had followed for much of the previous day.

From his vantage point on Dobbs, Sam was the first to get a view of the area into which they were headed. Over to the south-west, he could see the waters of a huge estuary, sparkling blue in the bright sunlight. A small number of sailing vessels could be seen sailing down towards the coast or making their way up the estuary towards the River Fal. Marching over the hill tops on the opposite shores were lines of wind turbines, their blades glinting every so often in the morning sun.

Joel and Berta drew alongside him, both exclaiming in turn at the view before them and enjoying the refreshing breeze that blew in their faces now that they were no longer sheltered by the lee of the hill. Joel fished in Dobb's panniers, eventually producing an ancient and battered pair of binoculars. He peered through them before passing them onto the others.

It seemed like an appreciable time before anyone spoke and then it was Berta who broke the silence.

"Have you ever seen ships rigged like that?" she exclaimed. Joel and Sam followed the line of her gaze.

"No," replied Joel. "They're certainly not like the ships we've seen off the Somerset coast."

Sam waited a moment before he spoke.

"I think I've seen them before," he said. "Only once or twice and they were always some way out to sea. I think I'd recognise those peculiar sails anywhere."

"Tell us more," said Joel.

"There isn't much more to tell. I mean, I don't really know any more. My dad says that they use both the wind and the sun to drive them along. I think that the sails work in much the same way as the sails on an ordinary sailing ship, but I don't know how the sun can help to propel something the size of a ship."

Berta was sceptical. "I have a job to believe that those flimsy looking 'sails' – if that's what they are – would ever work as well as the huge sheets of canvas that you get on a sailing ship."

"Well, take another look," replied Sam. "At the moment I can see four ships out there and none of them is an ordinary sailing ship, but unless my eyes were deceiving me, they are all making good speed."

Joel and Berta had to agree that he was right.

They continued to stare at the blue of the estuary, the green of the surrounding hills and at the wide rivers that fed into the deep natural inlet.

Finally, Joel turned his attention to the town ahead of them. "It's deceptive."

"How do you mean?" asked Berta.

"Well, if you look towards the town, it seems really close – but we still have some way to go."

Sam agreed.

"Being able to see the roofs of the houses and the sails of the ships makes me feel that we're almost there, but when I look at the road, I can see that we still have a bit of a journey."

"We need to get on," said Joel, and without further discussion, they began to move off down the hill.

The heat of the road was tiring and after they had been walking for some time, Sam brought them back to the subject that was uppermost in their minds.

"I'm beginning to feel the need for food."

Berta agreed. "It's doesn't seem long since we last ate, but I suppose that it must be several hours now. When are we stopping, Joel?"

Joel stopped in the middle of the road and consulted his map. "If we can walk for about another two hours, we should have quite an easy journey tomorrow," he said.

Sam and Berta both gave a very loud groan.

"Did you say two hours?" Berta looked at him with a pained expression on her face.

Sam remained silent but then, having all the while remained on Dobbs' back, dismounted and offered the saddle to Joel. Joel, however, still preferred to walk so that it was Berta who finally scrambled into the saddle.

Slowly they shambled into a walk which took them down the far side of the hill on a road that remained fairly straight, but which undulated along its route towards Falmouth.

They descended from the hill, and walked for a long time in relative silence, either gazing at the gradually changing countryside or else sunk deep in the solitude of their own thoughts.

During the previous day, the rugged rock-strewn moorland from which they had come had been gradually replaced by dense woodland, tracts of wild wasteland, derelict farms and settlements.

Now the landscape was changing again, and their route lay amongst the enclosed orderliness of farms that were still in use, although there were few animals to be seen in the fields, most of which seemed to be devoted to crop production. Extensive fields of ripening wheat stretched out to either side of their route, but as they continued, they also saw large areas of small trees which Joel identified as vines stretching in long, parallel rows away from the road. Clusters of ripening fruit could be seen hanging from the branches, although when Sam plucked a small bunch of grapes from a vine close to their path, they tasted sour and were clearly not yet ready for eating or for wine making.

Looking at the wry expression on Sam's face, Joel commented, "Don't be surprised. They won't be ready for another two months."

Spitting the remains out of his mouth, Sam said, "I've never seen them before. What did you say they are – 'grapes' was it? Is that what you said?"

"Yes," said Joel. "You should know that anyway. There are plenty of vineyards in Somerland."

"Well, if there are, I can't imagine why anyone would grow them."

From her perch in Dobbs' saddle, Berta was listening with amusement. "You'll soon change your mind when you've had a glass or two of wine."

"Oh, and how would you know?" Sam felt annoyed that grapes and wine seemed to be topics about which he knew less than either Joel or Berta. "Anyway, I've tasted wine!" he added indignantly.

"And what sort of wine would that be?" enquired Berta with a hint of amusement in her voice.

It was quite enough to irritate Sam still further. "Since you ask, my mum makes a very nice drop of elderflower wine every year." He thought about his statement for a minute and then added, "Well, nearly every year."

The subtlety was lost on Joel and Berta who were trying hard not to laugh.

In a voice that seemed to be rather strained, Joel commented, "I'm sure that your mum makes more than just elderflower wine...?"

"Oh yes!" agreed Sam. "She makes lots of different sorts. There's raspberry and blackberry for a start – and my dad's very fond of the parsnip."

"Yes, I'd heard that as well..." agreed Joel.

Sam, by now thoroughly launched on his subject, ignored him and continued. "My mum likes a drop too, you know. In fact, when she and my dad get the wine out – well, you should see them!"

Joel gave him a knowing look. Sam continued, encouraged by his friend's apparent interest.

"Perhaps I shouldn't say," he said in a confidential tone "but my mum once told me that it was whilst she and my dad were drinking one night that I..."

At this point, he became aware of peculiar, strangulated sounds that seemed to be coming from Berta. He looked up to see that she was hanging tightly onto Dobbs' neck whilst her body was shaking with tremors that she appeared to be fighting hard to control.

Sam was alarmed. "What is it, Berta?" he yelled. "What's the matter?"

The only response from Berta was a sort of muffled snorting followed by further convulsions and an even more determined clinging onto Dobbs' neck.

Dobbs tossed his head and gave a small whinny.

Sam looked across at Joel, seeking reassurance.

"Is she alright?" he asked. "What's the matter with her?"

Joel was struggling hard to contain his own amusement.

"I'm sure it's nothing," he said. "Or at least, nothing much. We have been on the road a long time. It could be the dust."

"Dust? What dust? Oh yes, I suppose it could be." Sam was thoroughly confused.

Meanwhile, Joel had pivoted round and bent double, had made his way with exaggerated steps towards a small ditch on the other side of the road. Here, he proceeded to cough loudly as though the mysterious dust was hacking at his lungs.

"What?" exclaimed Sam. "You as well? Oh dear, I knew we should have stopped. We should have stopped ages ago."

Amidst the strange behaviour of Joel and Berta, Sam became aware that Dobbs had also stopped and although Berta was still clinging tightly to his neck, he had reached down to some clumps of grass at the roadside and had begun cropping them.

Joel recovered sufficiently to straighten up though not to face Sam. Over his shoulder, he said, "It's still quite early but Dobbs seems to think that we've arrived. It looks as though he's chosen a pretty good field with plenty of grass. I think we could stop here. Why don't you go up to that house at the top of the field and see if you can get some water?"

"Well, OK," agreed Sam, "if you think you'll be alright with Berta."

"Yes, I'll be fine. I'm sure she just needs a drink of fresh water."

"Right then," said Sam, fishing a canteen from its place in the saddlebag. "I'll get going."

Joel waited until Sam was well on his way towards the house before he went across to Berta. By now, she was recovering although he noted that she uncharacteristically accepted his offer of help in dismounting from the saddle.

They both watched Sam's retreating back for several moments before collapsing in a helpless heap of laughter on the ground. Eventually Joel found the strength to say, "Come on now, it wasn't that funny..."

Berta looked at him in disbelief before gasping, "But it was! It really was!"

She collapsed into fresh paroxysms of laughter which continued for some time before finally she sat up, dabbing at her eyes with her sleeves.

"He could be gone a little while. Perhaps we should start putting up the tents?"

She nodded but then said, "Wouldn't it be better to wait until we know that we've got permission to stay here?"

"I suppose you're right," agreed Joel, "but no-one's refused us yet and, well, I feel obliged to Sam. He'll be feeling really tired when he gets back to us."

They agreed to begin putting up the tents but not to complete the task before Sam had returned.

Some minutes later, Sam arrived, struggling slightly with the weight of the canteen and something else that he was carrying in his other hand.

Joel went to help him. "I've heard that it's best to carry it on your head," he said, nodding towards the canteen.

"Ha, ha very funny!" retorted Sam. "I'd like to see you try it first. It's a good job I'm feeling pleased with myself. I managed to bargain with the farmer for another rabbit and a few more vegetables."

Joel did not think that it would be tactful to ask what it was that Sam had used to bargain with and simply resorted to saying, "Well done!"

Between the three of them, they finished putting up the tents and Joel began collecting wood and kindling for a fire. Sam, however, was temporarily exhausted and crawled into his tent, falling asleep on his blanket almost immediately just inside the entrance. Berta realised that she could not get past him without waking him up. She held back the flap of the tent whilst Joel peered inside.

"Oh look what he's done!" she exclaimed. "How am I supposed to get in?"

Joel heaved a sigh. "Pity," he said. "I was hoping that we could begin cooking a meal. Now I suppose we'd better wait."

Berta was not inclined to disagree. Together they drifted across towards the entrance to Joel's tent where he found a blanket and pulled it out onto the warm grass. He sat down, propping himself up with his left arm. Berta lay almost full length, facing him with her chin on her hands.

"Are you comfortable like that?" asked Joel.

"Yes," she said. "I'm fine."

"Funny," said Joel. "I can never find a way to sit comfortably when I'm camping. Sleeping's even worse. I don't know how you manage with two of you in a tent."

"It's not really a problem," Berta reassured him, "although it does get rather hot."

"I would imagine that it does..." agreed Joel.

"It can be stifling with the blanket across the middle."

Joel was not sure that he heard her correctly. "Did you say that you have a blanket across the middle of the tent?" he asked, trying to keep the surprise out of his voice.

"Of course we do," she replied. "We've all heard of brothers and sisters who sleep together when they're very small – but not at our age." She gave him a little smile as though she was amused at his mystification.

Joel meanwhile was still taking in the second of her revelations. "Are you also saying..." he asked in a voice that was becoming hoarse, "that you are brother and sister...?"

She looked at him seemingly a little surprised but with another faint smile on her lips.

"Well, most people think of us as 'half-sister' and 'half-brother'," she corrected him. Then another thought seemed to occur to her. She put out her hand and laid it on his arm. "Joel," she said, "you surely don't think all this time we've been on the journey that Sam and I were...Well, I could be shocked I suppose." She paused for a moment and then laughed, finally putting her fingers over her mouth.

"Really, Joel," she said. "What must you have thought of me – of us? I always believed that everyone on the Ridge thought of us as brother and sister."

Joel looked down at his knees. "I didn't know what to think," he said. Then he looked up at her. "I tried not to think about it at all."

There was a pause before he eventually continued. "So if you are 'half-brother' and 'half-sister', does that mean that you have the same mother – or the same father?"

"In our case, the same father," she replied and then added, as if hesitating to say anymore... "except that he wasn't really my father."

"Just a minute," exclaimed Joel, thoroughly confused. "Are you now saying that you're not really half-brother and half-sister after all?"

There was another pause before she said, "Yes, that's it. That's what I am saying – only Sam doesn't know, and I don't want you to tell him. We were certainly always encouraged by our parents to believe that we're blood related."

It was Joel's turn now to look a little shocked. "So why are you sleeping in a tent with someone you're not really related to – and who you're not married to, either?"

"Because I don't know what else to do! Besides, we only have the one tent between two of us – so we have to share even if, as you can see, it's well past its best. Sam and I have spent so much of our time together that he'd have thought it really odd if I'd made a huge fuss about wanting my own tent."

Joel was still not convinced. "Hasn't he ever tried to...I mean, if he's not your brother surely..."

"He hasn't even looked at me... well not in that way at least."

"Well, how about you? Haven't you ever looked at him in that way? Haven't you ever wanted him?"

This time she seemed distinctly annoyed by his question. "Of course not!" she exclaimed angrily. "We've always been around each other, ever since we were little children. In almost all respects, we've always been like brother and sister towards each other. Why would we behave differently now?"

Joel was about to explain that there were perfectly understandable reasons but then thought better of it. Instead, he decided to ask her yet another question.

"So how did you find out that Sam's father is not your father after all?"

"I found out because Sam's parents are not the only ones who like to drink a drop of wine."

As she told him this, she looked sideways to where Sam was sleeping. Joel followed her gaze. There were signs that he was beginning to stir.

She stood up. Joel also stood up, not really wanting her to go. She smiled at him her previous annoyance apparently forgotten.

"I'll tell you the rest of the story – at least as far as I know it – but it will have to wait until another time."

She set off back towards Sam who by this time was rubbing his eyes and attempting to sit up.

***

That evening's meal – predictably a stew of rabbit and vegetables – was one that they ate whilst reflecting that although eating was part of survival, on this occasion at least, it was also a pleasure. There was precious little left by the time that they had eaten their fill. The fire on which they had cooked their food flickered low amongst the embers, cheering them with its warmth and gentle flames. They had finished putting up the tents whilst they had waited for the vegetables to cook, so now they lay back on the grass staring up into the sky.

The long shadows of trees slanted across the field. Bats flitted about in the yellow and orange remnants of the light, and gradually, as if being lit one by one, came the stars of the night sky, hanging like tiny distant lamps far above them.

None of them had a watch. Watches were treasured personal objects that were now passed down through families and all were mechanical since electronic watches could be neither made nor repaired in the world in which they lived. The fading light, however, was more than enough indication of the time.

Sam rolled over so that his face was eerily bathed in the glow of the fire.

"How long do you think it will take us in the morning?" he asked.

Joel, chewing a blade of grass, rolled over to face him. "About two hours, give or take."

"Sounds like quite an easy walk then compared with some we've had lately," commented Berta.

"It certainly will be," agreed Joel.

Sam wanted to think ahead to the morning. "Where do we have to go when we get there?" he asked.

Joel fished a piece of paper from his pocket and, reading his father's untidy scrawl, he said, "We have to find the Carrick Warehouse, and someone called Edwin Dire – or at, least, I think that's his name. My dad's handwriting is hard to read."

"Oh great," said Sam, reacting to Joel's casual reply. "And I bet you don't know where this warehouse is?"

"Of course he doesn't. None of us has ever been to Falmouth before, but I'm sure we'll find the warehouse and this 'Edwin Dire' without any problem." Berta felt impatient that Sam suddenly seemed to doubt their ability to carry out what they hoped would be a straightforward piece of business.

Sam was not reassured but decided to settle for the satisfaction of being able to say "I told you so" when they found themselves lost and wandering in ever decreasing circles, the next day or the day after.

"I need some sleep," he announced, yawning and drawing a hand across his mouth.

He stood up but Berta was reluctant to go to bed whilst there was still light in the sky.

Sam was unperturbed. "Don't worry about it! I'll move your things through to the front of the tent," he called back to her.

For a moment or two Joel and Berta watched Sam as he headed for the tent before exchanging glances in the firelight.

It was Joel who spoke first. "I may be tired, but I really enjoy this time of day."

"Me too," agreed Berta. She looked up towards the sky. "Most of the stars are out now. Look. There's just a small part of the sky where there's still some light."

Joel was not looking in the right direction, so he manoeuvred himself round to face the same way as Berta. A small strip of sky, vivid in orange, yellow and gold was slowly receding into the purple of dusk. Together they watched as the last of the sun's light faded from the sky and then they were left alone with just the firelight flickering on their faces.

After a moment of two, Joel shifted so that he was propped up on one elbow, facing Berta.

"So are you going to tell me now about your family?" he asked.

She paused for a moment. "I only know so much – and I never really knew my dad," she said at last. "There was the bit that my mum blurted and then there was another bit that I managed to wheedle out of your granddad."

Joel looked back towards the fire and said, "Hmm, perhaps that's not such a surprise. A pretty face has always seemed to loosen his tongue."

She glanced at him briefly before returning to the subject. "Well, the first part I learned when my dad confronted my mum one night. They'd both been drinking, and he yelled at her something about being 'a slut' – just like her mother."

"Were you shocked when you heard that?"

"Yes, I suppose I was a bit – although I didn't know what it meant. It just sounded bad. Anyway, they carried on shouting at each other, and my dad accused her of being as bad as Janey, my grandmother, who, apparently, had slept with someone who was in the Army." She paused. "Then, if anything, it got worse."

Joel looked at her quizzically, prompting her to carry on.

"There was quite a lot more – something he'd been told about Janey whoring away with this soldier in the barn over at what's still known as 'Andrew's Farm'. Then he shouted at her that her big army 'hero' dad was buried up in the woods and did she know that? Did she ever go to look at the grave?"

"So what did she say then?"

"She didn't answer him directly but decided to do some yelling of her own. She shouted that my grandmother had only gone to him because she couldn't get what she needed at home. I think she was implying that she'd done the same."

"I won't ask what that was," muttered Joel, but Berta ignored him and carried on with her story.

"They were both getting extremely angry, and when he shouted at her that I wasn't his but someone else's child, it was a question of who was going to hit the other one first. But in the end, he just walked out. He disappeared for about a week – and, in spite of herself I think that she was quite worried about him. Anyway, he turned up at the farm on the end of The Ridge."

"Oh, yes," said Joel, "with Sam's mum, Nicola – I think I might have heard a little bit about that already. Didn't she lose her first husband in the fighting – you know, 'The Battle of the Ridge' as my parents call it? I thought he was Sam's dad."

She shook her head. "No he wasn't. He was quite a bit older than Nicola. My dad had been seeing her for some time and had probably been looking for a reason to have a row with my mum. Sam's only just a little bit younger than me. It also explained why my 'dad' – as I still sometimes think of him – was never very warm towards me. I was frightened when he left but now that my mum is happy again, I'm much happier as well."

Joel looked at her with a faint smile in his eyes. "So the person I've always thought of as your dad is not your dad. Also, the person you first thought of as your dad is not your dad but now lives with Nicola down at the end of The Ridge. Instead, your real dad was some bloke you've... well, whom you've never met." He paused. "So what was it you learned from my grandfather?"

"Some interesting things – I asked him one day about the 'Battle of the Ridge' and he told that me that before the battle, two army officers came to The Ridge to brief everyone about what they thought was going to happen and the sort of preparations that they needed to make. He remembered one of the officers in particular."

"Oh, so did he remember his name?"

"Yes, he did. He said his name was Robert Lawson, although most of the people on The Ridge just referred to him as Lawson.

Joel nodded. He had heard the same story from his grandfather.

Berta continued. "Anyway, your granddad didn't seem to think that it was his real name."

"Why was that?"

"He wouldn't go into any specific reasons. He just said that there was always something of a mystery about him and that although he played an important part in the planning for the defence of The Ridge, they never really got to know much about him. It seems all the same that he told them what needed doing – and they did it."

"So he had a lot of authority then – this man – the man who you think now was actually your grandfather?"

"I'm sure that he had," she replied.

Joel hesitated, as if in thought. "Does the fact that he was known as Robert have anything to do with your nickname 'Berta'?"

"Yes, of course, it has," she replied.

"But your real name is Jane. I've never known how you came to be called 'Berta'."

"That's because you've never asked about my second name."

"Which is..." he asked, feeling that he already knew the answer.

"It's Roberta, of course, after my mother – and her father before that."

"Oh, Roberta! Roberta!" he mimicked. "It sounds frightfully posh."

"Well we both know that it isn't!" She looked at him indignantly.

Tactfully, he decided to go back a step in the conversation.

"So 'Berta' is just what you've always been called on the farm?"

"You know it is," she replied, "although there is a bit more to it than that! It was Sam who first called me Berta. It was when he was very young. He couldn't get his tongue around the name 'Roberta'. My mum was generally known as 'Robbi' for a similar reason."

They became aware that during the conversation they had drawn closer to each other. Carefully and deliberately, Berta rolled onto her back and lay looking up at the night sky, her face still lit by the glow of the fire.

Slowly Joel moved towards her until his face was above hers. She seemed unsurprised but looked steadily up at him with a faint smile on her lips.

"So do I call you 'Berta' now – or is it 'Roberta'?" he asked.

"I don't really mind so long as you give me a kiss," she replied softly.

Savouring the smell of the meadow grasses in her hair, he bent carefully down and kissed her gently on the lips. She closed her eyes – and opened them again as he drew away.

"Do you think Sam's still awake?" asked Joel, suddenly remembering the friend whom he had for so much of the journey assumed was 'Berta's' boyfriend.

"No," replied Berta. "He usually goes straight off to sleep."

"So we don't need to rush then."

She looked thoughtful for a moment and then said, "No, Joel, we don't need to rush. But this evening isn't the right time."

He must have looked a little disappointed because she paused and said, "There will be other times for us – better ones than this – and they'll be soon, I promise you."

"I hope so," said Joel, smiling. She kissed him gently again, but then rolled away and got to her feet. He watched as she walked slowly towards the tent in which Sam was now soundly asleep. He felt sure she was right about better times for the two of them – but about the world around them, he had much less confidence.

* * *

Early the next morning they were on the road again, keen to reach the destination they had been travelling towards for nearly a fortnight. Two hours after they had broken camp, they found themselves making their way through the outskirts of Falmouth.

The well-maintained road contrasted oddly with the dereliction around them. Many of the buildings along their route had once been two and three storey houses, but now few of them were habitable. Most doors and windows had long disappeared so that dark spaces gaped upon the passing world like cavernous eyes and mouths. Here and there, houses had collapsed – or been demolished; it was impossible to tell. Either way, the disintegrating buildings must have been a useful source of building materials for the survivors of the catastrophe that had befallen the country in the early part of the century. Amongst the rubble of the fallen houses, there were signs that fires had been lit, some of which had clearly spread to neighbouring buildings which now stood out like black and jagged teeth. At intervals along the rows of houses and on either side of the road, there were the longer frontages that must once have belonged to shops, pubs and restaurants. Of these, just a single pub, 'The Ship' remained. Elsewhere, it was the same tale of destruction. Doors and windows had been stolen, smashed or had rotted away. Walls had been knocked down or driven in, and anything that could be useful to the living had been spirited away and the interiors left to the ravages of fire or water. Some were filled with rubbish, whilst many exuded a stench that suggested that they were used as lavatories by the customers of 'The Ship'.

Curiously, amongst this chaos, could still be found an occasional house where the present occupants took a pride in its appearance, where there were signs of recent repairs and where also, to the surprise of the three travellers, there were curtains at every window.

Whilst stopping to look every now and then at the buildings along the way, Joel, Sam, Berta and Dobbs drifted down the hill towards the town centre. As they walked, they felt a mounting sense of apprehension which was made still worse by their realisation that the road on which they were travelling had become a street and that they were approaching a huge wooden gatehouse that spanned its entire width.

As they approached, they could see that set within the wall of timber that confronted them was a huge pair of wooden gates. Suddenly, a wooden flap within was flung open with a bang and a voice bellowed from behind an iron grille.

"Step for'ard, strangers and state yer business!"

Joel, who had been leading the way, stepped forward.

"That'll do. Come no closer. Look up and be 'minded to tell the truth now!"

Joel did as he was bid and looked up. Along the ramparts at the top of the gatehouse, he could see that they were covered from every angle by crossbowmen.

"So who are yuh?"

"I'm Joel Hallam. These are my companions, Sam and Berta Capstick."

There was a certain amount of muttering and discussion behind the grille and then the voice bellowed again, "OK, stranger, maybe we know about you, maybe we don't! So tell us what's yer busyness?"

"We're here to get parts for our parents' wind turbine. We're bound for Carrick Warehouse."

The name Carrick Warehouse seemed to cause another bout of muttering and murmuring on the other side of the gate. Then the voice bellowed again, "OK! OK! Yer' getting warmer, boy – but yer ain't there yet – nearly but not quite. Now do you have a seal?"

They had anticipated this moment. Joel looked silently back at Sam who delved deep into one of Dobbs' panniers.

Other voices bellowed down from the ramparts. "Take care now, boy! No silly stuff!"

Sam fished out 'the Seal' – a large, bronze coin commemorating the Golden Jubilee of Elizabeth II, drilled and mounted on a red, white and blue ribbon. Then he held it aloft for all to see before passing it to Berta who passed it to Joel.

Joel held the seal up to the grille, taking care not to place it too close to the bars. He was surprised to hear a low chuckle from the other side.

"Alright, boy, alright – now just turn the seal around slowly, and hold it steady so I can look at it."

Once more, Joel did as he was asked, knowing that what the gatekeeper was looking for was a small impression of the Cornish flag which had somehow been stamped into the reverse side of the coin.

"Right, boy. Good, good! Seems like you'm one of us after all! Get those friends of yours right up to the gates. We don't want the gates open longer than need be."

Taking care that they were not trodden on by Dobbs, the three of them huddled closer to the gates. There were multiple sounds of bolts being slid back, of locks being unlocked and chains being unchained and then, slowly the huge gates were swung open, creaking and complaining loudly on their giant hinges.

Joel led Dobbs briskly though the gates, quickly followed by Berta and Sam. Once they were inside, the gates were swung back into place, the bolts slid into their sockets, the chains chained again and the locks systematically relocked.

Joel turned to see a short, fat man with wispy grey hair, ambling towards them. He wore a greasy brown jacket over a grimy faded T-shirt that looked as though it might have been bright red at one time and a pair of soiled grey trousers.

"Now let's see that seal again, just once more," he said.

Recognising the voice, Joel patiently held it out where it could be seen by the gateman who fished in the breast pocket of his grimy T-shirt and produced a monocle that, it could now be seen, was on a cord around his neck. Carefully, he inspected the impression again until he was satisfied.

Holding the monocle in place, he began to inspect each of them in turn at very close quarters. They bore with it until he finally came to rest with the monocle barely an inch from Berta's left breast.

"Excellent! Excellent!" He muttered more to himself it appeared than any of those around him.

"Yes, well, that's quite enough of that!" exclaimed Berta, turning bright red and moving hastily closer to Sam and Joel.

"Can't be too careful," said the gateman, once more as much to himself as to the people around him. "Get people comin' in h'yar in all sorts of weird and wonderful disguises."

The excuse caused looks of open disbelief to flit across the faces of the travellers, but then Joel interrupted the older man's bumbling.

"I think that there is an agent waiting to meet us here – someone by the name of 'James'?"

"Oh yes, yes there is. Good job too, else you'd never have got in, not even with that seal. Now just wait here a minute. I'll bring 'un out drekly but I think he's drinking tea in my shed."

He shambled towards a wooden lean-to which had been built against the stone wall of a house next to the gate. After several minutes, he reappeared, with 'James' in tow.

James, as far as Joel could tell, was in late middle age although his hair was already a distinguished mixture of grey and white. He was rather less than Joel's exalted height, barely reaching his shoulder. He wore a dark suit and slightly grubby shirt. He had a benign, rounded face which at that moment was lit with a smile.

"Welcome, welcome!" he said. "I hope you don't mind our little rituals, but they are necessary – very necessary."

Joel shook the agent's hand and moved aside so that Sam and Berta could also greet him.

The formalities over, James began to fill in some of the details that they had heard from their parents but had only half absorbed.

"I've arranged somewhere for you stay," said James. "The fleeces your parents sent with the messenger have paid for it all, so you have no need to worry about that. Whilst you're here, you'll be able to use these." He held out a handful of coins for them to inspect. "They're only good inside the walls of the town here, but that will be sufficient for your stay. I'm sure that you will find you have more than enough."

They mumbled their collective thanks, genuinely grateful that they would not have to worry about this aspect of their visit. They were more used to barter than to using coins but were confident that they would be able to use them without difficulty.

James now turned and led them at a brisk pace down through the old town, every so often waving his hands to left and right to indicate places that he thought it would be useful for them to know about. The first feature that he pointed out was a high stone wall running away in either direction from the gate through which they had come.

"The wall that you see," he said, "runs right round the old town. It's made of granite although in many places, houses form a part of it – probably the weakest parts. It took us over 20 years to build, but inside the walls, life is much safer and, I think you'll find, a lot more civilized."

"Why do you need a wall?" asked Sam, immediately aware that he probably knew the answer already.

"You have to go back some years now," replied James. "You may have missed most of the trouble in your isolated part of the world, but down here, we had people trying to move in from all over the country – not to mention other parts of the world."

It was not quite the answer that Sam had expected. "Why would they want to move down here?" he asked.

"Plenty of reasons – as you may have heard, in many parts of the world people were facing floods, drought, starvation, extreme heat – not to mention storms that nobody had ever seen the like of before. They were forced to migrate to places where they stood a chance of surviving. Of course, wherever they went, other people were already living there. There was a great deal of bloodshed – some of it around here."

Berta took up the questioning.

"So where did these people come from?"

James turned to her and shrugged, a look of hopelessness on his face as though the task of explanation was too big. Then, after a moment or two he said, "Where did they not come from? They came from India, Pakistan, China, Africa, the Middle East. They came from everywhere except anywhere that was north."

"Why not from the north?" asked Joel.

"Because, as you could have guessed, that's where most of them wanted to be," replied James.

"So they came here because this is a port, and they could get a boat from here to ...?" He let his sentence trail off into a question.

"Mostly to North America, particularly Canada, although some went to Scandinavia and the Baltic," replied James. "They were going as you might say, 'North by South-West'."

Berta wanted to get back to Sam's original question. "You said there was bloodshed here. Why was that if people were just passing through?"

"Even if they were just passing through there would have been plenty of trouble – but not all the migrants wanted to move on. Some wanted to stay here – some had simply grown weary of travelling and saw Falmouth as a place to settle."

"So why was that a problem?" asked Sam.

"Look around you," said James. "There's very little space here. It may rain for much of the year, but we still have problems collecting enough water for the town and most of the food that we have has to be grown in the area around us. We can feed ourselves and a few visitors, but we can't feed an army of people who decide that they're going to move in."

Joel thought that James had left out part of the explanation. "I had heard that people down here don't readily accept strangers."

James saw no point in denying it. "That's true," he said. "We don't readily accept strangers, even desperate strangers – but you have to remember that we were desperate too. There were several battles, big ones, and if you don't mind, I'd rather not go into the details. Terrible things were done on both sides, things that still haunt those of us who were there."

Berta made a subtle change of tack. "It seems peaceful enough here now. How did that come about?"

"Well, first," said James, "we Cornish have our backs to the sea. We weren't going anywhere – at least not on someone else's 'say so'. But we were prepared after a lot of fighting to let people through and that's how it came to be settled. We would let people through, but we had to be able to control the access to the town."

"Did any of them settle here?" asked Joel. "Usually local people will mix with people from other parts whatever happens."

"You're right, of course," replied James. "We're a very mixed population here now, as you'll soon see, but it's taken a long time for that to happen."

By this time, they had made their way down to the lower part of the town. James led them into a small cul-de-sac where two-storey half-timbered houses faced each other forming something that resembled an open courtyard.

"This is it," said James. "This is where we've arranged for you to stay. I hope you'll be comfortable here."

The sound of their voices had brought a short, red-faced and very rotund woman of uncertain age into the courtyard.

"This is Gwen," announced James. "She will take care of you for the time being."

They turned and Gwen did a little mock curtsy.

"Thank you, James!" said Gwen with a big, apple-cheeked smile. "And where can they find you if they need you?"

"Down at the 'Chain Locker' – it's an inn just down the way. But my advice is to rest after your journey and then we'll get on with our business tomorrow."

He nodded towards them and then strode away out of the courtyard leaving them with Gwen.

"Well, my dears," she bubbled, "I gather that you have travelled rather a long way, so I dare say you'd like some food and a bit of a rest. Our last visitors sailed two days ago so you can each have a room to yourselves, if that's agreeable?"

They nodded that it was 'agreeable'.

"What about Dobbs?" said Berta, thinking for a moment that he had been forgotten.

"Oh, no problem my dear. My young 'un Tom'll look after 'im – for a small consideration o' course. There's a stable at the end of the row."

Right on cue, a shabbily dressed Tom appeared.

"Right," said Sam who was holding Dobbs' reins and passed them to Gwen's rather pale and skinny son who took them confidently in his own hands, muttering quietly into the neck of horse that towered above him. Dobbs whinnied and shook his mane but was otherwise quite happy to clop away to his stable, confidently led by his small and most recent acquaintance.

Gwen led them into the building, which in previous times had been a small hotel. Joel could not decide how old it was. He guessed that it had been built in the middle of the nineteenth century, but the dark ceiling beams, studded walls and lattice windows were reminiscent of much older buildings.

They followed their host up a broad staircase that swept up to a landing. From there, they passed into a wide corridor lit by small lamps, mounted at intervals along either side.

"We're here," announced Gwen. "These are your three rooms, and these are your keys."

There were no numbers on the doors, but she passed each one of them a key; each one had been marked with a small loop of coloured wool.

"The keys are marked in the hope that if they do become muddled, you'll be able to remember which one is yours. I'll be leavin' you now but if you want anything else I'll be in the kitchen. You'll need to fetch your belongings up from the stable, but Tom will still be down there with yer 'orse for some time yet. He can give a hand if need be."

They chorused their thanks and then Gwen went off to her tasks. They decided to explore each other's rooms in turn. Joel and Sam were next to each other in the first two rooms, whilst Berta's room was next door to Sam's.

The rooms were all very similar. Each contained a fairly large bed with white sheets and covers. A small armchair, a chest of drawers, a small wardrobe and a rug next to the bed completed the furnishings. A window had been opened in each room to provide a draught of air on a day that had become hotter as it progressed.

They had reached Berta's room when she said, "I'm going to like staying here. Excuse me – I must make use of that washbasin. They may be short of water here, but it's been so long since I've seen anything as civilized as taps and running water."

She crossed the room to a small washbasin on the far wall of the room, turned on the cold tap and washed her face, luxuriating in the water's coolness.

Sam and Joel perched on the edge of her bed. Reluctantly, Joel reminded them that they needed to fetch their belongings from the stable.

Despite their fatigue, they agreed that they would go together. They found their way to the stable and to Tom who was conscientiously grooming Dobbs. Rather quaintly, he was standing on a large stool in order to reach Dobbs' head, neck and back.

"I've put his tack and the panniers over there," said Tom as they approached. He nodded towards the shadows.

"Thanks!" said Joel. "Are you alright there? He's a big horse!"

"Oh, I'm fine," said Tom. "I like 'orses – and this one's a beaut, ain't yer, fella?"

"Well, we're glad to know you're happy. Do you need any help?" asked Sam.

"No! No! I like this job," said Tom, "but there's one thing I would ask you. I'll look after Dobbs each day that you're here, but if you could pay me on the last day and give the money straight to me. My mum won't mind but if you give it to her, well...I might not get to see it."

"No worries," said Berta. "We'll make sure we pay you directly – or is that 'dreckly'?"

Tom grinned and they left him to his work and went across to the panniers. Although the sunlight outside was still strong, they found that they needed to bring a lamp across from the other side of the stable so that they could see what they were doing. Using what Sam called 'organized rummaging' they picked their way through the contents of the panniers, taking out their changes of clothing and wash bags. Then, saying 'Goodbye' to Tom for the time being, they made their way back up to their rooms.

Sam went straight into his room, calling back over his shoulder, "See you later!" Joel hesitated in the corridor, glancing down towards Berta. She too had hesitated at the door to her room. He read her lips as she said, almost silently, "See you later."

He let himself into the room, slipped off his shoes and padded in stockinged feet across to the curtains. He drew the curtains part-way across the window and then took off most of his clothes, intending to sleep in just his underpants. The covers looked much too thick for such a hot day, so he stripped them back until just a single sheet remained. Quickly, he crawled beneath it, enjoying its coolness until drowsiness overcame him and he fell sound asleep.

It seemed to him that he woke just a short time later but the light in the room had diminished and so it must have been rather longer than he thought. Something had woken him although he was not sure what it was. He lay with his back to the door but rolled over to see if anything on the other side of the room could have disturbed him.

Barely had he done so when he realised that someone had stolen into the room and was in the process of locking the door from the inside. He was about to call out when, despite the dimness of the light, he began to recognise the silhouette of the person who was now tiptoeing towards him. He lay still, feigning sleep, as his visitor carefully lifted the sheet and slipped in beside him.

Despite the heat of the day, her flesh felt cool. Joel turned fully towards the 'intruder', not needing to guess her identity, and ran his hands slowly and gently over her stomach and towards her breasts. The swollen beauty of their roundness and the firmness of her nipples made him ache for her. He slid his hands carefully back down again until the fingers of his right hand lay on her stomach again. If she was going to stop him from going any further, it would surely be at this point, but she made no move to prevent the progress of his fingers. Fighting hard to control his eagerness, he slipped his fingers just inside her. At that moment, Berta was not looking at him but had closed her eyes and drew in her breath sharply as she felt him gently exploring her. Carefully taking his hand away, he moved so that he lay above her but taking most of his weight on his forearms and lower legs. He had thought about this moment so much – had probably worried about it – but now that it was happening, his movements were entirely guided by instinct.

He fumbled a little to find her entrance. They were eager for each other and entering her was not initially difficult, but then for a moment, her body seemed to resist him. She gasped as once more, he pushed firmly into her, finally opening her eyes and drawing him down into a long and passionate kiss.

Some while later, they fell asleep, breathing slowly, quietly and lying side by side, no longer touching one another.

Joel thought that he had been asleep for some time but then realised that it had probably been only a few minutes.

Berta's eyes flickered open, and she looked sideways at him, smiling.

"That was beautiful, Jo." She hesitated. "It was the first time that I've done that."

She felt cautiously around in the sheets. "I think that some of this stickiness might be from me."

Joel was faintly amused. "It would be surprising if you hadn't made your own contribution," he said.

"No, I don't think you understand what I mean." Carefully she pulled back the sheets. They were slightly spotted with blood where Joel had lain between her legs.

For a moment he was slightly alarmed, wondering if he had somehow injured her or himself but then he realised what she meant.

"Sorry," he said. "I was a bit slow. It's my first time as well."

They lay gazing at each other for a few moments longer before Berta said, "You realise that what we've just done could cause a few problems."

Joel nodded. "It usually seems to cause more than just a few problems. But go on – let's think about what they are."

"The first one is that you might have made me pregnant."

"Of course," replied Joel. "But we both knew that from the start."

"Okay but we need to think about it a lot more than we have done so far."

Joel smiled faintly. "We've left it a bit late for that," he said.

"Not necessarily. We'll know in a few days."

"Why then?"

"Because that's when my period is due."

"Alright," said Joel. "Suppose that your period doesn't arrive. How will you feel – how will I feel then?"

"Whether I'm pregnant or not, I want us to stay together," said Berta.

Up to that point, Joel had remained slightly detached from the conversation but now he looked intently at her.

"I feel that way too. I've been thinking about you for a long time. But we need to be sure that we want to bring a child into a world such as this."

"Our parents must have had the same thoughts. I don't regret the life that they've given me."

"That might be because we haven't had much experience of life yet. We might feel differently even just a short time from now."

"But how can we know what we might think in the future? We have to make our decisions based on what we know now."

"Yes, we do," agreed Joel.

Berta drew closer to him. "I don't know how much more you want to talk about this – but there is someone else that we need to think about."

Joel could think of a number of people they needed to think about, but he knew who she meant.

"Sam?" he asked.

"Yes," said Berta. "I don't want him to resent us, and we still have a job to do – an important job."

"I agree," said Joel. "I think that we need to carry on looking out for each other in just the same way that we have on the journey here. We have no idea what might happen here – or on the journey back."

"Do we need to tell Sam about us?"

"Not at the moment," said Joel. "But I'd sooner tell him than just let him find out. So it won't be long before we have to tell him."

Berta lay back on her pillow gazing up at the ceiling, lost in her own thoughts. Joel found his own thoughts drifting back to a day when he had overheard an argument between his grandparents. His grandmother's voice echoed in his head.

"Joel is too naive. His father is too harsh. He should go on the journey himself."

His grandfather's voice echoed in reply. "It is harsh. I don't agree with the decision to send them, but if they don't go we'll have an even bigger problem with feeding everyone here."

"So that's it, is it? They have to make their own way because we can't feed them anymore. It's rubbish and you know it. I'd rather try every last thing we know before we send them into the barbarism and cruelty that we know is out there."

"Unfortunately, we're not the only voices. We're not even the decisive voices."

"I don't understand – I will never understand – how they can make such a decision about their own children!"

In his memory, his grandmother was almost screeching with anger. He sighed. He had crept away, not wanting his grandparents to know that he had overheard them.

The decision had been made plain to them eventually and here they were now, having treated the first part of their journey as though it had all just been something of an adventure. Joel let out a long breath. His father had taught him civility. Life on the farm had hardened him physically and made him strong. The adults around them had tried to educate as best as they could. He wondered if it would be enough or whether they would just be swallowed up now that they had come out here into the cruel and barbaric world that his grandmother feared so much.

He felt Berta's hand on his arm. "You're doing a lot of sighing," she said.

"Oh sorry," he said. "I was thinking about life at home."

"I think about it too," she replied. "But I'm tired of thinking about it. I want to do some more of what I did for the first time just a short while ago. Or have you already had enough?"

His reply came quickly, making her gasp again before losing herself in the pleasure of their actions.

* * *

Sam was almost at the end of the meal that Gwen had provided for them. It was some time since they had eaten fish, and the mackerel that she had served them was beautifully fresh. At home, they often felt as though they were still children eating at their parents' tables, but now they felt like adults eating the meal that she had prepared, like guests treated with respect in a civilized place.

Joel wondered if this feeling of 'civilization' was an illusion and suspected there was more to the town than had so far met their eyes but for the moment, he kept his thought to himself. Sam sat back in his chair with a satisfied look on his face.

"That was worth the journey to get here. Did you enjoy it?" Berta wiped her lips carefully on a napkin that Gwen had provided.

"Yes," she said. "It's been a long time since I've eaten a meal like that."

"You wouldn't be trying to say something about our cooking now, would you?" asked Sam, laughing.

"No, I would not!" replied Berta. "Just remember that the fish was almost straight out of the sea. Some of the food that we've had to eat on the journey was hardly fresh."

Joel glanced at Berta, pleased that there was no obvious sign that Sam knew about their afternoon activities.

"What are you two planning to do this evening?" he asked.

"Nothing much," said Sam. "I want to be wide awake tomorrow when we meet Edwin Dire – since that's why we came all this way."

"Me too," said Berta. "I'm still tired after the journey and I could do with an early night."

"OK," said Joel, "I feel tired too, but I want to talk to James before we meet him again tomorrow. There's a lot more that he can tell us about this place."

Berta was concerned. "Are you sure that's a good idea? We've been very careful every step of the way so far and now we're in a strange town, you decide to go exploring at night."

Joel smiled. "I'll be fine. James said it was just a short distance down the road – and I would really like to talk to him before we all get down to business tomorrow morning."

Berta was still concerned but thought that it was better not to make it obvious in front of Sam.

Finally she nodded. "Alright then – Sam and I will keep Gwen company and have an early night. We'll see you in the morning."

"Right you are," said Joel. "I won't get the chance tomorrow. We'll be too busy. Don't wait up."

"Not very likely!" exclaimed Sam. "See you."

Joel stood up to leave and made for the door. Berta followed him. She drew close to him, putting her hand on his arm. "I won't come to you tonight – but I will knock on your door later just to make sure that you've got back safely."

"That's fine, Berta, but don't worry. I'm sure this town is perfectly safe. I'll see you later. Now look out for Sam or he'll find out about us before we've had a chance to tell him."

Joel turned to give a brief wave to Sam and then made his way out into the street. It was still warm, and the evening twilight was still fading, although the first stars had just begun to appear. He would enjoy the short walk to the Chain Locker.

"So, what was that all about?" asked Sam as Berta approached.

"I just want him to be careful," she said.

"Yes, I heard you tell him that."

"I did say that I would check on him later – just to make sure that he got back safely."

Sam looked bemused. "Why?" he asked. "He's an adult, isn't he? We all are."

"I'm not so sure about that," replied Berta, a note of exasperation creeping into her voice.

Sam said nothing more but smiled faintly to himself. Her irritation tended to confirm what the last two days on the road had led him to suspect. Late in the afternoon, he had also knocked on Berta's door. There had been no reply, but the door was open. When he had looked in, the room was empty. He knew that she would not have gone far, and he was almost certain that he knew where she was.

He came out of his thoughts and stared after Berta. She was headed for the kitchen in search of Gwen.

Outside, Joel was enjoying the short walk to the Chain Locker. He guessed that the road he was following was separated from the harbour only by the line of shops and houses on his left. On his right, streets and buildings sloped steeply up the side of a hill. He had not gone far before he saw a narrow street running down to the harbour. A short way down was a half-timbered building displaying a peeling sign bearing the name 'Chain Locker'. He made his way down to it and found his way in.

The bar was dimly lit by candles. Despite the huge wind turbines reaching out into the sea, the town seemed to be short of electricity. Joel peered through the smoky gloom looking for James. Unless he had a liking for spending his evenings alone in his room, Joel felt sure that he would find him in the bar.

The bar was not crowded. A handful of men in the rough clothes of harbour workmen rubbed shoulders with each other. Two young women sat talking to one another and, like the men, drinking beer.

Joel presumed that most of them were local people who probably knew each other. As a stranger, he felt slightly intimidated by the feel of the place. His eyes scanned along the bar and came to rest when he spotted James sitting by himself at a small round table towards the far end of the pub. At first, he did not notice Joel, but sat pulling on his pint of beer and quietly absorbing the scene around him. Then as Joel moved towards him a look of surprise and then of pleasure lit his face.

"I didn't expect to see you until tomorrow. Come and have a seat. Can I get you a drink?"

"I thought I would get you one," replied Joel.

"That's good of you," said James. "But let me do the honours this time." He stood to go to the bar and pointed Joel again towards the seat beside his own, muttering in his ear as he passed, "It's a good idea not to let them see your money too easily in here."

Joel sat down and waited whilst James was being served. The young women had moved from their seats and were now standing at the bar talking to two men. Joel watched them for a moment or two.

Now that she was standing, Joel could see that the woman closest to him was wearing a short and fairly flimsy dress with a low neckline. There was something slightly insubstantial about her, a little careworn perhaps. As she talked to a short, older man with a comical face who was seated at the bar, she smoothed away wispy strands of fair hair that had fallen across her face.

Her friend was talking to a tall, burly, dark-haired man who was leaning on the bar. She seemed more confident, more obviously attractive to men. Her brown hair had been carefully cut and her dark dress showed a good deal of her arms and shoulders and ended a little above her knees. She looked confidently into his face, laughing and smiling and talking in an animated manner.

James returned from the bar, trying not to spill beer from the two glasses. He set them down carefully on the table where, to his surprise, Joel examined them carefully.

"We haven't lost all the knowledge of the old ones," said James. "We still know how to make beer glasses."

Joel smiled in response. "In the case of beer glasses, I'm pleased to hear it." He gestured round at the candles on the bar and the tables. "I thought that there would be electricity in here – especially with so many wind turbines out to sea."

"You can't believe what you see," replied James. "Most of those wind turbines are old. They're falling apart – although the ones that work are still a useful source of power for the town."

Joel was surprised. "That's not a good start. Perhaps I've come to the wrong place!"

"Oh no, no," replied James. "Getting parts for the turbines is not the problem. All the turbines that are working have probably been repaired a number of times, but we don't have enough people here to repair the number of turbines that are out there in the bay. There's hundreds of the things. But have no worry. The part for your parents' turbine is already here and waiting for you to collect it from Dire's warehouse."

"Where did it come from?" asked Joel although his parents had already told him.

"I thought you knew," responded James. "The part you've come to collect came from Canada. Some of them come from the States."

Joel had heard about the United States from both his parents and his grandparents, but they always seemed to be talking about a country that had existed in the past and were unable to tell him about the present day. He wondered if James could supply some of the pieces missing from his knowledge.

"My parents have always talked about the 'United States'. Is that the place that you mean?"

"Yes it is," replied James emphatically, "except that there's not much that's united about them anymore."

"I heard that it was the richest and most powerful country in the world."

"Yes it was – until everything collapsed, that is. Everyone – all the countries in this part of the world – used to take their lead from the United States."

"My grandfather says that he thought they would move in and take over when terrorists attacked the government here."

James looked thoughtful and rubbed his chin. "It could have happened – but none of it did. The United States fought a war with China. Both sides used nuclear weapons. On top of that they were having ever bigger problems with climate change. Every plague and disaster you can think of – they've had it."

Joel wanted to know more but James would only say, "I can only tell you so much. I was a sailor when I was younger and saw a lot of the Eastern seaboard but it's not safe to go there now. Many of the cities – what's left of them – are radioactive after the war with China. Civil order broke down, much as it did here and many of the survivors moved north."

"That's what this place is all about, isn't it," commented Joel. "Moving north?"

"Yes it is, Joel." James narrowed his eyes and lowered his voice. "But you need to be careful. You could find yourself 'moving north' as you put it whether you want to or not."

"What do you mean?" asked Joel.

"Okay," said James. "Take a look – a very careful look – over there. What do you think is going on?" With an almost imperceptible movement of his head, he drew Joel's attention in the direction of the women at the bar.

Joel looked briefly and turned back towards James. "Oh you know, men, women, drink, candle light – the usual things."

James smiled sarcastically. "Well, with those people there you might be right. But then again you might not. Some of the women round here are used by gangs to trap men."

"Trap them for what?" Joel was sceptical.

James' reply began in the form of a question. "Have you noticed the ships out in the bay?"

"Yes, of course," said Joel.

"Well, there are two main types – the very modern ones that have steel masts, electronically controlled sails and are manned by just four or five people. And then there are the old, traditional style sailing ships which need large numbers of men to sail them and where brawn is probably as important as brain. If you'd been on one you'd know why. You're a young man. Someone will already have noticed that you're strong and healthy. You need to look out for yourself."

"I will, don't worry," replied Joel. "Tell me more about the gangs."

"Alright," agreed James. "But we need to keep our voices down. And when I've told what I'm going to tell you, I think that we should move on."

Joel nodded and James continued. "The women are used to encourage men like those two at the bar to get drunk. They lead them into thinking that they're going to have sex with them, but later on when they've staggered out into the street or when they're lying in the woman's bed, someone comes from behind and hits them over the head. The next thing they know, they wake up with concussion on some old stinking tub of a sailing ship, miles out at sea and not a woman in sight."

"It sounds like something out of Cornwall's past."

"You're right. It is out of Cornwall's past. But it's also part of Cornwall's present – and you need to be on your guard."

Joel had not quite finished with his questions, however. "I thought that there was a legitimate trade here and a place from where passengers could sail to North America."

"There is," said James. "Most of those businesses here are legitimate, but I'm warning you that there's also a darker side to this town – and you'd do best to stay away from it."

"Thanks, James," said Joel. "I'm glad I came to talk to you." He looked about him. Most of the candles had burned low. "It must be getting late," he said. "I need to get back."

"I'll walk back with you," said James and seeing Joel about to object, he added, "I'm too well known here and there would be too many questions asked if they tried anything whilst I was with you."

Joel wanted to ask about the identity of 'they' but decided to accept James' advice, and together they walked back up the street towards Joel's lodgings.

***

James was already rounding the corner on his way back to the Chain Locker as Joel turned towards the door of the house, fumbling for the key he had brought with him. Then as quietly as he could, he opened the door and tiptoed in, locking the door once more behind him.

It took his eyes a little while to adjust to the gloom, but then as soon as he could see sufficiently well, he made his way across to the foot of the staircase and padded quietly up to the landing.

When he reached his door, he had to fumble for yet another key. He felt grateful that when he was at home on The Ridge he never had to bother with keys and locks but then moments later, he had let himself in. He quickly undressed but did not put his clothes away in the wardrobe; in the morning, he would be in something of a hurry so he placed them instead on a chair. The night was still warm and the sheets on his bed felt deliciously cool as he slid between them.

His head had hardly touched the pillow when there was a light knock at the door. He had forgotten that Berta had said she would check that he had got back safely. He slid out of bed again and tiptoed across to the door. He opened it carefully to find as he had expected that Berta was waiting on the landing. She slipped into the room, and he held her closely, kissing her gently on the lips.

She lingered with him in the kiss but then drew away. "Too much of that and you'll tempt me to stay," she said.

"Why don't you?" asked Joel.

"You know why not," she replied. "We talked about it earlier. I just wanted to check that you'd got back safely."

Then, frustratingly for Joel, she was once more at the door and was slipping out onto the landing.

Her voice drifted gently back to him.

"Good night, Joel. See you in the morning."

Joel drifted back to his bed, climbed once more between the sheets and in moments was fast asleep.

* * *

Breakfast the next morning was a hurried affair. Sam gobbled his way through several slices of toasted bread, whilst Joel and Berta ate some of the apples and plums that Gwen had placed in a bowl on the table. Temporarily ignoring his two companions, Joel was poring over a sheet of paper that he had extracted from an envelope.

"What have you got there?" asked Sam.

"You'll be pleased to know..." replied Joel "that yesterday, when we were delving through the panniers, I found some more instructions about how to get to the warehouse."

"Ah," said Sam with a glint in his eye. "I didn't think your dad would leave us to wander the streets of Falmouth."

Joel frowned but did not reply to Sam's comment. "The instructions might have come from the messenger or, possibly, from someone at the warehouse. Anyway, they're not in my dad's writing."

He looked up at the other two. "As soon as we've had enough to eat, we can get started."

They finished their breakfasts and Gwen came to clear away the breakfast dishes and reassured them that she would rather deal with the washing up herself than have several young people in the kitchen all of whom were itching to get away on their day's business. Sam went with Tom to fetch Dobbs from the stable. Joel and Berta checked that they had everything they needed for their business at the warehouse.

As they set out, it was another bright, hot summer's day but the shadows cast by the houses on either side of them, provided them with some relief from the heat. They wound their way along narrow streets between tall three- and four-storey buildings in varying states of repair. Most were shops selling such things as meat or fish, vegetables, clothing, hardware and chandlery, and were well cared for, but a few had not been in use for some time and stood empty, their windows and doors heavily barred.

They walked for some time until they were well past the centre of the town and were approaching a large archway leading down to the harbourside. They turned down beneath the arch, the clopping of Dobbs' hooves echoing eerily on the cobbled surface and came out into the bright sunlight reflected by the sparkling waters of Carrick Roads.

"Remind me who we're meeting here," said Berta.

"Well, as you know, the warehouse is owned by someone called Edwin Dire, but in the instructions I found yesterday, it says that we should be doing business with a chap by the name of Corin – Jim Corin."

"I don't think I've heard that surname before," commented Sam.

"No, I don't suppose you have," replied Joel. "But my dad said that long ago the Corins were miners down here in Cornwall. Anyway, we'll be there in a few minutes. You can talk to him about it yourself."

Even in the shadow of the large building they were now approaching, they were once more aware of the stifling heat, which seemed only to be amplified by the reflected glare from the water. Dobbs' hooves clattered along the road as they approached the entrance to the warehouse. A wooden door to their right opened and a fairly short man with greying hair stepped out into the sunshine.

Berta looked at his clothing, wondering how he could bear to be wearing so much on such a hot day.

"What on earth is he wearing?" muttered Berta to one side.

"I think it's called a 'boiler suit'," whispered Joel.

"I'll bet it is – on a day like this!" she commented tartly.

Sam was tempted to laugh, but by then the wearer of the boiler suit was standing in front of them.

"Can I 'elp 'ee?" he inquired politely. Sam and Joel barely understood what he was saying, but Joel had tuned in to the man's voice.

"I'm looking for Jim Corin," he said.

"Then I can 'elp 'ee," replied the man. "I am Jim Corin. I am he. You must be Joel."

"I am," confirmed Joel, "and these are my two friends, Sam and Berta."

"I bin 'spectin 'ee for a while," said Jim. "Yer father sent a message to say you was comin'. Anyway, I'm glad yer 'ere now cause I bin wantin' to meet yer."

By now Sam had also tuned in to Jim's way of speaking.

"Jim," he asked, "is 'Corin' a Cornish name?"

"Well, Sam, I'm not often asked that question but yes 'tis. There's still a few of us down 'ere – and in the Forest of Dean."

"Does your way of speaking come from down here?" asked Berta.

"Well, some of it does," replied Jim. "But the rest comes from the Forest. I spent a good part of my younger life up there."

"So, it's a mixture," commented Berta.

"Yes 'tis'," responded Jim. "A 'mixture'. Good word fer it. Anyway, come inside young 'uns. 'Tis a bit warm to be standin' around out 'ere. Bring yer 'orse an all. 'Tis a warm day fer 'im too."

Jim walked a little further along by the side of the warehouse and slid open a larger door, through which Dobbs trotted happily into the warehouse. Sam muttered his thanks. Berta and Joel followed.

Once inside, Berta began to appreciate why Jim wore his boiler suit. Inside the gloom of the warehouse and away from the heat of the sun, it was much cooler.

"Now," said Jim, suddenly more business-like than he had been outside. "The note from yer dad said you would 'ave something to pay for this part that you are wantin'. I did agree it with 'im at the time."

Joel nodded and went to Dobbs' saddlebags. With Sam's help, he took out the fleeces and laid them carefully on the ground.

Jim turned and went to a wooden box which stood on a workbench, several feet away from them. The three companions followed him. Jim removed the lid of the box so that they could see the part – essentially a large cog – wrapped in an oily cloth and sitting in a bed of straw.

"The fleeces don't seem much for this," said Berta. "It means a lot to us. We'll be able to have electricity again."

Jim laughed. "Good job 'twas Joel's dad doin' the bargainin'. You shouldn't tell the seller that he 'asn't asked enough!"

Berta smiled with embarrassment.

"Ah, take no notice 'o me, young woman," continued Jim. "I'll get a good price for those fleeces. We can't get enough of 'em down 'ere even with all the sheep that we 'ave. Those are good quality. Now are you goin' to have a problem with this thing? 'Tis quite 'eavy!"

"No, I don't think so," replied Sam. "Dobbs will be a bit unbalanced for a while but it's only a short distance back to the house. We can sort him out there."

Joel gazed for a few seconds at the cog, reflecting on the journey they had undertaken to collect it. Then, together with Jim, he closed the box, tied down the lid with some lengths of stout cord and loaded it into one of Dobbs' panniers.

This done, there was no further reason for delay.

"Right y'are then," said Jim. "I'll follow yer out. Watch the quayside when you get out there. Water's very 'igh this mornin'. I don't know if the walls will keep it out much longer. Gets worse every year. Lower town was flooded back in the Spring."

"Yeah," continued Jim as they stood together outside the warehouse. "'Tis high tide now. Just look at it!" He pointed to where the water lapped, not far below the top of the wall. "We can't keep buildin' up these walls. We don't have enough stone. One of these days – or nights – it'll sweep the lot of us away."

He paused in his thoughts for a moment and then said, "Funny thing though. This mornin' there was a dead body bumpin' against the quayside."

He looked up and mistaking the looks on their faces said, "Oh don't worry none. 'Tis not uncommon. Some gang fight over t'other side I 'spec. Best to stay clear, I say."

"Where's it now?" asked Sam, trying to make his enquiry sound as natural as possible.

"Oh, we pushed 'n off again. It'll be somewhere up there". Jim waved vaguely with his hand in the general direction of the rest of the quay. "Current will have taken it."

Although the thought of a dead body floating in the water brought out a streak of morbid curiosity in Joel, he thought that it was time they left. He turned to face the way they had come.

"It's been good to meet 'ee," said Jim, shaking each of them by the hand in turn. When he shook Joel's hand he said, "Give my regards to your father an tell 'im, 'tis good doin' business wi 'im. 'Ave a safe journey 'ome!"

Sam led Dobbs round and together they set off for the house, glad that they had only a short distance to travel in the heat. It had been a relief to deal with the business that they had spent so long travelling to do. It had also been interesting to meet Jim, and Joel felt a sense of satisfaction as they began their journey back through the streets to the relative cool of Gwen's house.

CHAPTER 21

NEWS FROM THE NORTH ATLANTIC

Sam and Berta did not feel like going out again. They were both curious about the town but knew that on the following day, they would have to set out on the long arduous return journey home. In these circumstances, Sam decided that he would prefer to work with Tom, preparing Dobbs for the next day and then doing some packing. Berta also decided to do some packing but then, rejoicing in the availability of clean water, went to plead with Gwen over the possibility of a hot bath or at the very least, an all over wash in hot water.

Joel felt, however, that once the heat of the day had died down, he would like to meet up with James once again. Gwen had prepared an evening meal for them which they all ate with gusto but once it had been cleared away, Joel announced to the other two that he wanted to go to 'The Chain Locker' to meet up with James again.

"You must like that place!" commented Sam.

"It's a good place for a drink and a chat," replied Joel. "Besides, James has been telling me quite a lot about events elsewhere. I'm hoping he'll tell me a bit more this evening."

"I'm very tempted to come with you," said Sam. "But Tom and I haven't finished loading the panniers yet and it seems a pity to waste the evening light."

Sam's conscientiousness made Joel feel a little guilty, but he felt determined to learn from James as much as he could about the situation in the outside world whilst the opportunity was available to him.

As soon as he reasonably could, he set off down the street once more, heading for the 'Chain Locker'. He found James seated at the same table as on the previous night, a candle flickering in the holder in which it had been set on the table before him.

"Ah Joel!" said James, shaking his hand. "It's good to see you again – although truth to tell, I thought you might be back this evening."

"Can I get you a drink?" asked Joel seeing that his companion's glass was nearly empty.

"Yes, thanks Joel, I will accept one this evening. At least the people in here know you're with me now so they won't try any of their funny business."

Joel went to the bar and returned with two pints of beer.

"Thanks, Joel. Cheers!" said James, raising his glass as Joel settled into the seat beside him. "Since you are here this evening, you'll have a chance to meet an old friend of mine, Joe Sorrel – although he's been generally known just as Sorrel almost since I first got to know him."

They had been sipping their beer for just a few moments longer when Joel became aware of a short, wiry man with a rolling gait approaching them through the flickering light of the bar. James immediately stood, holding out his hand in welcome.

"Sorrel, old friend, it's good to see you again! Come and sit yourself over here." He drew his friend towards a seat opposite Joel in which Sorrel quickly settled himself. "Can I get you a drink?" he asked.

Sorrel looked suitably gratified by the offer and James made his way to the bar. Joel reached across the table to shake the newcomer's hand and to introduce himself. Sorrel's grip was strong, and the skin of his hand was hard and horny. Without waiting to be bidden, he seated himself at the table whilst James went to get the beer.

Joel studied their visitor who was now gazing about him. His first impression was of someone who, despite his lack of height, possessed a certain rugged strength. He looked at what he could see of Sorrel's face and his first impression was that within his features could be seen both experience and intelligence. Although living in Falmouth was now enough to brown the skin of even an occasional visitor to the outdoors, Joel thought that the deep tan of their visitor's complexion suggested that their visitor spent most of his time in the open air.

James returned with the glass of beer. On taking it into his hands, Sorrel immediately raised the glass and took a long pull on the beer before placing his drink on the table.

James rejoined them. "I told Joel that you were coming," he said, nodding in Joel's direction.

Sorrel nodded in acknowledgement but seemed disinclined to open the conversation, so James continued, "Sorrel works on board 'The Spindrift'. It's quite a large vessel operated by the company for which I work, and it plies between here and North America. I rely on him for my news of what's happening there."

Joel thought that he saw a frown flit across Sorrel's face. Sorrel bent his head and took another pull of beer from his glass, giving Joel time to observe their visitor's greying hair and the deep nut-brown skin where his hair was thinning.

"Yes, well, it's not good news – although, in truth, the news has been getting worse for some time. It must be nearly a year since we last met!" Sorrel looked at them both.

"One way or another, I've sailed the Atlantic most of my adult life," he said. "But in the last few years, I've had plenty of time to see the ways in which it's changing."

James' face had begun to wear a puzzled frown. "Surely the sea is the sea is the sea...?" he commented.

"Until recent years I'd have agreed with you, my old friend," responded Sorrel. "I've seen the sea in all its moods and at every time of year, but now even a child would know that there's something wrong. It's the sea itself. It's in poor health. It's like an old man ailing. You can see and smell it everywhere you go. It's in your ears, eyes and nose anywhere you sail."

James' frown had become a look of bemused scepticism, but Sorrel could see that he had excited the curiosity of his companions, so he continued.

"Think about it, James. I'm talking about what's happening to the oceans now, and really most of us only get to see what's happening on the surface, but I dare say that the things we see at present have been developing for a long time. Just to take an example, how long is it now since any of us was willing to sail down towards the Gulf of Mexico between June and November? The Spindrift used to sail regularly to the Gulf even in July and August. It was always risky because of the weather down there – but now we wouldn't even consider it."

"That's not news," commented James. "The hurricane season is something we've talked about many times before. It's always been of concern to sailors."

"It has indeed," responded Sorrel. "But not like it is now. One of the few times that I've been genuinely afraid was the occasion I told you about at the time, some five years ago when we had to ride out a hurricane in the Gulf of Mexico. Fortunately, we were just on the southern edge of it for it went north and then ashore in the New Orleans area, but we were still lucky to ride out the storm. It was only the captain's experience and the strength of the ship that saved us. Even so, it took weeks to repair all the damage."

"Then what's different now?" asked Joel.

Sorrel turned his gaze to focus on him. "What's different, Joel," he said, "is the ferocity of the storms. You have no idea of the power of the sea until you've seen waves like the ones we saw in the Gulf that time. I've experienced some terrible storms in my time at sea and I have a due respect for them, but this was something else, something that I've never seen before. The power, the ferocity of it..." His voice tailed away into momentary silence.

James gently prompted him. "You've talked about that storm before, but I appreciate that Joel hasn't heard about it. Coming back to what you were saying, what makes you say that the sea itself is sick? What makes you say that?"

"Just exactly what I said before – it's like a sick person, like someone showing every sign of distress!" responded Sorrel vigorously. "There are many places you can go now where the sea stinks to high heaven! 'Bad eggs, rotten eggs' is how some of the sailors describe it, though others are more down to earth and say it's like there's been some gigantic fart from deep down in the bowels of the ocean."

James found it hard to suppress a laugh and Joel struggled to conceal a smile.

"Yes, well you may laugh, my friends," retorted Sorrel. "But when you see the other signs, you would know what I mean."

"Such as...?" asked James.

"Such as vast shoals of dead fish, many of 'em the weirdest creatures you've ever seen. They're not species you find in the upper waters of the sea. They're creatures from deep down – creatures that in the past we've only seen occasionally. Some of them look like they're from another planet. All the same, we've been seeing that for a long time now – although it's getting worse, much worse and much more common."

He paused, seeming to struggle with the inadequacy of words. "I can tell you about it," he said. "But what I can't put across to you is just how awful it is. Here, on dry land and in this country, there are long spells when you could be forgiven for thinking that nothing is happening, that nothing is out of its usual familiar old ways. It's because things change, but slowly I tell you! Out there–" he gestured in the general direction of the sea. "Out there, you can see and smell that our world is dying!" He hung his head sadly before taking another swig of beer. James and Joel could now clearly see that he was speaking in earnest and prompted him no more but waited patiently instead for him to continue.

Sorrel eventually resumed his story. "The strangest thing of all was that about four months ago, we were sailing north of the Grand Banks, towards the Hudson Bay. There's not much ice to be seen up there these days but we still have to be on the lookout for the occasional iceberg – even the small ones are big enough to sink a ship. It was very foggy, but again that's normal when suddenly there was a huge explosion and everything on the ship was shaken with the force of the blast."

"What on earth caused that?" asked James.

"It so happened that I was in good position to see," replied Sorrel. "I was up on deck and was looking down towards the bows when I saw what I can only describe as huge fireball. At first it exploded upwards into the sky, but then it seemed to race out over the ocean. The sound of the blast took an appreciable time to reach the ship, so I guess the explosion was a long way off. Had we been anywhere near it at the time, I guess we would have been nothing much more than cinders floating on the sea. Anyway, our business took us to Baffin Island and the captain was determined that he wasn't going to be put off by mysterious explosions in the distance – so we continued, but it wasn't a popular decision with the crew."

"Did you find out what caused the explosion?" asked Joel.

"We did," confirmed Sorrel. "We asked people on shore at Baffin Island when we landed and they told us that the explosions have been happening for a number of years now, but that recently, they have been getting a lot more common. A year ago, there was an explosion about the time that a fleet of fishing boats mysteriously disappeared and, of course, they blame the explosions, although it could be many things in that part of the world. From what they say, it's methane from under the sea. It still seems mighty cold to me up there, but the sea is getting warmer all the time and they say that the methane has been released from the bottom of the sea. It's been trapped down there until now by the cold temperature of the water but now that the ocean is warming, it's coming to the surface. When it hits the air, it explodes!"

"Sounds serious," said James. "I never came across anything like that in my sailing days."

Sorrel had not quite finished. "There are still some big places not far south from the Grand Banks – or at least, not far in terms of the distances you can travel at sea. There's Halifax and then Boston and New York – or what's left of them. Even so, a fireball off the coast of Nova Scotia or Maine could kill a hell of a lot of people."

There was a long pause while they thought about what Sorrel had said. Sorrel tilted his glass, draining down the last of his beer and then glanced at James.

"Look," he said, "I'm only ashore for about a week this time and I've got someone waiting for me at my place. She's already been waiting for me for months and beggin' yer' pardon but I think I ought to get down there."

"That would be Molly, I suppose," commented James. Sorrel nodded. "OK, Sorrel, it's been good to see you again. I'm sorry you couldn't stay longer. I'm glad you could come though even if it was just for a short while. Joel here is leaving us tomorrow and I just wanted him to hear whatever news you could tell him about what's happening these days, outside of this little place."

"Yes, I'm sorry I can't stay longer but after all these months, Molly is a bit impatient, if you see what I mean. Perhaps we'll meet again, Joel?"

"I hope so," replied Joel, knowing that it was unlikely but also feeling that he liked Sorrel despite the grim nature of the news that he had brought them.

James showed their visitor to the door whilst Joel cleared away the evidence of their drinking session.

"Strange man," commented Joel.

"Yes," agreed James. "He's a good source of news but his news is always like his name."

"How do you mean?" asked Joel.

Well, 'Sorrel's' a plant, isn't it – and to my knowledge, it's one you can eat – but it has a bitter taste!"

Joel smiled at James' comment but said nothing more other than, "I wish you good night…"

"You'll keep your eyes open for troublemakers?" asked James.

"Yes, of course," responded Joel and rose to make his way past the drinkers at the bar. He paused briefly at the door and turned back to see that James was still slowly drinking his beer, but then he made his way out into the street.

CHAPTER 22

DESPERATE MEASURES

It took Joel just a few minutes to make his way back to the street in which Gwen's house was situated. He turned into the square and began to fumble for his key, but then to his surprise he noticed that the front door of the house was slightly ajar. He pushed at it, and it swung open. For a moment or two he thought that it was simply a piece of carelessness on the part of those inside, but then as he fumbled his way forward, he realised that there were other things amiss.

He had expected that a lamp would have been lit for him but instead, the room was in complete darkness. He fumbled his way forward, temporarily unable to see in the very dim light that filtered in from the street. With a startled cry, he fell headlong, bashing his shoulder hard on the wooden floor. For a moment he lay dazed and then, as his sight became accustomed to the darkness of the room he realised that he had fallen over an upturned chair. He scrambled to his feet and raced up the stairs.

"Berta! Berta!" Joel yelled, unable to contain his anxiety as he ran along the passage in the darkness. There was no reply.

As he reached the door of Berta's room, he could see that it stood open. In Berta's room, at least, a lamp flickered, its dim light dancing on a chaos of bedclothes tumbled on the floor.

In Sam's room, the scene was similar; there was no lamp, but Joel could just make out the same signs of disturbance that he had seen in the other parts of the house. He turned back into the passage, his heart thudding and his mind racing over what he should do next.

It occurred to him that maybe Gwen and Tom were still in the house somewhere. He ran back along the passage. Cursing the number of steps on the staircase, he stumbled his way down them, leaping the last few and landing heavily on the floor of the lounge. He ran across to the kitchen, where the door stood wide open, its handle hanging by a screw from a large and jagged piece of wood which hung awkwardly out of the door. Saucepans lay scattered on the floor and Joel's feet crunched over broken pieces of china as he tried to push his way further into the kitchen. He turned to go back out the way he had come and saw lying on the floor a white cap that he seen Gwen wearing, earlier in the day.

Once out in the lounge, he quickly decided that further searching would be useless. Had there been anyone there, the sound of his own voice and movements would almost certainly have brought them out. He would have to get help and at that moment, the only person he could think of was James.

He ran back down the hill towards the Chain Locker, steering around stumbling rowdy groups of drunks and just managing to catch James by the arm as he was about to mount the staircase up to his room.

James' surprise at seeing Joel again and then at hearing the breathless story that he poured into his ears, was quickly followed by concern.

"There's no time to lose!" he said, pulling his coat around him. The landlord had begun locking up.

"Here, what you up to then?" he cried as James prevailed upon him to not lock the door before they had been able to make their exit; they leapt into the street only to hear the door being locked behind them.

"It's alright," said James, "I've got a key for whenever we get back."

They had returned to the main street and Joel stumbled along at James' side as they hurried between the shops and houses lining the road.

"Where are we going?" yelled Joel.

"We're going in search of a man by the name of McLennan – Alistair McLennan."

Joel did not have to reach very far into his memory to remember the rather eccentric individual they had met just a few days ago on their way down to Truro.

"I don't suppose there could be more than one Alistair McLennan?" asked Joel breathlessly.

"Not very likely!" James called back over his shoulder. "Not in these parts, at any rate."

"Why are we looking for him now?" asked Joel.

"Because he's the most likely person to know where your friends have been taken!" responded James.

"Taken? What do you mean, 'Taken'?" Joel yelled back.

"Just exactly that!" exclaimed James impatiently. "Hold onto your questions for now. I'll explain it all later. We're nearly there – so let's hope he's in."

They had entered a narrow street where the houses seemed almost to reach out to one another above their heads. James stopped at a door painted in gleaming black and in the middle of which was a large, brass door knocker. He seized it firmly and rapped sharply on the door. At first, nothing seemed to happen and then Joel was startled by the sudden sliding back of a small panel just above the door knocker. An eye appeared in the panel. Joel could almost feel its gaze roving over them as they stood in the street.

Then a voice, which Joel immediately recognised, boomed out from within: "What time do you call this?" There was no response from James other than three more sharp raps on the brass doorknocker.

Immediately there was the sound of a key in a lock and a heavy bolt being slid back. Then, in the flickering light of a lamp, McLennan appeared in the open doorway. He glanced up and down the street and said in much lower voice, "You'd better come in!"

As Joel saw him again still dressed in black and silhouetted in the doorway, he was reminded of a thin and rather sinister bird – perhaps like one of the cormorants that were found all along the coast.

They hustled into the narrow hallway and McLennan took them from there into a small front room, where he set his lamp down on a table. It reminded him a little of some of the rooms in his grandfather's house. Books and maps littered the chairs. McLennan swept some of them aside and onto the floor, waving to James and Joel to sit down.

"Now then," he said. "What brings you here at this time of night?"

James nodded to Joel, indicating that he should repeat the story he had told him just a short while before.

McLennan listened in silence, his only response, seemingly, a deepening of the furrows on his forehead.

As Joel came to the end of his story, McLennan shook his head. "I had hoped to meet you again," he said, "but not in circumstances such as these. I can help you, but it isn't going to be easy. We'll need some more help – the rough kind – because this could be very rough before we've finished."

"Will my friends be alright?" asked Joel, still not knowing what had happened to them.

"That could depend on how quickly we get to them," replied McLennan. "They were probably not taken until after dark so we should still have time to get to them before..."

Joel interrupted him. "Before what...?"

"Before Sam wakes up gagged and bound on board one of those ships out there in the harbour."

It was as Joel had feared but then he asked, "Right, but what could they want with the others – with Berta and Gwen and the little lad?"

"Two things," said McLennan. "One, they wouldn't have wanted to leave any witnesses behind. They wouldn't want Sam's fate to be known – at least not until he was well out to sea."

Joel was impatient. "You said 'two things'. What was the other?"

"It's almost a pity you had to ask," replied McLennan grimly, "but it'll probably be sex – unless they simply intend to kill them and didn't want to do it at the house."

He could hardly believe McLennan's words. His life at home had always been hard, a constant battle for survival – as it was for everyone – but it had never contained what he was meeting here. Until now he had liked what he had seen of the town, even in its decayed state, but the darkness and depravity to which McLennan had alluded was something that he had not encountered before.

"I wish we'd never come to this place!" he muttered between clenched teeth.

"Huh!" said James. "Better here than most places. In most places, they'd..."

McLennan interrupted, "Joel doesn't need to know that just now. We're wasting time. Come on! We'll go out the back way."

He led the way through the gloom of the house to a large wooden door. He opened it and ushered them out onto some large stone steps. Locking the door behind them, he took them down the steps to a small courtyard and then across to a gate in a high stone wall. Beyond the gate they came out into the darkness of a cobbled street which sloped steeply upwards to their left. He set off at a brisk pace uphill.

"Where are we going?" asked Joel.

"First, we're going to get help."

"Where's that?"

"Not far. We're nearly there. You'll have to wait a few moments – and then we can get on."

McLennan went a little ahead of them. They were now on the remains of what must once have been a coastal road that made its way just behind a line of cliffs towards the remains of an old castle on a promontory overlooking the sea. In the darkness, Joel could hear waves beating on the shore. On this side of the town, he thought, they were no longer next to the harbour. The sharp tang of salt in the breeze told him that the cliffs just beyond them overlooked the ocean.

"Wait here!" called McLennan. He went ahead and up the path of a large house on the left-hand side of the road. The house might have been a boarding house or a hotel in former times, although to Joel, it was simply another building that had somehow survived the ravages of conflict and civil breakdown, and which still managed to hold its place in a line of other, similar houses overlooking the Atlantic Ocean.

Joel thought that he saw the front door of the house open, and a shadowy figure admit McLennan inside.

James drew him aside and they waited behind a clump of gorse bushes. "There probably won't be anyone else coming along here," commented James. "But it's as well to be careful."

It was warm night, but Joel still felt himself shivering in anticipation of what was to come – and because inside him was a sharp knot of anxiety about the fate of his friends.

"What's keeping him?" he exclaimed.

"He's only been gone about two minutes," replied James. "He won't be a second longer than he has to be!"

They waited a similar time again. Then, just as Joel was about to make another remark to James, the front door of the house across the road swung open and three men, McLennan included, spilled out onto the path; Joel peered through the darkness, trying to catch a glimpse of his companions.

Moments later, they were all standing in a bunch and McLennan was saying, "Joel, meet Mick and Chick." He felt his hand grasped in first one bone crunching handshake and then another.

Now that they were standing next to him, Joel tried to get a better look at them. The only light was that of the stars, but as far as he could see they were two similar individuals – possibly brothers. They had rather square heads and jaws, close cropped fair hair and wore dark jackets and trousers. One – the one introduced to Joel as Chick – was a little shorter than the other, but they both looked as though they had been hewn out of rock and he was glad that they would be helping him and not fighting against him. "Some 'Chick'," thought Joe, reflecting on their names, "though 'Mick' is probably about right."

It was now Mick and Chick who led the way. McLennan explained that though they usually worked for him, they had a particular score to settle with the people they were going to meet and were only too pleased to have the opportunity.

He spoke for a moment to the taller of the two men – Mick. "I'm relying on you two. I don't know my way into this place."

Joel had been waiting to hear one of them speak and when Mick replied, it was a mild shock. "It's not a problem, Alistair," said Mick in a precise and clearly enunciated tone. "We've been watching this place for some time. We know it like the backs of our hands." In the darkness he spread out his own ham-like hand in front of their faces and then jogged back to join his brother, a short way further on along the road.

"What are we going to do?" asked Joel as McLennan returned his attention to him.

"Well, first," replied McLennan, "make sure that you stay close to James. He knows how we work. We'll need you two to stay back, a little out of sight and come up if we need you. They won't be expecting us. Surprise should be on our side. Can you handle one of these?" He shoved a gun into Joel's hands. It was a shotgun though its twin barrels were shorter than those of the guns that Joel had used before.

Joel was mildly shocked but said, "Yes, of course I can." He had learned to shoot on the farm, and it was second nature to him although the largest things that he had shot until then were deer or feral dogs.

"It's loaded and the catch is on. Here, you'll need these!" McLennan shovelled a clutch of cartridges – Joel thought that there were eight of them – into his hands.

"Thanks," said Joel suddenly a little in awe of someone who could dole out such rare things in a seemingly casual way. At home, cartridges were treated as though they were gold nuggets.

They walked briskly but in silence until Joel asked, "Who are these people who've taken Sam and the others?"

"They call themselves 'The Razors' – after one of their favourite weapons," answered McLennan. "Sometimes they call themselves 'The Hell Razors'. It suits them." He thought for moment and then said, "It could be worse, your friends could have been taken by 'The Eastside'. If it had been them, we'd have no chance. You're in luck – if that's what you can call it. These people are total perverts – but also complete amateurs."

It was small comfort to Joel. "So what's in it for you, Alistair – and those two?" He nodded towards the two men just ahead of them.

"For me?" said McLennan. "The Shipping Company – the legitimate one, that is, pay me to put these people out of business. And they pay me well." He made his last remark with a certain amount of vehemence.

"Right," said Joel. "But that still leaves Mick and Chick."

A frown stole across McLennan's face. "We're getting close to where we need to be," he said. "But all I'll say for the moment is that there used to be three brothers – until one of them was killed by The Razors." James, who had also been listening to McLennan, stepped forward and put a hand on Joel's arm, drawing his attention back to the two brothers.

Joel shifted his gaze away from McLennan and looked ahead to where he could see the angular outlines of Mick and Chick. Now that they had their backs towards him, he recognised the shapes of two crossbows, strapped across their shoulders.

At that moment, the brothers turned towards them, indicating the need for silence and plunged off down a small bank and onto an overgrown path amongst a dense growth of trees and bushes.

For some minutes, they walked again in total silence. Below them, Joel could hear the rhythmic sounds of the sea washing against the walls of the harbour. Ahead of them and down towards the water's edge was a long, low stone building. Mick led the way, eventually moving into a crouched position and then gesturing to the others to do the same.

McLennan leaned back so that he could speak to James and Joel. "I was right. They're not expecting company. There's just the one guard outside the building."

Joel wondered how they would deal with the guard, but his answer was not slow in coming. Mick had crept onto the path at the side of the building and waited until the man was in reach but had his back towards him. Swiftly, he stepped behind the guard, clamping a hand over his mouth. Joel waited, expecting a violent struggle but there was little to see, other than a sudden decisive movement of Mick's arm and the guard hanging limp and lifeless in his grasp. For a moment, he stopped to get a firmer grip on the body and then walked backwards, dragging it to one side of the shed and finally concealing it behind some piles of planking.

A grim sense of shock began to steal over Joel, but he had little time to think about it because Mick now waved them to follow him. He was quickly joined by his brother whilst McLennan, James and Joel scrambled down to meet them. No sooner than they were together outside the door, then Mick quietly swung open the large wooden door into the shed.

Immediately, they found themselves in a long corridor that ran the length of the building. It was not very wide, and they had trouble keeping out of each other's way. Chick turned right and, keeping low, went to investigate. The others watched as he crawled along the full length of that end of the corridor, pausing every so often to poke his head up and peer through windows that ran along one side. After a minute or so he reached the far end, stood up and walked back.

"Offices," he whispered when he reached them. "No-one there."

"Let's try the other end," breathed Mick. "Wait here."

Like his brother, he crawled along the corridor until he had covered about half the length and then stood up cautiously to investigate something he had found on his right-hand side. He motioned the others to move forward. They did so and joined him outside a large pair of wooden doors. In the upper half of each door was a small square window. Mick stood and peered through the window in the left-hand door. They were slightly surprised to see a faint light flickering on his face. Then, cautiously, he pushed open the door, holding it open so that the others could crawl through.

Once inside, they could see that the light was coming from behind a long series of panels that partitioned the length of the space in half and reached about two-thirds of the way to the ceiling. They could also hear voices – coarse, animated voices, talking excitedly. As quietly as they could, they crept across the intervening space towards the partition. There was a gap between the first panel and the wall. Mick positioned himself so that he could see round the panel and, in the semi-darkness, peeped cautiously out into the area beyond.

On the other side were three large workbenches. Shipwrights' tools hung along the walls, barely visible in the dim light. Seated at one end of the nearest workbench, three men were playing cards. Then, as his eyes adjusted to the dim light, he thought that he could see four other people, bound and gagged. Two lay bound, blindfolded and gagged in the shadows on one side. Mick guessed from their size and shape that they were Gwen and Tom. A third figure seemed to have been tied over one of the workbenches. Mick could not be sure but guessed that it was probably Sam. The fourth figure was moving – quite violently, trying to wrench the chains that fastened its ankles and wrists to thick iron rings set in the wall.

The card game seemed to be nearing its end and one of the players was becoming impatient.

"Come on! Play your cards. Fucking get on with it!"

The voices that had been indistinct before could now be heard clearly by Mick as he stood flattened against the panel separating him from the card players. Silently, he unfastened his crossbow and loaded it with a bolt.

"What you worried about? You had the boy, didn't you? But perhaps you're getting greedy."

"No greedier than you! You got to be desperate to go shagging old women!"

"Fuckin' shut it, you two. Let's get this finished!"

Peering from between two of the panels and hidden by the darkness, Joel watched as the third player laid his hand of cards gloatingly on the table.

The other two players looked in disbelief at them.

"How the fuck did you get those?" said the player nearest Joel. A moment later, he had scrambled away from the table, trying desperately to avoid the blade of a large knife that had nearly sliced open his right cheek.

The remaining player was not so foolish.

"Okay, okay, Jake!" he said. "She's yours. But we get her after you."

"You'll have plenty of time to work out who's next," came the reply." I ain't had one like this in a while." The speaker replaced the knife in its sheath slung from a strap which ran over his right shoulder and under his left arm.

He stood up and moved towards the shrouded figure straining at the chains. There were gasps and whistles, as he tore the shroud from the person imprisoned by the chains. Joel felt sick. It was Berta. He had felt sure that it must be her, but it was still a deep, inward shock to see her naked and vulnerable in front of the thugs who were now standing around her.

He began to move forward without knowing what he intended to do, but Chick swiftly put a large, restraining hand on his arm and gestured with his crossbow towards the three men.

The men were moving towards Berta. "Take her blindfold off. I want the bitch to see what I'm doing."

The smallest of the three men moved quickly forward and after some fumbling with the knots, removed the blindfold.

This caused a fresh outburst of futile straining against the chains and muffled cries from Berta, but the only response from the man in front of her was to begin unbuttoning his trousers.

"P'raps you'd like to see what yer gonna get!"

By now, his trousers had fallen awkwardly around his ankles, but he shuffled in closer, his erect member wagging before him.

Berta averted her head, jerking at the chains, her muffled cries becoming even more frantic but the next second there was a rattle from Mick's crossbow. Its bolt flew across the intervening space and struck the semi-naked thug in the neck. He fell to the floor, blood pouring from his mouth.

Almost immediately a second bolt, fired from Chick's crossbow, found its target in the chest of the man who had removed Berta's blindfold. Joel watched once more in shocked surprise as he fell immediately, almost noiselessly to the ground, his life ending without further gesture or sound.

Mick had begun to reload, but Chick, seeing that the third member of the gang might escape, ran forward, snatched up the knife which now lay on the floor and pursued him. Joel levelled his gun at the retreating back of the third gang member. He fired from both barrels of the gun in quick succession. The double crash echoed around the warehouse, momentarily deafening them all.

Despite Joel's action, Chick was almost too late. The third member of the gang had reacted swiftly and, although wounded by Joel's shots, was running towards a huge pair of sliding doors located on the far side of the workshop. He tore desperately at the bolts holding the doors in place, pushing one of them back and launching himself into the darkness beyond.

Chick was just a short distance behind him. McLennan too was now in hot pursuit. Just ahead of him, he heard a loud splash and an angry cry from Chick. Finally, he found Chick slouched against the wall of the workshop, holding his side in an attempt to staunch a flow of blood.

"Bastard had a knife," snarled Chick by way of explanation. McLennan tried to get a look at the wound, but after a moment or two, decided that they needed to move inside. With Chick's arm around his neck, they staggered back into the flickering light of the workshop.

Once inside, McLennan asked, "What happened?"

"He swiped at me with a knife, but he was off-balance. I stuck my knife in him and he went over backwards, straight off the harbour wall."

"Do you think you killed him?"

"I don't know," panted Chick, "Joel hit him as well. I doubt if he'll survive the swim, but you never know."

"Okay," said McLennan. "We'll worry about it later."

He cautiously peeled back Chick's coat and shirt which were soaked in blood, but which had given him a certain amount of protection.

After a moment or two, Chick having momentarily released his pressure on the wound, McLennan said, "It's a nice mess but we can fix you up. First, though, we have to get you back to your house. We can't do much here."

Whilst Chick and McLennan had been in further pursuit of the third gang member, Joel and James had gone to Berta. James found the keys to her shackles in the pocket of the thug sprawled on the floor in front of her.

As soon as she had been released from the shackles and the gag, Joel helped her to cover herself with the cloth that initially had been draped over her. She huddled on the floor, sobbing quietly with Joel's arm around her shoulder. James moved off, Mick going with him to release Sam, Gwen and Tom. Somehow, despite the shock of the violence that had been inflicted on her, Gwen managed to tell them where the thugs had put their clothes. Like Berta, they huddled, traumatised, in the coverings that had been flung over them earlier in the night.

A minute or two later, James found their clothes and having returned them to their owners, went to see what the situation was with Chick.

Mick also moved on to find out what had happened to his brother. Together, McLennan, Mick and James decided that, despite the risks, they would move Chick back to the brothers' house. McLennan would then stay with them whilst James and Joel took the rest of the group back to Gwen's house. McLennan and Mick between them weighted the bodies of the dead gang members and the guard and slid them into the waters of the harbour. Then, with the freed captives between them, they set off back along the route by which they had come.

The night had begun to seem interminably long. Their retreat was slow and although Chick's wound was not thought to be life threatening, it was giving him a great deal of pain. The other members of the group found it hard to hide their concern but knew that they needed to get back to the brothers' house before anything effective could be done.

Despite the shock that he had received through the treatment inflicted on him by the thugs, Sam began gradually to recover. Like the other captives, he had been humiliated and subjected to violence, but his fear and anger were gradually giving way to an enormous sense of relief. As they trudged back, he began to take a turn in supporting Chick along the path and back onto the road to the brothers' house.

After what seemed a very long time, they arrived at the house door. Mick assured the rest of the group that Chick would be alright, and that McLennan would stay with them in case they needed any further help. Once they had gone inside, James and Joel urged the others to carry on with the journey until many weary steps later, they rounded the corner of the street in which Gwen's house was situated.

Joel was first into the house. Gwen's presence of mind had stayed with her in spite of the treatment she had been given, and she soon found and lit a lamp which provided a dim, flickering light. For the time being, however, they all seemed to be almost too tired and shocked by the night's events to utter anything other than a few guttural remarks about needing to sleep before they could even think about doing anything else.

Berta wanted Gwen and Tom to share her room to which Gwen consented. Sam simply wanted to crawl into his bed. Joel similarly had no sooner laid his head on his pillow than he fell asleep fully clothed.

James, older than them all, stayed behind to secure the front door which he did with an arduous but determined thoroughness before finding a bed for himself in the room next to the one normally used by Gwen. Then they all slept, fitfully but exhaustedly, well into the next morning and long after the hot fingers of the sun had begun to trace their course across the floor of the front lounge.

* * *

Joel and James were the first to wake. Having slept in his clothes, Joel felt stale. The desperate events of the previous night had led him to temporarily forget the reason that they had travelled so far. Today, it was once more in the front of his mind and whatever problems arose from the previous night's rescue, he had to get them all safely out of the town and on the road home.

He forced himself to be patient whilst he peeled off his clothes and then stood in front of the sink to wash. A breeze through his open window warmed the room and it was no hardship to stand naked and wash himself thoroughly. Drying himself on one of Gwen's towels, he went to look for whatever fresh clothing he still had left in his bag.

When he had dressed, he made his way along the corridor and down the staircase. He sat at the table where he had sat the previous evening with Sam and Berta. It was something of a surprise to realise that it was only the previous evening that the three of them had sat there; it seemed much longer ago than that.

He looked up to see James heading towards him. His clothes gave him a slightly crumpled look and his face had the grey pallor of someone who has had insufficient sleep. Despite this, he walked past Joel and over to the window where he drew back the curtains, allowing the warm sunshine to flood into the room. He returned to sit briefly at Joel's side.

For a moment or two, neither of them spoke and then Joel said, "Did you manage to sleep after the events of last night?"

"Oh yes, it was no problem, although the bed in the small room there leaves a bit to be desired."

James looked at Joel, realising that he was worrying about what had happened. "What's bothering you?" he asked.

Joel sighed. "I'm confused," he said. "I'm relieved that we managed to rescue the others, but in order to do it, we had to kill three people – possibly four."

James frowned and then said, "Just listen to me carefully for a minute, Joel. It's not the first time I've had to deal with thugs like those who took your friends last night – though it's never come easily to me. But I know people in this town who would barely give it a moment's thought – and one or two who even enjoy killing for its own sake."

He paused and then said, "Do you have any idea what they would probably have done to Sam and Berta if we hadn't got there in time?"

Joel shook his head.

"Well, I'll leave you to think about it because I'm not going to sketch it out for you," said James. "But what I will say is that the town will be a better place without those thugs in it – although there's plenty more where they came from. They were like wild animals but animals that prey on their own kind."

Anger had crept into James' voice. Joel looked away, feeling that James was right and supposing that it was his own naiveté and inexperience that wanted there to be a happy outcome untainted by violence and guilt.

He looked up. "We'd better check on the others. I'll find out if Berta, Gwen and Tom are awake yet."

"No, let me do it," said James, placing a hand on Joel's forearm.

Joel looked at him quizzically.

"I should have told you. Gwen is my wife and Tom is my son."

Joel understood immediately but was unable to conceal his surprise at the suddenness of the revelation.

Mistaking surprise for incomprehension, James muttered with some vehemence, "They took my wife and son!"

Joel was left to stare after him as he strode across the room and launched himself up the stairs. The implications of what James had said were left to flood in upon him. He sat for a moment wondering why and how James had kept his relationship to Gwen and Tom so well concealed. After a moment's further reflection, he decided that other than the need to know about it, it was none of his business. He had wanted to find out about Berta, Gwen and Tom, but James would get to them before him. Then he remembered that on the journey home, Sam had been very quiet. He would check on Sam first.

Joel eased the door of Sam's room open to find his friend just beginning to stir. He eased himself into the room and sat on the foot of the bed. Sam propped himself up on one elbow.

"Oh," he said, "It can't be day already." Slowly he sat up and then he gave a groan as the memories of the previous night came back to him.

"Oh," he said. "Oh no!"

Joel waited.

"I feel useless. I feel like a fool!" exclaimed Sam. "I let those people in! How could I have been so stupid?"

Joel waited again whilst Sam explained. "We'd locked the door after you went to the Chain Locker. The others had gone to their rooms but a short while later, there was knock on the door. I looked out of the side window. There was this scrawny little man waiting in the courtyard. I thought I'd have no trouble dealing with him – so I opened the door."

Joel could almost guess the rest of the story but left his friend to continue. "He said he needed to speak to Gwen. He seemed to be alone, and I was about to call for Gwen when three more of them came tumbling in. They must have been hiding just out of sight on the other side of the doorway."

Despite his determination to listen to Sam without reacting, it was Joel's turn to give a groan.

Sam, however, ignored him and swept along by his memory, continued with the story.

"The biggest one, the one I last saw lying on the floor with an arrow through his neck, he put his arm around my neck and told me that if I made a sound, he'd cut my throat. Since he was waving a very large knife under my nose at the time, I believed him.

"The rest was simple. It took them just moments to tie and gag me and then they went for the others. When they'd bound, gagged and blindfolded us all, we were thrown in a horse cart, covered with a sheet of canvas and taken to...to, well, where you found us at the workshop, although at the time we didn't have a clue where they were taking us. We seemed to lurch about all over the place. I could hear the sound of horses' hooves on the cobbles."

Sam seemed to be struggling to tell his story, so Joel prompted him with a question.

"What were they planning to do?"

"Well, they'd already done some of it when you got there!" retorted Sam heatedly. "They..." He got no further because suddenly he was overtaken by sobbing. He tried again and managed to say "They..." once more before resigning himself to the tears that had begun to roll down his cheeks. Joel waited, wanting to say something that would help but knowing that there was nothing. He needed to let Sam talk. After a moment, his friend somehow found a voice again and said in words that were barely audible, "I'm not telling you what they did to Gwen and Tom. Anyway, you can guess what they did! They were like animals. No, I take that back! The animals I'm used to don't know what they're doing. Those people knew alright! They knew what they were doing! They were disgusting – the most depraved..." His voice tailed away again, and he was unable to finish the sentence.

Joel moved to put an arm round his friend's shoulder, but Sam motioned him away. Joel returned to his seat at the foot of the bed.

"If you and the others hadn't found us, they had similar plans for me and Berta. They kept talking about 'initiating' me, giving me a dose of what they said would happen to me once they'd got me on board a ship."

"Oh, so they planned to 'press gang' you?"

Sam looked at Joel, wondering what the term 'press gang' meant but then said, "Yes, I think that's what they planned to do. I heard them talking about putting me on a ship bound for the North – Canada, I heard one of them say."

Joel nodded and then asked, "And what about Berta? What plans did they have for her?"

"I'm sure you can guess," replied Sam. "They were planning to use her for their own entertainment and, if you and the others hadn't arrived, to carry on using and abusing her until they'd had their fill. And then, I guess, they might have sold her – if they hadn't already killed her by that stage."

Joel shuddered. The feelings of the previous night returned to him, and he felt sick again at the memory. Hatred and revulsion welled within him. It was some moments before he remembered that three of the thugs were dead – but then there had also been a fourth member of the group – and he might still be alive; it was important for them to remember that.

"Are you fit to move?" he asked.

"Yes, I'm a bit stiff," replied Sam. "But I'm OK. I'm glad we were able to talk about it. Now I just want to get moving. Let's do what we have to do and then get out of here!"

Joel nodded in agreement, drawing encouragement from Sam's desire to put the previous night's events behind them. They had dwelt on it enough, although the others had suffered the most – and they had yet to talk to them. For the moment though, he and Sam would have to put it to one side.

"You're right," said Joel. "We need to get Berta down here."

* * *

Dazed and weary, Berta was trying hard to focus on the discussion between Sam and Joel. The three of them were sitting around Gwen's dining table debating what they should do next. Until the events of the previous night, it had always been Sam who wanted to explore the towns along their route, but now he wanted to leave as soon as possible. Joel wanted a further day to prepare for the journey back, but Sam and Berta were convinced that whilst they remained in the town, they were in great danger.

Joel endeavoured to listen patiently as Sam explained his viewpoint.

"Ok," he was saying. "I agree that I was the one who wanted to explore every place along the route, but after last night's experience, I just want to finish what we came to do and get back to the Ridge as soon as possible."

Joel nodded and then looked at Berta, hoping that she would agree with him but realising that, if anything, her experience had been worse than Sam's.

"I can understand why you want a bit more time, Joel," she said. "But for as long as Sam and I are here, we'll be afraid that someone will want to kidnap us or take revenge for the killings."

Joel pursed his lips in reluctant agreement. "I can see how you feel, and I understand why. But the journey here was hard, and I would have liked longer to make sure that we were really prepared."

"We'll have to make the best of it," replied Sam. "Sooner or later, someone will want to know what happened to those thugs at the workshop. Although it may be hard to believe, someone will notice that they're missing. I don't want to stay here long enough to give anyone an opportunity to get back at us.”

“Alright,” said Joel. “We’ll leave this morning, but we need to get together some food, even if it’s only enough for the first few days.”

After their conversation, Berta went to seek Gwen’s advice about where to buy food and supplies. Following her suggestion, the three of them then spent a hot, anxious hour at a street market hurriedly buying food, oil for their lamps, darning materials for their clothes and items such as soap which would help to make the homeward journey more tolerable.

When they returned again to the house, they hastily packed their belongings into the large panniers that would be placed once more across Dobbs’ back. Tom had recovered enough to help them, although his former chirpiness had been replaced by a sullen determination to help with the work and no more.

They were all worried about Gwen. Other than provide Berta with advice, she had kept herself doggedly to herself. Berta decided to see if she could talk to her, however briefly, before their departure. She found Gwen in the kitchen, aimlessly shifting cups and plates from one place to another. She managed to draw her away from her pointless task and sat her at the table while she went to make her a cup of tea. The large black kettle had been bubbling away on the fire for some time and Gwen had ignored it. Berta returned with two steaming cups of tea and sat down at the table, next to Gwen.

They sat briefly in silence until Gwen eventually took a small sip of her tea and then said, “I’m surprised you wanna drink tea on a day like this. You need to get goin’ – and it’s already hot out there.”

“You’re right,” replied Berta. “But it’s cool in here. Besides, tea is rare in the village where I live. This might be my last cup for some time.”

Gwen managed a watery smile. “We grow it not far from here,” she said. “’Tis so warm most of the year now and the frosts that some people talk about – well, we never see ‘em ‘ere.”

She paused and then said, “But I guess you didn’t come to talk to me about tea or the weather.”

Berta had not thought about what she would say to Gwen but was driven more by a feeling that they needed to talk to each other. She waited, not sure what Gwen would say next and was unprepared for her sudden departure from the commonplaces of a moment or two before.

Gwen stared at the table. "I never...I never thought people could behave like those bastards yesterday," she said. She looked around her, partly blinded by the tears of anger and frustration that had begun to flow profusely. Her face became streaked and red, and she began to beat her fists and then her forehead on the table.

"I can't bear to think what they did to me and my Tom. I can't bear to think what those scum, those...filth did to me and my boy!" Her voice broke and she could speak no longer. She sobbed uncontrollably, her shoulders shaking and her tears pouring down onto the table.

Berta moved closer and put an arm around her heaving shoulders. She felt helpless but knew that Gwen was expressing an anger that they both felt. It was some time before Gwen spoke again, but eventually she said in a small, tight voice, "Do you know the worst thing? Do you know what makes me feel worst of all?"

Berta shook her head, waiting for Gwen to speak again.

"I'm glad Chick killed 'un cos' if he hadn't, I would've – even if it cost me my own life, I'd a killed 'un. I wanted to get that knife they had and..." She broke down in huge sobs again, leaving Berta to imagine what she would have done to the thug who had violated her. It took little imagination on Berta's part for she understood only too well the emotions that were tearing at Gwen.

Without relinquishing, Berta's arm, Gwen turned to look her full in the face. She said, "The thing is that in my heart, they've made me like them. I wanted to kill 'em, every one of 'em. And now they are dead, thank God. But I 'ave to live with how they've made me feel about myself – the filthy, disgustin' thing they've made me."

She put her head down on the table again, her tears flowing once more. Berta held her firmly around the shoulders, struggling with her feelings for Gwen, but also with the memories of the previous night that she had so far pushed deep down in her mind, but which had now risen once more to the surface.

Outside in the lounge, Joel could hear just sufficient to guess what was happening in the kitchen. James appeared but Joel motioned him away. They stood for a moment debating what to do. Joel was aware that it was many hours since they had last eaten, but food seemed to be the last thing on anyone's mind at that moment.

He knew that Berta had wanted to talk to Gwen, but now that the others had voiced their fears, he too was anxious to leave.

***

Sam and Berta picked at a belated breakfast that they had cobbled together from food in the kitchen. Joel and James joined them, but Gwen insisted that she did not feel like eating. Soon, they were once more in the courtyard, loading the last items needed for the journey into Dobbs' panniers. The cloudless sky above told them that it was going to be another hot, sunny day.

Tom seemed glad to be doing something and helped Sam to adjust Dobbs' load, all the while making a fuss of the big horse of which he had already become fond.

Finally, they were ready to depart.

Gwen was tearful, hugging Berta in particular. "It's been good to 'ave another woman 'ere. I'll miss 'ee," she said.

"At least you'll have James with you now," belatedly musing to herself that they made an odd couple.

"Yeah, an' I 'ope 'e'll stay this time," replied Gwen.

Sam and Joel solemnly shook hands with Tom and then waved their goodbyes. He stood at his mother's side, frowning and waving back at them.

Ironically, James told them that for the short time that it would take to accompany them to the town gate, he would leave Gwen and Tom at the house. No-one other than James thought that it was a good idea, but as they made their way through the narrow streets leading back to the gate, James was at their side.

They were soon at the gate and mildly relieved, though not surprised, to find that this time the guards were less attentive. Joel could see just a single guard on the rampart above the gate, and he was yawning and sunning himself rather than watching the latest group of travellers to be leaving the town.

"Oh – there is one last thing." James had hesitated before leaving them to move forward to the gate.

"The gate keeper will open the gate, but he will need the last of any coins that you still have left."

Sam laughed. "What a surprise," he commented sarcastically. "But they'll be no use to us out there anyway." He fumbled in his pockets to produce the last of his coins and then cupped his hands to receive the rest from Joel and Berta.

The appearance of the money seemed to stimulate action on the part of the gatekeeper. He shambled across to meet them, although in truth, the shamble was more of roll, as befitted his girth and general shape.

"Good mornin' to 'ee! James," he cried cheerfully. "An' to you young 'uns too!"

Joel was not too sensitive to smells but found it quite difficult not to register his discomfort as the man approached. The waiting group all quietly noted that he was wearing the same greasy brown jacket, grimy faded T-shirt and soiled grey trousers that he had been wearing when they had first seen him. Sam held out the coins towards him. A beaming smile lit up his face.

"Ah, I see that James has bin educatin' you in our ways," he laughed. "Well I 'ope you have enjoyed your stay in our little town?"

They nodded, almost in unison, not wishing him for one moment to get any inkling of what had happened to them. James maintained his own inscrutable facial expression.

Apparently detecting nothing, the gatekeeper shovelled the coins into the capacious pockets of his jacket and then turned to two guards who had now put in an appearance and yelled, "Open her up, boys!"

In response, the guards ambled forward, to unlock the locks and unchain the chains with as much clanking and rattling as before and soon the gates were being swung open for them to pass through.

"'Til we meet again then," said James, shaking Sam's and Joel's hands warmly before finally planting a rather whiskery kiss on Berta's cheek.

Then, taking Dobbs' rein, Sam led them forward until they were on the other side of the gates. They waved once more but as the gates closed behind them, they could just see that James had already turned and was heading back towards his house.

"So that's that!" exclaimed Joel. "And we've got what we came for."

"And a lot more besides..." replied Sam but with a frown on his face rather than a smile. Then, as an afterthought he added, "I hope that James and family are going to be alright..."

"James was telling me this morning that he has plenty of friends who will be keeping an eye on them," replied Joel.

"They're going to need them," responded Sam gruffly, sounding unconvinced.

Berta at first said nothing but then scrambled into Dobbs' saddle. "It must be my turn up here," she said. Neither Sam nor Joel were prepared to disagree and as the street beyond the gate gradually became the countryside, their sense of freedom, which had lain dormant and unremarked whilst they were in the town, now began to return.

They plodded along in silence for a while, aware only of birdsong from the trees and bushes at the roadside and the clop of Dobbs' very large hooves.

CHAPTER 23

HOT PURSUIT

It was early afternoon the next day. As usual, it was Dobbs' rider who was the first to see what lay ahead and at that moment, it was Joel's turn in the saddle. The dark surface of the road shimmered in the heat so that as he looked ahead he could not be sure whether he was looking at a mirage or the landmark that they had hoped to see for the past hour.

They continued until finally Joel felt sure that the copse from which they had turned onto the road some days before was now just a short distance away. Although they had many miles to cover, they had already decided that, despite their sense of urgency, they would take a short break to cool down. Joel ran his forearm across his brow and was unsurprised to find it covered in sweat. The sun burned down on his back and in all, he felt very uncomfortable. He peered from beneath the rim of his hat at his two companions.

Sam had pushed his hat back so that the broad rim sheltered his neck, and his forehead was exposed to the breeze that was blowing. Berta had found a white piece of cloth which she had placed over her head – but with the same intention of sheltering her neck and shoulders from the sun. All three of them were red in the face and longing for the shade that the copse would offer.

Joel found it daunting that the copse provided the last tree cover that they would see for many miles. Once they were out on the moor, the only shelter available to them would be the larger rocks and the tors. As they arrived at the copse they were relieved to see that the stream was still flowing, although the amount of water making its way between the rocks was visibly less than it had been a few days before. Dobbs seemed unconcerned and lapped at it greedily as soon as he was able to do so. Berta waited until he had finished and took two canteens that they had already emptied on their journey and refilled them from the stream. Sam and Joel, concerned about the distribution of weight in the hurriedly packed panniers, removed them from Dobbs and spent some minutes swapping items between them.

Rarely had the three of them found shade so welcome. They picked out much the same spot as the one in which they had snoozed several days before and lay down within reach of each other. Joel felt himself becoming almost immediately sleepy. Sam and Berta were not slow to follow. Dobbs too, having been relieved of his panniers, rolled briefly in the litter beneath the trees and then stood again, patiently waiting amongst the trees and flicking away the flies with his mane and tail.

Sam was the first to wake again. He lay looking between his shoes at the road along which they had come. In the silence of the afternoon, he thought that he could hear the faint thunder of horses' hooves. As he continued to look, he could also see a cloud of dust rising above the road and apparently travelling in their direction. He was more curious than worried, but it seemed strange that anyone should be in a hurry on such a hot afternoon. He shook Joel who groaned but then turned to look at him.

"What do you want?" he asked blearily, annoyed to have been woken.

"I think someone's headed this way – someone in a hurry."

Joel now sat so that he could look where Sam was pointing.

"Hmm," he said after a moment or two. "Riders – I can see them too."

"I wonder who it is?" mused Sam.

"I've no idea," replied Joel, "and we can't stay to find out." Joel turned and shook Berta's shoulder. She tried to wave him away but then reluctantly opened her eyes and finally sat up, trying to see what they were looking at.

By now the dust cloud was larger and visibly closer. The drumming sound had also become more clearly audible. All three of them had wondered since leaving Falmouth if they would be pursued. Now there was the possibility that it was happening.

Berta agreed with Sam and Joel that it would be better to leave immediately. Although there was little cover on the moors, flight along the track they had previously used was preferable to hiding in the copse waiting to be discovered. As quickly as they could, they buckled Dobbs' panniers back into place and then, gathering Dobbs' rein, led him rapidly down the track.

None of them wanted to risk mounting and galloping the horse along the track since it was so rough that they would almost certainly have injured him in the first moments of the attempt. Instead, they scrambled along as quickly as possible, hoping against hope that a small outcrop of rocks that they remembered as being just a short distance from the track would be able to provide them with a temporary place to hide. As they stumbled over the rocky path, Joel estimated that they had five minutes at the most before their pursuers, if pursuers they were, arrived at the copse.

They arrived at a point on the track which lay parallel to the rocky outcrop. From there they struggled over boulders, huge clumps of heather and coarse grass until they reached the shade of the rocks. The outcrop was much larger than it had looked from the track and even Dobbs was fully concealed. Joel fished in one of the panniers for the binoculars and looked back towards the road.

It was some moments before he saw the horse riders who were causing the dust cloud – but then he saw them clearly. They had stopped at the point where the track met the road. There were three of them. Joel was worried that they had left behind all manner of signs of their departure along the track, but the riders seemed to be debating which way to go. Eventually, one rider set off along the road, whilst the second went off on a track that led round the back of the copse and off on a north-easterly route across the moor. The third rider, however, began to pick his way down the track that Joel and his companions had taken.

There was a hurried debate amongst them as to what they should do next. Joel and Sam thought that they should get back onto the path and then try to outdistance the rider. Berta thought that they should remain hidden behind the rocks. As they talked, however, it gradually became clear that they could be visible to two of the riders. They decided to return to the track and hope that they would not be spotted until they had been able to give their pursuers the slip.

They returned over the heather, grass and rocks that lay between them and the track, hoping that it would be some time before the rider spotted them. All of them, including Dobbs, were sweating and breathing hard by the time that they returned to the track. For some minutes they were lucky. The bends and undulations concealed them until they had travelled some distance out onto the moor, but then as they descended a long slope, they realised that once the rider had rounded the bend at the top of the slope, he would then probably have a good view of them as they toiled along below.

"What do you think he'll do if he sees us?" asked Berta.

Joel frowned for a moment but then said, "That's a good question. He could call out to the other two, but we've come so far down the track that they probably won't be able to hear him."

"On the other hand," said Sam, "he might decide to take us on by himself."

Berta was not convinced. "Why would he do that? There's one of him and three of us."

Joel partly agreed. "Good point – but if he has a crossbow or a gun, the odds might not matter so much."

Sam and Berta frowned. They had not thought about the possibility that the rider might be armed. They looked back and realised with some dismay that the rider had now rounded the bend and had clearly seen them. He paused for a moment, sitting upright in the saddle. Then they heard him, calling to his two companions across the moor.

Joel wanted to make the most of their lead. "Even if they hear him, it will be some time before they can get here. Come on. We need to go as fast as we can!"

Together they ran and stumbled along the track, trying constantly to go faster but also aware that if just one of them injured themselves in the process, it would complicate an already difficult situation. Of the three of them, it was Sam who felt the need to look back at regular intervals at the rider who was pursuing them. He felt sure that he could hear the sound of the rider's voice and of the horse getting ever closer behind them.

"Come on, come on! Can't we go any faster!" he complained.

"Not unless you want one of us to break a leg," growled Joel.

Berta turned to follow Sam's backward glance and was horrified to see how close the rider had now come. All three of them could hear him spurring the horse forward and the thud of its hooves was becoming ever more audible.

Suddenly, there was a loud cry from the rider and a shrill whinnying from the horse. Sam felt disbelief turn to joyful relief as the horse went headlong into a somersault, catapulting its rider along the track before trying to scramble to its feet on legs that no longer seemed to co-ordinate with each other.

Sam stood for a moment to watch, but Joel and Berta urged him to keep moving.

They climbed as quickly as they could to the next ridge in the track. At this point, they all looked back to see what had happened to the horse and rider. The horse was on its feet but was clearly limping and unable to put any weight on its right foreleg. The rider had just begun to stir and was making vain attempts to get up from the position into which he had been thrown.

Having seen enough, they hurried on, believing that it was now all but impossible for their pursuers to catch them. They began to relax into their journey again although as they made their way ever further across the open moor, every step took a conscious effort.

Joel remembered their outward journey clearly and said, "It shouldn't be long now before we reach the river."

Berta was not so sure and looked up, urging the other two to stop for a moment. Her face was burning with the effects of sun and the wind. "I think we still have some way to go," she said. "It's so hot out here. I need a drink."

She found one of the canteens that she had filled whilst they were at the copse and took a long swig before passing it on to Sam and Joel.

Although he had lost his preoccupation with their pursuer, Sam still seemed distracted. He bent down to tug at a tuft of grass. It had the dry, slightly prickly texture of straw.

"Everything is so dry..." he commented. "It's almost like tinder. We need to be careful."

They all knew that in these conditions the smallest spark would be enough to cause a wildfire. The breeze of which they had been aware during their journey that day had now become much stronger.

Sam sniffed the air, his suspicions fuelled by whisps of cloud in an otherwise cloudless sky. He felt sure that he could smell the distinctive odour of burning vegetation. He turned to the others to see that they too were sniffing the air and peering a little anxiously at the sky.

Having recently rounded a spur on the track across the moor, they were unable to see the open expanse of rocks, grass, bracken and heather that lay behind them.

Joel watched as a pair of buzzards circled high above in the late afternoon sky but then his gaze was drawn downwards by more wisps of cloud – clouds that had a darker tinge to them and seemed now to be billowing upwards in ever increasing density. The smell that Sam had previously detected was now carried to them by a gradually strengthening wind.

"Those are not clouds!" he exclaimed. "That's smoke! There's a fire!"

The other two needed no further prompting. Berta hastily pushed the bung back into the neck of the canteen from which she was drinking and shoved it into Dobbs' pannier. Once more, they found themselves forced along at a faster pace than they wanted to go.

Sam yelled back to the other two. "I suppose it was only a matter of time. I wonder how it started?"

Joel felt that it was more or less irrelevant but yelled back, "Almost anything could have started it! For all we know, it might have been Dobbs' hooves!"

"How do you mean?" called Berta.

"Well, if you watch his feet, every so often he strikes a spark from one of the rocks. And remember, further back we were stumbling along as fast as we could go!"

"Sparks or no sparks that's what we need to do again!" replied Berta, glancing fearfully back over her shoulder.

They urged themselves on. In desperation, Sam yelled, "Wouldn't it be better if one of us rode Dobbs?"

"I can't see how!" shouted Joel. "But if you think he'll go faster with someone on his back, you can try it!"

Sam decided that he would try it and halted Dobbs for a moment or two whilst he scrambled onto his back. Hanging on to Dobbs' reins, he drove his heels against the huge horse's ribs, urging him forward at a trot.

It was difficult to achieve on the track, but the side of the track seemed if anything to provide a smoother path. Dobbs was fairly content to maintain the trot. Joel and Berta ran along behind, although it was soon apparent that they would not be able to sustain for very long the pace that Sam was setting on Dobbs. The gap between them was soon growing.

A breathless conversation began to take place between Joel and Berta.

"The wind's blowing really strongly now. It's pushing me along," panted Berta.

"Just as well," puffed Joel. "We're only running at about six or seven miles an hour."

"That's better than walking!"

The reply took Joel a moment or two, but he said, "Yes – but it's a lot slower than the wind."

Berta began to realise why he was concerned.

"How fast do you think the wind is blowing?" she asked.

"It's a pretty fresh wind now. Could be around 20 miles an hour." Joel struggled again to get the words out.

Sam was now well ahead of them but had slowed down. He decided that it might be better if he travelled at a pace closer to that of Joel and Berta. Slowly but surely, they managed to whittle down the distance between them. All the while Sam was turning anxiously in Dobbs' saddle looking back at the progress of the fire.

Driven by the wind, the fire was advancing in a rapid line through the grass and heather. Where the vegetation was more substantial, huge tongues of flame tore into the air. Above them the sky was turning to shades of grey and black as increasing amounts of smoke began to blot out the sun.

"How far is it to the river!" gasped Berta.

"Not too far. We should be there shortly."

The fire was closing on them, although it was still some little distance behind. Sam could see clearly the wall of flames moving towards them and everywhere there was smoke in the air. It was beginning to irritate their throats and eyes.

"We need to get there soon." Berta was almost wheezing now.

They laboured on, hoping that each rise in the path would fall away to reveal the course of the river crossing their path. Joel felt sure that it was nearby, but with the smoke swirling around them and his eyes now streaming, he was able to see little further ahead than his own feet. Sam was having a difficult time controlling Dobbs and found himself pushing down feelings of panic. He felt sure that he could feel the heat of the fire on his back and amongst the smoke, black fragments of debris eddied around them in the air currents driven before the flames.

Joel was just a little ahead of the others now and was sure that he recognised the downward slope in the path onto which they had stumbled. Still he could not see the course of the river.

Then suddenly from behind him, there was a loud, panic-stricken whinnying from Dobbs, and the sound of large stones being dislodged from the path and hurled into the grass and bushes.

Joel looked back and felt a trickle of cold sweat dislodge itself from his hairline and roll down between his shoulder blades. Dobbs had fallen and was threshing wildly about him with his enormous legs and feet. One kick from his enormous hooves would be enough to kill any of them. Berta's cries came through the smoke.

"Sam! What's happened?"

Joel clawed his way back through the smoke to find Sam fully conscious but lying on the track beside the panicking horse. Mistakenly, Joel thought that he had been injured but then he saw what had happened. Somehow, one of the straps in Dobbs' tack had worked loose and he had caught a foreleg in it, causing him to fall heavily on the track. Now, he lay on his side, his leg still caught in the strap.

Whilst Joel was still wondering what to do, Sam crawled forward so that he had his hand and arm on the horse's neck. He spoke gently but calmly, trying to reassure him and fishing for a knife that would cut through the strap and release the horse's leg. Dobbs made another huge attempt to get to his feet, his legs flailing lethally to one side and pitching Sam onto his flank. Somehow, Sam managed to get his legs back on to the track behind the horse and then to work his way into position again. Although Dobbs was momentarily calmer, he was still heaving his massive neck and head to and fro, threatening to pitch Sam into the range of his hooves again.

Despite the smoke, Sam had managed to find the knife but realised that with the horse's unpredictable movements, there was risk that either he or Dobbs could find themselves impaled on its blade. Deciding that it was a risk he would have to take, he kept the knife in its sheath until the last possible moment and then, with a deft movement, removed it and hooked it under the strap. Sharp though it was, the knife was not capable of cutting straight through the thick leather strap. With his heart in his mouth, Sam sawed at the leather until finally it parted.

It took Dobbs a few seconds to realise that his leg was free, enabling Sam, coughing and choking in the ever-increasing smoke, to slide the knife into its sheath and roll to safety. Rolling onto his knees, he was in time to see Dobbs lumbering to his feet, the pannier on his right side, hanging alarmingly close to his hind legs. Joel and Berta now ran round and, supporting the pannier between them, urged the horse forward and down the slope towards what they hoped would prove to be the river.

Sam staggered to his feet and, as best he could, ran after them. Moments later, they found themselves at the edge of the river, some distance from the old bridge they had used to cross the river on their outward journey. There was now only a small volume of water flowing between the rocks that lay along its bed. Urgently, they began to pick their way across the rocks and where they had no alternative, to wade through pools of water that lay in their path. Soon, however, they found themselves climbing up from the river's bed and onto the bank.

There, they paused for a moment to look back only to see in horror, that the flames were fast approaching the dry foliage that lay along the river's bank. With Joel and Berta still supporting the pannier hanging awkwardly from Dobbs' flank, they moved on again with Sam now once more firmly leading Dobbs by his rein.

Joel would not agree to them stopping until they were some two hundred yards from the river. From there, they could see that the river had temporarily halted the fire in its tracks. They flopped onto the parched grass at the side of the track and sat coughing and spitting out fragments of burnt vegetation. It was some time before any of them spoke.

Finally as Joel began to recover from a prolonged fit of coughing he said, "Well done, Sam. You were bloody amazing!"

Sam, who was still trying to forget that they had temporarily left him behind, visibly straightened and sat up with a pleased smile on his face.

Berta crawled closer and flung her arms round him. "Yes, Sam. Joel's right! That was an incredibly brave thing that you did back there!"

Sam submitted to Berta's hugs for moment or two, but then struggled free. "Okay, okay!" he exclaimed. "You or Joel would have done the same if you'd been closer."

He smiled shyly, leaving Joel and Berta to reflect that they had been almost as close to the horse as he had, but they had both been momentarily paralysed with fear of the enormous power unleashed by

Dobbs in his panic. He was the one, though, who had had the presence of mind to get behind the horse's heaving body and cut the strap that had trapped his leg.

There was brief silence and then Joel looked back towards the river and the fire. "We need to move on again. The river may not stop the flames for long."

Berta agreed. "There are sparks flying across. It only needs one of them to start a fire on this side.

Wearily, they got to their feet. Joel and Berta between them managed to tie the strap that Sam had severed so that they could once more walk without having to support the pannier. Sam returned to leading Dobbs by his rein.

***

Digging deep into their reserves of energy, they managed to continue travelling for about another two hours. At this stage, they had begun to pass through the margins of the moor and were descending into the wild and overgrown countryside beyond. As soon as they were able to find sufficient open space amongst the jumble of vegetation around them, they pitched camp, made a fire and put together a meal from the meagre rations that they were carrying with them.

When they had eaten, Sam and Berta sat for a short time by the fire, talking about the day's events.

"I wonder what happened to the rider who was following us?" said Sam.

"He'd have been lucky to escape. We only just escaped – unless of course..." Berta paused.

"Unless what?" Sam felt ambiguous about the idea that their pursuers might have escaped.

Joel, who had been lounging full length by the fire, found the energy to prop himself up on one elbow. "I think Berta means that our pursuers might have started the fire. The wind drove the fire before it so if they did start it, there would be a good chance that they would have got away safely."

"I suppose it was the only way that they could still get at us," reflected Sam.

"Yes," said Berta. "There was no other way that they could catch us."

Despite his comment, however, Joel still thought that they would never know how the fire had started.

"It's so dry out there. Almost anything could cause a fire. Even a spark from Dobbs' hooves..."

"Even a spark from Dobbs' hooves..." echoed Sam wearily, imitating Joel's repetitious comment and stifling a yawn. "I thought you two were exhausted and needed to get some sleep?" There was a note of irritation in his voice.

"Alright, alright!" Berta took the hint and rose wearily to her feet.

A muffled "Goodnight, Joel" drifted over her shoulder as she headed for the tent.

Sam followed with no more than a brief backward glance in Joel's direction.

Joel watched them as they went, remembering that he and Berta had agreed to keep their arrangements as they had been during the rest of the journey, but left now by himself, he wished that it was otherwise.

For the time being, he pushed away memories of the afternoon that he and Berta had made love at Gwen's house but longed instead for the end of their journey and for a safe return for all three of them to The Ridge.

He lay for some minutes longer, in the guttering light of the fire. The day had begun peacefully but the afternoon and early evening had been consumed in anxiety and fear. After their experiences on the moor, they had been reluctant to light a fire at all but had decided that their desire to eat cooked food outweighed any worries they might have about a camp fire.

He stretched out a hand and brushed at the dry grass on which he lay. It had certainly not been a lack of warmth that had led them to light a fire. He remembered many dry summers but never one quite as dry – and as hot, as this one. There must, he realised, be some variation from year to year, but in recent years, he could only remember summers that seemed to become ever hotter – and drier.

Weary of his thoughts he stood up and then, scooping up handfuls of dry, dusty soil, poured them onto the last of the fire's embers until he was satisfied that he had smothered them completely. As it was, he would still wake in the early hours of the morning, sweating and believing that he was being consumed by the flames of an inferno.

PART 4

CHAPTER 24

EMBERS

It was September. Joel, who was now approaching his 60th birthday, was in his daughter's house. His reason for being there that day was that although he had come to see his daughter, the house had previously belonged to his grandfather and he also wanted to look again at some of the books – and some of the objects that, out of curiosity and a sort of reverence, were still permitted house room.

Kirk and Alison had now been dead many years. Both had lived into their seventies, with Alison, the older of the two, being the first to die. Her death from cancer had been a protracted and painful one but one which, Kirk had sadly reflected, might have been alleviated or even prevented in the years preceding The Collapse. He was left for seven years to ponder the memories of their life together – which had been for the most part both happy and healthy and one in which they felt as though they were cheating the violence and disorder that lay beyond The Ridge.

If, through good fortune, obscurity and inaccessibility, the people of The Ridge were largely left in peaceful stability, the same could not be said of the climate which Kirk and Alison both lived to see becoming ever more chaotic. Cold winters such as those they had known in childhood became a rarity, whilst the heat of summer could be both prolonged and almost unbearable. Wildfires could often be seen burning out of control in the lands beyond The Ridge, their ravages only brought to an end by the violent storms that frequently swept across the landscape. At such times, flood rather than drought was then the threat that everyone dreaded. In some years, it was only ingenuity and unrelenting hard work that stood between the inhabitants of The Ridge and starvation.

The art and, for that matter, the science, of photography were almost dead although there were still photographs of Kirk in the house that had been his – and of Joel's grandmother, Alison. The photographs had undergone some interesting changes of colour, but Alison had eventually thought to keep them away from the light so that their condition was better than it might otherwise have been.

Joel's daughter, Emily, and her husband, Josh, had gradually extended the cottage and now kept two of the smaller rooms at the back of the house as something of a family museum. Emily tutored some of the children from the village – a job for which she was paid in farm produce – and sometimes used the resources in the museum to help with her teaching. Joel often felt protective about the various books and artefacts but reminded himself that his own rudimentary education would have been poorer without them.

Despite the use of the resources in the museum, many areas of previous learning were now deliberately neglected. Electricity, however, had continued to be of such importance that its generation and supply was still considered to be essential to the village. It was one of the few areas of technology in which care was taken to pass on existing knowledge to succeeding generations of young people.

A trick that Emily liked to show the schoolchildren was to switch on the old flat screen television set that had been owned by Kirk and Alison and then to watch the faces of the children as the electronic message 'No Signal' moved around the screen. At first, the children would be amazed – and then amused, before being finally bored and wondering why on earth there was nothing more to see. Occasionally, however, Emily's trick was enough to germinate the seeds of curiosity and investigation that lay in the minds of some of the children that she taught.

Joel had often pondered the fact that after so many years since The Collapse and the ensuing chaos that his grandfather had told him about, no-one had ever begun again to send signals and images out to the thousands, perhaps, millions of television sets that were probably still in existence. His guess was that neither the will nor the level of social organisation required had yet returned to the world beyond The Ridge.

Joel hated the phrase 'The People Before' but it was the form of words generally still used to refer to the people who had populated the world before the catastrophic implosion of civilisation that occurred in his grandfather's time. The people of his own time were as intent as ever to 'get on with their own lives', but if they did stop to think or talk about 'The People Before' any curiosity and wonder that they felt was also mixed with a degree of incredulity that such apparently intelligent and skilful people could bring upon themselves a disaster that had ended their civilisation– and reduced populations to tiny fractions of their previous numbers.

Despite the catastrophe, however, the legacy of the early part of the century was still everywhere to be found. One of its more obvious and tragic legacies lay in the bombs or mines that were occasionally discovered by hapless people or animals if they ventured across those parts of The Ridge that had been fought over in the infamous battle. Another was the fear and suspicion with which ideas from the twentieth and early twenty-first centuries were regarded, and it was to this that Joel attributed the 'No Signal' message on the television screen. There was no general will to re-invent a world that had led to such colossal failure – a failure, Joel thought, that had struck at the heart of so many beliefs embedded deep in the consciousness of those times. Ideas of unending 'progress' and 'development' now seemed risible in the light of the struggle to survive that now formed the lot of everyone he knew.

Joel's daughter, Emily, sometimes found herself to be the subject of suspicion in that the education she offered formed a link with the past. Opinion about the benefits of education was split along sharply contrasting lines. Joel had never been less than grateful for the learning that had been passed on to him through his parents and grandparents, but he also understood the deeply mixed emotions that thoughts and folk memories about 'The People Before' still engendered.

Other than the journey to Falmouth, undertaken in his youth, Joel had rarely ventured out of his tiny corner of the world. Instead, he had taken to observing the life about him, in the one small part of the world that he had come to know in great detail. When he was younger, the four seasons had still been fairly marked and resembled those that he read about in his grandfather's books, but as he got older, there seemed to be just two major parts to the year – a mild and very wet season corresponding roughly to the late autumn, winter and early spring of previous times, which would then be gradually replaced by a season of drought and often fierce heat which lasted from late spring through to early autumn.

Joel's daily need to get a living from the land around him had gradually encouraged in him an intuitive ability to predict the weather, at least for a short time ahead. It was this ability that now so often brought him the greatest pessimism and discomfort – and which made him wonder about the viability of life on The Ridge for his children and their young families.

It had been the year 2066, his grandmother had told him, when he and Berta and Sam had journeyed to Falmouth – a thousand years since the island of Britain had been successfully invaded by the Normans – but now the threat was different.

During the mild and often extremely wet winters it was difficult to get around the farm, and no one ventured down to the river when it was in full spate. In the land beyond the river, The Levels were permanently flooded, and never offered safe passage to travellers, even in the hottest summers. Water was no longer pumped away from them, and irrigation ditches had long fallen into disrepair. Many of the old watercourses, natural or artificial, were choked with the rubbish of many years and now contributed to the flooding rather than relieving it. When the river would let them pass, Joel and his friends would go out into The Levels in boats, in search of waterfowl, but it was quite a long and even dangerous journey, and he was always relieved to return. The Levels had become both moody and treacherous, a strange and watery wilderness sometimes becalmed in eerie mist, and at other times, lashed with storms that seemed to arise from nowhere. It was a place that played on the mind.

Summers, with occasional variations, seemed only to get hotter and in June, July or August, The Ridge became both hot and dusty. Blinding vortices of dust and torrid air would sweep across the open land of the farms picking up debris and sometimes causing minor damage to buildings. Conserving water became a vital aspect of life during the summer months and many ingenious means were used to store the water that fell from the skies in such abundance during the winter. The task was made harder by the fact that much of the water that fell on The Ridge eventually flowed or percolated to the areas below. Over the years, however, the inhabitants had built large wells and cisterns together with an ingenious network of irrigation channels so that nothing less than severe drought could cause hardship to the farmers and villagers.

Since the battle, people on The Ridge had become ever more suspicious of the world beyond its bounds. The central area was now protected by a large timber stockade that they had constructed over a number of years at great cost of wood and labour. There were also many tunnels, pits and traps which were well known to the inhabitants but, it was planned, would be lethal to any unwary invader.

The Ridge's greatest protection lay in its inaccessibility. The changing climate ensured that for many months of the year, the wetness of the surrounding landscape made it difficult to cross and for many miles around, the Levels were a formidable barrier. To the West, the expanses of moorland were still relatively open and in summer, large areas were frequently ravaged by wildfires, but paradoxically, as in long periods of their history, there were also many other places wet enough to harbour deep and treacherous bogs, and these were more than capable of swallowing terrified travellers.

As if all this were not enough, some of the sparse population in the South-West had returned to supplementing its livelihood by preying on travellers. Joel suspected that many of the tales he heard were exaggerated, but he still remembered choosing his routes with care when he had travelled to Falmouth with Sam and Berta. More decisively still, there were far easier East-West routes to the North and South of the Ridge so that only an obtuse or exceptionally curious traveller would have chosen to explore an isolated piece of upland like The Ridge, surrounded as it was by difficult terrain. As so often in the past, many travellers preferred to take their chances with the sea rather than risk the journey overland.

That morning, it was not the security of The Ridge that was uppermost in Joel's mind. Instead, it was the summer's dryness that was the source of his anxiety. Virtually all the crops from both farm and garden had suffered in the heat and it was proving to be a poor harvest which, in turn, would mean a difficult winter. The signs were that even foraging would be poor. None of this, however, completely explained his frame of mind.

Whilst the weather gave him many short-term concerns, it was the perceptibly changing climate and a sense that the weather was becoming ever more unstable that most perplexed him. Usually, he stayed at Emily's house to chat to his daughter and catch up on any news from the family or community, but this morning, he felt unable to talk to anyone.

It was a fairly short walk from his daughter's house to the farmhouse that he and his father had built. At that time, Roberta's pregnancy with their first child had added urgency to the task. Joel's father had been friendly with Will Capstick, Janey's first husband, but being much younger, was forever regarded as Will's apprentice. Joel always thought that he got his love of books and of knowledge from his grandparents but that his practical skills came largely from his parents.

His mother Emily, after whom his daughter was named, had always seemed almost too frail for the life that they led on The Ridge. She was not very tall and had long, black hair. Despite her slender figure and her gentle manner, however, she had plenty of energy and had been Roberta's main support when she was expecting her first child. Joel wondered vaguely if boys' ideas of beauty were in some way formed by early memories of their mothers; he had certainly always thought of his own mother in her younger days as being beautiful.

His father James was quite tall but also had a strong, stocky build that was well suited to his work around the farm. He had a good head of fair almost sandy hair, and an open, outdoor face that spoke of humour and robust good health. Joel sometimes found it hard to imagine that he was the offspring of Kirk and Alison, but much of his father's character could be attributed to the life that he led. Although James was essentially a practical man, Kirk had at least managed to instil in his son a love of learning.

This was not a common attribute amongst the inhabitants of The Ridge for whom life was generally ruled by the demands of physical labour and the unrelenting round of the farming year. It was, however, an attribute that Joel shared with both his wife, Roberta, and his friend Sam.

Roberta had never specifically objected to the nickname 'Berta' that she had been known by in her teens and early twenties, but it had gradually seemed less and less appropriate to the tall, graceful and shrewd young woman that she became. Sam too, so awkward and easily teased in his teens, had become a young man of quick intelligence who had made the most of the life that they had and who had gone on to marry a sprightly and pretty young woman from the Village. Sam was still amongst the closest of Joel's friends, although Joel's love of solitude in recent years was something that even Sam found hard to understand.

The September sun slanted through a window into Joel's cottage. There was forever something to do on the farm, but Joel slumped into a chair, one of a pair, intending only to be there for a few minutes but wanting time to think about his wife. It had been nearly 20 years since she had died in childbirth – the child had been stillborn – and he often paused to reflect that there was now so much about her that he only remembered when some person, object or event happened to trigger his memory.

Today the random object that set his memories loose was a crossbow. He had left it on his worktable, ready for the hunting trip that he was going to make. It took his mind back to a desperate night in his early life when Sam and Roberta had been kidnapped by thugs. He still struggled with his memories of that night, with the killings that had happened before their eyes. Then again, he wondered what would have happened to Gwen and Tom, Sam and Roberta if the gang members had not been dealt with by James' killers. He had dumbly assented to the killings by not intervening, but then he had not bargained for the ruthlessness of James, Alistair McLennan and the two brothers. He pondered for a moment the almost casual ease with which human beings could slip into savagery.

Over the next few days, he would hunt and kill deer, but he knew that he would give more thought to each deer that he killed than he had given to any of the men who had been killed during the rescue of his friends. His thoughts were interrupted by a cursory knock at the door, which he had left slightly ajar. A head of fair hair appeared round the door. It was his daughter, Emily. As she came into the room, Joel reflected almost subconsciously that she was the image of her mother.

"Hello, Dad," she said. "We need to talk before you set off."

Joel sat up in his chair, rapidly returning from his memories.

"Emily – sorry I didn't see you before I came back. I thought you'd probably be busy. I was hoping to catch you later."

She flopped into the armchair opposite him. "Dad, that's just an excuse!" She was indignant but it was a conversation that they could have had on almost any day in recent weeks. Although she was mildly annoyed with him, she was also concerned.

"The children were disappointed that you didn't drop in. You know how much they look forward to seeing you each day." She did not say that she also looked forward to her father's visits and Joel knew that his recent preference for solitude was worrying her.

"I'm not much company at the moment. I just want to get away for a few days and get my thoughts straight." Listening to himself, Joel thought that it sounded rather feeble, but it was what he wanted to do; he needed to go away for a few days, away from the round of farm and family life, and spend some time sorting out his thoughts, his concerns about the future.

She decided to take a direct approach. "What are you worried about, Dad? What's bothering you?"

He paused, knowing that if he tried to answer now, his replies would seem woolly and inconsequential. "What am I worried about?" He repeated her question. "I'm worried about all of us, about our life up here and the way it's changing."

Emily's inner resolution to listen, and not to give in to feelings about the predictable path of their conversation, was already beginning to fail her. "Dad, do we have to talk about this now? We must have discussed it hundreds of times."

She reflected that whilst her father had made sure that her childhood had been carefree, his worries about life on The Ridge had formed a more regular part of their conversations since she had become an adult.

Joel made no reply. His mind was already beginning to focus on the journey ahead. He would leave later that day, preferring not to have a full day's journey ahead of him.

"I want to come down and join you."

Joel dragged his mind back to the room in which he was sitting. He wanted Emily to join him, but he was not sure that she would be able to get away from the farm. "What about the children?"

"I'm sure Josh can manage for a day or two. Things are a bit slack on the farm at the moment."

"Well, if you are able to free yourself, you could come with me today!" It was not a serious suggestion, but he wanted her to be more precise about when she would arrive at the lodge.

"No," she said firmly. "I'm busy for a day or two, but I need a break as well. I'm looking forward to getting away from here even if it is only for a short while. Besides, you'll need help with all that food you're going to bring back for us."

Joel's journey would provide them with much needed meat to supplement their diet through the autumn.

"I could stay here. There are enough deer in these parts nowadays – far more than there were when your great-grandfather was alive."

"But there are many more, further south. You're much more likely to have a successful trip down there."

"That's true," agreed Joel. "There's also plenty of other game. In the end it may come down to how much we can bring back."

"I could ask Sam to come with me."

"Huh," said Joel. "He's hardly ever able to get away from that wife of his. Anyway, I'll probably make more than one trip this coming winter. I could do with him going with me when we get into midwinter. This time around though, it will be good for the two of us to get some time together."

"But you see me every day!" protested Emily.

"You know what I mean. You're at everyone's beck and call up here. It will do them no harm to fend for themselves for a few days."

She smiled at him. "You're just selfish. You want me to yourself – but you can be very persuasive. Not that I need much persuading. It will do Josh some good to be reminded that he's got two children."

"That's what I hoped you'd say." Joel felt satisfied. He would have his first few days of hunting and the solitude of which he felt so much in need and then some time alone with his daughter. He would not be gone long and if there was a dry spell during the winter, he would make another trip with Sam – by which time, the need to supplement their food supply would mean that their absence would be more readily accepted. Joel sighed. There was always a tension between the demands of life on The Ridge and the occasional need to go into the regions beyond.

Joel returned his attention to his daughter. "Are you sure that you'll be happy to ride down on your own?"

She laughed. "Well it's not exactly the first time, is it? And it's not like riding over the moors. I'll keep to the usual route. I've never had any trouble going that way."

Joel nodded. The route that they took kept them away from other people's farms and the area for which he was headed was now so thinly populated that he had rarely met anyone in its thickly wooded valleys. Every time that Emily made the journey alone, he wondered how wise it was for her to do so, but she had inherited a fierce streak of independence from her mother and Joel knew better than to try stopping her. All the same, he always had a residual anxiety about her.

"You'll bring a gun, won't you?" he asked.

"I will if I must. Bundle's not exactly fond of them." Bundle was the name of Emily's horse. He was strong, patient and well suited to the uneven terrain that her journey would cover.

Joel felt reassured to know that she would be riding Bundle.

"Bundle will be OK," he said. "He's got a good temperament. And I'll feel much happier if you have a gun with you."

She did not disagree. They both knew that she was a good shot, much quicker and more accurate than Joel.

"I suppose you'll be taking the crossbows?" It was a question she hardly needed to ask. Joel always preferred them. They were not easy to obtain but they enabled him to kill his prey swiftly and silently and without scaring every other animal for miles around.

Joel made no reply, other than a nod. She stood to go. Joel pulled himself to his feet and she kissed him on a very bristly cheek.

"Uggh, Dad!" she protested. "You need to have a shave!"

He let her go, briefly waving her off from the door of the cottage, having agreed with her that she would join him at the hunting lodge in about four or five days' time.

It was mid-afternoon when he finally got away. He had packed his saddle bags with just enough food and clothing to last him for about a week although some of it was there as a precaution. Most people from The Ridge knew enough to live off the countryside. His horse, Toby, a piebald cob, had been part of a complicated barter several years before. He had already been broken in by a farmer who specialised in catching and breaking in wild horses; Toby had been captured from a large herd roaming the moorland areas to the west of The Ridge. Catching such horses was difficult and dangerous, but Joel observed to himself that it often became a way of life for those drawn to it.

Toby would be well suited to the journey they were about to make. Although he was not a big horse – and Joel was quite tall – he was nimble and sure-footed, qualities that Joel had come to value when riding him in the countryside around The Ridge.

True to his earlier intentions, Joel had been to see Emily again and his two grandchildren, Daniel and Grace. Josh was still out making his rounds on the farm, but Joel had talked to him some time before about his intention to make his usual autumn hunting trip.

As soon as he could, he set off heading his horse towards the woods and valleys that lay almost due south from The Ridge. There were some hours of daylight still left and he would be well into his journey before he would have to make camp for the night. The first part of the journey took them along well-kept paths and being able to trust Toby gave him a certain sense of freedom. He allowed his mind to go back to his earlier preoccupations.

The weather that afternoon was unusually good for riding: warm sunshine, little cloud in the sky and just a gentle breeze that stirred only the uppermost tips of the trees. Joel was grateful to be making the start of his journey in such favourable conditions, not least because the weather could be so unpredictable and at times violent in its extremity.

He felt a small sense of guilt. He was carrying in one of his saddlebags an unnecessary weight – a sheaf of papers that was in the process of becoming a book. This was not, in itself, however, the reason for his guilt. He had toyed with the idea of telling his daughter about his writing, but at the last moment had decided against it. He rarely concealed anything from Emily, but this time he felt that he needed to write more – if only a little more – to enable her to understand the purpose of his project. All the same, he felt uncomfortable about not telling her.

There was a further feeling that he had about his 'book'. It was a feeling that, whatever its merits or otherwise as a piece of writing, it would be valuable to Emily, to her family and, perhaps, to the other inhabitants of The Ridge. She would need to know about it soon he mused, if only because it was not a book he could write by himself. It would have to be written by many people – but Emily could make the first contribution. He found himself wondering for a moment what would happen after that but 'after that' was not a problem that would be his. It was another reminder that he could not see into the future even though he sometimes deluded himself that he could.

His most important need was to pass on to Emily his ideas about the nature of the book, its purpose and the way in which it needed to be written. He had once seen in Kirk's house a copy of 'The Bible'. It was a book over which he had puzzled for many long hours. It seemed to contain so many passages that appeared to be nonsensical, that found no resonance in his world or his imagination – and yet there were many others that represented the collected wisdom of people who had struggled to survive and to understand what, if any, was the meaning of their lives. He drew from it what he could, not least because there was no-one looking over his shoulder telling him that he had to accept it in its entirety or as literal truth.

He thought a little longer. Although The Bible was generally referred to as a book, it had always seemed to him that it was, instead, a library of books, many of which were quite short – and not intended to be read from beginning to end unless the reader was so inclined, but to be used as writings that could be drawn upon as grist for thought and reflection. This was what he wanted for his own 'book' – except that it would not be his; it would take on a life of its own and would be developed by others, people of future times, people who were strangers and perhaps, as yet, unborn.

This presented him with something of a paradox. He hoped that there would be many contributors but also, that it would not be a book of enormous length. The only printed books that Joel had seen were those that had survived from before The Collapse. Printing as a means of disseminating writing was mistrusted and had, for a variety of reasons, all but disappeared. Anything that he wrote would have to be copied out by hand – a slow and laborious task. Despite the general suspicion, he would have to trust to fortune and hope that at some time in the future, copies of the book would find their way to a printer – and more than that, to a printer who would not mishandle or abuse the spirit of its creation.

He reflected that, given human nature, this was too much to hope. He paused for a moment in his thoughts and the pause coincided with a realisation that his horse had reached a point on the track where he had to pick his way forward with care. Part of the track had collapsed down the steep slope that lay to one side, although there was sufficient left to enable his horse to negotiate his way through.

The other side of the track was dominated by a line of trees and the long shadows they cast reminded Joel of the oncoming darkness. After some minutes, he reached the end of the line of trees and saw that there was still enough light for him to make camp and set up a simple shelter for the night. Finding a fairly level and sheltered place amongst a natural circle of rocks, he tethered Toby to a tree and set about finding materials for a bivouac, of which there were plenty nearby. Then he made a fire, a skill he had learned slowly, long ago but which he now knew how to do in a variety of ways, although the same ingredients were always needed – tinderbox, tinder, kindling and fuel.

Sometime later, he was drowsing by the embers which were still giving off a remarkable heat, reminiscing about a similar fire that he had shared with Sam and Roberta. The journey to Falmouth had been for them a rite of passage. After they had barely escaped the wildfire on the moors, Joel had always had a heightened sense of mistrust where fire of any kind was concerned. He had agreed with Roberta that they would do nothing more about the relationship that had begun to develop between them until they were back at home. It was an undertaking that had been easier to make than to keep. Sam had seemed unaware that his two companions had fallen for each other, but he was good at masking his feelings when he felt it was necessary and Joel still wondered how much he had known.

Staring into the embers, Joel was glad of the distraction that the warmth and comfort of the fire had brought him. Remembering his wife was always a bittersweet experience. Mostly now, he was able to remember much of their life together with some semblance of detachment, but there were other times when he still grieved for her. He stood up, pushing back the thoughts that he knew were just a short distance away. His instinct was to put out the fire, but this far from home he could not be too sure about the creatures that were living in the woods. He put enough wood on the fire to ensure that it would continue to burn – and that he could turn it into a blaze if necessary; then if any 'escapees' from wildlife parks came prowling round, he would have an answer to them – except that they were no longer thought of as escapees but as the descendants of animals that had adapted to life in Britain and now roamed and bred wherever they were left alone by human beings.

In his bivouac, Joel pulled a blanket over himself, mulling over the strangeness of the notion of a 'wildlife park'. It was an idea from another age – an age that from his perspective was difficult to understand.

***

Toby jogged along. They were entering the valley – a place that was very familiar to Joel. When the wind came from the south, it was possible to smell the sea.

Joel brought Toby to a halt on the bank of the river. The valley descended rapidly from where they stood, and the water flowed at speed over the rocks in its bed. Usually when Joel came to this place, it was with someone else, but today, his solitariness pressed in upon him.

He held Toby on a light rein giving the horse freedom to pick his way over the rough track. At this point in the journey, it would take only a moment's lapse in the concentration of horse or rider to send them both tumbling down to the rocks lining the river's edge.

Beyond the narrow confines of the track, the tree line rose again to a higher point on the hillside, allowing the warmth of sunlight into the valley. Although the autumn had begun to advance, the way before them was carpeted with wildflowers and insects droned in large numbers between them, making the most of the sunshine.

Joel looked ahead to where the trees advanced once more to a point just above the river bank, the point on the track through which he and Toby would have to squeeze before they came again to the lodge that Joel and his father had built many years before. It had always been a wild place but now Joel wondered how much longer he would be able to keep the incessant invasion of vegetation at bay.

Unerringly, Toby picked his way through the gap at the top of the river's bank, avoiding the stones and rocks that lay in their path. With relief, horse and rider turned towards the smoother, grassy track that would bring them to the path leading up the hillside to the lodge.

Joel remembered the many hours of labour that it had taken to clear the natural ledge on which the hunting lodge now stood. He and his father had removed rocks, stones, trees and undergrowth that was capable of ripping their skin to pieces. At first they had cleared just enough to begin building, but then, year after year, they had progressively opened up a larger area around the lodge so that there was now a distance of more than a hundred yards between the house and the tree line. Fortunately, most of the materials they cleared, they had been able to use for building.

Maintaining the area around the lodge was something to which Joel had to give attention and yet he found it hard to muster any enthusiasm for it; it was time that could not be spent hunting. Joel brought Toby to a halt for a moment. The horse had instinctively jerked his head away from a cloud of flies hanging over something that lay in the long grass to one side of the track.

Leaving Toby to crop the grass, Joel dismounted and went to investigate. Picking up a long stick and risking the unwanted attention of the flies, he parted the grass. The last remnants of a deer lay where the predators of the forest had left them. Deer were usually too fast for most predators but this one might have been injured. There was very little, just enough of a dark, bloodied mess to attract a thick coating of flies, taking a late meal before the autumn set in more fully.

Joel walked back to his horse, wondering what had attacked the deer. He suspected that it was a bear, although no doubt a number of other animals had picked over the remnants of the carcass. He knew that bears, the descendants of animals that had been held in captivity, had successfully bred in the forest and although they were few in number, they still represented a danger.

***

He decided to lead Toby the last few yards of the path that led up to the lodge. The path was quite steep and led between grassy banks that formed a natural gateway to the level area surrounding the house. Joel went slowly, warily, in case some other human being or creature from the forest had taken up residence whilst he had been away.

He went first to the stables, housed in a long rectangular building constructed of stone and standing along the further edge of the yard in which Joel and his father had built the lodge. Unlocking the door to the first stable, he opened it as far as he could, letting light and fresh air into the interior, and led Toby inside. A habit he had been taught from childhood was that before he tended to his own needs, he had to tend to those of his animals. It was not a task that Joel resented, since Toby was his trusted means of transport and also his only companion on a journey such as the one he had just undertaken. Toby waited patiently as Joel groomed him and then provided him with fodder. He had been able to lay in a stock of hay, and later, although pasturage took a certain effort to maintain, Joel kept a paddock for Toby and other horses owned by the family, next to the lodge.

The lodge itself was also built of stone, much of it gathered from the river valley below. Slates for the roof and glass for the windows had been brought piecemeal from the Ridge, although some of these materials had also come from the many derelict buildings along the route to the lodge. Having seen that Toby was content for the time being, Joel now stood before the large oak door, fumbling for the key to the padlock – an item that his father had commissioned the village blacksmith to make.

It was not a large building. Removing the second of two strong pieces of oak that were used to secure the door, he finally swung it open, feeling a cool draught of air move past him as he did so. He did not, however, go straight into the room before him. There were four fairly large windows, two at the front of the building and two at the back. The building depended on these for its light and so Joel went carefully around them, removing the shutters that were used to protect the glass and to provide further security.

He went patiently about his task, remembering the occasion when he had found an adder beneath his bed. Bats too had colonised the lodge. As with all the living things around him, Joel treated them with respect. He loved to watch them flying around the lodge at dusk but knew as well that they carried a strange disease in their bite – one for which there was no cure available. It was something that he remembered if he found one injured, as happened occasionally, and was tempted to handle it.

With the shutters removed, there was nothing worse to be seen than a certain amount of evidence that mice and rats had maintained their residence and bat droppings on the floor confirmed that they too had continued to occupy the roof spaces.

The internal layout of the lodge was simple. The living room at one end was the largest room. There was no ceiling so that the arched timbers and the boards in the roof could be clearly seen. A large stone chimney breast and hearth took up much of the space on the outer wall at the far end. A small well-lit annex attached to the front of the building provided space for a kitchen and a washroom, although Joel generally used the large hearth in the living area for cooking most of his meals. Hot water could only be provided by heating it over a fire.

The other end of the lodge had been partitioned, with timber walls, into two bedrooms. These both had ceilings so that those sleeping in them were spared the attentions of the creatures living in the roof. Winters were rarely cold, but Joel and his father had built small hearths, one of the few concessions that they had made to any kind of luxury, so these rooms which were some distance from the hearth in the living room could be heated on those rare occasions that the weather turned particularly cold. Joel had seen snow only twice in his lifetime and frosts were very rare, even in the heart of winter.

Sanitary arrangements for the lodge were basic. A path led from the living room door for about 50 yards to a small, stone-built outbuilding, roofed with slate. Here a small stone platform topped with a wooden seat concealed a hole in the ground which in turn led down to a spacious chamber below which Joel and his father had excavated years before. The stone platform had been both something of a joke between them and a luxury. Most privies on the Ridge consisted of little more than an enclosed 'hole in the ground'. Like the rest of the lodge, the latrine was generally populated with spiders, and creatures such as birds, mice and rats that made night-time visits rather more eventful than Joel would have wished. The latrine, however, had been built a further 50 yards from the edge of the forest so that larger animals would generally be disinclined to investigate. All the same, night-time visits were made laborious by the need to take a lamp and a crossbow.

The day was advancing into late afternoon. There would be several hours of daylight yet, but Joel had built a large fire in the living room hearth. The room had smelled dank and musty when he had entered it. A fire would provide some welcome warmth and the means by which to cook an evening meal.

***

Emily was waiting for Josh. She thought that he would be late back from the fields. Her intention to ride over to see her father at the lodge had not gone down well. Much of the harvest was in but, contrary to Emily's belief, there was still plenty of work to do. The meat that she would bring back with her father would be a welcome addition to their food supplies, but Josh did not relish spending several days looking after his children.

Daniel and Grace both helped their parents with the farm, but Emily also insisted that they spent time learning as much as she and her companions could teach them.

She was about to get busy in the kitchen when Daniel came in. He was a rather thin child whose prominent knees and elbows were forever getting bruised or grazed in the course of the daily activities into which he threw himself. His tousled hair was almost the colour of straw since he spent most of every day when not at school either chasing about outside with his friends or helping his father. After a long hot summer, his face was a dark brown and dappled with freckles.

He threw himself into a chair and called across to his mother. "Hey, Mum, is there anything to eat? I'm starving."

She looked across at him. "There might be if you can help me with the potatoes."

"Mum, do I have to?"

"Yes, you do, if you want to eat."

Daniel was used to helping but knew that his mother would want him to peel the potatoes. It was a job that he hated, especially since most of the knives in the kitchen drawer seemed to be blunt. Resigning himself to the task, he made his way across to the sink, pushed up his sleeves and began peeling the potatoes that his mother had left for him, at the side of the sink.

Emily busied herself with the pieces of mutton that she had decided to roast for their evening meal; seeing her, Daniel's enthusiasm increased.

"Mm, Mum! Meat! What's the occasion?"

"No particular occasion!" she said indignantly. "Your dad has been working since early this morning and he'll deserve something good to eat when he comes in!"

"I suppose so," replied Daniel. "He was in a bloody bad mood today."

Emily looked up sharply from the pieces of mutton she was cutting. "Daniel, I've told you not to use that word!"

"Sorry, Mum." He paused. "Freddie uses it all the time."

Emily sighed. There were times when she wished that the men who worked with Josh would save their swearing for when the boy was out of earshot.

The door into the house swung open and Grace, Daniel's younger sister, made her way along the hall and into the kitchen.

"Hello Mum, what you doing?"

"Cooking your food," Emily replied. "Want to help?"

Grace nodded. She really wanted to go to her room, but like her brother, she was hungry.

She sat at the kitchen table and Emily dumped peas for shelling and carrots for peeling in front of her. Grace was duly impressed. "Mum!" she exclaimed. "Who's coming to dinner?"

"Don't you be cheeky, young lady! Your dad's been working really hard today. He deserves a good meal when he gets home."

Like her brother, Grace had the dark complexion and straw-coloured hair of a child who had spent most of the summer in the open air. Emily ensured that she regularly cut Grace's hair, but it never seemed to be tidy. Her daughter, like Daniel, was thin and agile, but had not developed the same tendency to cut and bruise herself. She sat patiently shelling the peas.

"You know when you go away, Mum...how long will you be gone?"

"Not long. About four days."

"Are you going to help Grandad?"

"You know I am, Grace. We spent a long time talking about it the other day."

"Mum, I don't want you to go."

Daniel looked across from where he was peeling potatoes at the sink.

"Don't worry, sis, I'll look after you," he said in a mocking tone that he knew would annoy Grace.

Emily shot him a warning look. Smirking, he returned his gaze to the potatoes.

Grace was not usually given to making a fuss when her mother went off to help Joel. Emily felt slightly concerned.

"Why what's bothering you? I've gone off to help Granddad before – you know I have."

Grace paused for a moment. The thing that she wanted to tell her mother had been bothering her for most of the day.

"I was over by Wagg's Corner, today, with Ruthie. We were playing on the edge of the village – you know by the old tree stumps." Emily nodded. It was a place where the children from The Ridge often liked to play. "Well, we were playing 'Grandma's Footsteps' and as I was creeping towards Ruthie, I thought I saw someone on the edge of the wood."

Emily smiled reassuringly. "That's not so unusual," she said. "People from the village often go into that side of the wood."

Grace frowned, her nose wrinkling a little. "Yes, I know, Mum, of course. But it was someone I've never seen before – someone tall, a man. He dodged back when I looked at him. I don't think he wanted to be seen."

Daniel turned to look at Grace with a mocking smile on his face.

"I know who it is," he said. Grace looked expectantly towards him and as she did so, her brother contorted his face into an ugly grimace and clawed at the air with his hands. "It's Old Gurney, the Bogeyman, sis – the one who lives in the woods!"

"Daniel, why don't you go and find your father," interrupted Emily. "Give him some help until such time as the food is ready."

Daniel needed no further prompting. Barely drying his hands, he hurried down the hallway, through the door and out into the yard.

Emily quickly finished the potatoes and set the meat to roast over the fire.

"Come over here and help me find the pots for those vegetables," she said to Grace.

Looking a little sulky, Grace made her way round the table to where her mother was standing.

"I hate my brother!" she exclaimed, laying her head against her mother's side.

"No, you don't," replied Emily. "But he can be very annoying, I grant you."

She sat on a nearby stool for a moment and took her daughter's hands in her own.

"Why does no-one ever believe what I say?" continued Grace looking rather woebegone.

Emily looked at her. "I believe you, Grace," she said. "Tell me some more about this man you saw. What made you think that he wasn't from the village?"

"Because we know everyone from around here, Mum!" replied Grace. "I've never seen the man I'm talking about before. Besides, he was different."

"What do you mean, he was different?" asked Emily.

"Well, he was dressed differently from people in the Village. He had a sort of jacket and trousers made of animal skins. And he was carrying something. It looked like a bow."

"Was there anything else that you noticed about him?"

"No, as I said he dodged back into the shadows and then I didn't see him again."

Emily nodded thoughtfully. Wool was the most common clothing material in the Village. Seeing someone clad in animal skins was not unknown but it would have struck Grace as being unusual.

Quietly pleased that Grace had been so observant, she continued holding her daughter's hands and looking at her with a reassuring smiles she said "I believe you. You're right to tell me! I'll talk to your dad about it, this evening."

"Will he know what to do, Mum?"

"I'm sure he will. If nothing else, it can do no harm to have more people looking out for this man that you saw."

For the time being, Grace seemed reassured. Letting go of her mother's hands, she took a saucepan from a cupboard, went to the sink and began to fill it with water.

"Well done," said Emily. "The meat's cooking well now. It will be a while before Dan and your dad get back, but we may as well set the table."

* * *

Joel had finished the plate of vegetables that he had cooked for himself and was now sitting just outside the back door of the lodge. The light was gradually fading, but the warmth of the day persisted. Stars had begun to appear over the darkly silhouetted treetops of the forest. Hoping to have some fresh meat for his evening meal the next day, Joel reflected that he had only been able to spend a very short time that afternoon adding a few sentences to his book. He felt a certain tension between time spent writing his book and the time required to hunt and provide for himself and the family.

The bats overhead flitted about, their abrupt changes of direction signalling their pursuit of insects. Joel turned again to his earlier thoughts about the climate.

His concerns had steadily increased over many years. Wildfires on the moors were not unknown in his father's youth. Often they had been started deliberately but now, in the long, hot and dry summers, they often ignited without any assistance from human beings. Winters had also become warmer but, unlike the summers, were frequently a time of deluge - and flooding, even on The Ridge, was a common hazard.

Joel had mixed feelings about the flooding. It kept the eastern flank of The Ridge secure. Few travellers were sufficiently brave or determined enough to make their way through the extensive marshes that now covered that part of Somerset. The numerous tanks, wells and cisterns that were used to irrigate the dry uplands of The Ridge were also more than replenished during the winter months, but the vagaries of the weather brought huge uncertainty to the farming, hunting and gathering on which everyone depended.

Most of all, Joel feared the huge storms that could arise with incredible speed. He knew that human memories were faulty things and yet it was his clear impression that storms were both more frequent and more powerful than those he remembered in the younger part of his life.

The few travellers who were allowed into the settlement on The Ridge sometimes brought news of what was happening in other parts of the country. In many instances, the stories that they brought with them were of small outposts of civilisation, struggling against disease, conflict and the climate, to survive. There was occasional news too, of larger towns and cities which were now the provinces of ruthless warlords, willing to butcher anyone who contested their power or territory. News of such places was harder to come by since most travellers avoided them, and only a few were able to come and go without risking the wrath of local tyrants.

Joel knew as well from his sporadic contact with travellers to the coastal towns and villages of the South-West that sea level was rising. On the South coast, places that had been nearly a yard above sea level were now inundated. In recent years, travellers from such places as Portland through to Falmouth had all told of estuaries, low lying land and waterfronts that had been flooded and were now part of the sea's fiefdom. News from around the South-west coastline told the same story. Joel often had to remind himself that these rises in sea level would continue far into the future; it was easy to fall into thinking that the sea had taken all that it was going to take and that everyone could just adapt to the new boundaries that it had established – but such a notion was not consistent with the news that the travellers brought. Instead, the accounts they gave told of incessant encroachment and of the fear that this apparently unending process engendered. Those who chose to remain close to the sea's margins found themselves retreating ever further inland.

The only certainty in Joel's life was that of change. Although he was not yet 60, he thought himself fortunate to have survived so long and still to be in good health. Of the few older people on The Ridge, most had to endure the effects of ill health; with only rudimentary medical care available to them, they had no other choice. Joel reflected that life generally determined that most people he had known fell into two categories; those who were in raw good health and those who were dead. The longevity of his grandfather's years seemed to be a receding feature of life.

The darkness was now gathering about him, and a chill had crept into the air. Late home-goers amongst the birds were hurrying to their roosts and the eerie sounds of owls calling across the clearing brought a feeling of isolation, of a world that had been there before him and one that would continue without him. He withdrew into the house, bolting the door behind him, stirring the embers of the fire and putting onto them some of the wood that he had left to dry in the hearth during his absence.

He had brought with him a carefully calculated amount of the vegetable oil that he used to fuel his lamp. Ensuring that there was sufficient for several hours' light, he took the lamp over to the table on which he had left his writing and in the soft glow, began his work. He continued, pausing only occasionally to gather his thoughts, until fatigue finally overtook him, and he crawled away to his bed.

* * *

An hour before, Emily had decided that although Daniel had returned to the house with news of his father's imminent return, they could wait no longer. She told the two children to sit at the table and she served them their meal, deciding that although she was hungry, she would wait until her husband returned. Somehow she would manage to keep the food in a fit state to eat.

Josh returned to the house some while later, tired and irritable. Washing himself and changing out of his work clothes did little to improve his mood. The family, and principally Emily, always strove to keep themselves and their clothes clean; this was out of a need to preserve a sense of their own self-respect as much as the need for hygiene, in a world where medical care was very limited and where prevention had to take the place of generally non-existent cure.

Emily served Josh a good helping of mutton in gravy together with as large a portion of vegetables as could be spared at that time; she intended to set off the following morning and did not want to leave him smouldering about her absence.

Josh had arranged himself untidily at the table. Sitting upright in his chair was too much of an effort but he ate with an urgency that spoke of his need for food. Emily looked at his dark, outdoor complexion, reflecting that it emphasised the strength of his face. She forgave him his sprawling posture at the table; it was, at the best of times, rather small for his large frame. His dark hair was quite long and curly from exposure to the rain and wind. It had been a while since Emily had cut it.

With some food in his stomach, the aggressive mood in which he had entered the house began gradually to abate and a sense of satisfaction with his day's work was moving in to take its place.

Eventually managing to mop up the last of the gravy on his plate he said, "You been alright here today then, Em?"

Emily nodded. "Yes, it's been fine. Dan and Grace helped me with the vegetable garden this morning, then Grace and I did some clearing up in here. After that, Grace went off to play with Ruthie and Dan wanted to help you."

"Yes, he was useful," said Josh. "He helped make up for Freddie's lack of effort." He paused for a moment. "It's a pity Dan is still so young. Freddie's getting too old for the sort of effort we have to make out there."

"Makes him swear a lot, does it?" asked Emily.

"I suppose it does," replied Josh. "It can't be much fun for him these days. Why d'you ask?"

"Oh, Dan came out with a few bits of Freddie's vocabulary this afternoon."

Josh carefully avoided any sign of amusement, knowing that it would irritate his wife. He decided that a change of subject would be helpful.

"So when are you off to help your dad?" he asked.

"I want to get away tomorrow if you think you can manage here?"

Josh looked at her with a faint smile. "I guess so. I had a good day today and one or two of your dad's men have offered to help out."

"So you won't miss me then?" There was tinge of irony in her voice.

"We can manage the work," replied Josh. "But you know I don't like you riding off on your own."

Emily had done the journey numerous times and the worst hazard that she had ever encountered was a pack of feral dogs. She had needed to shoot two of them before they had retreated into the forest. Fortunately, the incident had occurred before she had married Josh and she had never wanted to mention it to him.

"It's very quiet down there – you know it is. Dad wouldn't ask me to go if he thought there was any real danger."

"True – but if there's ever a problem, what am I supposed to do then? Abandon the kids?"

"No, of course not!" she exclaimed impatiently. "You could ask Sam to come down. His so-called 'boys' are all men now. They can manage over there for a few days."

"I suppose so," was Josh's grudging response. He had often envied Sam's situation and wished that his own children were a few years older. "Anyway, you'll take the gun with you?"

"Yes, of course I will," replied Emily, "if you'll do something for me."

Josh looked up, waiting.

"I want you to check up on something Grace said this afternoon."

"Oh, and what's that?" He might have known that his wife would have conditions of her own.

"Grace thought she saw a stranger acting suspiciously just inside the wood, over by Wagg's Corner there. It could be nothing, but it was close to where she was playing with Ruthie. If there was someone over there, we need to know what they were up to."

Josh wearily agreed. He sometimes felt that the villagers' customary vigilance was akin to paranoia, but at that point, he was too tired to disagree.

"I'm going to miss you for the next few days," he said.

Emily regarded him with a slightly crooked smile on her face.

"Do you mean 'miss me' – or 'miss it'?" she asked with a hint of sarcasm in her voice.

"Come on," protested Josh. "You know you like it too. Besides I know you want another child."

"Do I?" Emily was by no means sure that she did. "There'll be another mouth to feed. And if you were the one who had to put up with the pain, you'd feel differently," she said.

He could hardly disagree. He remembered what she had endured giving birth to Daniel and Grace. It was almost as if all the sexual pleasure they had known during their lovemaking, had been rolled up and reversed in an equal and opposite outpouring of pain.

"So do you regret having children then?" he asked.

"Of course not – you know I don't!" Emily almost snorted her response though within herself she felt very uncertain about having a third child.

Josh retreated and went upstairs. Looking in on Grace, he saw that she was sleeping soundly. Emily went to check on Daniel.

"Asleep?" she queried, as Josh quietly closed Grace's door.

"Yes," he replied.

"Come on then. You can have what you want. But you have to promise that it'll be the silent version."

"Of course," he said in a stage whisper.

They crept into their bedroom and Emily was soon wondering if her husband, who now seemed to be in such a hurry, was the same person who had been protesting about his weariness when he had come in from his work. They both felt that it was fortunate that neither of the children awoke when Josh failed to live up to his promise of silence.

***

Joel slept until the first traces of light crept under his bedroom door. His mouth was dry and had a sour taste, so he crawled out of bed and went to get a drink of water. Then, deciding that he would be unlikely to get back to sleep, he went to the window overlooking the yard and the clearing at the back of the lodge.

His interest was immediately seized by the sight of a deer. It was a large female red deer – a hind. She was grazing at the edge of the clearing, moving restlessly from one patch of vegetation to another. It was still early in the season to be hunting her – but his family needed the meat. He felt he had little choice. He wanted to stay, to watch and admire her beauty, but he had to remember the reason that he had travelled to the lodge.

Hoping that she would continue to be occupied, he pulled on some clothes and went out of the lodge by way of the front door, making as little sound as possible. He was in luck. There was a slight breeze, but it was blowing from the direction of the forest and across the valley; it would carry both scent and sound of him away from the hind.

Crouching low, crossbow on his back, he crept across the ground that lay between him and the edge of the tree line. Then keeping downwind, he began to worm his way towards her, his heart racing at the thought that he could disturb her at any moment. Slowly, cautiously, he lifted his head. It was still something of a long shot. At that range, his accuracy was not guaranteed. He crawled on his stomach, worming his way forward until he had a clear view of her head and neck. It was enough!

He estimated that he was now well within 30 yards of her. He carefully planted his crossbow rest in the ground before him. Then he pulled the crossbow round into his grasp and, with the familiar effort but as silently as he could, drew back the string, taking care to latch it at the centre point. A glance told him that the hind was still grazing a few feet from where he had first seen her. He lowered the bolt into the track and lowered the crossbow onto its rest. He still had a good view now of the hind's head, neck and shoulder. He placed his finger on the trigger when, for the moment, she lowered her head to crop at the grass again. He breathed as slowly and silently as he could and then as she raised her head again, he held his breath and squeezed the trigger. Faster than his eye could follow, the bolt flew across the short space between where he lay concealed and where the hind was grazing. The bolt struck her full in the shoulder and she went down with a hoarse cry, threshing with her legs. It was a clean shot, but Joel was quickly upon her, striving to stay clear of her hooves, his knife drawn, thrusting it into her, ending her pain and then sinking to the earth, holding her as the last vestiges of life oozed from the now unconscious animal. The seconds and minutes passed. He crouched beside her, his fingers splayed in the coarse hair of her coat and feeling the heaving of her sides but waiting for the moment in which she would lie lifeless on the woodland floor.

The moment arrived. It never became routine. It was a moment for which the people of the Ridge had devised a ritual. Joel went into it now, bowing low with his hands and arms laid against the slaughtered animal then raising them again opened to the sky, crying aloud in a release of tension and celebration for the kill before bowing low again, uttering words of reverent thanks for the life sacrificed to preserve his own.

The ritual helped to ease his mood down from the exhilaration of the hunt into the less elevated feelings that followed. When he had first begun hunting, a sense of conflict had sometimes followed in which he tried to reconcile his reverence for the beauty of the animal he had killed with his need for food and with the hunger that drove him onwards towards the perfection of his hunting skills. Such early conflict now lay largely forgotten and in the moments of exhilaration that followed the kill, his gratitude towards these animals was akin to worship, to visceral feelings that he found hard to connect with those few vestiges of the previous civilisation that his people sought to preserve.

Now he had to get the slaughtered animal back to the lodge. She was the weight of a large man, but he decided that he would be able to drag the carcass from where it lay to the back door of the lodge.

From there on began the laborious work of skinning the deer then butchering and preserving the meat. It would begin by suspending the deer from a large wooden frame that he had previously constructed in the yard. There was a cold store on the north side of the lodge which he could use when necessary, although for longer term preservation, cold smoking was his preferred method.

Joel knew that these various processes would take him much of that day and some of the next, but that at the end of it he would have the beginnings of a supply of food that would help his family to get through the winter. A single deer would not be enough. He would have to hunt again – but it had been a lucky start to his expedition and one that would enable him to make good use of his time prior to Emily's arrival.

***

It had been an early start. Emily had decided to take two horses. She had saddled Bundle. Then, when the children had eaten a quick breakfast, they had helped their father to prepare Rhodri, a handsome bay cob. He would have an easy outward journey but would earn his keep on the return, carrying the meat that Joel had prepared.

Josh stood in the yard with Daniel and Grace, waving their mother off on her journey. Shortly she would join the trail that led almost south below the tree line following the contours of successive river valleys. The journey would take her almost two days but, despite having to leave her home and family, she was looking forward to the ride and to spending time with her father.

The rough track that she was following soon joined with the trail that Joel had followed southwards. It was a mellow autumn day and a mild breeze from the south carried with it the smell of damp vegetation and of the fields spangled with dew on the waving grasses and myriad autumn flowers. Bundle's steady gait made Emily's ride at this point an easy one and Rhodri was happy to jog along behind, seemingly content to be away from the confines of the farm and the stable yard.

The slow jog of the trail unwound around the hillsides. For a long section of the journey, Emily would ride through valleys that were now almost completely forested and where she would see little sign of the sun, but then, on the second day of her journey, she would emerge again into the river valleys further south. In that part of her ride, the tree lines would recede to further up the hillsides and the final section to the lodge would require care but would otherwise provide just enough challenge to make it interesting.

Although Emily had ridden the trail many times, she now reached the long section in which she always felt her spirits sink a little. The trees closed in on the path which now began to wind its way gradually up a long slope to her right. Here and there in the gloom, she could see the huddled, shadowy outlines of houses and cottages that had long been enveloped by the forest and whose inhabitants had, for one reason or another, left, died or been driven out.

As she gazed at the dense, dark woods around her, they prompted memories of books that she had inherited from her great-grandfather, in which there were several collections of children's fairy tales. Daniel and Grace had both loved having them read to them, although Josh was rather dismissive, saying that there was already enough around them to worry about without filling their heads with superstition. Looking around her, Emily thought that he had a point; the forest's twilight made it easy to imagine such things as goblins and elves or other strange creatures that would hustle her and her horses off the path and down some long, subterranean tunnel into the hillside.

The trail took a long turn to the left and wound downhill for a short distance before bending round to the right and making its way uphill again. The twists and turns in the track made Emily feel disorientated, although ahead of her, the path's direction had enabled the sun to send a long shaft of light down through the trees to form a large pool of light and warmth on the forest floor. For the short time it would take to traverse this well of light, Emily would enjoy the cheer that it afforded.

She scanned the way ahead, aware that both Bundle and Rhodri were becoming restive. They were both even-tempered horses, but their senses were sharper than hers and they usually became aware of problems that lay ahead well before their owner knew that anything was wrong. Emily peered into the gloom and towards the approaching shaft of light. To her bemusement, a small brown creature scampered on all fours across the path and into the trees on the other side. Suddenly, a much larger animal came lolloping down the hillside behind it and catching the smell of the horses came to rest on the path, before standing up full height, its enormous shape silhouetted by the sunlight behind. Bundle reared up and Emily had to hang on tightly to prevent herself from being thrown. Rhodri snorted and tugged vigorously at his tether.

Emily was used to seeing deer and even wild boar in the forest, but it was the first time that she had seen a bear. She guessed that the smaller animal she had seen scamper across the path was a bear cub and that the very large creature that reared its huge mass ahead of her was the mother.

The presence of the mother bear on the path continued to disturb both the horses. Good natured and resilient though he was, it was all that Emily could do to stop Bundle from bucking and throwing her off. She assumed that the bear was only interested in protecting her cub, but she also began to wonder if at some moment very soon, she would begin to show a more active interest in the horses.

She waited. The bear remained where it was, blocking her passage along the path and occasionally turning her head towards her cub, which was now some yards further down the slope and rooting about amongst the leaves, seemingly oblivious to the confrontation that it had caused.

Emily thought quickly. She could frighten the bear off with her rifle but the noise of the gun, particularly if she fired from the saddle, might spook the horses. She decided to dismount but not to tether the horses; if the bear decided to charge, she wanted to give them the chance to escape. Drawing the rifle from its long holster in front of Bundle's saddle, she unlatched the safety catch, raised the gun to her shoulder, and took aim. If she had thought that this alone might be enough to unsettle the bear and send it shambling off after her cub, she was wrong. To her momentary dismay, the bear broke into a gathering charge, heading towards her at a furious speed. Instinctively, she fired into the track just ahead of the bear.

For a brief second, her heart pounded as she thought that the shot had had no effect, but the bear was unable to halt its charge completely and instead, veered off amongst the trees and headed back at speed towards her cub. The crash of the gun was still echoing off the surrounding hillsides and rooks that had flown, cawing raucously, in huge numbers from their nests began now to return to their lofty perches. Emily remained motionless, her rifle at her shoulder whilst she peered through the sight at the rapid lolloping retreat of the bears, down through the trees lining the steep hillside.

Slowly, she lowered her rifle, watching until she was certain that the bears would not return. Then, finally satisfied, she turned to her horses, grateful that their training had paid off and that, with not much more than a little whinnying and shaking of their manes, they had stood their ground. She returned to them, patting them reassuringly on their necks and talking to them in an affectionate, gentle voice. Finally, she slid the rifle back into its holster and remounted. Knowing that the horses had the ability to sense what she was feeling, she kept them moving along the trail at a moderate but steady pace until she felt that they were out of any immediate danger and that her own heartbeat was returning to something approaching normal.

* * *

Emily was still too distant from Joel for him to have heard the sound of her gun. He was, in any event, engrossed in his work which had now progressed to the cold smoking of the venison. The previous night, he had spent long hours at his writing, and the warmth of the day and the smell of the smoke made him feel sleepy. He began to hope that soon he would be able to break off for a while.

He had pulled an old chair out of the house and into the yard. Drowsing in the autumn sun, he fell as so often into memories of Roberta. When they had returned to the Ridge after their journey to Falmouth, they had largely abandoned the discretion that they had previously shown and were not afraid to be seen around the Village together.

For a while, they became the subject of gossip and amused speculation. This had irritated Roberta, although Joel tried to ignore it, knowing that most people's interest would last until the next piece of gossip came along – and then would move on.

Sam, meanwhile, had soon sunk himself again in the life of the Village and of his parents' farm. There was general relief and some gratitude that the part needed for the wind turbine had been successfully fitted into place and that those households that received their supply from the turbine could begin again to use electric light and the limited amount of water heating that was permitted.

Joel tried to set aside his memories, but they continued to weave themselves amongst his thoughts. He intended to hunt again the next day and needed to prepare for his expedition into the forest. As he went about his work, he wished that Roberta was there to work beside him, as she had been in the early years of their marriage – a short, precious time that had ended with the birth of their second child – a boy who had not survived more than a few hours. He tried again to push his memories away but still they came to him with a deep heaviness in which his enthusiasm for the tasks around him began to ebb into a sense of futility.

He forced himself to concentrate on one activity at a time. Knowing that his daughter would probably arrive the following day helped to focus his thoughts. Although winters were rarely harsh, they needed to eat, and they would only do so if he and the other adult members of the family were able to provide enough food to sustain them until well into the new growing season. There had been winters when the whole community had come close to starvation. The memories of those times reminded him about the reason for his journey and about why his predecessors had relearned skills that had lain largely neglected amongst them for some 200 years.

He prepared the crossbow and the bolts that he would take with him. He would set off as soon as it was light, taking just the things that he would need for the hours that he would be away, and returning in time for his daughter's arrival later in the day. That evening, he would return to his writing but would have then to set it aside after just two or three hours because of the need to make an early start the next day.

He looked at the position of the sun in the sky, realising that the day was now well advanced and that he was hungry. He decided to eat a little of the venison. It would be a warm evening, so he could cook and eat in the yard at the back of the house. The fire pit in the yard was a little distance from where he was smoking the meat that he wanted to preserve. He began collecting together kindling and small pieces of wood with which to start a fire.

***

Later, he had eaten the venison straight from the spit on which he had roasted it, savouring it to the last morsel. He sat back, finally full and satisfied. Soon he would have to go into the house and light the lamp so that he could begin writing again. Shading his eyes, he looked towards the setting sun and then into the deepening blue of the sky to the east and the south-east, trying to assess how long it would be before night fell. As he looked, he saw a very curious sight, an immense glow that was growing and lighting the sky above it. He judged that the source of the light was some considerable distance away to the south-east and that he was seeing only those parts of it that were reaching far up into the Earth's atmosphere. He continued watching, bemused by the strength of the light which, even at the distance from which he was watching, was almost blinding. He glanced away, not daring to look straight into its intensity which, as far as he could tell, was still growing. Then, seemingly further away again, came a dazzling flash and once more, a glow that grew in size and intensity, reaching far up into the sky and illuminating the atmosphere above it. Whatever had caused the flashes, he thought that had he been anywhere close to their sources, he would have been blinded by them.

He felt deeply unsettled by these phenomena, wondering whether they were natural or the result of human activities. He found it difficult to believe that human beings could produce anything with the power to illuminate the atmosphere so far above the Earth, but neither had he seen any natural phenomena that would produce such an effect. He had been told during his piecemeal education that human beings could produce explosions of enormous magnitude – a single explosion being enough to destroy an entire city, but Joel now lived in a world, he thought, where most people struggled simply to get enough food to eat each day.

The lights from the east persisted for some time. Joel tried to divert himself by clearing away the remains of his meal, taking care that no scraps were left to attract animals from the forest, but every so often, he would look anxiously into the eastern sky until finally the glowing in the atmosphere had disappeared from sight. He wondered, with deep trepidation, if whatever terrible thing had taken place so far away would come to visit its wrath on the country in which he lived.

He thought about his writing, the aim of which was to help others to survive, but now there was the possibility that people far across the

Earth's surface were setting out to destroy rather than preserve life. He found his lamp and lit it with a taper from the fire. He could not allow himself to be diverted from his task. It was now all the more essential that the knowledge needed to sustain human life was itself sustained.

Further across the globe, in regions of Europe and the Middle East that Joel would never see, firestorms were raging, incinerating everything within their irradiated compass. Climate chaos had propelled, rather than weakened the expansion of human conflict and suicidal competition.

The embers of Joel's fire were guttering in the fire pit as he tried to calm his thoughts, but it would be many days before the fires far to the south and east declined to the extent that they were no more than the radioactive embers of a civilisation that had clung on but could not finally defeat enemies that were as old as the human species.

$$***$$

The encounter with the bears had made Emily more wary than usual. She had travelled on further than she had intended, looking for a place to camp overnight, a place where the tree line would not be too close to her bivouac and where she could keep a good fire burning. She also tethered her horses close by; they would soon become restive and give her warning if animals from the forest approached. She kept her gun next to her loaded but with the safety catch on, in case she should need it during the night.

Like her father, Emily had also seen the intense light in the sky to the south-east. She was puzzled by its brightness but supposed that perhaps it was part of an enormous thunderstorm or that there was a huge volcanic eruption somewhere. Eventually, when the glare began to fade, she preferred the idea that it was an atmospheric effect connected with a thunderstorm, although the intensity of its initial brightness continued to puzzle her.

In her own mind, her suspicions were confirmed when several hours later she heard what she took to be thunder rolling across the landscape. There was something about the sound, however, that did not seem reminiscent of thunder; it tolled, like some analogue of hatred and rage, across the dismal shadows of the night, pushed out as if in waves from a distant, resonating source.

It was a warm night, and she was finding it difficult to sleep. Her bed was less than comfortable, and the incidents of the day kept playing through her head. It was almost with relief that she saw from the entrance of her shelter, forks of lightning blaze down from the sky to strike the tree-topped hills. Here, after all was the storm that she had expected. The thunder had seemed unusual, but she had become accustomed to storms of great ferocity and to atmospheric effects that dwarfed anything she had been accustomed to seeing in her childhood.

She pondered the onset of the storm, hoping that it would last just long enough to cool the air and lay the dust of the trail on which she had been travelling. She had built her shelter carefully, but she was not confident that if the storm was accompanied by strong winds and heavy rain, it would be able to withstand them.

The first heavy drops fell, splattering the dust in front of her shelter. Then within moments the initial, hesitant drops had become a downpour of water, drilling into the land below and spitting through the many gaps and holes in her bivouac in a fine spray that soon began to soak her clothes and bedding. She crouched in the entrance, weighing up a decision to move herself and her horses to the edge of the tree line.

The storm was now very close. An instantaneous spear of lightning flashed in the sky above the forest, illuminating the trees in its baleful glare, a clap of thunder following fast behind and rolling out across the hills and valley. Emily debated with herself whether she and her horses were more at risk out where she was in the open or at the edge of the forest.

The fury of the storm was making a decision inevitable. There were risks whichever course of action she took, but the fine spray inside the shelter had now become a cascade, soaking everything within it. She decided to take her chances with the lightning and make for the edge of the forest. Bundle and Rhodri had both begun tugging at their tethers and, with some difficulty and a certain amount of hazard, she released their tethers and, stumbling forward, led them both towards the tree line. Sheltering in the forest would bring its own risks but she felt that she was more likely to cope with those than the risks of being out in the open.

The wind had strengthened and was pushing the storm away to the west, but the rain fell with ever more ferocity. Emily was soaked to the skin by the time that she led her horses under the trees. The river, which was a little distance below her camp site, had also now swollen to a torrent which hurtled down the valley, submerging its rocky bed and tearing at the earth and vegetation in its path. The valley was steep, and it seemed unlikely that the river would reach far outside its banks, but if there was a flash flood emanating from further up the river's course, the area in which she had camped might be vulnerable.

The lightning flickered now across the darkness to the west. Peals of thunder came crackling back across the hills, shaking the earth beneath her feet. She watched with a morbid fascination as the sweep of the river's torrent began to edge towards her campsite, waiting to see if the bivouac would be borne away.

The rain continued for some time and then it began slowly to falter, giving way eventually to dank silence and aromatic darkness. Emily dozed against Bundle, wondering if there was anywhere dry enough or safe enough to sleep. She would try again to light a fire but this time using whatever material she could find that had not been soaked by the rain.

She led the horses away from the trees and returned to a position just a little further up the slope from the area she had chosen for her bivouac. Tethering the horses once more, she set about building a new fire which, after repeated attempts, she managed to light. The wind by now had abated but had chased away the clouds sufficiently to allow the moon to shed an eerie light on the trees and the still-swollen river.

Emily returned briefly to the edge of the wood, keeping her rifle at the ready but making her way into the gloom until she found some large, dry branches that she could drag back to the fire. Aided by the breeze, the fire was now well established and was able to take larger pieces of wood which she fed carefully into its blazing maw. She turned away briefly to rummage in the saddlebags, which fortunately had not been penetrated by the downpour. There she found the cloth which she generally used as a towel and some dry clothing. Then, in the solitude, she took off her wet clothes and hung them from pieces of branch that she had managed to push into the earth, near the fire. She towelled herself and then stood naked before the flames, warming her goose pimpled flesh and feeling revived by the fire's heat. When she felt sufficiently dry and warm, she pulled on the fresh clothes and tried to improvise a seat, using a log that she found nearby. With her knees raised and her arms on her knees, she managed to doze for a while and then sleep, only to awaken a short time later with a stiff neck and a continuing feeling of weariness. She fell asleep again as the first fingers of dawn were creeping into the sky.

* * *

Joel had left the lodge before dawn, taking with him his crossbows and enough food and water to sustain him until the later part of the day. He returned by mid-morning, pulling behind him a young stag he had killed an hour or so before. It was a fine animal, and he was pleased with the kill; it would provide his family with a good quantity of excellent meat in the weeks ahead. Hunting and then pulling the stag back to The Lodge had made him both hungry and dirty, so that as soon as he returned, he had washed and then breakfasted on strips of bacon that he had brought with him, grilling them on sticks placed over a fire in the yard.

Having eaten and then briefly rested, he set about butchering the stag. It was a task that took him much of the morning. Then the long process of cold smoking the meat lay before him.

Smoking the meat sufficiently would take many hours. Like most of the other structures around The Lodge, the smoke house was stone-built whilst other materials needed in its construction such as pipes and metal fittings had been taken from the many houses that lay derelict along the trail to The Lodge. Smoke was piped into the smoke house from a small burner a short distance away. Joel had previously cut and dried a supply of oak, which he would burn to supply the smoke.

He arranged the meat on the racks in the smoke house and then when he was satisfied with it, lit the wood in the burner. A short while later he was gratified to see smoke emerging from the small chimney on top of the smoke house. His task now would be to ensure that the burner continued to do its job efficiently.

He went about his work using skills that he had learned and practised over many years. Hunting the deer made him aware of how much he and his family depended directly on the natural world of which they were a part. Some of the people in the Village talked about the cunning required to hunt and kill the animals that they ate for food, but Joel preferred to think of it simply as knowledge – knowledge of the creatures' ways of living and of their habitats. Although Joel hunted deer, he never lost his respect for them. His knowledge of them and of the weapons that he possessed gave him an initial advantage, but once alerted the deer were faster than he could ever be, could remain elusive within the forest for long periods of time and could survive in the wild without any protection or shelter other than that provided by the herd and their natural habitat.

His admiration for the plants and animals around him, gave him a sense of his own place in the natural order and of his dependence upon it. There was also in Joel no belief that the world around him existed for his exploitation and convenience. Instead, he had a sense of wonder and of a perfection that he could not find in anything made by human beings.

Late in the afternoon, there was finally little more that he could do other than wait. He washed himself thoroughly and then sat on an old log and gazed out past the lodge and across the valley. He decided to eat out in the open again, anticipating that Emily would arrive in the late afternoon or early evening.

He sat gazing around him, vaguely discontent with his own inactivity. As his gaze swept round past The Lodge, he noticed that a small section of fencing along the boundary of the horse paddock had been blown down in the storm, the night before. He wandered over to it, thinking that it would take him just a few minutes to mend. As he approached, he realised that the storm had done quite a lot of damage and had blown down several lengths of wood onto the ground. He picked his way amongst them, intending to pile them on one side whilst he had a better look at the rest of the fence.

As Joel bent down to pick up the wood, there was suddenly a harsh, raucous squawking from bushes bordering The Lodge and a loud clatter of wings. Involuntarily, he stepped back only to stand on something sharp that pierced through the sole of his boot and deep into his foot. Through his shock, he realised that he must have stood on a nail in one of the planks from the fence, which then nearly upended him as it remained nailed to his boot and foot. With considerable effort, he somehow managed to wrench it away and went hopping about the yard, cursing and trying to distract himself from the pain.

His foot still throbbing, he looked back distractedly to where he had been standing. He could see clearly the offending nail projecting from the plank on which he had stood. It was a further annoyance that no matter how many times he encountered pheasants, the sudden way in which they broke cover always startled him and made his heart pound.

He hobbled back to his seat on the log, carefully removed his boot and sock and inspected the puncture wound that the nail had made. There was a certain amount of blood in his sock but it had bled less than he had expected. The wound, however, was another matter. Some of the rust from the nail had discoloured the entrance to the wound, and he could feel that the nail itself had penetrated deep into his foot.

The pain was making him feel light-headed, but somehow he managed to get a bowl of water, a clean cloth and some of the homemade soap he had brought with him. He hobbled back to his seat on the log because there, the light was good, and he could see what he was doing. Carefully and rather gingerly, he washed the wound until there were few external signs, other than a small hole, of where the nail had entered his foot.

He went into the house, to the box of items that he kept for minor emergencies, found a bandage and bound up the wound. Then he found a fresh pair of socks and having put them on, finally put his boots back on as well and hopped out to the yard. There he rummaged in a wood pile that lay to one side until he found a length of branch that he could use as a crutch. Choosing a branch that had a convenient fork in it, he trimmed it with an axe until it fitted neatly under his armpit and he could use it to get back to his seat on the log.

He sat for a while, musing that his plans had been curtailed by the intervention of a simple nail. It was fortunate that Emily should be arriving shortly and that she would be able to help him make the preparations for the journey home.

He drowsed for a while, the pain in his foot having subsided to a throb. He drifted briefly into a sleep where he dreamt of pursuing deer through woodlands in which they were somehow protected by areas of ground on which he dare not tread, when suddenly he was struggling to wrench himself out of his dreams and back into wakefulness.

***

Emily tethered Bundle and Rhodri and came hurrying over to see what, if anything, was wrong with her father. It was unlike him to be sleeping when she arrived. He was usually bustling about in the yard, preparing for her arrival.

She stood by his side casting her shadow over him. He had woken with a start and sat gazing up at her, his eyes still momentarily unfocussed.

"Dad are you alright?" she enquired anxiously.

It took him a moment to think about his reply. "Yes...yes, I think so."

He stood awkwardly, hugging his daughter to him and giving her a kiss on the cheek.

"It's good to see you," he said.

Emily returned her father's hug but then stood back to look at him more carefully. There were small beads of perspiration on his forehead and his face had an unusual pallor. Something had happened, she was sure, and she needed to know what it was. Despite this, she decided to wait for a suitable moment before trying to find out more and said instead, "It's quite hot out here. Wouldn't you rather be inside?"

Joel smiled for a moment. Emily was her usual self, fussing over him in her familiar way. "I'm fine. I've been hunting and I was just taking it easy for a while. Come and sit down here beside me."

"Ok, I will do, but first I need to see to Bundle and Rhodri."

Joel nodded, hardly able to disagree and then dozed in the sun whilst his daughter led the horses away to the stable.

It took her a little while to groom and feed them. Joel was awake when she eventually came to sit beside him on the log. She looked sideways at him and then asked, "What's happened then, Dad? I can see you're not your normal self."

"Oh, it was nothing much. I had a bit of an accident." Joel did not really want to talk about it.

Emily, however, persisted. "What sort of an accident?"

"I was over there," Joel gestured towards the gap in the fence. "I stood on one of those fallen fence rails and a nail went into my foot."

Emily winced in concern. "You should let me have a look at that. There might be something I can do."

Joel looked at her resignedly. "Ok," he said. "But I've already given some attention to it."

Gently, she helped her father to remove his boot, and looked carefully at the wound, which by then was rather inflamed. Her father always kept a quantity of salt for preserving meat and it took her just a short time to make a salt solution with which to bathe her father's foot. Joel jumped involuntarily when she applied the solution to the wound but then waited patiently whilst his daughter found a bandage and bound up the wound, saying that she would look at it again the next day.

As he settled back again on the log, Emily was satisfied that he looked more comfortable. They chatted for a while, and she recounted her experiences with the bears and with the storm the previous night. Joel nodded but then said in a slightly agitated way, "Did you see the lights in the sky? You must have seen them. They were impossible to miss."

"Yes, I did," replied Emily. "But I just thought that they were something to do with the storm."

"No...no, I don't think so, Emily. I almost wish I did believe that, but I don't think it was anything to do with the storm."

"Then what do you think it was?" She managed to sound at once both sceptical and a little anxious.

"Well, for a start, I think that whatever it was, it was happening a long way from here. I'm sure that we only saw it because it was something huge, a phenomenon well outside the things we usually see."

Emily rummaged through her memories of the various phenomena that her father or her great grandfather had told her about.

"So, what do you think it was?" she asked. "A volcano? A large meteor? Perhaps it was one of those satellite things hitting the Earth?"

"I suppose it could be any of them – although trying to guess from what we saw I don't think so. A satellite would have a large impact but what we saw was something colossal. It could have been a meteor or, given the enormity of the glow in the sky, a small asteroid – but then I think we might have seen some sign of it, however brief, before it hit the Earth. A giant volcano is a possibility, but the glow did eventually fade and unless it was some kind of violent, volcanic explosion, I think that it would have persisted longer."

"Then what do you think we saw?"

Joel shook his head, his face full of sorrow.

"Even from the huge distance that I think was involved, I thought I saw some strange effects amongst the clouds – strange phenomena that for me only recall some pictures that my grandfather showed me in one of his books. I think we were seeing the effects of nuclear weapons."

Emily did not want to believe it. "An enormous thunderstorm could produce the sort of clouds you're talking about."

"I agree, Emily – but this was much more than the sort of anvil shaped clouds that you get with thunderstorms. The effects seemed to be more regular than that, geometrical in fact. I know that nature can produce such things, but this was also connected with the intense light. Anyway, I don't think we were seeing what was happening close to the Earth's surface. It was too far away. I think we only saw the effects that were produced high in the Earth's atmosphere."

Emily shook her head. "You could be right, but it is only guesswork, isn't it? And from the little you've told me about such weapons, we have to hope you're wrong. There are other explanations, I'm sure – and I don't see any particular reason for believing what must be one of the very worst of them. This may sound very selfish, but if it was as far away as you say, then surely it can't harm us here?"

Joel looked doubtful. "I'm not too sure about that."

"What do you mean?" asked Emily anxiously.

"Well, if I'm right, there is a danger to people right across the world."

"Dad, what can that be – if this 'whatever it was' happened so far away?"

"If I'm right, even people huge distances away could be affected by radioactive fallout."

"By what?"

Joel thought about how he could best explain what he was saying. "The explosion, if it was an explosion, could have thrown millions of poisonous particles into the atmosphere."

"It might – but they would still have to get here – and if you're right about the distance, they would have to travel a very, very long way."

Joel looked at Emily, suddenly wondering why he was persevering with such a horrifying topic when, as Emily had said, he was probably wrong and, if so, he was only causing both of them anxiety that was completely unnecessary. He decided to break away from the conversation they had been having.

"You make me feel very selfish," he said after a long pause.

"What do you mean?" asked Emily, hoping for some relief.

"I mean that I've got you to come all the way down here when you have a husband, two young children and a farm to worry about."

"After what you've just said, Dad, this is not the time to remind me – but then, I have been coming down here ever since you first brought me as a child. As far as Josh and the children are concerned, it's never been any different."

"I know," replied Joel. "But things are changing."

"I don't see how," retorted Emily.

"Well for a start, there's more to worry about in terms of the animals living in these woods now."

Emily started to respond but Joel continued.

"There are far more predators here than there used to be. Their numbers have increased because there are so many deer. Meeting up with bears is a serious matter."

Emily nodded,

"You're right, Dad, but we don't grow enough vegetables to live on them all through the winter – even if we wanted to. And we've had such a drought this summer that it's been a poor year on the farm. We need the meat that we can get by coming here."

"We could hunt closer to home."

"That's true, but the game is more plentiful here. There are too many people hunting in the areas around the Village."

Joel felt defeated. "So what do you suggest we do?"

Emily thought for a moment. "Perhaps it's time for other people to do this then you could spend more time working on your ideas for The Ridge."

"Who do you have in mind?"

"Well, for a start Josh could come here with some of the others from the Village."

"Josh always has too much to do on the farm."

"Until now," agreed Emily, "but in a year or two Daniel will be able to do far more than he's doing at present – and he's already pretty useful. Grace can help too, although since she's that much younger, it will be several years before she can do a lot more."

Joel looked thoughtful. He was reluctant to give up both the hunting and the solitude that it brought him, but he was beginning to be persuaded that Emily had solutions to some of their problems.

"Hmmm," he said. "It could work."

"But..." responded Emily.

"But what?"

"You know very well. You're still not happy. I can see it by the expression on your face."

Joel frowned. "You know what it is. We've talked about it many times. The climate's changing."

Emily sighed. "Dad, it's always changing. It's changed throughout history. It's even changed since I was child. It's the whole reason that we now live the way we do!"

Joel had sometimes given up at this point in the past, but this time, he decided to press on.

"You're right, of course, Emily, but how many summers have we had like this one? How many winters have we had to dig deep into our reserves of food and water? And it isn't the same year after year. We know that every year it's getting hotter and drier in the summer, and every year it gets even wetter in the winter. The time is not far away when we won't have any reserves to dig into."

Usually Emily disagreed with her father, but this time, her disappointments over the poor harvest of both root crops and cereals led her to feel that he was right. A sense of helplessness – and almost of fear – returned to haunt her from previous occasions that she had stopped to think about it.

"So what can we do?" she asked. "What can we do that we aren't already doing?"

Joel had already given a good deal of thought to the problems.

"Well, for a start, we could do a lot more work to improve irrigation on The Ridge. We're running out of space for more cisterns, but we could do more to pump up water from below. It always strikes me as odd that on The Ridge we're suffering through lack of water whereas below The Ridge, there's far too much of it. We could find ways to pump some of that water up onto The Ridge."

Emily nodded. It sounded feasible and the inhabitants of The Ridge had always needed to be both inventive and resourceful. She added a thought of her own. "We could move," she said.

"Where to?" asked Joel.

"Well, we could move down to the Levels."

Her father looked sceptical. "The reason that we've all stayed on The Ridge is that it can be easily defended."

"Yes, Dad," agreed Emily. "But instead of living in what has become a hill fort, we could live in a village built on stilts. It would be just as hard to attack, and we'd have plenty of water all around us."

Joel laughed. "It's been done before, you know. There was a time in the distant past, when people in our part of the world lived in villages on stilts," he exclaimed.

Emily was indignant. "I know that. It was you who taught me about it, if you remember. All the same, we would have fish and wildfowl all around us – and we could still farm The Ridge, although instead of travelling to the Levels, we would travel to The Ridge."

Joel laughed again but this time with a greater appreciation of the neatness of her idea.

"So we'd have the whole of The Ridge as a kind of allotment..."

Emily looked bemused so he explained. "Your great-grandfather used to have one or two of his vegetable plots some distance from his cottage. He always referred to them as his allotments."

Emily smiled, understanding now what he meant.

Joel, however, returned to frowning. "There would be some problems that were not necessarily there in the past."

"What do you mean?" asked Emily, a little wearily.

"Well, for a start, large parts of The Levels used to dry out in summer, whereas now, they never really dry out despite the droughts that we have. Another problem..."

Emily sighed.

"Another problem is that the storms we get now are almost certainly much worse than anything experienced in the past."

"We don't really know that", replied Emily, deciding this time to disagree. "We don't have access to much information about the weather in previous times."

"No, you're right," agreed Joel. "I shouldn't suppose things when I don't actually know much about the past. All I think I can say is that there seem to be more severe storms and that they occur much more often now than when I was a child."

"How do you know that Dad? Have you kept records?"

"No, I haven't, but I do have to pick up the pieces after each storm – somehow try to fill the hole that's been left by all the food that's been lost through damage to crops and repair all the damage done to the farm."

Emily could tell that he was intensely frustrated, but then perhaps it was because as he became older he was growing weary of the incessant hard, physical work required in almost all areas of their daily life. "Perhaps we should move away from here," she said. "Not just move to the Levels but move right away."

"But where to?" asked Joel. "Where would we go? The weather doesn't affect just one country. The weather patterns must be changing everywhere."

"Of course," replied Emily. "But if the changes in the climate here are making life harder, perhaps there are places in other parts of the world where they've made life easier?"

Joel did not reply immediately. Instead, he sat remembering his conversation long ago with James in Falmouth, a conversation about people emigrating to Canada.

"There may be such places," he said at last. "And some of those places may be inside the Arctic Circle."

Emily remembered that he had told her many times about the journey that he had made to Falmouth with her mother and with their friend Sam and that from Falmouth people made the long sea crossing to North America.

She decided to break away from their thoughts. She was hungry and had not eaten since early in the day.

Seeing her stir, Joel felt a twinge of guilt. "You've been here all this time, Emily, and I haven't offered you a thing to eat."

"No, you haven't," she agreed. "And I'm starving!"

"Well. I'd better do something about it then, right away!" With a considerable effort Joel got to his feet and began hobbling towards the lodge. Emily watched him and realised again that the injury to his foot was giving him considerable pain.

"It's alright, Dad!" she called after him. "I can cook something for both of us." She sprang up and went quickly across to him.

As she drew level, he looked at her and said, "The most I'll agree is that we cook the meal together."

She smiled in consent, though hoping that he would at least have the sense to sit down if the injury to his foot made it necessary. Eventually, she persuaded him to build a fire in the fire pit for which most of the materials were already close by, whilst she went in search of the ingredients for their meal.

***

Despite her hunger, Emily decided that they would make a stew. The smell of the food whilst it was cooking over the fire made them impatient to eat, although they knew that the meat needed some time to cook properly. Joel hobbled about, aided by his makeshift crutch, ensuring that the stove for the smoke house was kept well fed with fuel. Emily pottered at a variety of tasks such as checking the horses, inspecting her father's arrangements for the venison, and making sure that their beds would be comfortable enough. Eventually, when they were able to leave their work for a while, they sat and chatted until the stew was ready. Then they both sat with a plate of steaming food which they ate greedily and of which they made sure that they ate every scrap.

Finally, when their hunger was satisfied and they sat staring into the flames and the heat of the embers, Emily decided that it was a good time to broach the subject of their return to The Ridge. She had intended to stay several days whilst they continued hunting, but now it seemed to her that because of the injury to her father's foot, it was more urgent for them to return. Joel's hunting had already provided them with enough meat to last them into the beginning of the winter. Perhaps by then Sam and her father would be able to return to The Lodge to replenish their supplies.

"Dad, I know that we planned to stay here for several days but do you think that it would make more sense now to return home?" She thought that the question would probably irritate him, but instead he sat for a moment, thinking about his reply.

"I don't know," he said. "Let me see what I feel like in the morning. If I get a good night's sleep I may be alright. All the same, I can't see myself chasing deer with a foot in this condition. We may have to settle for what we have and hope that Sam and one or two others can get down here during the winter."

"I think you're right, Dad. You're having enough difficulty just getting around the yard. Getting around in the forest would be a lot harder."

Joel neither agreed nor disagreed but sat slumped on the log, still gazing into the fire. Emily looked away to the evening sky, lit now by the sunset. "At least it looks as though we won't get another storm tonight," she commented.

"Call that a storm. I barely noticed it."

"That's easy for you to say," replied Emily. "You weren't camping out in it."

Joel smiled at her. "No – I was trying to sleep but I imagine that you got a good drenching."

"I did," she confirmed. "But I agree that it was nothing compared with some of the weather we've had this summer."

The fire flickered steadily lower in the pit and the last of rays of light radiated into the darkening sky from behind the crenulations of the forest treetops.

Emily went to check the horses before the light disappeared completely and then headed for a bed that could only be more comfortable than the log on which she had tried to sleep, the night before.

Joel raised his hand in acknowledgement as she passed him on her way into The Lodge.

He planned to write for some while that evening despite the prospect of the journey the next day. However trivial his accident might have been, in the back of his mind was the thought that it only made the completion of his contribution to the writing more urgent.

The lamp had flickered low before Joel finally extinguished the wick and crawled away to his bed. The pain in his foot had not receded; if anything, it was worse. The night was warm, and it took him a little while to get to sleep. When at last he fell asleep, he dreamed that he was still writing, struggling with a passage in his book, a passage that was never quite completed and to which he returned endlessly.

***

Although it had been late when he had gone to his bed, the morning seemed to take a long time to arrive. At daybreak, he was briefly aware of the first rays of light filtering through the shutters on his window; the arrival of the light seemed to reassure him and, curiously, helped him to sleep more deeply, finally leaving behind the repetitive dream that had so wearied him.

He was next aware of Emily shaking him.

"Dad! Dad! We need to get moving."

Reluctantly, he dragged himself awake. Emily stood in the doorway for a moment as if to check that he was not simply going to turn over and go back to sleep. She was reassured when she saw him raise himself to a sitting position and then prepare to get out of bed.

Unlike her father, Emily had slept well. Her lack of sleep the previous night and the subsequent ride to The Lodge had made her very tired and she had fallen asleep moments after getting into bed.

Before Joel had begun to stir, she had already washed, dressed and been out to feed the horses. She was now preparing breakfast, taking a little more care over it than usual. Hunting through the food that her father had brought with him, she had found the ingredients for pancakes and had started to make them when she went to check on her father.

Joel made his way through to the washbasin, hoping that cold water would help to drive away the weariness that he still felt. Some minutes later, he was feeling a lot better – fresher and cleaner – and, for the time being at least, the pain in his foot was no longer distracting him. The smell of the pancakes, wafting through from the fire in the hearth, motivated him further; soon he was dressed and shuffling around the table where they would eat their food, slicing up fruit to follow the pancakes.

She was pleased to see him occupying himself with something that did not intrude into her space around the hearth. Unless she was working with her children in her kitchen at home, she found it difficult to share the area around her when she was preparing food.

They took a little time to eat their breakfast, knowing that it would be some hours before they would be able to eat again. Emily sat enjoying the fruit that her father had sliced, whilst Joel made the most of a large slice of bread spread with butter which had retained its freshness and flavour through being kept in the well.

Feeling refreshed, they then began their preparations for the journey home. Neither of them returned to the question as to whether they should stay longer or return to The Ridge; Emily could have continued the hunting but was concerned about her father's injury and Joel felt sure that they had enough meat to last them at least until the next expedition. He also felt a renewed urgency about the completion of his writing and wanted to be back in his cottage where, for a short time at least, he could neglect some of the everyday tasks around him.

They were well used to packing at the end of their hunting expeditions and although it took a little time, they at least had a well-practised routine for it. Having assembled the clothes and equipment that they needed to take home with them, they brought the horses across from the stable and tethered them next to the lodge. From there, they loaded the saddlebags, taking care to distribute the weight as best they could. Much of the venison they loaded onto Rhodri, although it was also necessary to use Toby and Bundle to carry some of it as well.

***

Whilst Joel got on with boarding up the windows and checking round The Lodge, Emily busied herself with final adjustments to the horses' tack and to the saddlebags. When they were ready, she mounted Bundle with Rhodri tethered behind her as, with some difficulty, her father swung himself into Toby's saddle. Moments later, they were making their way along the rocky track that led at an angle down the hillside to the path they would follow, just above the river.

At the junction of the path and the track, they paused briefly to look back at the lodge, giving themselves a brief opportunity to remember anything that they had forgotten, but also indulging, if only for a moment or two, in small feelings of disappointment that the expedition had not gone entirely as they had planned. Their feelings were alleviated a little by the anticipation of the ride home which they hoped would enable them to arrive safely with the venison and to feel again, that they had played their part in the family's survival and well-being.

CHAPTER 25

GATHERING STORMS

Grace watched as small group of youths from the Village took part in their sport of axe throwing. They had gathered during a short escape from their work around a large oak tree at the centre of the village green. A dry, dusty patch of ground from which most of the grass had been worn away, separated Grace and her friend Ruthie from the group of youths. Whilst Grace was curious about them, she had made sure that she chose a seat well back from the spectacle. Ruthie, meanwhile, was lying on her front, carelessly chewing a blade of grass, strands of black hair falling across her face. She was rather taller than Grace and had turned her pale, oval face towards the group.

As usual Grace was not interested in the young men or their sport, but rather, was worried about her mother's reaction, if she came across her watching them. Ruthie, however, had no such compunction and would have preferred to be sitting a good deal closer.

She said, "I like that one over there." With an interested smile, she nodded towards a thin, dark-haired youth who was at that moment stepping up to a short post embedded in the ground. Ruthie was several years older than Grace and sometimes made comments about boys that she did not understand.

"Phwaw," exclaimed Ruthie. "Look at those muscles!" The youth had taken his shirt off, revealing a well-developed torso.

"S'nothing," responded Grace. "Most of the men on my dad's farm look like that – or at least, the younger ones do. They often take their shirts off." She did not understand her friend's fascination but was determined not to be outdone by her comments.

Ruthie laughed. "I'd better spend more time on your dad's farm. Need any extra help this week?"

Grace began to feel irritated, so she returned to watching the youths.

Their 'game', if such it could be called, entailed throwing small hand axes at a target fixed to a large oak tree at the centre of the village green. Most of the young men in the Village possessed a throwing axe, objects on which they lavished a good deal of care and attention. The target, made from a thick piece of wood, had been fixed to the tree at shoulder height, some five yards from where the youth was standing. Concentric rings, at the centre of which was a bullseye, had been marked on the target, with the tip of a hot iron rod.

The thrower stood making slow motion throwing movements in the direction of the target and then brought his arm swiftly forward, watching as the axe cartwheeled with dazzling rapidity through the air and sinking with a satisfying thud into the innermost circle. Whoops and yells rose in applause from the group gathered behind the thrower, two or three of whom ran forward to examine the precise point at which the axe had embedded itself in the target, but the axe thrower was there before them, pulling the axe out of the target with a well-practised tug.

"He's a sharp one!" commented Ruthie appreciatively, referring to the thrower rather than the axe.

At that moment, a stocky, rotund figure appeared on the other side of the green.

Ruthie groaned. "Oh no! It's Petty – come to spoil the fun, as usual!"

Grace had no watch but knew that the youths taking part in the axe throwing had probably overstayed their lunch break. This time she understood Ruthie's comments. 'Petty', as he was nicknamed – otherwise known as John, or sometimes Farmer Pettifer – had a reputation around the Village for intervening at a time when others had just begun to enjoy themselves. With a certain amount of grumbling, the group of youths began to disperse, making off in different directions towards the places in which they worked. Grace was not completely surprised by Petty's intervention, since several of the youths worked for him.

Grace watched her friend gazing after the object of her admiration. "He's Sam's youngest lad," she commented in response to a question that she felt was hovering in the air.

"Is he now," replied Ruthie, adding, "not that I asked! When you say 'Sam', you mean your great-uncle Sam?"

"Of course – there aren't that many 'Sams' around here."

Ruthie looked as though she was about to dispute the point when Grace added, "Besides he's not really my great-uncle."

"Isn't he?" queried Ruthie. "I always thought he was. Still, it's complicated in your family. Now my lot..."

Grace was not yet at the age where she might enjoy disentangling family relationships, so she said quickly, "Do you fancy going to the den?"

Ruthie mulled it over for a moment or two and then said, "No, think I'll stay here."

Grace was not particularly surprised. Her friend seemed to be changing although as yet, in ways that she could not quite identify to herself.

"OK," replied Grace. "I'm not due back at home for a little while yet so I think I'll go round that way."

Ruthie nodded, only half interested. "See you later," she said.

"Yeah, see you later," replied Grace.

She drifted away from the patch of grass in which she had been sitting with her friend. Behind the Village was an area of woodland which ran north and south, but which tailed off in the direction that Grace was heading. There were times when she felt like a prisoner because a stockade had been built around the Village and the farmland that covered upper parts of The Ridge. It was during the building of the stockade that the land on which the Village now sat was cleared. Before that time, there had been just two small cottages in a clearing, the owners of which had set out to make more space in which to grow food and pasture their animals. An agreement drawn up amongst the inhabitants of The Ridge had stipulated that all adults should spend a prescribed amount of time each year helping to build and maintain the stockade. The work had begun when Grace's father was still a boy and had continued throughout the early years of his adult life.

The timber for the stockade had all been taken from the area around the clearing in which the cottagers had first begun to clear a space for themselves. Since that time, rudimentary businesses had sprung up together with small buildings in which the villagers could live and work. The geography of the clearing and The Ridge determined that the houses ran in a horseshoe (or 'Crescent' as it was known amongst the more pretentious) around the space that had become a village green. From the first, the village green had been adopted as one of the few available spaces in which people briefly get away from the grind of daily life, where they could gather for games, sports, music and dancing events, or simply to exchange gossip.

Unlike the town of Falmouth, which Joel had visited in his youth, there was no currency in The Village. Any goods or services that the inhabitants of The Ridge could not provide for themselves they obtained through barter. Having seen the use of currency, Joel thought that the use of barter was both complicated and clumsy, but its use had persisted because no-one on the Ridge had come up with a system of currency that did not use valuable, and therefore scarce, resources and which could not be easily forged.

The villagers were proud of what they had built. The services offered in The Village had come to include a blacksmith, a herbalist, a shoemaker, a carpenter, a plumber and a workshop in which parts for wind turbines and other pieces of machinery were made and repaired. The blacksmith had originally spent most of his time shoeing horses, but his family had now extended into forging tools and weapons. A doctor, midwife and undertaker all worked from discreet premises at one end of the Crescent. The doctor and midwife had settled in the Village although they had trained in Bristol, and it was from there that some of their medical supplies still came. They were kept busy throughout the year, although the undertaker's work generally reached a peak during the winter and, despite the regular passage of couriers to and from Bristol, both the doctor and midwife struggled with a chronic lack of medicines, equipment and expertise.

Grace, however, found the small world in which she lived both isolated and suffocating. Some of this frustration came from the reading which her mother Emily had encouraged her to do, but also from an imagination that could not be encompassed by a stockade. She drifted along, kicking at stones in the dust and wondering if the storm of a few nights before had damaged the den. It would be her first visit since her mother had returned from the hunting trip with her grandfather.

When she and Ruthie had first built the den, they had made sure that it could not be seen from the path along which she was walking. At the time, they had wanted a place in which they could meet and where they could get away from brothers whom they both regarded as irritating. Now it seemed that Ruthie was developing other interests. Grace kicked hard at a stone and sent it flying into the bushes.

Even now, she sometimes found it hard to locate the entrance to the den. The vegetation was prolific and only rarely did either she or Ruthie take time to clear away the undergrowth that ensured not only the den's obscurity but also its secrecy. She looked for the birch tree that stood just behind and to the right of the den and then, after a short search, began to push her way along the barely perceptible track that lay beneath the overhanging leaves of bushes and ferns. The wickerwork door that covered the entrance to her lair blended readily into the surrounding undergrowth. After a moment or two, she located it and pushed away the bracken that obscured it from view.

With a certain amount of effort, she pulled the wickerwork door from its place and set it down carefully to lean against the wall of the den. Peering inside, she could see that rain from the storm had penetrated the roof and left small puddles on the floor but then, as she ducked through the entrance and saw her pieces of 'jewellery' and her magic charms sitting on her stone shelf to one side, she was drawn again into the world of her imagination. Moving into the centre of the den, she could stand full height. Reaching just above her head, she unfastened some small pieces of cord which held in place a square of wickerwork. Pushing the square upwards, it hinged back onto the apex of the den's roof. A small shaft of light fell instantly into the centre of the den, illuminating the stone fireplace and the remnants of the last fire that she and Ruthie had lit there.

She stooped again and sat on a small chair, one she had 'borrowed' from a derelict house in the woods and sat opposite a similar chair usually occupied by Ruthie and began to wonder how long she would continue to come to this spot, which had been for two or three summers now, her most secret and private place, a place that she loved and which she shared with no-one other than Ruthie.

She sat for a while, trying to think her way forward, to guess what would happen next in her world, but her prevailing mood was one of restlessness. Somehow, that morning, the privacy of the den could not encapsulate her. She got to her feet, replaced and secured the vent in the roof, and then ducked once more through the doorway. Replacing the door always took a little bit of effort and patience, which was something that in her present mood she could barely manage, but as she left, she looked back to satisfy herself that it would remain secret.

The track to which she returned took her on through scrubby woodland towards what she thought of as the edge of The Ridge. The boundary between the upper area and the sharp slope that fell away steeply down to the wild area below was delineated by the stockade. Sighting its timbers amongst the trees and bushes, she made her way over to the wall of thick and sharpened stakes. From her initial vantage point, it had not looked very tall but now it towered above her. The stockade was sporadically patrolled, and the passage of feet had left a track inside its perimeter. She followed the track for a short distance, now and then pushing at the timbers, feeling their solidity and thinking once more that although the intention was to protect the Village and the farms on The Ridge, it made her feel as though she was a prisoner.

In anger and frustration, she pushed with all her might at the section of stockade closest to her, only to find herself tumbling outwards on top of four large timbers that fell together away from her, crashing to the ground in a cloud of leaves and dust. For a moment, she was aghast, believing that her pushing had damaged the stockade, then she scrambled forward to the other side, a sense of freedom but also of vulnerability, making her heart pound. She continued forward, crawling halfway down the timbers until she could jump off them and onto the ground below, steadying herself against them so that she did not fall into the deep ditch that ran all the way round the external perimeter of the stockade. Then, positioning herself carefully, she tried to lift the outermost timber, hoping that she would be able to heave it back into position. It took her only two or three futile efforts to realise that its weight was much greater than she could manage. She sat, red faced with exertion and panting for breath, trying to list her options.

Her first thought was that she did not want to be blamed for the gap in the stockade and that she should keep it a secret and come back with one or two of her friends to lift the timbers back into place. It did not take her long to dismiss this idea because she thought that, even together, they would be unable to lift the heavy wooden stakes. She toyed with other ideas such as getting her friends to bring ropes and haul the stakes back into upright positions or, more feasibly, to bring one of the farm horses down through the woods to do the necessary heaving. Eventually, she dismissed each of her ideas because a further thought was nagging at her – which was the possibility that someone had deliberately loosened the timbers in order to weaken the defences.

To test her thought, she returned to the inside of the stockade and began pushing at the timbers on either side of the gap left by those that had fallen. No matter how hard she pushed, shoved, tugged and heaved, they remained immoveable. None of the fastenings to either side had been impaired. As she pushed for the final time at the stake on her right, it seemed increasingly likely to her that the timbers had only been loose because someone had made it their business to loosen them. With something of a sinking feeling in her stomach, she remembered the stranger she had seen trying to conceal himself in the wood next to the village green.

She clambered up onto the fallen timbers once more and looked down through the trees and undergrowth to the valley below. Although the ditch at the top still presented a considerable obstacle after a long and exhausting climb up the steep slope of The Ridge, if someone wanted to get inside the stockade, this was a way they could do it.

Conflicting feelings tugged at her. She did not want to be blamed for the gap in the stockade, but she also felt an urgent need to tell someone – an adult – about what she had found. She decided to tell her father. She was certain that he would be angry with her because he hated any distraction from his work, but this time, she would have to take that risk.

Grace ran through the undergrowth to the track that she had been following and then headed for the path that would take her back to her parents' farm. It was quite a long run and one that she had not attempted before. She would have to pace herself, a discipline that she would find all the more difficult because a growing sense of urgency was now driving her on.

***

Emily was worried. It was now more than a week since she had arrived back with her father. Josh had surfaced from his work long enough to show an appreciation of her return and of the meat that she and her father had brought with them. He had even taken a little time to help her stow it away in the cold store so that it could be safely preserved until they needed to eat it. Now, however, he was once more engrossed in his work, repairing an irrigation ditch that had caused a temporary drought in one of the fields, and she needed to talk to him about her father.

During the first two days back at The Ridge, her father had seemed rather withdrawn. At first she had put it down to a project that she knew he was working on – writing that she had occasionally seen him concealing beneath other pieces of paper when she approached. Whilst Emily always took an interest in her father, she tried not to be intrusive. She was intrigued to see him using paper – which was a scarce commodity, and which was always recycled elsewhere and brought into the Village – but she assumed that he would tell her about the writing when he was ready. Now, however, a different matter was bothering her.

That morning, her father had not stirred from his bed. The wound in his foot was still inflamed although Emily had regularly bathed it. He was running a high temperature, was sweating and had complained several times of a stiff neck. She thought that the symptoms were all related to the wound in his foot but that whatever the disease was that was taking hold of him, it was beyond her knowledge or ability to treat it. She began to worry that the situation was running away from her. Her thoughts returned to her husband and finally decided that she would not wait but instead would go immediately to the doctor.

She hurried back from Joel's cottage, quickly saddled Bundle then mounted and rode at a gallop towards the Village. Those villagers who were going about their business were surprised to see her riding at speed along the track that led into the Crescent and then amidst a cloud of dust, down the street to the doctor's door.

She dismounted in haste and banged the door knocker loudly so that it was almost immediately answered by the doctor's assistant, Mrs Sawyer, who quickly took Emily through to the front room of the surgery and away from the eyes of curious onlookers.

"He's out on a call at the moment," she explained as soon as Emily had told her about her father's symptoms.

"Then when's he expected back Marion?" asked Emily, a note of desperation creeping into her voice. Marion, the doctor's assistant, was a fairly tall, slim woman whose dark hair was streaked with grey although she was still in early middle age. She smiled at Emily, hoping to reassure her.

"He's been gone about an hour now. I'm expecting him back shortly. I'll tell him as soon as he gets in and he'll come straight over." She said this with some confidence, knowing that his calls that afternoon were routine and realising that Joel's symptoms were such that he would be concerned about them.

Confident that Marion would do as she said, Emily quickly mounted Bundle and rode back to her father's cottage. As soon as she arrived outside his door, she swung from the saddle and went in to check on him again. He was sleeping though rather fitfully and still sweating a great deal. She went to the tap and moistened a cloth with cold water, placing it on her father's forehead and then finding a chair so that she could sit by the bed and wait for the doctor to arrive.

* * *

Joel had only been vaguely aware of the time for which his daughter had left him alone. He was not delirious, but his thoughts went back to times in which he had been happier. He remembered his return from Falmouth and the pleasure it had brought to the families to have their young people back amongst them again. Joel, Sam and Berta were subjects of great attention by the Village's children and other youngsters who had rarely been away from home.

Sam soon drifted into his own orbit of work in which he began to develop a small farm of his own on land that had previously been farmed but which had become neglected in the years after the destruction brought about by the infamous Battle of The Ridge. Clearing the land and setting up with crops and animals took Sam most of his waking hours, and for a long while, he saw his friends only occasionally.

When Joel had made love to Berta at Gwen's house, they had both been worried about Sam's reaction if he found out. Joel always wondered how much Sam knew or had guessed. Neither Joel nor Berta had ever mentioned it to Sam, but Joel was also aware that Sam knew them both very well and might have picked up on any changes that he noticed in their behaviour. Their pursuers and the fire on Bodmin Moor had forced them along on that part of their journey faster than they had anticipated, but it had still taken several more days before they had found themselves gazing once more on the long, elevated piece of land rising steeply above the Somerset countryside which they had always known simply as The Ridge.

Joel's semi-conscious mind drifted over memories of the dawning relief that he had felt when Sam had immersed himself in building up his farm. Joel and Berta were also kept busy by their families, and it was not always easy to steal away to see each other, but they met as often as they could.

Both of them were relieved that their love making in Falmouth had not made Berta pregnant. The return to their families had made them both more cautious but had also tended to inflame their desire for one another, and even in the extremities of his illness, Joel remembered with a faint smile, those times when they had given into their feelings.

The Ridge was a small place and had Berta known just a little more about her mother's past, she might have chosen not to take Joel into the same barn in which her mother had conceived her during her lovemaking with Robert. There was, however, just as much chance that she would have chosen not only the same barn but the same spot in which to lie with Joel; attitudes on The Ridge to those who fell in love with each other gave her a sense of adversity and, like her mother, there was something of the rebel in her.

Finding that Berta's desire matched his own, Joel began to think that it had better not be too long before they went to their parents and to the Village Elder to seek approval for their marriage.

Even so, it had been about a year before they plucked up the courage to talk to their parents about their wish to marry. There was no opposition from either family and, behind the scenes, only relief that two young people who had been thinking that their clandestine meetings were a secret could now be more open with those around them. Bertie Jameson, who had then just recently been elected Village Elder, was only too pleased to have the ceremony to conduct since, in his eyes, it would do his credibility no harm and would help him to establish himself. Some details were always left to the bride and groom, although certain key elements such as the vows and the conclusion of the ceremony were deemed to be 'essential'. So it was that Joel and Berta became the first couple during his term of office to recite their poetry to one another and to sing for their guests before making their vows and walking through the ceremonial arch into married life.

Berta, or 'Roberta' as she now preferred to be known, had not easily fallen pregnant. It was over a year again before she missed her period and Emily was born in late summer. Roberta's grandmother, Janey, had acted as midwife and had seen her own granddaughter safely into the world. Despite Janey's experience and the training she had received before the Great Collapse, it was an anxious few hours, particularly since both pain relief and medical support were in short supply.

Joel had come hurrying back from the fields but had been made to wait in the next room since in the circumstances of the time, Janey had an abiding concern with the hygiene that was needed by mother and child.

He had fretted away until finally, in late afternoon, Emily had vented a sturdy pair of lungs and an exhausted Roberta had sunk back on her pillows, profoundly relived that the immediate trials were over and that she was now the mother of a healthy daughter.

For several years, their happiness had been very great. Even at those early stages, Joel had still worried about the farm and about the changing patterns in the weather, and over time, to the climate, but the changes were gradual when seen in relation to a human lifetime, and for long spells, Joel's mind focused mainly on the everyday concerns of farm and family.

In those years, it had seemed to Joel that they had led a charmed existence. Roberta was the centre of his daily life and Emily was a source of both pride and pleasure to them both.

Although Joel was only semi-conscious, his memories gradually began to take a restless and sinister turn, taking him back to the time in which he had fallen from this state of grace in which he had lived with his wife and child and during which he had tumbled to the kind of earthly, and often grudging consciousness in which most of his friends and companions seemed to dwell. Emily had been just four at the time. She had been taken at the time to Joel's parents so that she would not be disturbed by the ordeal that her mother would pass through. Janey, Roberta's grandmother, had agreed again to act as midwife in the delivery of her granddaughter's second child.

At first, everything had seemed to go well but it was not long before Joel began to be aware that his wife was suffering a level of pain that she had not endured during the birth of Emily. Sam, who had called by to provide Joel with moral support, found it necessary to get his friend out of the house for a while where he could not hear his wife's cries so clearly. It had been a while before Janey, ashen faced, had emerged to explain that there were complications and that he needed to ride for the doctor with all possible speed.

Joel had ridden faster than he could ever remember riding before or since, encountering the doctor on the track that led back to the surgery. Together they had turned their horses and raced back to the house. The doctor went in immediately, but it was not long before he had emerged again with the tragic news that both Roberta and the baby had died.

The experience had shattered Joel, Janey and Roberta's mother, Robbi. The doctor had reassured Janey that she had done all that she could, but she had lost both her granddaughter, her great grandchild and her confidence as a midwife. Joel never fully recovered from the loss of his wife and saw his years after her as the years in which he hung on, in which he simply persisted with daily life.

Now his thoughts were returned savagely to the moment in which he was living. Although he was semi-conscious, he was aware that his symptoms were becoming worse. He could feel strange muscular spasms in his face and severe pains in the muscles of his neck and throat.

Emily watched over him anxiously, thinking that the doctor was taking an interminable time to arrive. Suddenly there was a rap on the cottage door. Emily hurried through to answer it and was relieved to find Dr Ripley waiting with his medical bag, his horse tethered to a tree just outside the cottage.

"Ah Emily, I'm sorry it's taken me a while to get here but I came as soon as Mrs Sawyer was able to give me your message."

He stooped to enter the cottage and Emily showed him down the passageway to her father's bedroom. Emily studied the doctor's face as he began to examine her father, but even after watching him carefully she could tell little from his facial expression. His look of studied professional concern remained much the same whatever message he would have to deliver to concerned relatives or friends.

Carefully removing the bandage that Emily had placed around Joel's foot, he looked at the wound made by the nail. Next, he checked Joel's temperature, listened carefully to his heartbeat and placed a hand on his forehead. Then, returning to his bag, he produced a long wooden spatula with which he gently probed the back of Joel's throat. Involuntarily, Joel bit tightly on the spatula and the doctor had to wait patiently until he could remove it again.

He looked across at Emily, but she anticipated him.

"Can you tell me what it is?" she asked.

"Yes," he said. "It's tetanus."

"How do you know?"

"The diagnosis is based on the nature of the wound in his foot, the various symptoms and your father's response to the test that I did with the spatula."

"Is it serious?" Emily had heard of tetanus but had not encountered it before.

"Yes, I'm afraid it is," replied Dr Ripley. "He needs treatment – as quickly as possible, but unfortunately we don't have the right medicines in the Village."

Emily's anxiety began to increase. "Then what can be done?" she asked.

"I'll need to send someone to Bristol – but the return journey may take as much as four days. If you know someone who can go, that will help. Whoever it is needs to be a good rider."

Emily thought for a moment. "There is someone" she said. "Sam could go."

The doctor nodded. "Get hold of him as quickly as you can and send him to the surgery. I'll leave a letter with Mrs Sawyer. You'll also need to arrange payment for the pharmacist."

Half an hour later, Emily had found Sam who agreed at once to ride to Bristol. In an hour, he was fully ready together with Len Brewer, one of the younger men from the Village. They had collected the letter from the doctor's surgery and then, side by side, had ridden up to the gate that would admit them into the world beyond the stockade. The guards waved in salute before swinging open the heavy wooden gates so that the two men could gallop through the gateway and down the steeply sloping road that would take them north-east and around the Levels.

***

Josh was angry. "I don't expect much, Emily. It's taken me all day to fix that pipe. Now that I'm home, the least you can do is to have some food on the table."

Emily was not inclined to placate him. "I've already told you," she said. "My father is ill. I couldn't leave him because it's serious and I've only come back now to get the meal started. Daniel and Grace will have to help."

Emily and Josh did not often argue, so the two children realised that it was a day on which it would be better not to make a fuss. Daniel began to get out the cooking pots.

Josh had wanted to say more since he often felt that his father-in-law took up too much of his wife's time but, knowing that Emily was not prone to exaggeration, he decided to go out to the yard and find another job to do until such time as the food was ready.

As he went out through the back door, Grace was returning from the well with a bucket of water. Seeing her father, she thought quickly. Should she try to tell him now about the gap in the stockade? She had already made one unsuccessful attempt to tell him whilst he was still out in the fields, but he had angrily shooed her away and told her to wait until later.

Deciding that she had to make every effort and that it would be best to try again, she put down her bucket and ran across to him.

"Dad!" she called. "Dad, I've got something to tell you!"

Josh glanced at her briefly and then said, "Not again, Grace. I've got too much to do!"

"But Dad, it's important – really important!"

Her father turned to glower at her, making no attempt to hide his irritation. "Yes, I know, Grace. Strangers in the woods again I suppose. Look, go and help your mother. That way we might get to eat before bedtime!"

Stung by his remarks and feeling tears pricking at the corners of her eyes, Grace picked up the bucket of water again and made her way to the back door. Her mother opened the door to let her in and she hauled the bucket through to the kitchen where she put it down, spilling a little of it on the floor as she did so.

"Oh, Grace!" exclaimed her mother. "Look what you've done! Mop it up quickly before someone slips on it!"

She went in search of the mop, wishing that she had decided to stay in the den. She had been utterly convinced as she ran back from the stockade that her mission was urgent – but now it seemed as though there was nothing she could say that was of the least significance to the other members of her family.

As soon as the food was cooking over the fire, Emily left the two children to keep an eye on it and hurried back to her father's cottage. She did not like leaving them in charge of the evening meal, but she was deeply worried about her father and felt that she needed to be in his cottage taking care of him. She could tell that there was something Grace was desperate to tell Josh or her, but for the moment, it would have to wait. Fortunately, the doctor had at least been able to leave some medicine to relieve her father's pain.

***

Sam urged his horse onward. There was still an hour or so of daylight left and he wanted to make good use of it. He was still recognisably the same person who had made the journey with Joel and Berta to Falmouth except that now his long thin frame was slightly stooped, and his formerly black hair was almost completely white. If his previous naiveté had been eroded, his humour and optimism still largely persisted.

He slowed his pace a little to allow his companion to catch up.

"If we can ride for the next hour or so," he said, "we'll be well placed for the rest of the journey tomorrow."

Len drew alongside of him, grinning in spite of himself. "Tell it to my legs and backside," he replied. "They'll be ready for a break long before then."

Len was not as tall as Sam but was broad across the shoulders. He was invariably Sam's companion around the farm. They had worked together since Len's mother had died when he was still in his early teens – although he was not sure of his exact age. He shared much of Sam's humour and optimism but was also capable of being shrewd and detached when occasion demanded it.

"Tell me again just why we're doing this," said Len, hoping for a moment to forget about the painful sensations in the lower half of his body.

"Well, I'm doing this for Joel," replied Sam. "Why are you doing it?"

"I couldn't stand another night in my lovely soft bed with my missus." He waited for a response from Sam but there was none, so he added, "I don't want to see a friend die a painful death. Emily must be beside herself."

Sam nodded, his usual good humour leaving him for a few moments.

Noticing his silence, Len knew the lever to pull, the topic that would get his companion talking and take his mind off their present discomfort.

"You and Joel go back a long way...?" He knew that Sam would seize willingly on the chance to talk about the journey he had made in his youth; although he had made many others since, it was this one to which he most happily returned.

Sam seized the conversational baton he had been handed, losing himself in his memories. Someone less good natured than Len might have tired of the story, but he contented himself with a distraction that would take them through to the moment when they would both roll out of their saddles and make camp for the night.

Early in the morning on the fourth day after Sam and Len's departure for Bristol, Emily lay drowsing, listening to Josh's snoring beside her and waiting for it to be light enough for her to make the short journey across to her father's cottage. She began briefly mulling over the doctor's visit to her father and the events that had flowed from Grace's revelations about the stockade.

On the previous evening, she had made sure that Josh had a good meal in front of him when he returned from his day's work. The pain relief that the doctor had given her for her father also seemed to be working. Together with her persistent efforts in cleaning the wound in his foot, the medication had allowed Joel to sleep, and during the previous day, he had been well enough to tell her about his book and to insist that she knew where the manuscript was so that if he was unable to complete his writing, she would at least be able to find it and to make decisions about what should happen to it next.

For a while, he had been lucid enough to set out his own beliefs about what should happen to the manuscript and then, worn out by the effort, he had fallen asleep. She had taken it back with her, feeling confident enough for the first time since his symptoms had first appeared, to leave her father to sleep. Her mood recently had been such that she had carefully spurned Josh's sleepy attempts to make love to her but, that night she let his hands wander where they would until finally they were both sufficiently aroused to lose themselves in each other. Long after he had rolled away from her, she lay musing on her role as someone whose task it seemed to be to get men off to sleep.

Now, as the cockerels began to crow, the dawn chorus filled the air and the first light of another day stole across The Ridge, her thoughts strayed to Joel's anxieties about the climate and about the ability of her family and the other families around them, to provide the necessities of life for themselves. Briefly she wished that such worries would go away but knew that this was the inheritance that had been left them and that there was nothing she could do about it. Survival was the uppermost concern of them all and was the reason why her father was so obsessed with his book. She knew he was hoping, against hope, that he was beginning something to which others could add, a cumulative collection of wisdom that was different from that which had prevailed in the past, and which would represent at the last possible moment, an opportunity for learning from the colossal mistakes that had been made. She had always thought of her father as a pessimistic man – but the book seemed to represent a kind of optimism, a kind to which she found it difficult to subscribe, wondering why, if human beings had been so far unable to respond to anything other than the short term, they should suddenly begin to do so now.

Her thoughts drifted back to Josh who was still slumbering and snoring at her side. They were at peace with each other for the time being, but her husband's obsessions were always with the 'here and now' of his work. There were times when his short-term view of life infuriated her.

It had been early in the morning after Josh had upset Grace that her daughter had found her and poured out her message about the stockade. Emily had found herself wondering how on earth she and Josh had managed to ignore their daughter the previous evening. Grace had been sitting on her mother's lap and Emily had looked carefully at her. The shadows under Grace's eyes and the state of her hair had told her mother that she had endured a sleepless night.

Grace had taken the exhausted child back to her bed to catch up on her sleep. Then she had set off in search of Josh. She had found him still working on the field drain that had taken up so much of his time in recent days. When she had finally been able to pass on Grace's message, he had made matters worse by suggesting that Grace never told him anything and that she was a 'mummy's girl'. Emily had hotly retorted that Grace had gone to him first, but that he had ignored her feelings and that it was small wonder that she had not wanted to try again.

When they had both calmed down, Josh had understood the urgency of Grace's message and had ridden into the Village to tell Herbert Haskins, the stockade foreman, about the situation. If he had expected an immediate response, he was disappointed. Herbert had thought that it would be at least a day before he could get anyone to carry out the repair. He had then suggested that perhaps Josh could take some men and a horse and set about the work himself, to which Josh had responded that he had already carried out his quota of work on the stockade for that year, at which Herbert had shrugged and walked away, calling back over his shoulder that he could see what he could do.

Despite a sense of frustration and futility, Josh decided to make a detour and return to his farm by way of the gap in the stockade. Following the instructions passed on from Grace, he soon found it. He had then returned with two men and a horse. They had been able to make temporary repairs with the materials that Josh had available, but when they had finished, he had known that it needed more work because a determined intruder or even the weather would soon flatten the loosened timbers again. He had then ridden into the Village to tell Herbert what he had done. The foreman had grunted his thanks and assured Josh that he would see that the repair was made fully secure. Feeling then that he had done his duty, Josh had ridden back to the farm and returned once more to working on the field drain.

Emily mused for a few moments more on Josh's account of the work done to repair the stockade, wondering just how adequate it was, and then slipped out of the bed and went downstairs to wash herself and get ready to check on her father before anyone in her own house was awake. A few minutes later, she opened the front door and set off down the path to her father's cottage.

* * *

As Emily entered the cottage, she noticed that her father's papers were strewn across the table that he used for writing. She immediately thought that he must have been working on them during the night. The thought made her briefly angry. She had made great efforts to help him recover and now it seemed as though he was indifferent about his own health.

She decided not to call out in case he had gone through to the bedroom and fallen asleep, although she wondered how, even in the early stages of the illness that was afflicting him, he could sleep because his symptoms seemed both painful and frequent in their occurrence.

Her guess had been correct, and her father lay sleeping, although Emily noticed that even as he slept small spasms continued to affect the muscles of his face. She hoped again with a certain amount of desperation that Sam would arrive back that day with the medication her father needed. Looking around there was little else that she could do for the moment, so she returned to the door and set out on the path back to her cottage.

She had been just moments on the path when she thought that she heard the sound of a bell ringing. She had only heard the sound before after a major storm had taken place when the bell in the village hall was used to call the people of The Ridge together so that mutual help could be organised in the clearing up and repairs that were always needed. Now, however, there was no sign of any storm, and she wondered what emergency had occurred that warranted the ringing of the bell.

For a moment she dithered between running back to her father and running the other way to her own cottage where her husband and children would probably now be waking. Deciding that for the moment she knew how things stood with her father, she directed her steps along the path towards her husband and children.

She entered the cottage quickly. So far there were few signs that the other members of the family were awake, although when she stood to listen for a moment, she thought that she could hear Josh moving about in their bedroom.

Moments later, Josh appeared at the bottom of the staircase, his clothes showing every sign of having been put on hurriedly.

"Why's the bell being rung?" he asked as soon as he saw Emily.

"I've no idea," she replied. "I've only just heard it myself."

"Emergencies," muttered Josh half to himself, half to Emily. "They only ring the bell in emergencies!"

"We need to find out what's happening," said Emily. "One of us needs to go into the Village."

"The children will look for you first. I'd better go."

"You're right," agreed Emily. "One of us needs to be here – and it had better be me. How are you going to get to the Village?"

"I could run but it would be quicker to take one of the horses."

"Which one?" asked Emily.

"Rhodri – he's faster!" Josh quickly pulled on his boots and went out through the front door, heading for the stables.

Emily went in search of Daniel and Grace. Daniel was already awake and was sitting up in his bed, stretching and yawning. Grace, however, was still asleep and Emily had to shake her.

Daniel quickly became aware of the bell, its chimes still echoing out over the fields and woodland of The Ridge. He appeared at the door of Emily's room.

"Mum what's going on? Why's the bell ringing?"

"I don't know, Dan. Your dad's gone to find out. Meanwhile you need to get dressed. We have to be ready for whatever's going on."

Hearing Daniel's voice, Grace had gone under the covers of her bed.

"Come on, Grace! This is no time to play games!" It might be a little while before they knew what was happening, but Emily was determined that they would be ready for it.

After persisting for some minutes, she managed to ensure that both children were dressed and quickly eating some breakfast which that morning consisted of no more than bread and butter.

Emily's focus on her morning routine was broken by the sound of galloping hooves. She went quickly to the front door, thinking that it would be Josh returning with news of what was happening. Instead, when she opened the door, she was in time to see one of the teenagers from the Village reining in his horse though not dismounting. His fair, curly hair and fresh face helped her to recognise him as one of the boys she had taught in her school. "Edward, Edward Harvey!" she called out to him. "I haven't seen you for a while. What brings you over here?"

"Urgent business, ma'am – The Ridge is under attack! Your husband cannot get back at the moment! You are to take your children and your father to a safe place and wait there until it is safe again. He will get a message to you."

"What attack? Who's attacking us?" She was aware that she was almost spluttering out the questions, but Edward was already spurring his horse on again.

"No time to explain!" he yelled back over his shoulder. "Go somewhere safe and stay there!" She was left gazing after him as horse and rider disappeared at speed down the track and back onto a path that ran round the edge of the woods.

She had a huge number of questions inside her head, but they had to wait. She ran into the cottage and almost immediately collided with Grace and Daniel heading towards the door.

"What's happening, Mum?" clamoured Daniel.

"Yeah, Mum, what's going on?" Grace looked anxious.

Emily caught hold of her daughter and also looked into Daniel's eyes to ensure that he was listening to her.

"We're under attack. The Ridge is being attacked. I've had a message from your dad. We have to find somewhere safe to hide."

Daniel immediately started towards the door again, so she caught his arm.

"I want to go out there! I want to find Dad!"

"No, Daniel! That was his message! That's what he wants us to do! We'll find him later!"

Daniel looked inclined to argue again but Grace said, "Will he be alright?"

Her mother frowned. She saw no point in being dishonest. "I don't know. I hope so. For the moment there's nothing we can do except what he's told us to do! Now we need somewhere to hide."

Daniel continued to wear a sulky look on his face, but Grace was already thinking about what her mother had said.

After a moment she looked up. "Here!" she cried. "There's a place here where we can hide!"

Emily waited for her daughter to speak again but remembered her father's words about how people responded to fear. He said that they always chose between 'fight' and 'flight'.

At that moment, she could not fight and with her two children at her side, the urge to flee was very strong. But if they fled there would be a time when they would have to be out in the open – and that would be a considerable risk. It would also be a needless risk when there was a concealed place right here in the house. They were losing precious time! She had to decide.

She fought down the urge to panic – a reaction to danger that her father had somehow forgotten to mention.

***

Josh had ridden Rhodri straight to the village. Although he had responded quickly to the clanging of the bell, he was by no means the first one there. Already as he swung from his saddle, there were some 20 others there – men and teenagers rubbing shoulders with each other.

Josh's eyes scanned across them, as he thought to himself that they were a motley collection of individuals. Most of them had already been preparing for a day's labour when they had heard the alarm call and had come straight to the green dressed in drab and dirty clothes that they wore for their work.

Amongst the crowd of men and boys there were a few horses – perhaps seven or eight – tethered or held by their reins. There was also a clutter of weapons and farm implements – scythes, pitchforks, sharpened stakes, swords, spears, axes, longbows and crossbows.

Josh sighed deeply, wondering how well they would be able to defend themselves and their families if the people coming against them were organised and well-armed. This was a day that had long been foretold but which most people on The Ridge had hoped would never arrive.

Somebody had placed a large wooden box to one side of the crowd. The man who had now been Village Elder for the past two years, scrambled onto it and turned to address them even whilst more men continued to arrive from the Village and from the various outlying parts of The Ridge. Josh had voted for Thomas Forton, the current Elder, believing that he would be a good leader and someone who would push forward the many projects that were needed to ensure that they could feed, clothe and protect themselves. Of these priorities, the first two had been well served but the third was about to be tested.

Forton waited a few moments, turning his large head of unruly hair this way and that as if trying to spot people he was waiting for in the crowd. He was stocky rather than tall, but his thickset figure had a certain forcefulness about it which had been known to carry weight in Village arguments where plain reason seemed unlikely to prevail.

"Men!" The buzz from the assembled crowd fell silent. "Men, the guards on the stockade told me about 20 minutes ago that a large force of people is headed towards The Ridge. It looks as though they've crossed The Levels and..." He was momentarily cut short by a buzz from those who had always thought that The Levels were their main defence in that direction. There were immediate cries of "Quiet!" or "Shut up and listen!" from others who realised that they had very little time. Forton began again.

"They're headed straight towards The Ridge. We think they'll be here in about an hour. The watchers in the marsh think there are about 150 of them..." He was momentarily interrupted by a fresh outbreak of noise from the crowd and renewed angry calls for quiet. "If that's right, we can hold them off or do enough to drive them away. But it will take every one of us to hold firm and fight!"

Angry determined cries broke from those standing before him, defiance, fear and courage mingling inextricably together. Josh felt his stomach churning with all three, but with others in the crowd, held his hand aloft to signal to those around him that they needed to listen and then get on with preparing to meet those who were advancing towards The Ridge.

There was a plan – of sorts – and they had practised a few times for such an event, but attendance had been dilatory, and the demands of daily life had often been given priority. Now there was little time for regrets. They would have to make the best use of such preparation as they had been able to carry out.

Josh tried to suppress the sinking feeling in his stomach and direct himself instead to the instructions being given by the Elder. Forton's voice was already sounding hoarse, but Josh was able to hear above the barely suppressed din the instruction to go to their assigned leaders. Men and teenagers alike made their ways towards the people they had learned to recognise as their 'marshals'. Josh fleetingly wondered how long the distinction he made in his mind between 'men' and 'boys' would last. By the end of the day, of those defending the Village, there would be no 'boys' left; of that he was grimly certain.

When Thomas Forton had finished speaking, there had been about 60 people assembled before him. As they broke away into their respective groups, their numbers seemed pitifully small. The largest and most practised group, known a little fancifully as 'Vanguard', made its way rapidly towards the main gates in the stockade. It was here that it was anticipated the heaviest attack would come. Two further groups, both designated 'Standfast', had the task of fighting anyone who broke through the defenders at the gates. Those wealthy or fortunate enough to own a horse had been organised into the 'Cavalry' which, though meagre, was expected to give first warning of any attacks on the long perimeter of the stockade and also to provide reinforcements wherever they were needed. Other than 'Vanguard', the 'Cavalry' had rehearsed their role the most times, although some practices had been curtailed because villagers had complained that they were in danger of being ridden down.

Four of the riders had been assigned to patrol sections of the stockade. With such small numbers, Josh felt that they could hardly be spared, but with the main effort concentrated at the gate the riders represented the only way in which the 'Standfast' teams could be warned of an attack from other points along the stockade.

Lookouts high up on the stockade yelled down to the marshal of Vanguard that a messenger – one of the watchers – was approaching at speed. It was a pre-arranged tactic which had to be managed with careful timing; the watcher approaching the gates would be the last person to be allowed inside the stockade. Anyone else would be assumed to be hostile and would be turned back or killed. The huge gates were swung open just long enough to admit the rider and were then swung shut again with unprecedented urgency. The rider galloped on, across to where The Village Elder was standing.

His horse was barely at a standstill before he had swung from the saddle. He handed a leather pouch containing a brief written message over to the Village Elder. Forton stood for a moment, reading the message, before shouting an order across to the marshal of Vanguard. The marshal responded by calling his men into formation around the gate. It seemed as though the awaited attack was now imminent.

So far everyone had followed the agreed sequence. The most immediate information had required action from the marshal, but there was other more detailed intelligence that was needed by Forton. His role now was to muster the Standfast groups, although this also gave him just a little more time to take in what was happening around him and to make decisions about where to focus the fight.

Rhodri pawed at the ground; Josh steadied him, knowing that the men on foot found the presence of the riders reassuring, but for men and horses alike the tension was mounting.

They had not long to wait. The attackers had approached the stockade in silence. One of the lookouts on the gate poked his head above the timbers and was immediate felled by an arrow that struck him in the face. His inert body fell with a heavy thud from the rampart.

There was barely time for a groan from those around him before smoke and flames began to issue from the bottom of both gates. There was no point now in silence on the part of the attackers. Instead shouts, thick with oaths, could be heard from the other side of the stockade. Soon, the fire set at the foot of the gates was taking a secure hold and flames were licking high up on the timbers.

The defenders could do little other than wait. One of the teenagers had previously succeeded in killing an attacker with a bolt from his crossbow but had then been struck in the chest by an arrow. His body was slumped across the spiked timbers of the stockade in full view of those below.

The marshal of Vanguard yelled at his men to concentrate their effort on defending the gate from below the ramparts. When, as now seemed inevitable, the attackers burst through the gates he wanted as many men as possible to be able to combat those coming through. The gates were very solidly constructed, and the gateway was narrow; it would not take much to block it. The obstruction that the marshal had in mind at that moment was a large pile of enemy bodies although he also had a large farm cart waiting just to one side.

It soon became clear that the gates would not be quickly weakened. Impatience started to get the better of the attackers and they began battering at them with heavy timbers they had brought with them, although at times, the fire they had set at the gates also threatened to engulf them as well as the gates.

Despite the orders of Vanguard's marshal, a large rock had somehow been manhandled up the ramparts and with a remarkable and rapid effort had been heaved over the stockade and onto the heads of the small group bent on ramming the gates. Screams and oaths from the other side of the stockade indicated that serious damage had been done. Answering oaths and shouts from inside greeted the attackers.

The situation seemed to be reaching stalemate when suddenly the right-hand gate started to show greater signs of movement. Then, a loud splintering sound heralded the weakening of the timbers where the gates met, and the fire began to pry its way into splintered sections of wood.

Once more, this time with the marshal's agreement, a heavy rock was manhandled up the ramparts and launched onto the heads of the attackers. The oaths were even louder and more profane, but the gang of men ramming the gates was forced to retire to a short distance from the stockade.

The defenders, however, could do nothing to prevent the fire from strengthening its hold. Attempts to put out the flames with buckets of water were abandoned when one of the defenders was hit in the shoulder with a bolt from a crossbow.

Soon the hinges of the right-hand gate were separating from the retaining timber and the gate slumped diagonally across the space it had previously filled. The ramming of the gates began again but the defenders could do little about it because by this time, smoke and flames had forced them from the ramparts. At the orders of the marshal, the farm cart was pushed into position across the gap and its brake jammed in position.

He then ordered the defenders into the positions they needed to deal with any attackers who got through. He also had a further trick up his sleeve, although it was a rather desperate one and he knew that it would do little more than delay the onslaught.

Three wooden hurdles were drawn across behind the small group of defenders. Behind this barricade, additional men from the first of the Standfast groups sheltered with longbows and crossbows at the ready. Minutes later, the right-hand gate crashed to the ground in a shower of sparks and embers, partly crushing the cart and forming a ramp over it. Clouds of smoke obscured the view of attackers and defenders alike. Two attackers who risked venturing through the smoke were immediately met with a volley of arrows and died in their tracks where, as planned, their bodies partly blocked the gateway.

The Vanguard defenders began to feel hopeful. The situation was looking slightly better; if they could inflict enough damage on the attackers at the gate, some of them might be available to fight elsewhere. Words of mutual encouragement passed amongst them.

A sweet, sickly smell of roasting human flesh pervaded the air. It had proved impossible for the attackers to remove the bodies of the fallen men. As the marshal had calculated, the attack was further delayed, giving still more time for the extra men from Standfast to move into position and to prepare themselves for the renewed onslaught that they knew was inevitable.

Forton was now mounted on his horse and watching the conflict from a vantage point some distance from the gates. He had readily agreed to the release of extra men from the Standfast group. The sporadic and seemingly chaotic practices they had held were paying off after all. With something of an effort, he drew his mind away from the scene still unfolding at the gates. There were two further concerns that were distracting him.

The first was that having shut the gates, no further news of the situation outside could get into the settlement. Reports coming back from the defenders on the gateway ramparts indicated that there were, at most, 40 attackers contained in the restricted area outside the gates. Where, he wondered, was the rest of the attacking force and what were they doing? The second concern was, at that moment, the lesser one and arose from a completely different source. In some ways, it simply added more uncertainty to an already desperate situation. He looked beyond the stockade and the woodland lining the top of The Ridge. The light of the sun was gradually being obscured by enormous banks of black cloud – clouds, he was beginning to realise, that were nothing to do with the fire at the gates.

He had seen many storms in his lifetime, but the clouds that he now saw massing on the horizon were darker and more ominous than any he had seen before. A strange twilight was falling over The Ridge and it occurred to Forton that they might all soon be fighting in semi-darkness. He had no idea which side, if either, this phenomenon would aid. There were pitifully few defenders, but then as he continued to think about it, there might even be a glimmer of hope within this second anxiety. The defenders were at least fighting on their home territory – territory that was thoroughly familiar to them.

His thoughts were interrupted by renewed shouts from the gateway. The attackers were making a fresh attempt to break through. From his vantage point, Forton watched grimly as one of the few tactics they had been able to rehearse began to unfold.

The fire had finally done its job and both gates and the wreckage of the farm cart now lay still burning on the ground. The flames that were spreading along the ramparts were being left to burn, whilst attempts were being made to douse the burning gates. Water was brought forward and poured over the charred timbers. A token volley of arrows flew into the ranks of those pouring the water, but the attackers were not deterred. Through the clouds of steam and smoke, they could see only a remnant force, a few of whom had bows but who were otherwise armed with swords and spears alone, with which they would be forced to engage in close combat – something that suited the attackers very well. They prepared to pour through the gateway against what they saw as a small number of poorly armed defenders.

The marshals of Vanguard and Standfast groups timed their effort to perfection. As soon as the gateway entrance was packed with the rampaging enemy, they melted away to the sides, the hurdles behind them were thrown down, and the force of bowmen and crossbowmen behind them fired in rapid order straight into the oncoming assailants. Soon a number of bodies lay slumped across each other in the area just inside the gate. Two of the Standfast defenders fell where they stood, brought down by sword thrusts, the perpetrators of which were hacked to the ground by the remaining Vanguard force. The attack began to falter. It seemed as though the resistance being met at the gateway was more than had been anticipated. The depleted force began to fall back, tempting the less disciplined amongst the defenders to surge forward. The marshals, seeing the potential danger, barely pulled them back in time, but having done so, were gratified to see at least a dozen bodies lying in the area just inside the gate. The attacking force at the gate had been reduced to less than half of its original capability – and now seemed, for the moment at least, to be melting away beyond the brow of high ground outside the stockade.

Forton wheeled his horse away from the scene at the gates. The marshals had a grip of the situation there, but now there was a pause in which he had a chance to ponder the lack of news from the riders who had been sent off to look for attacks on other sections of the stockade. The gathering storm in the sky above brooded over his head as he waited for a messenger to return. It seemed inconceivable that the attack at the gates was the main effort the enemy would make. He scanned the tracks along which his messengers would have to gallop. There was no sign of any of them – and still no news. The twilight around him seemed to be thickening by the minute.

* * *

Emily had hung on at the cottage with her children, waiting for the promised 'word' from Josh. The urge to get away from the cottage was still strong. If invaders managed to get into the settlement, it would be an obvious target. There was, though, an alternative.

Her great-grandfather had spent a great deal of time adapting the cottage for the increasingly difficult times that he had envisaged. One of the adaptations had been the building of a large cellar beneath the cottage; it had always been intended for use as a store for vegetables in the long months of winter and early spring. Already there was a large stock of vegetables down there in readiness for the coming season.

She stood for a moment weighing the risks of finding somewhere else to hide and of the cellar being discovered. She needed to move her father and in his present state, he could not be moved far. Then again, in trying to save her father she could not allow herself to jeopardise her children.

The cellar was their best option. The cellar door was well concealed and even if someone broke into the house, they would not necessarily be discovered. First, though, they would need to get her father out of his cottage and then down into the cellar.

The two children had not seen their grandfather in the last two days and his condition would be a shock to them – but she would have a job to manage him on her own. Daniel and Grace had both persistently asked her why they were not allowed out of the house and now seized on the chance to do something – even if the news about their grandfather did not sound good.

Together they crossed to Joel's cottage. As they scurried along, Emily could hear distant shouts and cries, and then chillingly, above the other sounds, an agonised scream. The two children had also heard both the sounds and paled as they realised that fighting must now be taking place within the settlement. She gave them no time to think further and hurried them on again.

The light was dim in Joel's cottage. Emily led the children through to the back of the house where their grandfather lay semi-conscious in his bed. Emily felt his brow. It was hot and clammy.

Emily turned to her son. "Daniel, bring me a damp cloth and a cup of water," she said.

Daniel immediately did as he was told, whilst Grace stood awkwardly to one side.

"Come on, Grace, give me a hand." Carefully she eased her father into a more upright position, moving his pillows to support him. From the other side of the bed, Grace followed her mother's example.

Daniel returned with the damp cloth and the cup of water. Without needing to be told, he placed the cloth on his grandfather's forehead; Joel's eyes flickered open for a moment and, on seeing Daniel, the ghost of a smile stole across his face. Emily held the cup of water. He drank, carefully and gratefully, before slumping back again on the pillows.

She had already told the children that they were all going into the cellar together. The noises they had heard on their way had only reinforced their sense of urgency. It was a warm day outside, but Emily realised that it would be cool in the cellar, and they might have to hide for many hours.

"Grace, fetch your grandfather's long coat." Grace went out immediately to the pegs in the hallway where Joel's hats and coats were hanging and returned with the long coat that he wore in the colder months of the year.

As soon as she returned, Emily said to the two children, "Well done, Grace. Now I need help from both of you. We have to be quick!"

Between them, they manoeuvred Joel into an upright position in which he was sitting on the edge of the bed. With a little help from Daniel, Emily got Joel into his coat and then drew him onto his feet. With Daniel and Grace propping him up on the other side, Emily helped her father through to the living room and towards the hall.

Her father's lips began to move. She had to bend close to hear what he was saying.

"The book – we must take it with us!" His voice was thin, and speaking at all was an effort, but there was no mistaking the emphasis he placed on his words. Grace and Daniel hung onto their grandfather whilst Emily hurried across to the desk. The papers were still scattered where her father had left them. She shuffled them quickly together and pushed them into a leather bag which she found at the side of the desk.

Shutting the door of the cottage as they left, Emily urged them all along the path as fast as they could go. She felt pathetic and useless, thinking that there was surely a better and faster way to get her father across to the cottage, but it was only a short distance and would not take long. Despite his illness, Joel did all that he could to walk along the path. Soon they were at Emily's door.

Pushing the door open, she urged them inside. Then from along the path leading out of the wood, she heard a cry and then the sound of a galloping horse. She hesitated. It could be the messenger that Josh had promised – or it could be an enemy intruder.

"Get your granddad into the cellar!" she ordered the two children. At any other time, such an instruction would have seemed completely unreasonable but now, they got on with their task, leaving their mother to conceal herself at the door, waiting to find out if the approaching rider was friend or foe.

The rider emerged at speed, galloping towards the cottage but then suddenly, for no reason that Emily could see, fell from his horse, a foot still caught in a stirrup. His frightened horse galloped some yards further along the road before coming to rest, tethered by the weight of the fallen rider.

Emily watched from the doorway, her heart pounding in her chest. A small group of men broke from their cover at the edge of the wood. She saw raised arms and the glint of metal as they made sure that the rider was dead. Then she waited no more but bolted the door behind her and, with the bag containing her father's book still in her grasp, rushed through the house to where the cellar door was hidden beneath the staircase. With considerable effort, she raised the heavy door and set her feet on the top step of the steps down into the cellar. A thunderous crash from the front door spurred her on. Wishing that there was more she could have done to conceal the cellar door, she rapidly lowered it behind her and went in search of her father and the two children.

Although it made her heart race all over again, it was almost reassuring that she could not at first find them. It was large cellar, and the small amount of available light only illuminated the area around the grille through which it came. Everywhere, there were stacks of boxes and crates, either containing vegetables that had already been harvested or still waiting to be filled with the present season's crop. She stumbled her way along to the far end of the cellar, trying to guess where they would be. Eventually, amongst the various piles of sacks, both empty and full, she saw a hand raised and beckoning her towards the place that Daniel and Grace had hidden with their grandfather.

Getting down onto her hands and knees, she crawled beneath the cover that her children had improvised from some of the empty sacks. Her father lay propped up against a stack of harvested potatoes, but otherwise also covered over in the same manner. His breathing was laboured and shallow, but for the moment, he seemed to be about as comfortable as could be expected. Their hearts pounded. The thick stone floor of the cottage prevented them from hearing anything other than occasional sounds from above, but from outside, they could hear the harsh shouts of men intent on plundering what they could from the cottages and gardens they were pillaging. Emily prayed that the grille providing ventilation for the cellar would not be discovered behind the weeds and bushes that, over many years, had gradually obscured it.

The shouting continued for some time. They seemed to be in no hurry and Emily guessed that they were systematically working their way through both houses. Involuntarily, she found herself listening to every sound from outside.

Soon, however, a new cause for anxiety moved in to replace their fear of discovery. This began with a burst of coarse laughter, followed by the clatter of horses' hooves. Thinking that it was now unlikely that anyone would find the door into the cellar, Emily crawled out from beneath the sacks and still on her hands and knees, crept along to the end of the row of sacks to where she could look across to the ventilation grille. As she watched, tendrils of smoke could be seen weaving amongst the shafts of light that penetrated down into the cellar.

Until then, the atmosphere in the cellar had seemed cool – even cold – but now all four of them began first to feel warm and then hot to the point that the air was stifling and filled with the stench of burning. Anxiety was steadily replaced with fear and Emily prayed a new prayer – this time that the stone floor above would protect them from the heat and the flames that she guessed must now be engulfing the cottage.

* * *

The frown on Forton's face was deepening by the moment. A messenger had finally arrived, and the news was bad.

"They've breached the stockade!" The messenger was yelling his news to Forton because the gang of men outside the gate area had returned and were mounting a fresh attack. The archers and crossbowmen of Vanguard and the first Standfast group were running low on ammunition and had begun taking casualties again. Three of their number lay between the battling forces where, at that moment, they could not be retrieved.

Despite the renewed attack at the gate, Forton turned again to face the messenger. It was important that he did not misunderstand the message that was being delivered and seeing the man's face would help.

"How many have got through?" he demanded.

"By my reckoning, it's about a hundred men!" If the messenger expected some obvious response from Forton there was none. He remained impassive. The messenger continued. "They're marching this way. They'll be here in about five minutes!"

Forton glanced back to the fighting at the gateway and then back along the track that the invading force would surely follow.

"How in hell's name did they get in?" he finally demanded of the messenger.

"They removed some of the timbers in the stockade about half a mile from here!"

Forton nodded grimly. So now a new attack was coming from the opposite direction. It was to be expected. He wondered briefly why it had been so easy for the attackers to breach the stockade, but then immediately redirected his thoughts. There was no time for an inquest – and less than five minutes to prepare for the arrival of a much larger force than the one that was besieging the gateway.

"Get the rest of the riders here!" he shouted back to the messenger. "We need everybody here!" The messenger wheeled away but galloped off down a track that would not bring him face-to-face with the invaders.

Forton rode his horse across to the marshal of the second Standfast group, rapidly relayed the news to him and then moved on to give new orders to the marshals defending the gateway. The marshals ordered their men into a defensive square so that they could resist attacks from all directions if, as seemed probable, that became necessary.

The seconds ticking by seemed elongated into minutes. Forton glanced away to the west. Billows of smoke were rising into the air, and he guessed that someone's farm had been set alight. He looked around to see if Josh had returned yet, since it was probably his farmhouse that was on fire. So far, there was no sign of him. The smoke was rising against an even darker sky, the colour of which drew Forton's attention once more. It was looking increasingly likely that they would find themselves fighting in the middle of a storm.

The enemy gang trying to fight its way through the gateway had been only partly successful. A few of their number were now inside the stockade, but so far, there were no others to provide them with support. Spears, swords and axes were now coming into use. Forton felt only satisfaction as the remaining archers and crossbowmen finished off those invaders who had been brave or foolish enough to break through. He guessed, however, that the main purpose of the force at the gates had been to distract the defenders, and that once the main force arrived, there would be a renewed attack from those still outside the gateway. The small, depleted force at his disposal would be committed to fighting on two or more fronts at once.

Shouts from the men in the defensive square heralded the approach of the main attacking force. Forton had been given no information about them other than their numbers, so their appearance was something of a shock. He had imagined that at least some of them would be wearing armour or protection of some kind. It had seemed a reasonable assumption although none of those attacking the gates had worn any kind of armour. Instead, as the front ranks began to approach, Forton could see that they were mostly naked to the waist and that their torsos were decorated with tattoos and elaborate patterns painted in a blue dye. They were of all shapes and sizes, but the overall effect of their collective appearance was one of savagery and barbarism, and their impact one that was calculated to strike fear into the hearts of anyone opposing them. Forton had time only to reflect that they were like throwbacks from Britain's ancient past and then the enemy were upon them.

The marshals did well to prevent their men from fleeing outright from the ferocious onslaught that struck the meagre ranks of the defensive square. Perhaps the desperation of the defenders stemmed from the impossibility of retreat, although in moments large gaps were carved in their ranks. The marshal of Vanguard was hacked to the ground, but the men in his group closed around his fallen body and fought back the thrust of the attackers. The superior numbers of the enemy were sufficient in themselves to overwhelm the defenders, but they fought on and soon there was a litter of bodies from both sides surrounding them. Then, for a reason that the defenders could not at first discern, the invaders fell back and something akin to silence fell over them. A tall warrior – a giant in relation to the rest – strode forward, surrounded by a small body of other warriors. For brief moments the defenders seemed dumbstruck as if wondering how this object of terror could have remained concealed amongst those attacking them.

Their thrall was soon broken. The giant warrior strode close enough to the defensive square to draw probing jabs from the spears and swords of those in the front rank. Swinging a huge axe that had remained almost hidden at his side, he swept off the head of the nearest defender. Forton ordered the few remaining archers to loose off a volley of arrows – which they did, only to see them lodge in shields of the giant warrior's bodyguard. Now the giant strode forward again, sweeping aside the defenders at the front of the square and leaving behind him a bloodied trail of dead and dying.

Forton realised that the appearance of the giant could lead almost immediately to a rout. Wheeling around, he looked for an opening to attack only to see that his horse would trample his own men because the giant and his bodyguard were now wading amongst them, thrusting, slashing and scything away the defenders, on every side.

A heavy rain was beginning to fall. At first neither side seemed to notice, but then with the minutes going by, the downpour became torrential. As the battle continued, the ground beneath them quickly turned to mud. Many of those lunging and thrusting at each other slithered and fell so that soon the fallen became a confusing mass of both the dead and the living.

A flash of lightning seared between earth and sky, followed by a resonating thunder clap. The fighting continued unabated, but the darkness shrouding both sides was making it impossible to distinguish friend from foe.

Of the identity of one warrior, however, there was still no doubt. Sam's youngest boy, Jonathan, like so many around him, had slipped in the quagmire beneath his feet and lay soaked and covered in mud amongst the other fallen bodies; as he tried to recover his feet, he suddenly found himself staring across at the giant. As if taunting the defenders, he had thrown back his head and seemed to be laughing, glorying in the flash of the lightning and the tolling of the thunder.

Jonathan could not afterwards have said how he did it, but whilst the lightning still flickered, he had snatched his throwing axe from his belt and launched it at the head of the giant. The throw was not a good one by his usual standards because the axe went a little below its target, striking the warrior not in the head but the neck. Its effect though was none the less dramatic for its inaccuracy. Coming so suddenly from one side, the attack took the bodyguard and the giant completely by surprise. Briefly, the huge warrior wrestled with the axe embedded in his neck, eventually tugging it free only to release a cascade of blood on those around him. He fell, like an enormous toppling tree, face down on the earth.

Seeing their talisman slain in front of their eyes, the bodyguard began to look for a way out. Those defenders who were still managing to keep their feet fell upon them with a desperate ferocity. Of the six members of the bodyguard, just two escaped back into their own ranks – but it was only to carry the news that their leader was dead.

Conditions, if it were possible, were becoming even worse. The downpour had become akin to a waterfall, but one that was driven from behind by a wind strong enough to sweep everything before it. Continuation of the battle was increasingly irrelevant – and impossible. The attacking force melted away to seek shelter where it could, to lick its wounds and revel in such plunder, rape and abduction as there had been time to commit. The defenders had not won but neither had they been defeated. The huge storm moving in from the south coast had enveloped them all and living things in its path were united in the need to survive against an enemy mightier than any of them.

* * *

Sam and Len had taken shelter in a derelict barn at the side of their route.

"This is some storm!" exclaimed Len. The wind was driving the rain almost horizontally before it. "Are you sure it's safe to be in here?" Sam could see the point of his question. Some of the boards on the windward side flapped and crashed, suggesting that they might be torn away, and the whole building was creaking and groaning as if it might collapse at any moment.

"We can stay here near the door in case we have to get out in a hurry," replied Sam.

Len's reply this time was a grunt. In the relative shelter of the barn, his mind drifted away from the incessant movement of riding.

He had wanted to get away from the restricted life of the farm for a few days, but he had not been impressed by some of the sights that they had seen during their journey. His thoughts went back to the squatters' camps on the western side of Bristol.

"Surely they can do better than that?" he had commented to Sam.

"With what?" Sam had asked. "They have next to nothing, just the things they can scavenge from rubbish tips. They probably had to fight for these patches of land that they live on."

"I guess you're right," said Len. He had heaved a sigh as he watched small children, ragged and barefoot, chasing each other amongst the shacks, 'lean-to' buildings and middens. Smoke from a fire over which an elderly woman was cooking food drifted across the road on which they were travelling. The sound of a domestic argument spilt its discordant notes into the afternoon. Sam had noticed that their presence was attracting attention. He had urged his horse on, and Len followed, hoping that it was not far to the place they were seeking.

The memory brought him back and he returned from his reverie, thinking that as soon as the storm was over he would be glad to be back amongst the peace and order of life on The Ridge. In Sam's saddlebag was the medicine Joel needed, and both of them fretted about the delay forced on them by the storm.

"I hope Joel can survive a few more hours without this medicine," he commented to Len.

"I hope so too," replied Len. "It was damn long way to go." He let his remark hang in the air for a moment but then diplomatically followed it with a question.

"Have you two been friends all your lives?" he asked.

"Oh yes," replied Sam. "He's a little older than me but we played together as children, and we've never ceased to be friends since."

"Well," said Len peering out into the twilight, "we could take our chances on the road again."

Sam gave a snort of derision. "If we went out there we'd be lucky even to see the road. And if we wander off it here, we won't get a second chance!" As if to reinforce his comment, squalls of hail began to batter at the old building, rattling loudly on the roof and bouncing off the road's compacted surface.

"No" he continued resignedly. "Looks like we're here for a while – at least until this lot clears."

They settled their horses as best they could and then arranging their saddlebags and blankets on the floor, lay down to catch some sleep before travelling on again.

* * *

The answer to Emily's prayer was not long in coming; the stone floor which formed the ceiling of the cellar, protected them from the fire in the house above – although while she waited she worried that it would only give them protection for a short time and if the fire got into the supporting timbers, the floor and burning debris from the cottage would all come crashing down upon them.

Red faced with the effort, they strove not to cough in the smoke that was still pervading the cellar. Emily thought that the men who had set fire to the house had left, but she could not be sure, and it would be worse than ironic if they were discovered now. It was quite some time later when the atmosphere in the cellar had become almost unbearable and the children were almost beside themselves that she heard a number of loud crashes and heavy thuds. The fire must have gutted the cottage and she assumed that the sounds were those of falling timber and masonry.

She waited a while and then almost because there was nothing else that she could do, she took to listening again. There were sounds coming through the grille and from above her, but they were not those that she connected with either men or fire. She decided to risk moving closer to the grille so that she could get a better idea of what was happening outside.

Despite her attempts at stealth, she found herself stumbling over sacks and inadvertently barging into piles of stored vegetables. The gloom in the cellar was becoming deeper. For Emily, the grille was above head height and she had to pile three large sacks against the wall before she could reach, but then she pushed herself as close to it as she could. Finally, she was able to press her face against its metal bars. The foliage that had helped to conceal them now obscured her view, but she moved carefully about on the sacks, patiently trying to find out what she could.

There were no signs that the fire above them had continued to rage. Instead, a strange, damp, acrid smell was finding its way into the cellar. The reason was not hard to find. Heavy rain was falling. Her mood lifted a little. The rain was surely so heavy that it would extinguish the fire. She moved back from the grille. If they were cautious, they might now be able to risk getting out of the cellar. The rain spattering through the grille began to make her face quite wet and her feet were also beginning to feel uncomfortable. She looked down to see that accumulating around the bottom of the sacks was a small puddle that had its origins in a trickle of water running down from a lower corner of the grille.

She felt slightly perplexed. The cellar had been built to be waterproof – a dry, cool place that could be used for storage. Now water was leaking through the ventilation grille. She could only suppose that the rainfall outside was truly exceptional and that the ground was unable to absorb such a sudden downpour.

She climbed down from her perch and returned to her children and father, this time with less stealth. They were still concealed beneath the sacks. Daniel hissed at his mother in a loud whisper, "Can we get out of here yet?"

"Yes, Mum, is it safe to get out? My legs have gone to sleep." Grace was not to be forgotten.

She returned their whispers and tried to humour her daughter. "Poor old you, Grace – I think it is safe to get out, but we have to be very careful. The soldiers may still be around."

She slid past the two children to look at her father. He lay sleeping and barely stirred when she placed her hand on his brow to check his temperature. He was hot and his skin was clammy. They had managed to get him down into the cellar but getting him out again would be a lot more difficult.

Her father's condition was not the only problem facing her. Daniel had been quick to point out to her that at several points, water was spouting from the wall at the end of the cellar. The cellar had always been dry in the past and she had no idea why this was happening now. Perhaps the deluge of water from the storm was greater than anything that had preceded it. Perhaps the fire had created cracks in the cellar wall so that water could now penetrate. Whatever the cause, the effect was the same. The floor of the cellar was slowly becoming covered in a thin film of water.

Waking her father took a little time – and some patience. The water continued to creep across the floor, adding urgency to her attempts. Finally, he stirred, opening his eyes but at first appearing not to recognise her.

"Come on, Dad, we have to get out of here! We'll help you! Here, put your arm round my neck!"

Strong though she was, her father was a big man and his temporary inability to help himself made her task all the more difficult. Daniel caught hold of his grandfather's other arm and gradually began to pull him to his feet. It all seemed a little brutal, but the incessant advance of the water was pushing them to hurry.

Joel gradually understood what they were trying to do and despite the considerable pain that he was experiencing, tried to support himself on his feet as much as he could. Between them, they managed to launch themselves into a collective stagger towards the stairway and door at the other end of the cellar.

It took them roughly three minutes to travel the distance that would, in other circumstances, have taken them seconds. Halfway to their target they all had to rest against a pile of filled sacks.

At last, they arrived at the stairway up to the door. Emily went ahead, leaving Grace and Daniel to support their grandfather against the foot of the stairs. At first, she pushed cautiously at the door, still fearing that their enemies could be close by, but her efforts yielded no result. Gradually abandoning caution, she began to push harder and harder, but still the door refused to budge. Finally, in her desperation she called down to Daniel to join her. Helping his sister to manage their grandfather to the floor where she could prop him up, he then scrambled up the stairs to join his mother and together they pushed with all their might at the door. Still it was stuck and for all their pain and perspiration seemed likely to remain so. In her frustration, Emily wept, trying to suppress her sobs so that her children would not hear her but inevitably Daniel said, "Mum, don't worry – we'll get out of here!"

"Yes, of course we will!" she replied. "We'll try again in a minute when we've got our breath back."

They sat listening to the sound of their own breathing then Grace called up to them again. "Will it take long, Mum? We're getting wet down here!"

Emily was taken by surprise. She had seen the water leaking into the cellar at the far end, but it had seemed sufficient only to cause them discomfort if they remained where they were. Now Grace was complaining about it at this end of the cellar.

She listened carefully. The sound of running water had been audible before but now it sounded much louder. After a moment's thought she said, "Daniel, can you go back there and find out what's happening?"

Daniel needed no prompting and rapidly descended the staircase, landing with a splash beside his sister. Grace and Emily listened as he paddled his way to the far end of the cellar. The returning splashes were much more rapid.

"Dan, Dan, what's happening?" called Grace as he returned to the foot of the steps, but he ignored her and rushed up the ladder to where his mother was sitting.

Emily immediately noticed the awe and horror in his voice.

"Mum it's unbelievable! A big piece of wall has collapsed. The water's pouring in! It's like a waterfall!"

For a moment she did not reply. Then she called down to Grace, "Are you alright down there?"

Grace's reply was hesitant. "Yes, Mum – but the water's still coming up. We're getting really wet!"

"Ok, Grace, just hang on! Daniel and I will have another go!"

Turning towards Daniel she said, "Come on. We've got to put everything we can into this. And this time, we've got to succeed."

***

It was barely light, but Sam and Len had both spent one of the most uncomfortable nights of their lives attempting to sleep in the derelict barn. They snatched a meagre breakfast from the small amount of food they still had in their saddlebags and then saddled up and rode out into the rain. The weather had barely improved overnight. The rain was still falling heavily, and the wind was still blasting across the land with an unrelenting roar. Their misery was compounded because soon they were soaked to the skin, but their determination to get Joel's medicine to him and their wish to be back in warm, dry surroundings drove them on.

Travelling in such conditions in the twilight of early morning was both difficult and treacherous. There were hazards everywhere. In several places, they came almost to a halt as they picked their way across small rivers that had carved a course through the road. On either side of them, the fields were flooded and although it was far from dry, the road was the only way forward across a wilderness of water. Fear plucked at them as they rode on. If the rain continued, it would not be long before their route was also inundated. On one of the few sections of road not already disappearing beneath small lakes of water, Len brought his horse up alongside Sam and called across at him.

"It can't be long now? I'm sure I recognised those buildings back there!"

"I think you're right!" yelled back Sam. "We should soon be on the road across to The Ridge!"

Their thoughts were confirmed when, a short while later, the road which would take them north of The Levels and across to The Ridge appeared to their left. Turning his horse onto it, Len shouted to Sam, "I wonder if this road is flooded!"

Sam did not attempt to make any reply other than a grin and a shake of his head. He had already had enough of trying to talk in such wind and rain. He was satisfied that they now had only a few miles to ride. Soon, with any luck the storm would pass, and all would be well again.

The storm continued, though, and the sounds of wind and rain drowned out everything else. For a long while they rode on, aware only of the roaring in their ears, the discomfort of their rain-soaked saddles and of water that seemed not merely to penetrate their clothing but simply to go straight through everything.

At last, the huge mass of The Ridge came into view on their right and grew steadily in size as they approached. Soon its precipitous sides rose before them and the river which followed its course around the Ridge on that side, raged in brown and white-capped fury between the road and the foot of the steeply sloping escarpment.

Sam had no doubt that the crossing would have been washed out by the torrent, but for the moment, it seemed too big a problem to discuss even though they had now ridden into the lee of The Ridge and conversation would have been possible once more. In recent years and after persistent problems at that point, the people of The Ridge had built a causeway to carry the road high above the river so that it remained drier than the surrounding terrain.

Neither Sam nor Len could have guessed that a useful surprise, one of very few that day, awaited them just round the bend that preceded the crossing. Len, who was now a little ahead of Sam, was the first to see it and his mouth dropped open.

"I don't believe this!" he shouted back to Sam.

Curious, Sam rode up beside his friend and looked across to the point at which he would normally have expected the large flat stones of the crossing. In the water's spate, he could not see them at all; that was not the surprise. Len's amazement sprang instead from the bridge that now spanned the river's width. He gazed up at the thick ropes suspended from trees on either bank and at the gangway of stout timbers lashed into a solid but slippery route cradled between further ropes and sections of planking.

Although the swollen river had long since overtopped its banks, it had not succeeded in washing out the bridge's structure which stretched from just below the road across to a point high on the opposite side. When Len found his voice again he asked, "Who on earth put that there?"

Sam shook his head. "I've no idea. I don't remember any talk of it before we left."

Cautiously they rode together across to the bridge.

"Looks solid enough," commented Len.

"Think it'll take a horse?" asked Sam.

"Don't see why not." He had already slid from his saddle and was placing a tentative foot on the timbers of the bridge that were nearest to him.

Gazing up, Sam wondered how they had missed seeing the bridge from further back. The concatenation of suspension ropes ran high up into the trees on either side of the river so that the arc of the wooden causeway cradled at its centre, swung just above the surging torrent of angry water.

Len was rarely one to hesitate in such a situation and made a trial foray across to the other side, leaving his horse with Sam. Returning more confidently than he had gone, he was soon at Sam's side again.

"It's a bit dicey in the middle" he commented. "But even with a horse it should be alright. We'd best not go together though."

Sam nodded. "Ladies before gents then?" he asked. He was referring to Len's horse. Len took it in good humour and led the mare he was riding to the start of the bridge. It would be treacherous because of the incessant rain. The horse's weight would also cause the bridge to sag by an amount greater than he had experienced on his trial run. Sam's heart was in his mouth as he watched.

Leading his even-tempered mare by the rein, Len edged over the sodden timbers towards the centre of the bridge. There was a brief moment when the horse seemed to lose her footing and be about to sit on her haunches, but at the last moment, her hooves found just enough purchase to enable her to reach the centre of the bridge. Here Len paused briefly with his horse, waiting for the pounding of his heart to subside a little. The surging water of the torrent raged beneath them, perilously close to the sodden timbers of the bridge.

Then it was the moment to scramble up the slope of the bridge's decking to the other side. Len pushed forward again, grateful for his horse's obedience. His heart began pounding once more as they scrambled over the sodden timbers sloping up to the far bank. His mare slipped – and Len's heart thudded in the brief moment that it took for her to regain purchase on the wooden laths but then, quite suddenly, he was splashing through the puddles on the opposite bank, his horse trotting behind him, happy once more to be on a surface that did not sway with every step.

Sam's gelding was both a little heavier and more inclined to be skittish than Len's mare. Feeling that hesitation would not help, Sam stepped onto the bridge leading his horse by the rein. The gelding was tentative, seemingly uncertain about the wet, sloping timbers. Then gradually, it stepped onto the bridge, almost forced on by Sam's firm but insistent tugging. All seemed well until, as they reached the middle, the central slats seemed almost to dip to the river's foaming surface. The horse sat on his haunches and refused to move. In desperation, Sam pulled repeatedly on the reins, but the downpour fell both harder and faster whilst the slats became even more slippery than when they had set off.

He was still tugging at the reins when suddenly a flash of lightening crackled to earth. It was followed almost immediately by a clap of thunder.

In panic, the horse bolted forward so that Sam floundered and lost his hold of the reins but then, flailing around in desperation, grabbed hold of a support rope at the side of the bridge. He was then suspended, one foot almost dipping in the river's foaming torrent whilst he strove to wrap his opposite leg around an adjacent rope. His horse, seemingly more sure-footed now that he had panicked, surged past him and scrambled over the sodden timbers to the safety of the opposite bank. At some risk to himself, Len managed to grab at the horse's flailing rein and bring him once more under control; quickly, he fastened the rein around a stout, low dipping branch. Praying and cursing to himself at one and the same time, he fervently hoped that the thunder and lightning would not recur until Sam had been able to recover.

Driven by his suspension just above the river's foaming roar, Sam found a strength he hardly knew he possessed. Using his arms and the leg that he had managed to wrap around the suspension rope, he hauled himself back onto the sodden timbers of the bridge. Then, forcing himself not to think about the lack of purchase provided by his boots, he clambered, crawled and scrambled over the slippery wooden laths until at last he found himself falling from the last timber of the bridge into a pool of muddy water on the far side. Spluttering and cursing, he rolled to one side in time to see Len's face pass from concern to stupid grin and then into outright guffaw. For a brief moment, Sam felt the urge to leap to his feet and hit him, but then the humour of the moment began to penetrate and, in the still pouring rain, they both found themselves roaring with laughter.

✱✱✱

They were now so thoroughly soaked that it hardly seemed to matter anymore. Water cascaded down to meet them as they urged their bedraggled horses up the steps that would finally lead them onto the steep slope below the village gates.

As they came within view of the gates, their eyes opened wide in disbelief.

"What on earth...?" Sam left his sentence trailing away into nothing. At first both men were too amazed by what they saw to make any comment. When they found their voices again it was only to ask more questions.

"What the hell has happened here?" Len had reached the gateway and was striving to heave aside one of the gates so that he could lead his horse through.

Sam stared down at the tattooed body of one the dead attackers. "Who are these people?"

Len motioned Sam forward until he stood beside him. He pointed to the top of the stockade where one of the first casualties of the battle still lay slumped over the wooden ramparts.

"I think I recognise him. Isn't that the blacksmith's lad – Mark – Mark Ebdon?"

Sam stared grimly upwards. "Yes, it is," he said slowly. He turned to stare about him.

"Now we know how the bridge came to be there! There's been a fight – a battle whilst we've been away! The invaders must have used the bridge to cross the river."

Silently they began to pick their way amongst the bodies piled at the gateway, recognising some of the dead but staring in sullen amazement at the corpses of the assailants.

Sam was about to step past the last of the bodies in the gateway and onto village territory when he felt Len's hand on his arm.

"Best go carefully," he said. He gestured towards one of the dead attackers, pierced through by an arrow and lying face down inside the gates. "Some of these people may still be about."

Sam nodded. He did not attempt to remount but led his horse by the rein. He was tempted to clap his hands in an attempt to drive off the carrion birds that were picking at the corpses, but then he remembered Len's warning comment. They did not want to draw attention to themselves.

Any other time he might have been interested in the various birds pecking at the bodies strewn about on what appeared to have been the battlefield. Crows, kites, buzzards and magpies competed to pluck at the flesh of the dead, whilst foxes too were tearing at the grisly remains.

Some of the scavenging birds flew into the air as the two men approached. Sam could well understand how people in the past had believed that such creatures bore away the souls of the dead. Misery deepened on their faces and in their hearts as they recognised a friend here, a neighbour there.

Wandering away from Sam a little, Len made his way to where the battle must have been at its most intense. It was as much as he could do to prevent himself from retching as he scanned the scene of severed heads, limbs and bodies with gaping wounds, many now covered in heaving swarms of flies. Despite his growing nausea, however, he eventually came to a point where he turned and beckoned to Sam.

Absorbed in his own private world of horror, it was some moments before Sam noticed him. Then seeing Len's gesticulations, he led his horse amongst the serried ranks of the slain. Drawing alongside his companion, he understood why he had signalled to him.

Lying before them was the body of the largest human being Sam had ever seen. He guessed that he was well over seven feet tall, although his height was only part of the story; his bones and physique were on a scale to match. The huge corpse was already locked in the rigors of death, the flesh discoloured by a day and a night spent in the open. A snarl was frozen onto the cadaver's lips which lay not face down like so many others, but half twisted onto its back.

"Look at this!" exclaimed Len. He pointed to a gash, both long and deep, in the giant's neck. Despite the rain and the mud all around them, it was clear that a great deal of blood had been spilt and remnants of it were still visible on what little grass remained after the churning of the ground by the combatants' feet.

Despite the rain and relative cool borne in on the tail of the storm, the wind brought with it a stench of death. They decided that they had seen – and smelt – enough. Sam began to lead his horse away from the carnage towards an open area that led on one side across to the village green.

Stunned and sickened though he was, Sam's mind was still working its way through what he had seen – and also through what he had not seen; there were several people who had not been amongst the dead – or at least, amongst those that they had been able to recognise. There would be survivors. There must be a number of them, probably hidden away in what remained of The Village and the outlying farms.

A movement away to his left caught his eye. He looked around quickly. There was a horse grazing at the edge of the woods; relieved to get away from the carnage, Sam climbed onto his horse and rode across to where it was cropping the grass. He dismounted and walked forward, hand tentatively outstretched towards the rein of the straying horse. Already he recognised it.

Len cantered across to join him and swinging from his horse's saddle, hurried over the sodden turf to where his friend was now patting the animal's neck. He too recognised it. "It's Josh's horse, isn't it?" he said.

"Yes, it's Rhodri," confirmed Sam. "But where is Josh?"

They searched about at the edge of the wood but failed to find any sign of him. Then, mystified, they turned back towards the scene of the fighting. Something lay amongst the grass midway between the wood and the carnage they had recently left behind.

Sam recognised Josh's body from some yards away. Dropping his horse's rein, he walked across to where it lay. Len rode up to join him, waiting while his friend looked carefully at his dead neighbour and the area in which he had fallen.

The grass around the body was heavily trampled and in places, the ground beneath had been churned into mud. Looking up at Len, Sam pointed to a bloody gash in Josh's side.

"Probably done with a spear – and it looks like he was set upon by several people!"

He pointed to separate tracks converging through the grass, whilst Sam brooded over the body and the possible way in which his friend had met his death. For the moment it was more than he could stand. He put a hand over his eyes and wept quietly to himself muttering, "Bastards! The fucking bastards!"

Len watched from a short distance, barely managing to hold onto his own emotions, but then his thoughts returned to the living.

"Sam," he said gently. "There's nothing we can do for Josh right now, but we do need to get to Joel with the medicine. Josh's wife and kids may also need help – not to mention our own families. Let's hope we're in time for them all!"

Sam turned away from Josh's body. "You're right!" he said. "We'll have to attend to Josh later. Let's get to Joel. If Emily's there she can do what's needed and we can get away."

It was no more than a few minutes' ride from the scene of battle across to Joel and Emily's cottages. The rain had slackened to a thin drizzle, but everywhere the ground was sodden. As they rode past some of Josh's fields, they could see that many of them were inundated with water.

"Huh!" snorted Sam. "If I remember correctly, Josh had just repaired the drainage system. Now look at it!"

Ahead of them, their view of the cottages was obscured by woodland until they were just a short distance away, but then as they approached, Len exclaimed, "My God, look at that!"

Sam needed no prompting. Together they galloped their horses over the remaining yards to the charred wreckage of the neighbouring cottages. The chimneys, which had been built of stone, stood out like lonely sentinels amidst broken walls, rubble and tumbled, blackened timbers which were largely all that remained of the houses themselves.

For some minutes, Sam searched about amongst the ash and carbonised remnants of his friend's furniture. Mercifully, he found no signs of Joel. Then, although he was some distance away, he heard Len calling to him.

"Hey, Sam, get over here!"

Leaving his horse, Sam ran across to where his friend was searching about amongst the ruins of Josh and Emily's cottage. As he rejoined him, Len said, "I'm sure I heard something."

"Like what?" asked Sam.

"Like a thud," Len replied. "I think it came from over there." He pointed across to where the remains of a staircase could be seen. With difficulty, they stumbled across, picking their way amongst large timbers which had fallen from the ceilings and roof. Shovelling some of the ash away with one of his boots, Sam thought that he could see the outline of a door. The pervading ash made it almost indistinguishable from the surrounding flagstones, but he found childhood memories coming back to him. He drew Len away. If his guess was correct, the door led down to a cellar – to somewhere in which Joel, Emily and her children might be hidden.

"I used to play here as a kid," he said. I think that's a door there!" He returned to trace the outline of a rectangular shape with the toe of his boot.

"I think you're right!" Len could see it quite clearly now that it had been pointed out to him. "Why don't we call out to them – let them know we're here."

"Yes, of course," agreed Sam. "But that door is thick and solid. When old Kirk put it there, he didn't want anyone crashing through it into the cellar below. If Emily and her family are in there, they will probably hear us, but they won't be able to tell who it is. They won't know if we're friend or foe."

"So what can we do?" asked Len, a hint of frustration in his voice.

"If I remember correctly, there is a place here from which they could hear us."

"Well, where is it then?" demanded his friend, gesturing with his hands to indicate his diminishing patience.

By way of reply, Sam began picking his way through the ash, masonry and chaos of blackened timber to where there was a drop down over the side of the cottage.

"So what's down there?" Len's exasperation with Sam's step-by-step approach was getting the better of him.

Jumping down onto ground just below the floor level of the cottage, Sam pushed his way down into a hollow that lay between the side wall and the garden. It was now largely overgrown with weeds and bushes, but Sam's memories came surging back to him. He continued pushing downward between the vegetation and the wall until at the bottom of the dip, the ground flattened a little. Kneeling uncomfortably between a large bush and the wall, he finally made out what he was looking for – the metal bars of a ventilation grille.

"Emily, Daniel, Grace, are you in there?" He hoped that from where he was kneeling, they would be able to recognise his voice. There was a pause and then to his great relief, the voices of all three came clamouring back – though they seemed oddly muffled. There was another pause and then he heard Emily's voice again. It was rather faint, and Sam wondered why she did not come to the grille. There was the same muffled effect as before, but he thought that he heard something about 'water' and being 'trapped'. That would explain it. To test his suspicion, he lobbed a small stone through the grille. There was the sound of a splash from inside. The cellar had flooded.

Moments later, he stood once more amongst the burnt ruins of the cottage. The timber that had fallen across the trapdoor into the cellar was heavy and it took a good deal of heaving and tugging to pull it clear.

"Try the door now!" yelled Len. There was no response.

"Damn! They can't hear you!" exclaimed Sam. He scrambled once more through the debris, leapt down into the dip and yelled through the grille into the cellar as loudly as he could. For a further moment, it seemed as though again there would be no response. Then, slowly the trapdoor began to open. Len leapt forward and seized on it, pulling it open to reveal Emily on the top step, blinking in the daylight.

Whilst Sam came stumbling back across to him, he put out a hand to help her out of the cellar. Then, with some difficulty, Len and Emily pulled Joel out and seated him on a fallen timber. Sam sat beside him, propping him up whilst the other two returned to help Daniel and Grace.

There was relief that they had been released from the cellar but then, hot on its heels came distress as they gazed around at the devastation of the two cottages. Finally, leaving Len to take his place, Sam had to take Emily aside and tell her about Josh. He held her about the shoulders, but she sank to the ground, her body shaking with sobs. After some moments she forced herself to get up and walk across to Daniel and Grace. With as much control as she could muster, she told them that their father was dead, killed in the battle that had taken place. Then they sat in a grief-stricken huddle in the ashes of their house whilst the rain began to fall again.

Sam debated what he should do. After brief deliberation, he walked across to his horse, retrieved the medicine that he and Len had brought from Bristol and returned to where his friend was sitting with Joel. Carefully, he tended to Joel and then discussed with Len how they could manage the situation.

They quickly agreed that Josh's family should not be left to fend for themselves so, desperate though he was to see his own family, Len offered to stay with them. That decided, Sam was once more aware that it was already the middle of the day and there was a pressing need to find out what had happened to Len's wife and to his own wife and children.

He once more mounted his horse and rode off along the path that he hoped would bring him to a happier situation than the one he was leaving behind.

* * *

The news that greeted Sam when he got back to his own house was that his wife was safe and that two of his sons – Jonathan the youngest and George the eldest – had survived; his middle son, Michael, however had been killed at the height of the battle. Those around Sam realised that the situation could have been far worse, but Michael had been very dear to him, and his death was an enormous blow.

It was fortuitous that when both Sam and Len had been absent on the journey to Bristol, their wives had been spending more time in each other's company than usual. On the morning that the attackers had broken into the settlement, Sam's wife Anne had planned to be at Len's house with his wife, Kate. Although they lived some little distance from the centre of the Village, they had both heard the tolling of the Village bell signalling the imminent attack. George and Michael had gone to find out what was happening, leaving their mother with Jonathan, but then Jonathan had slipped out after them, following at a little distance. George had eventually seen his brother tagging along behind them and had angrily told him that once they had discovered what had led to the ringing of the bell, he would have to return to their mother and tell her what was going on, but then all three of them had soon found that they were unable to escape and instead were caught up in the fighting.

Left alone in the cottage, Anne had waited for her sons to return with news but then anxiety had overcome her, and she decided to find out what was happening to Kate. She had also arranged with her two older sons that if for any reason they were unable to get back, she would go on to Len and Kate's house and that if they returned after she had left, they should follow her there. Len and Kate's youngest child, Sophie, had only recently learned to walk and Anne knew that if there were serious problems, she might have difficulty coping.

It was Anne who had first seen the enemy riders, intent on their task of destruction. She had barely reached Kate's house when three of them appeared at the end of the long lane leading up to the cottage. Immediately she ran inside, calling to Kate, telling her what she could in the short time that they had, and then pushing both mother and child out through the back door and into the margins of the woodland behind the house.

They had not long to wait. The men had ridden up to the front door and then set about pillaging the house. As Anne and Kate watched, they completed their rampage, finally setting the house on fire; flames had begun to shoot up from the front of the cottage. Kate was distraught but Anne drew her, with Sophie in her arms, deeper into the wood.

Shortly after that, rain began to fall. Hardly knowing what to do, the two women remained within the cover of the trees but began skirting the margin of the wood and following the Village boundary. The din of the battle taking place on the other side of the village green came clearly across to them as they tried to make their way through the dense, gloomy undergrowth amongst the trees. Despite the intensity of the storm outside, the tree canopy above them was such that very little of the water pouring from the skies penetrated through to them. Neither of them mentioned the terrible shouts and screams that they could still hear coming from a short distance away, but then they saw ahead of them someone who was clearly unaware of their presence. Signalling to Kate that she should stay back with Sophie, Anne crept forward. Despite the gloom she recognised the girl, or young woman in front of her. She was not someone Anne knew well but she had seen her around the Village a number of times with Grace, Josh and Emily's daughter.

Anne hissed the girl's name. She did not hear her, so she tried again, this time more loudly. The girl swung round in alarm, one hand on her chest. Anne went forward quickly, surprised to find that she backed away from her, a look of terror in her eyes.

"Ruthie, it's alright. I'm Anne, Sam's wife." She wanted to reassure her, not cause her any distress.

For a moment the frightened girl had seemed unable to recognise her as someone from the Village, but then at last, a small flicker of relief crossed her face. Anne was able to put an arm round her shoulders and make an attempt to calm her.

Ruthie, however, continued to shake like a leaf. As Anne's eyes adjusted to the darkness in the wood, she could see that Ruthie's dress was badly torn, that her face was smeared with dirt and that there was blood on her arms and fingers. At first, she seemed to be babbling, but then Anne could discern the words:

"They killed my dad and my brother! They killed them right in front of me! My family, my family – killed them for no reason!"

There was little Anne could do but listen and hold on to her. After a while she began to calm down. Anne wondered what had happened to Ruthie's mother but feared that she would become hysterical again if she asked, so she took hold of Ruthie's arm and asked gently, "What happened to you?"

"One of them, the youngest tried to..." She could not get the words out.

Anne thought that she could guess what Ruthie was trying to say. "Is that how your dress was ripped...?"

Ruthie seemed not to hear Anne's question but ploughed on with her own explanation. "I didn't want his filthy hands on me! I scratched him all over his face. Then my dad...oh my dad, what they did to him! Poor man, he was trying to save me! Jed flew at them – knocked one of 'em down – but they stuck a knife in him!"

For a moment she could speak no more, lapsing into uncontrollable sobs.

By this time, Kate had come forward but hung back a little, not wanting Sophie to be distressed by the sight of the sobbing woman.

Eventually Anne said, "Look, Ruthie, we need to get away from here!"

At first Ruthie refused to respond to her, shouting instead, "What do I care! What do I bloody well care!"

"We all need to care!" hissed Anne urgently. "They're still about – everywhere."

Ruthie looked away and refused to engage with her, so she turned to Kate. "The storm's getting worse out there. If we don't make a move, some of them will be sheltering in here and we'll be caught."

Kate could understand the urgency but could think of nowhere that they could hide. "Is there anywhere that's safe from these scum?" she asked in frustration.

Sophie, not used to hearing her mother speak in such an emphatic way, clung more tightly round her mother's neck.

Ruthie seemed to notice the child for the first time and was temporarily distracted from the horrors of the past hour.

"I know somewhere," she said.

Momentarily, Anne thought that she had misheard but then seized on Ruthie's comment. "OK," she said. "So where is it? Tell us!"

"I can't tell you! You'll never find it! I'll have to show you!"

Anne moved back a little, leaving Ruthie to show the way.

Somewhat to the surprise of the two older women, she began to lead them to the edge of the wood.

"I can't take Sophie out there!"

Anne could readily understand her friend's anxiety. The storm was reaching unprecedented fury. The rain had begun to resemble an unrelenting wall of water rather than something composed of single droplets and a ferocious roaring wind was showering the edge of the woodland with flying branches and debris.

Ruthie, however, seemed to be diverting her grief and anger into a contest with the storm.

"Die here then if you want to!" she yelled in Kate's face.

Anne caught Kate's arm. "Come on! We have to trust her! Follow me!"

Kate hesitated a moment longer but then seeing her friend disappearing into the downpour realised that she would be left alone if she did not go after her. She ran out into the storm, striving to catch sight of the two women ahead of her in the torrent of water that was blasting all around them. She could just make out two shadowy figures running along the path to her right. She launched herself forward with Sophie clinging tightly round her neck.

It was fortunate that she had not hesitated further for she had barely leapt forward when a large branch, torn away by the howling storm, crashed with an earth-shaking thump to the ground where she and Sophie had been sheltering only seconds before.

They ran...on and on...Then quite suddenly she was on top of Anne, crashing into her and falling out of control into the mud. She managed to let go of Sophie, who sprawled to one side. Grimly, Anne paused to pull her friend up and then turned back to Ruthie who had dropped to her hands and knees, just in front of her.

Kate's clothes were soaked through and through. Colliding with Anne brought all her anger to the surface. She retrieved her wailing child from the huge puddle into which she had fallen and yelled at her friend, "What the bloody hell are you doing?"

Anne was about splutter her own angry reply when Ruthie suddenly loomed before them. "It's here! I've found it! Come on!"

The last few yards of their journey were, if anything, almost worse than their dash through the storm. They were just a very short distance from the place to which Ruthie was taking them but trusting her under such dreadful conditions had tried the patience of Kate and Anne to the limit. Now, however, she stood gesturing towards something that lay to their right, hidden amongst the sodden vegetation. Without explanation, she plunged in amongst the wildly thrashing branches and bracken before her, returning some seconds later, tightly clutching a wooden hurdle.

Anne and Kate thought for a moment that, in her grief she had taken leave of her senses, but then Kate yelled urgently in Anne's ear that she could just make out the shapes of men and horses, hurrying along the track that they had left a short time before. Anne supposed that they were retreating from the battle and the storm, but her arm was seized, and she found herself being dragged forward into a rickety shelter buried amongst the foliage. She looked around wondering about Kate and Sophie, but already Ruthie had gone back for them and returned, pushing them ahead of her, through the low entrance to the shelter.

Crawling again on her hands and knees, she retrieved the hurdle that she had set to one side and fastened it in place. Praying that their movements had not been seen by the cavalcade of men hastening through the storm, she slumped onto one of the seats that she and Grace had improvised the summer before.

Despite the alarming lurches of the shelter and the incessant water cascading onto them through the many gaps in the structure around them, Anne's anger was steadily replaced by anxiety that even then, the soldiers would somehow discover them. Ruthie sat, shivering with cold, her teeth chattering and her body shaking. Barely an hour before, she had seen her father and brother murdered. Now she had saved Anne, Kate and Sophie from an enemy that was retreating but taking with it everything that could be wrested from the clutches of the storm. She did not refuse the arm that Anne placed about her shoulders. Together, the three women huddled together with Sophie between them, trying to share what little body warmth they had.

They spent one of the most miserable nights that Anne could ever remember. As soon as it was light the next day, Ruthie removed the hurdle covering the door and crawled through the sodden undergrowth and the dying ravages of the storm to the junction with the track along which they had fled, the day before.

There was no sign of the enemy now – a piece of information that she quickly took back to Anne, Kate and Sophie. Having entrusted her with their lives neither woman sought to dispute what she said and shortly, they were all heading for Sam's house – which mercifully, although it had been plundered and damaged internally, had not been set alight. It was here that Sam found them all when he came galloping along the track, early in the afternoon.

***

CHAPTER 26

CONCEPTION

It was early summer. Emily watched as Thomas Forton rode away, making his rounds as had become his custom in the aftermath of the battle. Her heart felt lighter every time he spoke to her, and their conversations were one of the few things that had given her comfort since Josh's death.

She looked around, preparing to check on her father's wellbeing when she noticed that Grace was sitting under a nearby tree with a deep frown on her face. Telling herself that her father was now well enough not to need her constant attention, she walked across to where Grace was seated and, tucking her skirt about her, sat down by her daughter. At first Grace made a show of ignoring her but then finding that her mother simply waited patiently, she said,

"I don't like you talking to that man!"

Emily thought for a moment wondering why, of all the men she had needed to speak to in recent times, Grace should suddenly take exception to Thomas Forton. Grace was not sure either, but she quickly found a reason – one that was not altogether false. It was something that had troubled her continually ever since the day of the battle, the day on which her father, like so many other men from the settlement, had died.

"You were talking to him about the den! I heard you!"

Emily thought for a moment that she understood. "I know that it was your secret place, love," she said. "But really I was telling Mr Forton about Ruthie – and how brave she was." The thought of Ruthie's courage only added another barb to those that were already pricking Grace's sensitivities.

"If you had listened to me in the first place there might have been time to mend the stockade properly!"

Emily could understand how Grace felt but could not agree. "Your father did his best. I told him about the stockade as soon as you told me. I don't think he could have done any more."

Grace lapsed into silence and Emily remembered that she had been trying to tell Josh about the stockade the evening before but that he had taken her to task for pestering him. Emily guiltily remembered that she had also ignored signs that Grace wanted to tell her something by asking her to mop up some water she had spilled on the kitchen floor. It was true that some hours had been wasted and that the work on the stockade could have been done much more effectively. Emily did not blame Josh for the failure of the temporary repair that he had done, but wondered instead why the stockade foreman had not acted with more urgency when Josh had gone to see him. Despite Grace's fragile mood, Emily briefly gave in to her own feelings of anger and despair.

"The people attacking us were determined to get in! They would have broken down the stockade anyway! There was nothing anyone could have done!"

Grace's eyes filled with tears. She did not usually argue with her mother but today, she was at the end of her tether.

"My dad is dead! Half the people from the Village have been killed! Our houses have been burned down – and still you don't want to listen to me! Still you're angry with me!"

"No, Grace – not with you. I'm not angry with you and I do want to listen to you. You know I do." Grace had never spoken to her in such a way before and she was taken aback.

"Sometimes you do! Even Dad used to listen to me sometimes but there have been so many other times – when you're too busy and you think I'm in the way!"

Emily waited, deciding that it was better to let Grace say what she had to say.

"The den was mine – mine and Ruthie's! It's where we used to go when no-one else wanted us around. The last time I went to the den, before Ruthie took half the Village to our so-called 'secret place', was the day that I discovered the hole in the stockade! Now everyone knows where it is! Now I've got nowhere I can go!"

Emily could say little. She put out her arms to her daughter, wondering if she would push her away, but reassuringly, Grace threw her arms round her mother, her body shaking with heartfelt sobs as Emily drew her closer. Grace continued to sob for some minutes until finally she had cried out her immediate anger and frustration. Then another feeling – one of emptiness – began to creep in upon her. Her father had very rarely held her, but now that he was gone, for all the times that he had sent her away, she remembered those few times when he had put his arms around her and she had felt that she was truly his daughter. Now that her father would never, could never, hold her again, grief filled her heart, and she was racked afresh by deep sobs. Sensing that Grace had moved beyond her feelings about the den and was now grieving for her father, Emily drew her daughter still closer, stroking her hair and waiting.

For that moment, she was patient and calm because the needs of her daughter came first. She had worried many times in the past months that Grace had seemed withdrawn and uncommunicative, but now at least she was dragging out into the open some of the feelings that she had kept buried away, deep inside herself.

Later, there would be another time for Emily, a time when she was on her own, when she would be gripped by a sense of conflict, wondering how long she should wait before more obviously responding to the growing attentions of Thomas Forton and how much longer again it would be before she would be able to tell Grace and Daniel anything about the feelings that she felt were beginning to unfold between her and someone she had barely known before Josh's death.

***

Sam's brow was beginning to furrow as he listened to Len's account of a conversation that he had overheard between some of the younger men of the Village.

"Yes, if they leave," said Len, "life here will get even harder than it has been."

"So who exactly was taking part in this conversation?" asked Sam.

Oh, you could almost guess – there was Joe Harvey, Fred Davies, Tom Wilton and Jed Paterson."

"Sounds like that lot that used to get together on the village green," commented Sam. He paused for moment, realising that there was a member of the group that Len had not mentioned.

He drew a sharp inward breath. "Len, are you getting round to telling me that Jonathan was there?"

Len looked warily at his friend. "I'm afraid so. I hate to say this but, young as he is, he seems to be the leader. Ever since the battle, he's been something of a hero to them all."

Len waited for his friend's reaction. It was not long in coming.

"Hero he might be!" exclaimed Sam. "But he's still too young to know his ass from his elbow!"

Len waited but then shook his head. "No, I don't agree about that," he said. "That little group are probably the smartest of the young people in this Village. If they go, they'll be a real loss."

Sam nodded. He knew that Len was right. "So what else did they say? Did they talk about why they want to leave?"

"They did," confirmed Len. "It was quite a list of things, but basically with the problems of farming here now and the fact that this place is not the fortress we used to think it was, they want to find a better life somewhere else."

"And did they say where this 'somewhere else' might be?" Sam almost snorted the question at his friend.

"It was nowhere around here. But then you've probably guessed that. No, they're talking about working their passage from Falmouth and going to the north of Canada. It seems that the climate there now is more like it used to be here."

"Yes, I've heard that too – but then, we all get our news from the same people – the messengers. I guess you're going to say that it's all the fault of me and Joel – and Berta for that matter!"

Len looked sideways at Sam and nodded uncomfortably. "There are some who say that. But I don't go with that myself."

"Then what do you think, Len?"

"I think that people here only say that because many of them have hardly been out of this place. Anyway, you went on your little adventure to help your families, whereas Jonathan and the others are talking about going for good."

"When do you think they'll go?"

I think it's already too late this year. If they do decide to leave, it'll probably be early next Spring."

Sam looked directly at his friend. The truth was hard to bear but he knew that Len's candour was based on true friendship. Just in the moment that he least wanted it to do so, his mind went back to Michael, killed at the height of the battle with the invaders.

"Why is it always the strongest and the best that have to go?" asked Sam in a voice that was broken and barely audible.

"I loved Michael almost as well as you – but you know that's how it is," replied Len sadly. Then, no longer thinking of the battle but of the hardships that young people leaving the Village would face, he said, "They're the ones who can make it – if anyone can."

Slowly, Sam turned away, not wanting Len to see the tears that had begun to form at the corners of his eyes. But Len had noticed anyway. It was not a sight that he could ever recall seeing before.

***

Emily reflected that a year had not yet elapsed since Josh had been killed in battle. Now she had donned her cleanest dress and her best cloak and was riding Bundle, on her way to see Thomas Forton. It occurred to her that Thomas might have seen Josh die. It was not something that she had so far been able to bring herself to talk about.

Bundle picked his way forward through the long grass. Emily held him on a loose rein. He already knew the way to Thomas' cottage. There had been periods in the winter months when she had seen few people other than her two children and her father.

Pictures of the winter ran through her head. It had been a wet, thoroughly depressing time – a time that she had spent caring for others, feeding them, washing and clothing them, trying to ensure that they survived the sodden rawness of the season. She was not self-centred or self-pitying, but in the long winter nights and the hours before she had to force herself to begin another day, she was aware of the cold space all around her in a bed that now seemed too big.

She worried about Daniel. Although Josh had been a less than ideal husband and father, it was to him that Daniel had most naturally related. Now his mood at home was dark and sullen. He preferred to spend time with Sam's two surviving sons and with the few men who could be spared from time to time, to help in the rebuilding of the cottages.

Grace sometimes crept into her mother's bed at night. They shared each other's warmth and the solace of each other's company. Whilst Daniel in his perpetual sullenness had become almost estranged from his mother and sister, Grace now also worked many hours helping her mother with whatever tasks had to be done – and so they spent a good deal of time each day and night in each other's company.

Emily was aware that she had begun to confide in Grace to a degree that was not in keeping with her daughter's years or with her ideas about treating both her children equally. Grace, for her part, innocently relished the new degrees of closeness that she now shared with her mother. It was a closeness that further repelled Daniel and which, since he knew of no way to share in it, went to seek the company of others.

Despite all this, Emily was still aware that Grace could not fill the spaces left by Josh's death. Sam and his wife had been more than good to her and the two children, and for many weeks she had kept her feelings at bay, but the reality of her situation had gradually forced its way in upon her. Then, one morning, when Grace and Daniel were both out of the house, she had found herself sitting in front of her bedroom window, weeping aloud and wondering what the future could possibly bring that would once more bring her happiness.

She had wept until the futility of weeping brought her tears to an end. Then she had dried her eyes and had made her way downstairs and across to the outbuilding that had been adapted for her father. He was recovering now although it had been a long struggle against both his illness and the winter conditions. There had been times when she had thought that he would not survive, when the struggle would become too much, but then she had sensed that he still had something that he wanted to achieve. At first, she had worried that the hours that he spent writing would exhaust him, but she began to be less anxious about it as she saw that it gave him a reason to fight his way into another year and all that it might bring.

She paused in her thoughts as Bundle hesitated. He was picking his way through the bracken on his way across to a track that led up to Thomas Forton's house. Occasionally, the scant remains of men who had been killed during the battle were still to be found around the margins of the woods, but this time, to her relief it was nothing more than a large branch that had toppled from one of the nearby trees.

Bundle negotiated his way around the branch and resumed his course towards the track leading to Thomas Forton's house. Emily, now that the house would soon be in view, resumed her thoughts. Even now, her heart beat a little faster as she remembered the morning on which Thomas had come to her door. She remembered the feeling of shame that she felt when he had stooped beneath the low doorway to enter the poor cottage that had been so rapidly built by his men so that Emily and her children could have some measure of independence and gradually proceed with the reconstruction of their lives.

He had offered to take them under his own roof, but Emily would not hear of it. Despite the poverty of her living conditions, she was learning to cope on her own and although she often felt the loneliness, she also preferred at that time to be in control of her own affairs – such as they were.

At first, she could not make up her mind about Thomas. He was quite large and squarely built. His long and slightly curly hair fell almost to his shoulders. His face was just a little too serious and intense to be handsome, and yet it had a strength that drew her in. Just once she had stared into his dark eyes but then had glanced quickly away again, embarrassed that she had done such a thing.

Bundle rounded a curve in the track and Thomas' house loomed into view. It was a large, two-storey building built of wood and stone. Emily thought that it resembled some of the Tudor buildings, pictures of which she had seen in her great-grandfather's old books.

Despite the size of the house, Emily reflected that she had been unable to see it until just the last few moments of her journey. It was tucked away at a remote end of The Ridge – which might explain why it had escaped the ravages of the invaders. That morning, it was eerily quiet. Usually there were farm workers bustling about, but now there were no signs of human activity and the circular forecourt of the house was empty.

She reined Bundle to a halt in front of a large oak door, then dismounted and walked across to rap loudly, and more confidently than she felt on its exterior. It was some moments before the door creaked open and there stood Thomas, his fine, slightly pallid complexion contrasting with the gloom of the hallway. Emily noticed that his hair was combed and fell neatly to his shoulders, that he had on a clean shirt and smart, grey tunic and dark trousers tucked into black leather boots.

He stood for a moment gazing at her, noticing the care that she had taken with her appearance, her womanliness making him slightly breathless. Then he found his voice and said, "Good morning, Emily! Do come in and make yourself at home! I'll take your horse round to the stable."

Emily returned his greeting and then went into the hallway and through to the spacious front room looking out onto the forecourt.

Thomas quickly attended to Bundle, ensuring that he had plenty to eat and a stall in which he would be content for a while. Then he returned to the front of the house. It would have been useful to have some help that morning, but he had ensured that all the farm hands had tasks to do in other parts of the farm. So far, he and Emily had only been able to enjoy brief, or even snatched moments together, but now this morning he wanted to have a long conversation with her, one that, as far as he could arrange matters, would be without interruption.

***

Events on The Ridge proceeded slowly. A little more than a year had elapsed since Emily had ridden to meet Thomas alone for the first time, in his house. She looked at her father as he lay on a bed beneath an awning under the trees. It was a hot, almost cloudless day and he watched as a small team of Thomas Forton's men worked on the rebuilding of his farmhouse.

In most respects, Joel had recovered from his illness in the early part of the previous year, but it had left him weakened and he could no longer work for long periods without resting. It was in these circumstances that he had given a large area of his farm to Thomas in exchange for the labour and materials needed to rebuild the cottages.

"Thomas' men are doing well," he said. "I should be helping them."

Emily gave the idea short shrift. "You'll do no such thing. Even a slow walk down the lane exhausts you. What do think that would do?" She gestured towards the men who were busily sorting and moving masonry so that they could re-use it.

"I suppose you're right," sighed Joel.

"Tetanus is no joke! You were lucky to recover."

"I never would have done, had it not been for Sam and Len taking a ride to Bristol."

"You're right, Dad – but it was lucky for them too! They're still alive when so many others are not!"

"They weren't to know. No-one could accuse Sam and Len of running away from danger!" retorted her father with indignation. Emily was often brittle these days but her remark had strayed beyond the bounds of reasonableness.

"No, you're right, they weren't to know, were they?" she echoed. "But then none of us, including Josh, were to know what was about to happen."

Joel waited. Now that she had been angry, she would calm down again and be sorry for her loss of temper.

"I was pleased to see Thomas here. He's a good man."

Emily sensed that her father was trying to placate her, but it was hard to disagree with a thought that was so in tune with her own feelings. Even so, it was some seconds before she felt able to reply.

"Yes, Dad – he is. And he's had a good influence on Daniel."

Joel looked across to where Daniel was working alongside Thomas Forton's men.

Emily decided to change the subject. She did not want to talk to her father about Thomas at that moment, although she knew that she would not be able to postpone such a discussion for much longer.

"There has been a good side to the fact that you've not been able to charge around so much!"

"Oh and what's that?" her father asked with a hint of sarcasm in his voice.

"I gather from what you said that you've nearly finished your contribution to 'The Book'."

"Yes," responded Joel, his tone changing and becoming thoughtful. "I have..."

* * *

A little later, Emily left her father to sleep. She wanted to see Thomas. Grace had gone to visit Ruth and for a short while, there was nothing that Emily felt she had to do. Something that she had wanted to tell her father but could not quite bring herself to do so was that she and Thomas wanted to marry. Daniel gave most of his time now to working on the farm or to helping rebuild the cottage. Grace too was finding that she had more time to visit her friends. Emily, in turn, had been spending more time with Thomas – to the extent that they both knew they were the subject of gossip around Thomas' farm. It was only a matter of time before the gossip got back to her father – and she wanted to tell him about her feelings for Thomas before he learned about them by other means.

She mused with a smile on her lips that the gossip was not without foundation. She had spent several afternoons alone with Thomas at his house – long warm afternoons in late spring and the hotter afternoons of early summer. Now, Emily was becoming sure that, as a result of their love-making, she was pregnant.

***

On the evening of the same day, Joel lay once again on the bed beneath the awning. The shelter had been improvised for him by Emily and Grace, and was suspended from the overhanging branches of trees.

He lay drowsing. The weather had been hot and dry for some days. During the winter, he had spent some time with Emily in her rudimentary cottage and other spells with Sam and his family. It had not been easy because most of the families on The Ridge were still in the process of rebuilding their houses after the havoc wreaked by the invaders. More recently, he had been able to spend a good many nights in a large tent that Len and Sam had set up for him a few yards from where the building work was taking place. It lacked the amenities of a cottage, but Joel liked having the ability to sit on his bed and watch the light fade at the end of a long day.

Despite Emily's concerns about his health, he generally felt much stronger than he had felt in the previous year. Whilst he drowsed, he was also waiting for Emily to reappear and was almost asleep when he felt her shaking him gently by the shoulder.

"Wake up, Dad! I've brought you some food."

Joel blearily awoke, swung himself into a sitting position and waited whilst Emily placed on his lap a dish of boiled vegetables with a few small pieces of mutton. She then sat on a nearby tree stump and watched as he ate it hungrily.

"Your appetite's certainly improved in recent times," she commented. Joel did not reply but concentrated on eating.

A few minutes later, he said, "That was good. I can't remember when I last enjoyed a meal so much."

"I think you say that about every meal I bring you," observed Emily drily.

***

The day was receding and as on so many occasions in the past, they sat in the deepening twilight, looking up at the sky.

Pointing west across to a bright point of light a little to one side of where the moon, half full, had risen, Emily said, "Look, the evening star!"

Joel looked where she was pointing.

"It's not a star," he commented. It was an observation he had sometimes made to Emily before.

"I know. You've told me. It's a planet – Venus, isn't it?"

"Yes – we often call it 'the evening star' – although it seems to get forgotten that Venus also appears in the east before sunrise. Then, as you might expect, people call it the 'morning star' – but it's the same planet appearing at a different time."

Emily gazed up at it again, thinking that it looked very beautiful. "No wonder it's called Venus," she commented.

"It does look beautiful, but you probably think of it that way because it's so bright." Joel had often thought about the dual nature of Venus' appearance.

"So why is it so bright, if it's not a star?"

"Because it's very hot – so hot that nothing can live there. Your great-grandfather used to tell me that it traps the sun's heat, like the greenhouse that he had in his garden – but that there was nothing to stop the temperature spiralling upwards."

"Her beauty is deceptive then?" suggested Emily.

"I'm afraid so. From a human point of view, she has more of hell about her than heaven."

Their conversation died for a few moments and Emily thought that her father was looking sad.

"What's the matter, Dad?" she asked. "Is it all this?" She gestured towards the rubble, timber and masonry that still covered the site next to them.

"Yes, it's that..." he agreed. "But it's many other things as well." He paused, deciding which of his thoughts to share with her. Eventually, he said, "Jonathan's been telling me about the battle. It seems to me that we've slipped back in time, not just a few years but centuries. Those barbarians who broke in here – they were like something out of Britain's ancient past."

"I've had the same thought, Dad," Emily replied. "There have always been the savages amongst us. It's just that now there's nothing to oppose them. There's no longer the 'rule of law' that you used to talk about. There's no-one to stop the murder, the rape and plunder."

There was a long pause. She seemed almost philosophical but given the events of the recent past, he wondered how she could possibly seem so detached. There were so obviously aspects of their conversation that she was avoiding. She never seemed to let her feelings out, and ever since the invasion of The Ridge he had been worried about her. He looked at her, hesitating for a moment, wondering what response his next remark would bring, wondering whether to make it at all – but then he said, "You always sound very detached, Emily. But all this has affected you as well. You must have feelings – the deepest feelings – about it all, just like the rest of us."

Emily was taken by surprise and felt tears pricking at the corners of her eyes. Her reply was angry and vehement. "Of course I'm affected by what's happened! My husband has been killed! Our houses have been all but destroyed! Many of our neighbours have been murdered! How can you even think such a thing – let alone say it?"

Joel was silent. It had been Emily who had first wanted to know how he was feeling, but even though she was his daughter when he, in turn, wanted to know she felt – she would not readily open her heart to him. Sometimes he had to provoke her into doing so although, at that moment, he wished he had set about it in a more tactful way.

He waited, knowing that she would have more to say.

"This is not a situation any of us wanted to be in – but we are! So now we have to get on with it! Besides, I could say the same to you! I see you worrying all the time about what's happening – but what's the point of that when you can do nothing about it?"

He was briefly stung by the remark. For many years, he had tried to find ways to influence the people around him, but they had always seemed more concerned with, if not consumed by, daily events.

Still he remained silent, refusing to respond, in turn, to Emily's provocation and knowing that she would speak again.

After a long pause, she said wearily, "I'm sorry. But the things that you worry about are taking such a long time to happen – at least, it's a long time compared with the amount of time for which most people live. Most of us can't be bothered with anything that takes longer than our own lifetimes. We're like the kids I used to teach. We have a concentration span of about five minutes – or less."

"I think you're right," replied Joel, "though the thought gives me no pleasure. I've never really agreed with the idea that we're too stupid to survive – as someone once said. But I do think that Nature could hardly have come up with a set of problems more likely to play on the weak points of human beings."

"If you don't think we can do anything about the changes in the climate, then what hope is there for any of us? Perhaps I should poison myself and the kids and put an end to all this!"

The strength of Emily's reaction took Joel once more by surprise. He was torn between explaining his thoughts truthfully to her and not leaving her in a state of despair.

"Of course I don't think that you should do such a thing! Whilst there are human beings on this planet we must never give in to despair! That's why the book I've been writing is so important to me. It's all about surviving in the world as it is – and as it may become. I haven't given up and I don't think any of us should. But the 'game', if something so serious can be called a 'game', has changed. It's no longer about trying to prevent climate change. The chance to do that disappeared in my grandfather's lifetime. It's about adapting to it!"

Emily wanted to talk about something else; a subject that was connected to her father's thoughts but also to the way that she was feeling. "Do you remember that some while ago we talked about the whole community here moving to 'The Levels' or even moving somewhere else completely?" Joel nodded. "Some of the young people are talking about leaving."

"I'm not surprised," said Joel.

"They've been talking about travelling west and then trying to get a passage to Canada. Some of the older people are blaming you and Sam – and your stories about Falmouth."

Joel gave a scornful laugh. "They forget that we only went because our parents wanted us to go! Now it seems that parents don't want their children to leave!"

"It was completely different, Dad! You were on a mission for your families and intended to return. The young people I'm talking about want to leave for good – to find somewhere else to live."

Quite apart from the dangers to which the young people would be exposed and the sense of loss that would be felt all round, Joel readily understood that the departure of even a few young people would cause enormous problems in the community. Without younger people to help with the work and to re-populate the settlement, life on The Ridge would come to an end. There was a long silence.

"Where are they headed?" Joel said at last.

"I don't think they know exactly," replied Emily. "The messengers who ride through here are their only sources of information. They say that places south of here – Africa and Southern Europe – are getting hotter and that some of them are already unbearably hot. The people in those places are moving north, trying to find water and places where they can still grow food. Animals are on the move as well, some of them in huge numbers."

"So everyone – and everything – is moving north?" Joel had talked to the messengers himself, but it seemed that now, others on the Ridge were beginning to understand what was happening.

"It seems like it, Dad. Fortunately, the news about the far north is different. Although it's warming more quickly than other parts of the Earth, it's thought it will be much cooler than places south of here for a long time to come."

"It still seems like precious little information on which to base your whole future," commented Joel.

"There's nowhere that's going to be safe! We all know that, especially after the battle. Many of the young people feel that they have little to lose – and maybe a lot to gain."

Joel looked up as she referred again to the community's young people. "Are Sam's boys planning to leave then?" he asked.

"George is staying, but Jonathan – and the other lads who used to gather on the village green – are all planning to go," replied Emily.

Joel nodded, thinking that after the loss of Michael, Sam would feel Jonathan's departure very keenly – but then he could readily understand how the young men felt.

It occurred to Joel that Emily was still young enough to seek a new life for herself elsewhere if that was what she wanted so he asked, "What are you going to do?"

"I'm staying here. This is my home. It will just continue changing slowly. Besides, Thomas is staying here and I want to stay with him. The children will decide what they wish to do when the time comes, but they'll both be here for the next few years."

"You've obviously talked to Thomas about all this then…?"

"Yes, I have," admitted Emily. "But I'll have to tell you about it tomorrow. At the moment, Grace and Daniel are waiting for me to get back. They're staying over at Sam's tonight."

She stood, bent to kiss her father on the cheek and then set off along the path that led away from the site of the cottages.

***

Joel watched as his daughter disappeared into the dusk and lay back on his bed, staring up at the sky. It had been a hot day and he knew that he would be more comfortable under the awning of the tent that night.

He had shared more with Emily than for some while and it had led them into a difficult conversation. Even so, it had not given him an opportunity to talk further about the tipping point that he believed had been reached a long time before – probably back in his grandfather's time. The ability of human beings to influence the climate had passed. Now the Earth would reach a new 'balance', a new equilibrium, but there was no saying where or when that would be. His only hope was that sufficient human beings would survive long enough for the planet to return to conditions more like those that had prevailed before his grandparents' time. There was, he thought, just a chance that such a thing would happen.

Then his thoughts became darker again. If he and Emily had previously witnessed the manifestations of a distant nuclear war, countless thousands of people had probably died as a result. Drought and famine had already killed millions, if the messengers were to be believed. Conflict as people competed for food and other resources might account for millions more. There was a risk that if global climate change did not directly destroy the last human beings, then they might destroy themselves.

He listened to the cries of tawny owls in the trees around the clearing. He often caught himself thinking only about the planet's human inhabitants, but there were profound consequences for all life on Earth. It was true that people on The Ridge had begun to live in close harmony with the natural world around them – but it was only because circumstances had forced them to do so. They still saw the plants and animals as being there for their convenience rather than as having their own right to exist in the great web of life that reached throughout the atmosphere, the oceans and the continents of Earth.

He shifted uncomfortably on his bed. It was such a hot night. He looked up again at Venus' bright orb burning in the sky above him and his mind went back to the huge pyres that had been lit to dispose of the dead after the battle against the invaders. He pondered the word 'crematorium' because it was known to him from his grandfather's time and because space on The Ridge was at such a premium that the practice of cremating the dead still persisted. The tragic thought occurred to him that the Earth could be in the process of becoming a 'crematorium of the species'.

Joel gave a heavy sigh. He desperately hoped that a tragedy of such incomprehensible proportions was not waiting out there in the future for all life on the Earth. When space exploration had been taking place in his grandfather's time, other planets capable of supporting life had been discovered but no life had actually been found. If life on Earth became extinct because the planet had become yet another searing hot cinder hurtling through space, then a cosmic miracle would have been extinguished.

His thoughts returned to his own time. He was angered profoundly by the foolishness, the inner blindness that had led everyone – and everything – into the situation around him, but he had not wanted to see all but a few residual vestiges of the previous civilisation disappearing into history. It seemed such an enormous loss of the products of human effort – and when he thought of literature, art and music, of science and technology – an enormous loss of human genius. Now his grandfather's collection of books, records and other artefacts lay amongst the ashes of the two cottages, entirely destroyed when they had been razed to the ground.

He had just one small consolation. Stored deep in the bowels of Len's house had been an old vinyl record and a wind-up gramophone. As Joel's friend, Len had loaned them to him, hoping that it would help him to recover from his illness but extracting from him elaborate promises about the safe-keeping of such valuable objects.

Joel wound up the gramophone and despite the darkness, managed to see sufficiently well to lower the gramophone's needle carefully onto the surface of the record. It was an early Oscar Petersen recording. He lay back, enthralled by the magic of being able to listen to music from another time, the unerring fluency, speed and sheer inventiveness of the piano playing that poured out through the darkness.

He was back to perceptions of beauty again. He lay with Venus fixed in his gaze, pondering the ambivalence of her beauty and wondering if all the living things upon the Earth would now inevitably be forfeited to provide her with a sister. Despite the music, a profound sadness fell once more upon him.

Printed in Great Britain
by Amazon

19771229R00278